LIMESTONE GUMPTION

A BRAD POPE AND SISTERFRIENDS MYSTERY

LIMESTONE GUMPTION

BRYAN E. ROBINSON

FIVE STAR
A part of Gale, Cengage Learning

GALE
CENGAGE Learning

Detroit • New York • San Francisco • New Haven, Conn • Waterville, Maine • London

GALE
CENGAGE Learning·

LIBRARY OF CONGRESS CATALOGING-IN-PUBLICATION DATA

Robinson, Bryan E.
  Limestone gumption : a Brad Pope and Sisterfriends mystery /
Bryan E. Robinson—First edition.
    pages cm.
    ISBN-13: 978-1-4328-2778-6 (hardcover)
    ISBN-10: 1-4328-2778-2 (hardcover)
    1. Fathers and sons—Fiction. 2. Psychologists—Fiction. I. Title.
PS3618.O3223L56 2014
813'.6—dc23   2013031869

First Edition. First Printing: January 2014
Find us on Facebook– https://www.facebook.com/FiveStarCengage
Visit our website– http://www.gale.cengage.com/fivestar/
Contact Five Star™ Publishing at FiveStar@cengage.com/

Printed in Mexico
1 2 3 4 5 6 7 18 17 16 15 14

For Sisterwoman, Glenda Robinson Loftin, for her
enduring love and support

ACKNOWLEDGMENTS

This book is a long time in coming, and there are many people whom I wish to thank for their physical and emotional support while I cut my teeth on my debut novel. First and foremost, my deepest appreciation goes to Sisterwoman, Glenda Robinson Loftin, a writer in her own right, for her encouraging words over the years and for reading the manuscript at various stages of development. And to all the members of her book club, "The Lake Norman Book Club," for asking me to read early drafts of the manuscript and for their interest and feedback.

I want to thank Julie Maccarin for rekindling in me the spark I needed to finish the manuscript and for her steadfast support, reading draft after draft of the manuscript. I extend my appreciation to Jena Levasseur, my Microsoft Master, for her technical insight and substantive direction, which helped make this novel stronger in so many ways. And I am indebted to my hand surgeon, Christopher Lechner, MD, for saving my writing fingers.

Special acknowledgment goes to the professional assistance of Tommy Hays, Vicki Lane, and Chris Roerden—whose expert guidance taught me how to write fiction. Without their wise direction, this novel would have never materialized. Plus I want to give a shout out to Ron Rash, Terry Hoover, Del Shores, and the other professional writers who endorsed this novel. Stephanie Wilder, Pam Kotler, Faison Covington, Linda Hamilton, and Patty Siple read versions of the manuscript and also gave me valuable feedback. And to my dear friend, Polly Paddock, who was kind enough to read the manuscript and believe in me with such strong and valuable support.

The WPC's cookbook at the end of the novel came from the assistance of many, especially Jamey McCullers for providing recipes attributed to Gigi, Lick, Gladys, Wilma-May, Betty-Jewel, Jackie, Shirley, Vasque, and Glenda.

Then there's my stable of dedicated readers and listeners who indulged my need to solicit critical feedback on early drafts of the manuscript: Sylvia Brackett, Nancy Chase, Kevin Davis, Karen DuBose, Tom Forrest, Lynn Hallman, Eddie Hallman, Linda Hamilton, Shonie Luckhardt, Corina Maccarin, Jamey McCullers, Debra Rosenblum, Susan Shaw, Patty Siple, Marie Stilkind, Ashley and Nicki Taylor, Sara Thompson, Rick Werner, Sharon Bono, Harry Schmitz, Kristen Shea, and Ann Sherry. And last but not least, The Golden Girls: Belle Radenbaugh, Ruth Schlesenger, Betty Kirby, and Ann Hawk.

A special recognition to my writing group, who supported me through the ups and downs of revision after revision: the discerning eye of Jon Michael Riley, and a special "thank you" to the creative slant of Janna Zonder, who meticulously read many drafts of my manuscript, and Katina Rodis for her valuable feedback. Their feedback enriched the words on the page.

I want to thank my agent, Sally McMillan, for her tireless efforts in supporting my work over the years. And to all the river dwellers on the Suwannee River for always making me feel at home. Last, but not least, I want to thank all the teachers in my life who have shown me how and where to find my own limestone gumption.

"If you can't surrender to life's hard knocks,
you're like the limestone arguing with the Suwannee.
When a river comes up to a stone,
do you think the stone spends all its time trying to push
the water back?
No siree.
The limestone yields as the Suwannee encompasses it
and becomes one with the rushing water.
The Suwannee carves the limestone into shapes and
images,
and it becomes a feature of the river.
In time, the limestone becomes a smooth, well-polished
cavern.
And the strength of its true character is revealed.
That's Limestone Gumption."
—Voodoo Sally

PROLOGUE

Big Jake liked to poke danger with a stick.

But now the slam of his heartbeat against his chest told him he should've waited for his student instead of attempting this dive alone. When he'd thrown on his dive gear an hour earlier, he'd ignored the partner rule, wiped sweat from his brow, and plopped recklessly into the mouth of Suwannee Springs for a solo dive. Now lost and nearly out of oxygen, he must stay focused on finding a way out of this underwater cave.

Big Jake had turned his thrill-seeking into a career, mapping north Florida's treacherous underground rivers and tunnels. Eleven months ago, his discovery of a ten-thousand-year-old Mastodon molar landed him on the front page of the August twentieth *Whitecross News*—a glory he'd begrudgingly split with dive partner Willard McCullers.

On this July trip, since his chicken-shit student hadn't shown, he'd decided the spotlight would be all his. He would discover a fossil that'd have Whitecross buzzing for years. At one-thirty p.m., clutching his underwater lamp, he'd descended into the cold waters of the springhead and slipped through a narrow gap of sand and rock, barely wide enough to accommodate his two-hundred-ninety-pound bulk. The tight squeeze twisted and turned before emptying him into the belly of an underwater chamber as wide as three football fields, tall as a ten-story building.

Tied at the mouth of the springs, a white nylon rope would

guide him back, trailing behind him now as he swam past eerie lime rock formations—gargoyles and screaming faces—carved by underground rivers that had cut through prehistoric limestone.

A black tunnel beckoned him. He kicked his swim fins like a frog, angling himself deeper into the passageway. As he skimmed along the bottom, he uncovered a handful of seashells and several oddly shaped bones, gingerly placing them one by one into the dive bag. Without warning, his lamp flickered, then dimmed.

Shit! He pounded the bottom of the lantern until it brightened again.

He swam deeper, farther, stirring up silt clouds. His lamp dimmed again; his world faded to black. As he pulled against the trusted dive line, he felt it loosen.

What the fuck? Adrenaline shot through the roof of his brain.

Now he knew he shouldn't have come here alone, but he'd wanted that damn newspaper article. Calming himself, Jake concentrated on his breathing.

In. Out. In. Out. No big deal.

Maybe the guideline was just loose, not broken.

As though reading Braille, Jake fingered the guideline, hoping it'd lead him back in the right direction. But he kept circling the maze of pitch-black tunnels.

Trembling.

He jerked frantically on the rope until it looped into his arms, causing him to panic. He slung the dive bag away, flailed his hands, kicked his feet, and entered one dead-end passageway after another.

His heart hammered his ribcage. His breathing, fast and hard, gobbled up his dwindling oxygen supply.

Frantic fingers slid over rough-carved limestone, poking for a portal, his neck slick with sweat. Some faint instinct told him to dig his way through the tons of rock, and he fumbled for his knife, stabbed at the porous limestone.

Choking. Gasping.

The thought of what put him here flashed through his mind. *Brad Pope, you son-of-a-bitch!*

He muzzled his welling-up urge to scream into an agonizing guttural sound from deep inside—like death belching its bitter taste from the cave's hungry throat.

The big man ditched his knife, clawed the cave walls until blood gushed from under his fingernails. Terror swallowed him, kicking, twisting, swirling.

One last howl . . .

One long pause . . .

One final breath . . .

Then his heart stopped, body stilled.

Big Jake—face bloated, eyes bulging, mouth gaping—took his place alongside the gruesome gargoyles beneath the Suwannee River.

CHAPTER 1

In my opinion, Big Jake got what was coming to him. That might sound cold-hearted for a psychologist, but down here on the Suwannee there's an old saying: *Evil carries the seeds of its own destruction.* I stood on a boulder, peering down into the mouth of Suwannee Springs. Needles of sunlight shot through overhanging cypress branches, danced across the translucent green waters below. My wavy reflection mingled with schools of golden-orange sunfish and grass carp darting near the sandy bottom.

Brad Pope, I mused, *what the hell are you doing back in this god-forsaken town?*

I thought I'd put the past behind me.

At least I told myself I had.

But my childhood grief had strapped its tentacles around my heart. I'd lost myself in work, unsuccessfully chiseling away at the past that held me in its grasp. But grief doesn't release you until you face and befriend it. My training as a psychologist had taught me that.

That's what brought me home.

Grief.

And rage.

A chance to heal.

And a chance to settle the score with my daddy, who'd snatched away the boyhood I'd so dearly loved—watching the river roll by, catfishing on moonlit nights, exploring the riverbanks for Indian artifacts.

To this day, Whitecross, perched high on the east bank of the Suwannee River, was a sleepy town with a population of 1700, one caution light, and a new Walgreens that had crept to the edge of town. Locals were online and computer savvy, but if asked about blackberries, they'd think cobbler, not wireless. And townsfolk usually died of natural causes, not murder.

Until now.

I hurled a rock across the water. The ripples spread toward the left riverbank where mourners had stacked piles of notes and flowers, a shrine to Big Jake's memory. Then I reluctantly hiked up the riverbank and climbed into my green Pathfinder. I pulled onto the paved road, heading for Jake's funeral behind a tractor-trailer belching a cloud of black smoke. When I drove through town, I winced at the words on the marquee out front of Bowen's Funeral Home, *Big J Lives On In Our Hearts.*

I nosed my car to a squeaky stop in front of the small wood-framed church underneath the shade of a sprawling live oak. Even the massive tree seemed to mourn. Its embroidered branches drooped with heavy beards of Spanish moss, stretching low to brush the lush summer vegetation. And the monotonous droning of tree frogs added a woeful dirge that warned of rain.

Scattered over the passenger seat and floor of my car, the *Whitecross News* splashed "Foul Play" across the front page. A disturbing photo of dive partner Willard McCullers, grinning ear-to-ear, stared up at me. The article said that Willard had led a two-day dive search before discovering the football hero floating against the ceiling of a large underwater cavern—his arms and legs splayed wide like a scarecrow, his guideline cut.

Looked like he'd been screaming, Willard was quoted as saying, *like he'd seen the devil hisself.*

I tore my eyes away from the newspaper, gazed through the

propped-opened double mahogany doors of the packed church. Mourners overflowed from the chapel into the vestibule, down the brick steps, onto the sidewalk and church grounds. Thank goodness my grandma was saving me a seat.

The sweltering heat pressed against my car windows. Over the crooning of Thelma's Gospel Hour from the radio, I angled close to the blasting air conditioner vent, savored the coolness against my face. When I looked up, a Piggly Wiggly delivery truck zipped by in a whoosh. On the rear roll-up door, a fan had scribbled in the grime, *Jake Will Be Missed.* I rolled down my window, swiped at my face with a coat sleeve to block the blanket of heat.

And I spat.

As I put the window back up, broadcaster Vasque Gaylord announced that more folks might become Christians so they could go to Heaven and be with Big Jake. That's when I killed the engine.

No one in town knew the dark secrets that Gladys Nunn had been hiding about her husband, Big Jake.

Except for me.

In my role of psychologist, I'd had access to the town's underbelly for the past year. To most townspeople, Big Jake was a god. To me, he was the devil incarnate. I'd decided to attend his funeral mainly for Gladys's sake, partly for my own. I'd hoped the service would put an end to the spinning doubt in my head: *Had I had a hand in his murder?*

I stepped out of the car to a low rumble of thunder. Off in the distance, low-hanging storm clouds were gathering. A black thunderhead swirled in the direction of the church. Already, I felt a few drops of rain.

As I made my way up the rain-spattered church steps, the clouds tore.

Darkness hovered.

Images of Big Jake's agonizing death barrel-rolled in my head like a gator caught in a net. I was supposed to meet him for a dive lesson the day he drowned. After an emergency session with a client had run over, I was half an hour late. By the time I had gotten there, he'd gone on without me. *If I'd shown up on time, would he be alive today? Or would I have died along with him?*

Going back to Suwannee Springs had only made the haunting questions worse. *No matter what happens from here on out,* I told myself as I entered the doorway of the church vestibule, *you need to get a fucking grip!*

CHAPTER 2

Inside the cramped sanctuary the closed casket rested in front of the altar blanketed with a spray of red roses, the Widow Gladys's favorite flower. Scents of yellow carnations, white Lilies of the Valley, and dozens of fragrant floral arrangements sweetened the still air. All of Whitecross had turned out to honor Big Jake. Honking noses and wails of amen punctuated Ibejean Martin's morose, off-note piano version of "Rock of Ages." I crawled over knees and feet in the second pew, dropping beside my black-clad Grandma Gigi. Her neck circled in pearls, she looked every bit the proper Southern lady.

"Bunch of hypocrites." She promptly whispered in my ear. "Whitecross has got holes in the soles of its shoes from parading to church and holes in the seat of its britches from backsliding."

"Shhh." I brushed a finger against my lips when I noticed the preacher's wife, Edna Black, lean in from behind us.

"Brad, don't you shush me." Gigi elbowed me in the ribs. "You know I don't have much use for religion. The only time I set foot inside a church is for weddings and funerals. I'm getting weary of going to the same person's wedding two and three times. Thank goodness folks only die once."

"You've been saying that since I was little," I murmured. "You're the one who made me go every Sunday before I went off to boarding school—you and Mama."

"That's before I saw through it," she mumbled in her low,

gravelly voice. "All you find is a bunch of phony, squabbling back-stabbers."

"Yes ma'am, but please keep your voice down." I bent over and tugged at my socks to avoid the craning neck and curious eyes of Sylvia Wynn, the pharmacist.

My reprimand made Gigi scrunch up her nose, tighten her lips into a straight line. Her real name was Madge Pope, but Gigi—my boyhood failure at pronouncing "grandma"—had stuck. Pretty soon, everybody in town started calling her "Gigi," which she thought was a much hotter name than "Madge."

I squeezed her boney hand, noted its cinderblock roughness against my smooth, well-manicured fingers, then rested it on the hymnal between us.

I both loved and resented Gigi.

I loved her because as far as family went, she was it. That and despite her seventy-three years, she could do anything. Fix the carburetor on my Nissan when it skipped. Wield an ax to cut firewood for her wood stove. Or whip up a chocolate cake in no time flat. Her motto was, *Never pay folks to do for you what you can do for yourself.*

Then there was her crusty exterior, a natural scab to a hard life that hid a soft side. She delivered Friendship Trays to shut-ins, donated free merchandise from her thrift store, and stuffed extra bills into the pockets of field hands. But there'd been a tense undertow between us. I still hadn't forgiven her for not visiting me during my ten years at the Asheville boarding school and for not being more forthcoming about my daddy's whereabouts. Plus, more often than not, her opinions were bitter pills to swallow.

Even now, as she pointed to the mahogany pew across the aisle, she didn't hold back. She curled her palm against my ear, her spearmint breath cooling my cheek. "That's Myrtle Badger in the red. She fixes the departed's hair and makeup so they look like they're asleep. Works part-time as corpse dresser for Bowen's and full-time as town bigmouth."

"Isn't that a wee bit like the pot calling the kettle black?" I elbowed her and smiled.

Gigi made a face, a small crease between her brows.

I wiped a bead of sweat from my forehead. The air conditioner was apparently on the blink. I leaned slightly forward. Over waves of rustling funeral memorials and flapping paper fans— with pictures of Jesus on one side, Bowen's Funeral Home on the other—I had a direct shot of Myrtle. Deep lines of disapproval etched a frown, and fat arms folded into a cradle across her stomach as though she were nursing contempt. A haughty ring finger boasted a humongous fire opal; an angry swollen foot tapped time to Ibejean's rendition of "The Old Rugged Cross."

Gigi elbowed me again, dropped her voice. "Myrtle's nothing but a big show-off. She blowed and waved at the caution light yesterday, just so I'd notice that jaw-dropper-ring of hers. She got it from swindling her blood-kin out of their grandmamma's will."

I glanced around for signs that Gigi's voice was carrying. Seeing no curious eyes or straining necks, I settled back on her. "Yes ma'am, but can we talk about it later?" Wilting from the heat, I undid the collar button of my once-starched shirt, loosened my tie, furtively wiping moist palms down my pin-striped suit.

Gigi shifted her body and pulled at the bottom of her black skirt. "Myrtle's miffed because the coffin's closed, and she won't get recognized for her so-called artistic achievements." Gigi made a low grunt, then continued. "After Gladys viewed Big Jake in private, she said Myrtle'd made a mess out of him. Said his swollen face and bulging eyes were layered with thick makeup and his mouth had a gash of red lipstick. Said he looked like a drag queen." Gigi chuckled and slapped her knee.

I double-blinked, surprised that my grandma knew about drag queens, although I knew Gladys did. In one of our therapy sessions, Gladys had shown me a picture of her sister's boy in Tampa dressed up as Cher. "Bless his heart," she'd said, "he oughta dress that way all the time. He makes a much prettier girl than he does a boy."

Gigi continued in her raspy whisper. "To top it off, Gladys said Myrtle laid Big Jake out in a white suit, blue shirt, and white tie, identical to the outfit Elvis was buried in. Said Big Jake ought to look like the celebrity he was. Problem is, Gladys never cared much for Elvis."

I nodded and patted her hand hoping she had finished her tirade.

Just below the music, I could hear soft accolades humming like a low-voltage wire across the flock of mourners: "He was a man's man . . ." "Wasn't afraid of the devil . . ." "Put this town on the map . . ."

As my eyes swept the congregation, I was alone with my frustrating thoughts. Jake had made All-American with the Florida Gators, even appeared on a National Geographic special with the dinosaur bone he'd discovered. Since then, the whole town acted as if he walked on water. If only they knew what I knew. But that was privileged information from my therapy sessions with Gladys.

I unwadded the funeral memorial, glanced at Big Jake's picture on the front, and used it to fan away the stale church air. When my attention landed up front on the sealed casket, it triggered images of Big Jake's bulging neck muscles choking for air as he lay stiff inside his container, his cardboard face drawn tight, his mouth pulled down as if it were tied to the bottom of his coffin to hold him there.

He had always been bigger than life—too powerful to be

pinned down. I could picture him fed up with these restraints like King Kong, raging against his captors. It wouldn't have surprised me one bit to see that casket start rocking back and forth. And Big Jake thrusting his bloated hand into a space . . . prying the lid from inside . . . popping it off with a loud bang . . . clamping both sides of the coffin and springing out of it . . . flying into the congregation.

Though the lid remained closed, the coffin sternly still, I wondered, *Had I helped put him there? Had I wanted Gladys to do to him what I'd been unable to do when Daddy was beating Mama?*

A grinding headache made me feel as though the ceiling had collapsed on my head. The room began to whirl and spin. A booming voice from the pulpit and Gigi's finger in my ribs brought me back to the service.

Shuddering.

Sweat-soaked through to my skin, I slid off my jacket, braced my head in my hands.

"Brad, what's wrong?" Gigi rubbed her palm against my damp back, the way she used to do when I was little. "You sick, son?"

"It's the heat."

"I was saying that Pastor Black's long-winded." Gigi had been taking a swatting spree at Reverend Ollis Black's eulogy. "I don't have much use for the man. He's been having an affair with Myrtle Badger for over a year."

I took a deep breath, straightened, then focused on Preacher Black's slick-backed pompadour. He had preached himself hoarse. Drips of sweat trickled off his nose onto the pulpit like beads of baptismal water. Coke-bottle thick spectacles magnified his eyes. His vision was set in two directions—one eye headed toward the Gulf, the other toward the Atlantic.

Gigi balled her fist into a megaphone, put it close to my cheek. "His insight is as bad as his eyesight. Word is, last week he pulled into the new Walgreen's drive-thru pharmacy window. He ordered a Big Mac, order of fries, and a Coke." She chuckled, then grunted, her voice softening. "No matter, I figure the poor soul could stand a good meal. So I fixed a mess of chicken and dumplings to take over to him and Edna after the funeral."

I gave her an approving head nod and two thumbs up. One of the things I loved about Gigi was her heart was always in the right place.

Preacher Black went on for another thirty minutes praising Big Jake high and low. He ran his fingertips down a scrawny black tie, wiped damp palms across the opened Bible on the lectern, his quivering jowls underscoring his remarks. "No finer husband, father, or friend existed in Whitecross. One thing's for sure: Today, Jake Nunn is diving the caverns of Heaven."

"Caverns of Heaven?" Gigi nudged me, her pale blue eyes sparkled like marbles catching sunlight. I shot her a wry smile.

A loud roll of thunder rattled the little church. Intermittent flashes of lightning lit the stained-glass windows. After reading several verses of scripture, Preacher Black turned the service over to the purple-robed choir, who sang "Blessed Assurance" and "In the Sweet By and By."

Our disdain for Big Jake was common ground for Gigi and me. She nodded her head at the casket, mumbled beneath the choir's hymns. "Gladys scraped the bottom of the barrel marrying that man. He was nothing but a glory hog, poking around in our caves, ruining the natural balance."

Before I could put a finger to my lips to shush her again, her voice trailed off on its own. Reluctant tears rolled down her parched cheeks, dripping onto her dress. She was overcome by her own maternal grief at the sight of Big Jake's mother weeping uncontrollably, throwing her head back on the shoulder of her only-surviving son, Eldred.

With her crusty nit-picking, my feisty grandma had tried to harden the loss of her only child, Ada Lea, my mother. But now, she'd let her guard down, revealed her true nature. I put my arm around her and squeezed. Her body went limp; her head gently fell onto my shoulder, the scent of lavender wafting over me.

With a knot in my throat, I watched the rest of the service through my own tears.

I glanced around the chapel, studying the Bible stories depicted in the six stained-glass windows. While friends and relatives dabbed their eyes, I was keenly aware of Jake's widow, Gladys—dry-eyed, stone-like in the front pew, her knees almost touching the casket. She stared at the pine plank floor, just like she'd done in our therapy sessions.

Hard-smacking pellets of rain pinged off the aluminum steeple. At the loud clap of thunder, I stretched my neck around. Mourners who'd stood outside made a mad dash to a green Bowen's tent in the graveyard beside the church.

Following the final prayer and benediction, I leaned into Gigi and a sea of hunched shoulders under thumping umbrellas as we scuttled from the sanctuary to the gravesite. A lightning bolt snapped at our heels, moving us faster down the sidewalk across the churchyard to the cemetery.

"The wrath of God has descended upon us." Wilma-Maytag Church sputtered behind us in quick, measured steps around the mud puddles. I felt a tap on my shoulder. It was her. "Doctor, how'd you like my page-turning?"

During the service, Wilma-Maytag—named after her parents' finest possession, a spanking new washing machine—had saddled herself into a chair beside Ibejean Martin at the piano and turned the hymnal pages. Gigi had told me that the choir director booted Wilma-May out of the chorus because she couldn't carry a tune, but he let her page-turn as a consolation prize.

I looked back at her and smiled. "You were flipping those pages so fast I could've sworn I felt a few jets of air all the way over to where I was sitting."

Gigi chimed in. "Wilma-May Church, what's this I hear about you page-turning for Ibejean and the Glory Bees when they travel to that recording studio over in Gainesville to cut their new CD?"

Wilma-May shot us a toothless grin. "That's right. It's called, *Jesus is Coming Soon.*"

"I look forward to getting a copy," I said, squeezing under the tent against Gigi and the sour-smelling clothes of mourners.

I clasped my hands in front of me. Willard McCullers and five other pallbearers, faces strained against the blinding rain, transported their heavy cargo from church steps to the tent that whipped wildly in the wind.

I glanced at Preacher Black. In his final tribute to Big Jake, he insisted that the Heavens had opened up and the raindrops were the tears of Jesus.

"Tears of Jesus?" I rolled my eyes at Gigi as hers rolled back at me. Even though I respectfully bowed my head for the final prayer, what I really thought was how screwed up this whole scene was.

As Preacher Black prayed for Big Jake's soul, everyone at the graveside seemed touched by the service—everyone, that is, except for the members of the Women's Preservation Club, who peeked at each other over bowed heads.

In addition to Gigi, Gladys, and Wilma-May, there were three other founding members. Shirley Gilchrist, one eye closed, flashed the opened one at Gigi. One hand pushed on her oversized artificial hair bun, hanging lopsided from its lofty perch. The other fanned the dead air away from her face.

Another club member, Betty-Jewel Iglesias, peered over black-rimmed glasses at her club sisters. She cocked her head to one side as if she were trying to understand Preacher Black's heavy Southern drawl, mashing the spectacles up the ridge of her nose with her middle finger.

Between peeps at Gigi, poufy-haired Jackie Priester snapped gum and furiously filed her nails. She flipped her right palm back and forth checking her work. Jackie looked up, blazed her thickly mascaraed eyes at me, and winked.

Gigi had founded the Women's Preservation Club when I was a boy to preserve Whitecross's way of life and its natural beauty. According to her, the founding members started out calling it the Society for the Prevention of Cruelty to Culture but claimed the initials SPCC had too many letters, making it sound Hitlerish. So they ended up calling it the Women's Preservation Club—WPC for short.

"WPC sounds more American," Gigi had once told me. "More like a name FDR would give it."

The six women referred to themselves as "sisterfriends." Somewhere between fiftyish and seventyish, they'd all met at a prayer circle back when Gigi was into religion. The WPC's biggest claim to fame was the garden they'd planted at the welcome sign on the outskirts of Whitecross.

When I turned my head toward the thick bushes at the graveyard's edge, I startled at a pair of dark-circled eyes watching me. Dressed in bib overalls, the familiar figure moved from tree to tree in the shadows of the woods. He was shaggy-haired and whiskered, twenty maybe, with a bad leg that made an odd shuffling sound as he dragged it through the brush. During frequent stops, he squinted and blinked. His gaze traveled the length of my body, raising prickly hairs on the back of my neck. He laughed, mumbled to himself; his body twitched.

I noticed Gladys cutting him periodic glances between

condolences from well-wishers. *Could her relationship with this man be more than she'd told me?*

Though his real name was Rufus, locals nicknamed him Lick Skillet because he fished leftovers and table scraps from garbage cans. A gravedigger for Bowen's, he terrified the townspeople. Anytime something went missing or was mysteriously wrong, fingers pointed in his direction first. Already, rumors were flying that Lick had something to do with Big Jake's murder.

As mourners trickled out of the cemetery, rain drummed a rat-a-tat-tat on the tent. I lingered for a few minutes, noting the silent exchanges between Lick and Gladys. Then I walked over to Preacher Black and shook his hand, thanking him for the service. Gladys flicked her eyes back and forth between the woods and Gigi, who was giving her a good finger-wagging.

The sound of their conversation carried. "You keep your mouth shut, Sisterfriend." Gigi's dangly ear-bobs, timed with her rapid-fire head nods, swayed back and forth. "Don't you breathe a word. I got the say-so. You hear me?"

"We have to tell him what we did." Gladys propped her tightly clenched fists on her hips. "He's got a right to know."

The other women of the WPC huddled around the twosome, clucking their tongues. When I stepped closer, they scattered like roaches when the lights come on. Gigi dropped her finger; Gladys removed her fists from her hips. Both strained artificial smiles at me. I cupped Gladys's cold hands, offered my condolences.

"Thank you." Gladys stiffened, shrugged her shoulders. Face blank, eyes dry, she shielded her fingers over her mouth and spoke softly through them. "I have to tell you what we did."

CHAPTER 3

The loud-smacking windshield wipers smeared away a light drizzle as I neared Gigi's place three miles outside of town. Gigi had agreed to host the funeral reception to take the burden off Gladys.

I nosed the car off the blacktop onto the dirt road that led to Gigi's double wide. The white, sandy Florida roads reminded me of how deep my roots run in this town. When Great-Great-Grandpa Henry Pope, a railroad tycoon, brought the railway to the port of "Suwannee Bluff" in 1886, all the roads were unpaved. That same year, he built the train station in the heart of town at a white sandy crossroads and changed the name to "Whitecross."

Back then Whitecross had become a port for steamboats, ferries, and cargo boats that lured settlers as diverse as the early Timucuan Indians and pioneers and log sawyers. Now, it drew cavers from around the world. Some dove the Suwannee for sunken logging boats containing two-centuries-old wood—valuable lumber by today's standards. Others explored the underwater caverns for the colorful marine life or just plain adventure.

I pulled the car to a spot alongside the dirt road, turned off the motor. Gigi's driveway was so packed with cars that it looked like the parking lot of a Blake Shelton concert. Well-wishers in black streamed in and out of the narrow metal front door carrying containers of food. I wondered how many of them were curiosity-seekers, bearing funeral casseroles, gallons of sweet tea, and home-baked desserts, in exchange for a peep show of the grieving widow falling apart.

Boy, were they in for a surprise.

My hands were empty, but my heart was full. I would offer Gladys my condolences, then split.

The white sand and gravel driveway had crumbled into a brown mud under my feet. I mounted the front steps, scraped my shoes on the doormat before entering the house. It was a Southern courtesy Gigi'd taught me as a boy—muddy or not—to make that scraping sound out of respect before entering somebody's house.

I slid through the front door, surveyed the room. The house smelled of home-baked food co-mingled with aftershaves and perfumes. Just below the steady hum of conversations, I picked up bits and pieces of Willard McCullers fielding questions in a corner of the living room: "I heard the fish ate his eyes out . . ." "Why was he diving without you . . . ?" "Always was a daredevil . . ." "They said it was foul play . . ." "Who do you think done it . . . ?"

Out of the corner of my eye, I noticed Myrtle Badger holding a paper plate stacked with what looked like banana pudding. Between bites, she licked her fingers and gestured wildly.

Although cozy and homey, you'd never know that it was a mobile home inside. Gigi had become a packrat, living alone after three failed marriages. The house was a painful walk down memory lane for me, her life stamped on everything in it, a museum of ups and downs documenting my childhood.

An Old Gold Cigarette sign hung over a small TV set in one corner, a La-Z-Boy facing it. Lace-crochet doilies adorned the side tables, overpopulated with family photographs. *Save the Suwannee* bumper stickers strewn on the coffee table. Old newspapers and magazines stacked floor to ceiling. Empty jugs of *Tug-a-Love Window Cleaner* lining the hallway to the bedroom.

She'd named the cleaner after her pet term for me, *Tug-a-Love*. She'd bottled it in her kitchen sink, stocked it on the shelves at Madge's Mess, her secondhand shop. When I was little, she'd let me measure a cupful of blue waxy-looking detergent flakes into a glass jug. Then she'd fill it with tap water and slap a sticky label on the side. She called it *Tug-a-Love Window Cleaner: Cleans and Shines in No Time.*

The first thing I had to do was run to the bathroom. Gigi still hadn't turned the calendar that hung above the commode. Here it was July and it still showed May.

Curled on the vanity, a golden heart locket caught my eye. It had belonged to my mother. I clamped it in my palm, leaned against the bathroom door, and fought back the sudden swell of sadness rising in my chest.

When I'd let myself feel the long-suppressed rage I carried for my daddy, it salved the grief. I made myself feel it now to drive back the rush of tears. It wasn't the best therapy, but it did the trick until I could face him man-to-man for what he'd done to Mama and baby sister, Lydia.

They said he'd dropped out of sight after Mama's death in 1981. Nobody'd seen him since. There'd been an ongoing investigation that had turned into a cold case. So I'd done some digging of my own. The online searches and conversations with folks in Whitecross had led to dead-ends. I'd even made a special trip to the State Office of Vital Statistics in Tallahassee a few months back. After searching property tax documents and birth and death certificates, I'd found a birth certificate for Johnny Devillers but no death certificate. I figured the bastard still had to be alive somewhere.

Every time I asked Gigi about Daddy, she'd change the subject or say she didn't want to talk about it. I'd tried to keep my simmering resentment toward her under wraps, because I didn't want to lose the only family I had left.

I threw water on my face, dried off with a perfume-scented towel, then threaded my way through the crowded hallway. I eased into the den and signed my name in the funeral register that stood in a corner.

Across the room, Gladys sat in the La-Z-Boy, comforted by condolences from huddled guests. Gigi received friends standing in line nearby. At forty-nine, Gladys was young enough to be Gigi's daughter. The other sisterfriends, all strange bedfellows, stood around a fold-up table in the adjoining dining room sampling the chow. Unlike Gigi who said and did as she damn-well pleased, Shirley Gilchrist— short, dumpy, and sixty-something—was a slave to social conventions. Her eyes landed on me, and she made a beeline my way, her giant-sized artificial hair bun tilting to one side.

"Glad you could come, Dr. Pope." Shirley braced her bun with one hand, and brushed something off my shoulder with the other. "Such good taste in clothes. I like your matching blue shirt and tie."

"Why, thank you, ma'am."

"With your blond hair and all, has anybody ever told you that you favor Brad Pitt?"

"I get that once in a while."

"Well, you do." She nodded emphatically, her bun teetering on the brink. "Dr. Pope, this whole thing with Big Jake has got us so jittery. I desperately need somebody to talk to. I was wondering if you were available."

I reached in my suit pocket, pulled out my iPhone, and checked my schedule. "Next Wednesday is my first available." She was agreeable, and we booked it.

"Thank you, Dr. Pope." She grabbed my arm, as if to steady me. "Now, don't slump your shoulders and stand up straight." Then she turned and headed toward the food table.

I felt a jab in my back. Gum-snapping Jackie Priester had

high-tailed it over behind Shirley and cornered me. The plus-size Jackie looked like a clown in a pup tent: hair teased into a helmet, thick pancake makeup, a ballooning floral muumuu that dragged the floor. But she had the fizzy good spirits of a newly uncorked bottle of champagne.

"Dr. Brad, I hope you don't hold my fingernail filing at the service against me. You can hold anything else against me, though." She shimmied her shoulders and raised one of her Marlene Dietrich eyebrows, heavily carved in dark eyebrow pencil, then moved in closer. "I gotta move, never could be still for long stretches."

"No harm done." I took a step back. "It was a long time to sit on a steamy afternoon."

"I guess I could've done worse things." A seductive smile split her ruby lips and rouged cheeks apart. She blew a bubble and popped it. Then her tone took on a weight. "Dr. Brad, I need to see you right away. The problem is . . . well, you see it all started with Big Jake . . ."

"Hold on, Jackie." I pulled out my planner. "Let's wait until we can talk in private."

"Okay, suits me. When would that be?"

We made an appointment for the following Thursday. I thought it odd that both women would pull me aside, urgency in their voices, and want to talk to me. In a town where people who go to therapy are considered "crazy," why would they risk that label? The smells of homemade biscuits and fried chicken drew me away from thinking too much of it at the time. I joined the other sisterfriends, who were standing around the food table, shoveling food into their mouths.

As I dunked a carrot stick into the spinach-artichoke dip, Wilma-Maytag Church latched onto my arm. "You've gotta taste my bean salad, Doctor." She scooped a spoonful of her creation onto a sturdy paper plate. "If you don't eat anything else, you gotta taste this."

At Gigi's insistence, I had conducted an intervention with this sixty-five-year-old woman a week earlier. She had struggled with alcoholism and shoplifting over the years. The church elders had accused her of coming to Sunday service with liquor on her breath and stealing money from the offering plate.

Gigi, who had no use for religion, had bonded with this foot-washing Baptist and insisted on helping her. Wilma-May loved country music and had written a country-western song based on her life, "I Don't Have Teeth, But I Got Two Eyes That Say You Been Cheatin' on Me."

Wilma-May stared at me while I sampled her dish. When my eyes widened with delight, her toothless smile captured my heart. I overheard the other women behind us. As they filled their plates, they talked about crime popping up in Whitecross.

"What about that Forney Fowler?" Shirley pushed against her bun to keep it from going askew. "He fell from that ledge to his death the other day. I read all about it in the morning paper. Weren't you watch-dogging him, Jackie?"

"We'll talk about it at the next WPC meeting." Jackie turned crimson, shifted her feet, downing the rest of her punch. "The man was a damn bastard! That's all I gotta say!" Her deep honking voice carried across the room.

"Jackie, watch your language," Betty-Jewel Iglesias said. A dour, strait-laced nerd, whom Gigi often accused of being a stick-in-the-mud, Betty-Jewel mashed her black-rimmed glasses back up her nose. "The reverend's right over there." She made a congested snort-like noise. Then she brushed her finger under her perpetually red nose in the direction of Preacher Black, who was hunched over, patting Gladys's hand.

"Anyhow," Shirley continued, "the paper said Fowler's death was an accident, but the robbery at the Hurry Hut a few weeks ago sure wasn't. And they never caught them, either."

"They're talking about putting metal detectors in the courthouse," Wilma-May said, "at the main entrance to the Suwannee County Courthouse to screen the public."

"That's because a paroled convict snuck into the courthouse's ground floor with an assault rifle. Held Ibejean Martin hostage for several hours," Jackie said.

"Bless her heart," Wilma-May said. "It made Ibejean so nervous she had to go on pills. Her piano playing at church has been rickety ever since."

"If I'm elected, you can bet your bottom dollar things are going to be different in this town." Betty-Jewel straightened the campaign button on her lapel that read, *Vote for a Jewel for Town Council.*

"Well, he got his," Jackie said. "After the sharpshooter nailed him, he ended up on Gladys's floor at the VA. So the WPC put him on our watch list."

"Are ya'll talking about my patient?" Gladys sauntered to the table, dished out a plate of food. "Sam Grimes?"

"Um hums" resounded from the sisterfriends, who circled the table, shoving food into their mouths.

"He was a handful all right. I dreaded going into his room, but he was on our watch list. Even though he was hooked up to an oxygen mask over his mouth and nose, he cursed me. Ordered me around. One day I was giving him a sponge bath, and he had the nerve to ask if I'd check and see if his *testicles were black*!"

"Lord have mercy," Wilma-May cried. "What'd you do?"

"I told him I most certainly would not. He threw a bed pan at me and rung for the charge nurse. When she came in the room, he took off the oxygen mask and asked her if she'd check and see if his *test results were back.*"

"For god sakes!" Jackie hooted so loud heads turned from around the room, and the sisterfriends bent double laughing.

"The next thing I knew he was dead," Gladys said, killing the laughter into pin-drop silence. She paused, looked past the food table through a window that framed the Suwannee. "Strange, isn't it? One minute he was chipper as they come. Then, all of a sudden, he was deader than a doornail."

There was an uncomfortable lull of coughing and body shifting, then dead silence among the sisterfriends.

"What're you girls chewing my grandson's ear off about?" The laughter had drawn Gigi. She strolled up, took me by the elbow. "Son, I need to talk to you alone."

She steered me into her bedroom. A few loose tresses flopped against her back. They had fallen from their bleached-blond perch where bobby pins—speared North, South, East, and West—had carelessly held them in place. I could tell something was up with her. Only a few days ago, her in-your-face hair color had been a tired, mousy-brown, her version of a mood ring. Tomorrow? She might be a redhead or bald, depending on who pissed her off. When she worried about things, she might dye it black. No siree. She wasn't the kind to pretend her hair had any natural color, when everybody knew that at seventy-three there's only one shade: pure white.

"How's Chris?" she asked.

"Fine." I crossed my arms, took a step back from her. I knew what was coming.

"Now, wouldn't it be nice if she were here at a time like this? She could meet the sisterfriends, and we'd be one big happy family."

I rolled my shoulders.

She pressed on. "When do I get to meet her?"

"Don't know." I avoided her eyes, tapped the shag carpet with my wingtip.

"You've been hiding her from me for . . . how long?"

"We've been together for three years, but I haven't hidden

36

Chris from you."

"Hell, I've never even seen a picture of her."

"I don't carry one." I looked into her face. "And I haven't shown Chris yours, either."

"So you're ashamed of your backward old grandma. I reckon I'm not good enough for your city-slicker friends."

"No ma'am, that's not true."

"Then how come you go up to Charlotte to see Christine but never bring her home?"

"Chris is a flight attendant, schlepping through airports at all hours. Whitecross is in the boondocks. Jacksonville is the closest airport—two hours away."

"Guess I'm old-fashioned." She paused, cleared her throat, then raised her voice. "When two people love each other, they ought to be together. It's high time she was here is what I think."

"Is that what you think?" I uncrossed my arms and closed the door. Then I unloaded on her. "Listen, Gigi, I'm a grown man, not one of your clingy club sisters. It's time you stopped trying to run my life."

"Brad . . . I . . ."

"And one more thing." I aimed my finger at her. "If you really believe loved ones should be together, where the hell were you when I was in boarding school? Where were you when I needed you? I thought it was 'high time' then, but you weren't there."

"Son, there's no call for getting so upset." She dropped her voice, spoke softly. "Family's family. You and I are all each other's got left."

"Really?" My voice pitched in a sarcastic tone. "Then you must know what happened to Daddy. Or where he is."

"Don't start that again." Her arms dropped against her hips. "Just let sleeping dogs lie."

"You've been hiding him from me for . . . how long?"

"Oh, for Heaven's sake." She whacked a golden lock of hair that flopped in her eyes. "When you pull something up by the roots to see how it's growing, you kill it."

"Sometimes when you don't, it rots on the vine." I squared my body with her. "Tell you what, Gigi. When you deliver Daddy to me, I'll deliver Chris to you."

Her face was peculiar, not her usual judgment-flogging look, but one that made it droop under the weight of my offer. She put her arm around me, called me by her pet name, "Tug-a-Love."

When I pulled away, she didn't miss a beat. "I ought to know my future granddaughter-in-law's all I'm saying."

"Stop pushing, Gigi."

"For crying out loud." She jerked the door open and marched out of the bedroom.

I threw a glance at my reflection in the dark yellow-spotted mirror over the dresser. Four old Eva Gabor–style wigs on Styrofoam headstands glared back at me, reminders of the many sides to Gigi's personality. I wiped both hands over my face, pressed my eyeballs into their sockets, blew out a long sigh.

When I stepped back into the den, Gigi waved me over. "Come here, son." Ringed by her sisterfriends, she brushed crumbs off her fingers, then slid her arm around my neck. "Mayor Smiley Bishop just told me the manatees have come upstream to the middle Suwannee. How about you and me taking a look tomorrow evening?"

"I'm all about that." Masking my bruised feelings from our conversation, I avoided eye contact and shrugged out of her hold. "Always wanted to see one."

I was glad to get the feelings off my chest.

Finally.

But I didn't want to hurt Gigi. Plus, I figured she'd be a captive audience on a manatee trek, and it would be a peaceful time to talk and get answers without interruption.

"I wanted you to meet Smiley, but he had to scoot to a meeting," Gigi said.

"Next time." I reached my hand toward Gladys, who stood beside Gigi. I offered my condolences once again, then looked at Gigi. "See you late tomorrow. Six o'clock okay?"

"That'll work." She twirled a lock of yellow hair.

I rubbed my palms together, vaguely aware of whiffs of English Leather and Estée Lauder from endless handshakes. As I turned to leave, the psychologist in me studied Gigi and her sisterfriends. They stood in a semicircle, shoulders brushing, hanging on to one another. It struck me that the WPC moved in a herd, afraid to veer off on their own. My training had taught me that when people cling, like a troop of monkeys, they're usually afraid of something.

I wondered what was up with these tight-knit women.

According to Gigi, none of her sisterfriends had traveled far from Whitecross. Not a single one had ever been on a train, much less an airplane. Gigi had told me when Shirley took a Greyhound bus to visit her sister in High Springs, it was the talk of the WPC for weeks. You'd thought she'd gone to Egypt. To hear Gigi tell it, you'd think flying to Asheville to visit me in boarding school would've permanently infected her with some kind of contagious disease. She'd explained it away by saying the sisterfriends had taken some kind of pledge to stick together.

I left my cantankerous grandma and her sisterfriends—elbows and fleshy wide hips wrestling for space in the herd—gaping at me, whispering behind shielded hands as I stepped through the door.

Though my psychologist mind staggered, I knew enough to trust it. But I still descended the steps scratching my head.

What could the antsy herd of club sisters possibly be concealing?

CHAPTER 4

On the way home, the drizzling rain had cleared. I turned off the windshield wipers and drove through a hazy mist rising from the pavement. When I passed Big Jake's old hangout, I grimaced at the cluster of black balloons bouncing against the sign *Britches Bar* and tried to ignore the chill that was lifting the hairs on my arms.

My mind seared with a memory from several months back when Gladys had introduced me to Big Jake. He'd been waiting for her after a therapy session. Gladys and I had stepped into the waiting room. The well-built Jake had stood to shake my hand. His arms bulged and twisted like a winding rope, a pack of Marlboros folded into the right arm of his short-sleeved shirt, the way my daddy used to carry his. His red curly hair and beguiling grin, plastered across a freckled face, gave him the air of a good-natured, happily married man.

Until he spoke.

"I put my foot down on her drivin'." He looked down at Gladys with a shit-eating grin. "She drives like a bat out of hell. I won't have her dentin' my new Yukon."

I rubbed the back of my neck and looked over at Gladys. "How will you get here?"

She shrugged, looked up at Jake.

"Oh, hell, I don't mind bringin' her." The big man had chuckled, talking for his wife as though she were not in the room. "I'll let her come as long as you can get her to mind me."

I winced at the thinly veiled anger behind his smile and couldn't resist tossing him a grenade. "She's got a pretty sharp mind of her own."

"Yep, a little too sharp, Doc." His eyes beaded at me; veins popped to the surface of his red neck. "Needs bringin' down a notch or two."

He pulled out a cigarette and started to light it until I put on the skids. "This is a nonsmoking facility, Jake."

He blanched as if I'd slugged him, and a slight twitch in his right cheek restrained a scowl. "Okay, if you say so." He twisted his jaw, stared at me for a few heartbeats, then slowly rolled his cigarette pack into his shirt sleeve.

"Big, let's just go." Gladys pulled on his sleeve.

"Okay, sweets." Grinning again, he grazed his fist against my shoulder. "I'm countin' on you, Doc. Straighten her out, now."

As we said our goodbyes, he gripped my hand extra hard. He had the handshake of a man who'd snapped a lot of chickens' necks, a harsh judgment for a first impression.

But Gladys's story had skewed my opinion.

In our first session, her stony hangdog face had reminded me of Mount Rushmore: salt-and-pepper bangs, a permanent frown tattooed into her forehead, down-turned lips tightened into a slit.

She had slumped into the far end of my overstuffed sofa, stared at the floor, as if she were waiting for me to do oral surgery. At the start, it *was* like pulling teeth. Lots of silences and one-word answers.

She said she was a registered nurse at the VA Hospital in Lake City. Pause. She had been married to Big Jake for twenty years with one grown son. Pause. Big Jake was a cave diver at a satellite center of the Geological Division of the University of Florida out of Gainesville. Silence.

When I had asked about her son, Gladys stonewalled. "Leave him out of it," she'd said, gazing into the wooden floor, never mentioning him again.

She spoke mostly about the other people in her life, especially Big Jake, whom she called Big for short. When I'd try to guide her inward, she'd divert attention away from herself to her husband.

"Big says I have the cold, wet puppy syndrome because I take in every stray in the neighborhood."

"Sounds to me like you've got a big heart."

"Not in Big's eyes. He said if I brought another cat home, he'd soak it in kerosene and throw a match on it, like he used to do for fun as a boy."

I flinched, but we weren't there to discuss Big Jake's childhood. "Tell me more about *you*."

"Well, let's see." She pressed a finger against her teeth. "I've been having these bad dreams and can't understand why."

"What about?"

"I'm lost . . . down deep in an underwater cave. Lost, and can't find my way out. Then I start suffocating and wake up gasping for air."

"Dreams mirror what we think and feel just below the level of consciousness." I rubbed my chin for a slim minute, noting that even the subject matter of her dreams belonged to Big Jake. "It makes me wonder if you've felt trapped in some way."

"Trapped?" She dropped her head, released a reluctant groan. "Did you see Big's picture in the paper after he found that ten-thousand-year-old fossil?"

"No, but I heard about it."

"Let me show you something."

She unzipped her handbag, reached inside, and tugged out a clipping from the *Whitecross News*. The headline read, "Local Hero Discovers Prehistoric Molar of Mastodon." The photograph showed Big Jake, fossil in hand, suited in dive gear with sidekick, Willard McCullers. I figured it was another ploy to divert attention away from her to Big Jake. I was mystified that she could love such an egomaniac, but in my profession I'd seen lots of women fall for men like him.

"You really admire your husband, don't you?" I asked.

"Hell no. I hate the bastard." She gaped at me through hard brown eyes—eyes pooled with deep resentment.

The notepad I'd been holding slipped between my fingers, tumbled to the floor. As I reached down to pick it up, I said, "You *hate* him?" I wasn't sure if I'd heard her correctly.

That had been the start of Gladys opening up more, taking charge of her therapy. Over the course of several sessions, she became a great navigator, describing in chilling detail why she'd felt trapped in her marriage. I acted as her rescue line, tracking intently, braced to bring her back in a moment's notice.

"Four months into our marriage, Big started browbeating me, shoving me around. After I told him I'd had my fill and threatened to leave, he puffed up like a frog, pressed me up against the icebox with his hairy bare chest. He grabbed my bangs and shoved his face in mine. The stink of his Skoal-smelling breath made me sick to my stomach. Then he dug his right thumb through my petticoat into my navel and made a slash across my stomach like a knife blade saying, 'If you leave me, bitch, I'll rip your guts out!' It was a side of him I'd never seen before, a side that was like my daddy when he'd get drunk. I didn't know how to fight back, so I just caved in."

I could feel my emotions starting to rupture. I'd had contempt for wife beaters and had dealt with abused women before, but it was always hard for me to stomach. As Gladys spoke, my hatred for Big Jake almost overtook me. A geyser erupted in my throat; tension pulsated in back of my neck. But

I pushed down my own feelings so I could stay present with hers.

"Big never let me forget that I was ten years older than him. One night after we'd been married for a few years—I was thirty-two and our son was still a baby—he came home drunk, narrowed his eyes, and smirked, 'I married a middle-aged fat, ugly woman and I don't like it. I don't like the way you look, and I don't like you.' "

Gladys took a deep breath and sighed before pressing on.

"I started telling myself it must be my fault that Big was so miserable. When he'd hit me, I figured I deserved it, so I tried to fix some bad part of myself that I couldn't put my finger on. I wore my hair his way, dressed like he told me to, cooked and reared our boy his way. Even had sex with him his way. Bit by bit, I despised him for *his way.*"

I nodded to encourage her. "Go on."

"One day Big went to Lake City for surgery on his right foot. The next day he flashed me a devilish squint, said he'd dreamed I was having sex with another man while he was under the knife, said he knew dreams had a way of telling the truth about things you can't know any other way. I was sitting in front of the mirror, running a comb through my hair. Before I knew it, he grabbed the comb, dug it into my scalp, and pulled me backwards onto the floor. 'Woman,' he said, 'If you make me bang my foot, I'll beat you double hard.'

"He protected his sore foot by planting it behind him. I threw my arms over my face begging him to stop, but he beat me. Hard. Then he yelled at me to shape up, slammed the front door, hobbled into his Yukon, and took off. I cradled my head and backtracked everything I'd done that could've made him so mad. He stayed out all night drinking at Britches. After he left, a man called for the third or fourth time that week and talked sexual talk to me. When I told Big about it, he said it was mighty strange that the man only called when he was gone. He was convinced that I'd been carrying on with Lick Skillet.

"The only thing I was guilty of was sneaking the boy Big's old clothes and feeding him like one of the stray cats and dogs that showed up on my back doorstep. But there was no convincing Big. Even though the boy put him on a pedestal, Big was cruel when he saw him. He would motion the boy over, stick his mouth against his ear, and holler, 'Retard.' The poor boy would jump plum off the ground, but it wasn't long before he started cowering around Big like a scared puppy.

"After shopping one Saturday, Big and me pulled into our driveway, and a pair of my panties was nailed to the garage door. He dragged me into the house and beat me worse than ever, claiming I'd been having sex with Lick again. He raped me too. That time I landed in the hospital, and Big told everybody I'd fallen down the back porch steps.

"When he visited me at Lake City General, he had this droopy look on his face. He whimpered in my ear that when he made me cry, it made him feel like a man. Then he looked me directly in the eye and promised to never hit me again. That's when I realized how weak and pathetic he was.

"On my second day in the hospital, Sandy Nelson, my next-door neighbor, popped in for a visit. Sandy hadn't even slid that pot of yellow mums onto the bedside table before she started whispering, 'I saw him do it.' She dragged a chair up to my hospital bed, leaned into me, and mumbled, 'I saw him do it with my own two eyes. Then he hopped back in his car and squealed off so fast his tires left skid marks. I wondered what on earth he was doing nailing a pair of step-ins to your garage door. It was Big Jake.' "

Looking back, Gladys said it all made sense. Jake had let her out at Walmart, saying he was driving over to Lowe's to pick up lumber for a dog house she'd wanted him to build.

"I was in Walmart no more than forty-five minutes. It would've taken him nearly thirty minutes to drive to the house and back to the parking lot. When I got outside with groceries, he was waiting there smoking a Marlboro, pretty as you please. I wondered why I never saw any lumber or a dog house. Lying in that hospital bed, I thought about what Sandy had said, and it dawned on me. It was him or me. One of us was going to die, and it wasn't going to be me."

I felt a deep stirring clawing its way into my chest—the same rage toward Big Jake that I'd felt for my daddy. I held down the twist of nausea in my stomach. Gladys's story had unearthed memories of Mama, who was Gladys's age when Daddy beat her to death. But my training told me if I was to prevent a similar tragedy from happening to Gladys, I had to maintain my objectivity. I felt the stirring settle as it dawned on me that by helping Gladys I'd be helping my own mother. It wouldn't bring Mama back, but it might help me find some small measure of relief.

"Dr. Pope, why would Big want to make me look bad?"

I drew my attention back to Gladys as her helpless, searching eyes caught my gaze. "Gladys . . ." I spoke slowly. "When he beats you, he doesn't feel guilty because if you're to blame he doesn't have to think about his part in it."

"I'll be." She put her finger against her teeth, stared at the floor. "So he's off the hook."

"That's right."

I realized I was walking a fine line between empowering Gladys and turning her further against her husband. Her feelings had to be hers, not mine. Then an idea popped into my head. "Did you ever see a 1944 film called *Gaslight* with Ingrid Bergman and Charles Boyer?"

She put her finger against her teeth again, obviously an

unconscious nervous habit. "No, can't say I remember it. How come?"

"The movie is about a man who drives his wife to the brink of madness, making her think she's losing her mind."

"What's that got to do with me?" Her eyebrows crunched up.

"Your story reminds me of that film. It popularized the term 'gaslighting' to describe a situation where someone makes another person doubt their own sanity."

"Gaslighting." She tried the word on for size, studied the office floor. "You mean there's a name for it?" She batted her eyes as if waking from a deep sleep. "Big has been gaslighting me."

"From what you've told me, it sounds like it."

She looked up, her big brown eyes searching me for answers. "What can I do? Everybody knows everybody in Whitecross."

"What about police protection?"

Her stony face loosened at the absurdity of my question. "That's like asking a fried chicken chain to protect their chickens. Most of the officers on the force are Big's friends, and they think he hung the moon. One of them is his first cousin, the other a dive buddy. Besides, Big told me, 'If you leave, I'll hunt you down, and you'll be one dead whore.' "

Without Gladys's permission, I couldn't notify the authorities, and she was too scared to give it. As far as public opinion went, battered women's shelters were as unnecessary as alarm systems because those kinds of problems didn't exist in Whitecross.

Over the next several sessions, Gladys began to get more in touch with her feelings.

"Dr. Brad, I rented that DVD—*Gaslight*—and watched it twice last week. It made me so all-fired mad. But then it lifted something in me. It made me feel better than I have in twenty years."

"I'm glad you feel better."

"I put attention on Big for so long, I lost count of myself. When I saw the same thing happening to Ingrid Bergman, it made me madder than when it was happening to me."

"That's because the film helped you see from the outside what you couldn't see from the inside."

A smile curled her lips up instead of down, lighting her from inside, pumping life into her stone-statued body.

Over time, Gladys became a force to reckon with in her own way. Even though she sported an occasional black eye—most recently from Big Jake because she'd had her hair dyed and styled at Bernice's Hairport without his permission—her body moved with a slight fluidity of confidence and defiance. Bernice had cut Gladys's bangs and swept her hair off her face. A henna rinse, applied to the tired gray that had made her look burdened, gave her a more youthful, almost pretty look.

In her last therapy appointment, Gladys had returned to speaking in bits and pieces, making it difficult to follow her train of thought.

"Dr. Brad, I'm worried. There are things I haven't told you." She spoke softly, her eyes traveling the wood-grain lines in the floor.

Her faint smile had faded back to Mount Rushmore. It made me think of when you look at a statue, and it seems to move or smile for an instant.

"What things?"

"There's a time in our lives when we have to do what's right." She absentmindedly preened her newly styled hair. "Even if it looks wrong from the outside."

I leaned forward in my chair. "I'm not following you, Gladys."

"I ought to be able to tell you everything, but your grand-mamma says not to involve you in it. She helped me out of tight spots when nobody else would, and I owe her."

She looped her handbag over her shoulder, her body language hastily ending the session.

"I think a lot of you, Doctor, but there'll come a day . . . when you find out . . . that you won't think much of me."

"What do you mean?"

"Let's just leave it at that." She hoisted herself out of the sofa. "I've got to skedaddle. Got to feed the animals and fix Big a meatloaf. He gets riled up when supper's not on the table at five o'clock sharp."

Her shoulders drooped. Before she closed the door behind her, a heavy clump in her walk made every step look effortful. I threw on a pot of coffee, put her file away, and rested my face against the cool metal file cabinet. That's when the questions began to swirl: *What was Gladys keeping from me? By emboldening her, had I pushed her into dangerous territory?*

Later that evening, I'd been catching up on paper work at my office when a banging on the door startled me. I swung it open. There stood Big Jake Nunn, eyes bloodshot, reeking of alcohol.

"What's up, Jake?"

His head protruded forward, top-heavy with anger. "Doc, you haven't done a goddamn thing to help my wife."

He swayed back and forth. The twitch in his cheek released a scowl that did a nasty dance across his face.

He was so shit-faced I probably could've punched him out right then. "I don't know what you mean."

"The only thing you've done is turn her against me." He raised his balled-up fist. "I'm gonna put a hurtin' on you, you won't never forget."

Then he lunged at me.

"Whoa, hold on." I blocked his body slam with the door and held it shut. "Damn it, Jake, calm down. We can talk this out."

"Talk, shit." He kicked the door hard. "I'll teach you to fuck with me."

"I said calm down. You're welcome to come to a session with Gladys. We can sort this out."

"Oh, hell yeah. So the two of you can royally fuck me over?"

"I give you my word I won't let that happen."

I heard him stumble back from the door. For a long minute, neither of us said anything. "Tell you what, Doc, I'll pay you a visit if you'll pay me one first."

"Pay you a visit?" I opened the door and faced him. He'd relaxed his fists on his hips. "Where?"

"A dive lesson. I'll show you my world, then you can show me yours."

"Sorry, Jake. It's a conflict of interest for therapists to socialize with family members of clients."

"What the hell does ethics have to do with goin' for a fuckin' dive?"

He lit a cigarette before I could stop him. "Conflict or not . . . " He made a zero with his lips, exhaled a smoke ring. "If you want me in therapy that's the deal."

"I'll think about it." I rubbed the tension in the back of my neck and wondered, *Would I be putting myself at risk?*

I'd heard no reports of violence toward anyone other than Gladys. And this man needed serious help before he killed her or she killed him. The clincher for me clicked again. Although I couldn't stop Mama's murder, it'd be worth the risk if I could prevent the same thing from happening to Gladys.

He took another drag off his cigarette. "Are you a pansy or somethin'?"

I laughed. "Will you agree to come with Gladys to at least three therapy sessions?"

"You got my word on it."

"Okay, deal." I reached out my hand, agreeing to meet him at

Suwannee Springs the next afternoon.

As he sealed his word, the steel squeeze felt reluctant. Of course, I knew he was afraid of my world and that toughness hides fear. Truth be told, I had some healthy fear of his world, too. But I had handled roughnecks like Big Jake before—tough on the surface to protect their tender underbelly.

I'd hoped that the dive would lay groundwork for healing the animosity between Gladys and Jake.

But it was too late.

The next thing I knew, Big Jake had been murdered. Gladys was a no-show at her next appointment.

And I didn't see her again until the day of the funeral.

CHAPTER 5

"I haven't lifted my legs this high since my last honeymoon." Gigi swung thin legs over fallen logs that blocked our path, stomping right by me through the prickly palmetto palms.

"Gigi." I playfully admonished her, marching dutifully behind.

"Get the lead out, slowpoke." She directed me forward with a palm wave.

I trudged faster. "I'm coming. I'm coming."

Though outspoken, Gigi didn't fit the ornery stereotype of the grizzled and bent granny. Trim and spry, she moved with the agility of a woman half her age. She attributed her vitality to natural herbs, hiking, and yard work.

The right hip pocket of her sand-smeared jeans was stuffed with a single glove, the left with a handkerchief. She sank deep into the soggy Florida swamp, gunk almost sucking off the knee-high rubber boots.

Gigi had taken me on several manatee safaris as a boy, but I was sent off to boarding school before ever spotting one. As she gently parted fern branches, scrub oak limbs, and palm fronds in front of me, my heart thudded in anticipation with each slushy step.

"You're no grand young'un of mine until you've seen a manatee." She stopped dead in her tracks and faced me. "You got your mind on books and other folks' problems. Your mama—God rest her soul—sent you up yonder before she had you off her tit. And you lost count of our ways. Your Great-

Great-Granddaddy Henry Pope would turn over in his grave if he knew you left all this behind." She circled the hot July air with her arms.

"I was nine, for god sakes." Katydids, screeching through the river birch, amplified the sting of rejection.

She'd already turned her back on me and spoke over her shoulder. "Let's get cracking." She tramped the ground harder, letting the branches smack me in the face.

"Ouch." I shrieked, trying to keep up but straggling behind.

She stopped again, waited for me, and spoke with real affection. "Son, you know I love you. You didn't have a say in the matter. But you turned right around, moved to Charlotte, and got all citified."

"I had a career. I was building a better life."

"Better life my hind foot." She threw her hands in the air. "Where can you find a better life than this? It made you uppity."

"Uppity? I . . ."

Dismissing me again, she forged on, belting out her favorite by the Dixie Chicks, "Wide Open Spaces."

I didn't know the words to her songs. Lady Gaga and Adele were more my style. I couldn't keep up with her music any more than I could match her quick-stepping gait. Even the new boots I'd bought at Whitecross Hardware felt unnatural. I kept tripping like a schoolgirl trying to walk in her first pair of heels over tangled roots welded into the earth.

Gigi felt I'd turned my back on her precious way of life. And I felt like she couldn't understand mine. She was so quick moving I could barely keep up with her, much less talk to her. But that was Gigi. She expected *me* to keep up. After all, I was thirty-eight years her junior, and she wasn't the kind to wait for anybody.

"Just a speck more." Nearing the river's edge, she coaxed me with her middle finger, exposing the missing index finger from her right hand.

She'd lost that finger because of her third husband, Melvin. Or as she put it, because "her relationship picker was broken." Her biggest failure in life was picking weak, dependent men with no backbone—men who took advantage of her good nature and hard work ethic.

Although she'd married three times, she'd proudly kept the Pope family name. She claimed it was the one thing no man could take from her. Widowed at a young age by my grandfather, her first husband, she'd divorced the second and vowed never to marry again after dumping Melvin, whom she called no account.

Gigi had told me about an afternoon several years ago when Gladys Nunn came crying to her that Big Jake was having an affair. Gigi consoled her by pointing across the room to the La-Z-Boy where Melvin sat day and night glued to the television. "You see that son-of-a-bitch? He's been cheating on me for years." Melvin didn't flinch or turn around; he just kept watching TV and scouring the obituaries for dead people's names. Then he'd look them up in the phone book, draw through their names with red Magic Marker, and smack his lips in some kind of warped self-satisfaction.

On one of his week-long drunks, he'd threatened to pull the loaded shotgun out from under the bed and do himself in. Gigi toyed with going to Walmart, maybe leave the barrel sticking out from underneath the bedspread, just to give him a little hint. But she'd thought better of it. She hadn't wanted blood and brains splattered all over her new gold shag carpet and the white vinyl walls of her double wide. Then she would've never gotten rid of him.

While *The Price is Right* blared on the TV set from the living room, she'd gotten down on her hands and knees and reached underneath the bed to pull the gun out and hide it from Melvin. She stuck her index finger inside the barrel of the shotgun. As she dragged it toward her, she heard Bob Barker belt out, "Let's spin the wheel and see who the lucky winner will be!"

The trigger snagged on the carpet, discharged, and blasted off her index finger.

But no matter where the spin of life threw her, Gigi managed to land on her feet. She'd turned her four-fingered fate to her advantage. Her middle finger became a scepter that endowed her with a sovereign authority to judge right from wrong, poke blame, or direct people's lives.

A week later she kicked Melvin out.

She claimed she carried on just fine without him since he was no help anyway. She could just wheel her 1983 Pepto-Bismol–colored Eldorado into Whitecross, hop out, and wiggle her emblem of authority at the Mexican men. She recruited them as if they spoke Chinese.

"Workie, workie?" She'd wave her scepter back and forth, "Ten dolla for workie workie."

When Gigi gave the middle finger, churchgoers were horrified. But it never occurred to her that she was flipping them the bird. Even now, she wagged her scepter at me as we approached the river.

The closer we came to the Suwannee, the more I had the eerie feeling that somebody was watching us. My neck felt like cold eyes were drilling holes into the back of it. As I whipped my head around, I saw a figure moving briskly through the briars and tangled vines, keeping pace with us. The human form rustled a thicket of wax myrtle, snapped twigs underfoot, trailed us toward the water.

"Somebody's following us," I said.

Gigi twisted her head in the direction of the sound. "Oh, that's just Sally." With disinterest, Gigi inhaled the humid breeze, snatched the handkerchief from her hip pocket, and swatted the mosquitoes that buzzed her ears. "These are her stomping grounds."

I froze.

A green lizard scurried beneath a rock. Gigi's mouth was moving, but I didn't hear words. And the sweet sounds of the Suwannee were abruptly mute.

Voodoo Sally? I thought. *Holy shit, Voodoo Sally!*

The name alone steam-shoveled into my core, unearthing all my boyhood fears.

Voodoo Sally was a black woman who lived in a dilapidated shack on the edge of the Suwannee. Legend had it that she was a root doctor who conjured up spells against people and midwived. Or, as she called it, "caught babies." She had caramel skin and large green eyes set in a wild gaze beneath untamed white hair that flew in all directions. The old barefoot woman wore a skirt turned upside down, the hem tied around her waist, the waistline tapered at her knees. I drew back my neck into itself and looked wide-eyed at her.

She peered at us from behind a clump of cabbage palms; her big eyes rolled around in their sockets like they'd been greased. She showed her face for a fleeting second. When her eyes met mine, she disappeared behind the palms and rattled the fronds with a twitching hand. As we continued toward the river, I kept a bead on the sorcerer.

The shrill sirens of the katydids echoed louder through the Sabal palms. Butterflies played tag in the sunset. Mullets flipped somersaults midair before smacking the water. Clumps of Spanish moss, cascading from the cypress trees, framed our view of the slow, meandering Suwannee and its sandy limestone ledges. Tannic acid from flatwoods and swamp vegetation darkened the water to a brewed tea color.

Gigi closed her eyes, raised her arms over her head. She

smiled and swooned like an evangelist slain in the spirit. As she inhaled, she seemed to imbibe the wonder of creation, her own holy place. I could tell from her silence that words were unwelcome, that they might spoil this sacred moment, so I remained still and paid my respects, too.

I jammed my hands into my jean pockets, inhaled muted scents of wild jasmine and wisteria. All the while, I kept a close eye on Voodoo Sally, who'd begun spinning and chanting, "evol wanga obeah, evol wanga obeah." Though I heard the sounds, I tried to push them away.

"You realize we're in the lap of Heaven here." As she came out of her contemplation, Gigi let her arms slap against her hips. "But I'm afraid it's dying out. The deer and manatee are dwindling." She pointed to the other side of the riverbank. "Look at that patch of bare land. Loggers have chopped down the trees. Logging and turpentine companies are dumping chemicals in the water, changing the natural drainage of the river. And now, Big Jake's murder."

Her eyes slid over me as if to vilify me, a look that stole my breath away. *Did she suspect that I had something to do with it?* I glanced toward the river, kicked the dirt, shook off what I imagined she might be thinking.

"Well, I sleep with my door unlocked here. I couldn't do that in Charlotte."

She wrinkled her brow at the instant a grasshopper pole-vaulted from the ground to a willow branch. "It's just a matter of time until everybody'll be installing alarms and putting up fences to hide behind like in Atlanta. Outsiders are moving in, ruining our land, spoiling our ways. But I won't live in a prison of fear. And the WPC won't put up with it."

"The WPC?" I bristled. "What on earth can the WPC do about it?"

"We have our ways." She smacked the dirt off her hands.

"Oh yeah?" I snickered and looked at her sideways. "Such as?"

"We have a watch list of outsiders we keep an eye on."

I stared at her, my mouth hanging open. "Are you snorting crack?" I jerked the brim of my hat into an awning from the sun. "You know, when I was little, Daddy used to talk that way about people who were different. 'Just bomb the Russians, ship all the queers off to an island, send the niggers back to Africa,' he'd say. That solves everything—everything but your prejudice."

"Don't compare me to that bastard!" She shook her scepter in my face. "I'm nothing like him. And you know it."

"I didn't say you were." It *was* a low blow, but I was so irritated with her holier-than-thou attitude that I didn't care.

"You don't know squat. Your daddy's the reason I quit the church."

"Why would you turn your back on the church because of him?"

"I never turned my back on the church. It turned its back on me. Every time Johnny'd beat your mama up, she'd go to Pastor Abrams for help. He'd tell her she wasn't trying hard enough. 'Go back and work on your marriage,' he'd say. Well . . ." She swatted a fleet of mosquitoes. "Your mama did that . . . worked so hard Johnny finally killed her. I reckon the pastor would say she worked herself to death."

My heart splintered. "I never knew that." I exhaled through my teeth.

"I know you didn't. And I'll bet you didn't know that Pastor Abrams ministered to your daddy for weeks after he killed your mama. Said all Johnny needed to do was accept Jesus Christ, and all would be forgiven. Even hid Johnny from the law until he could save his soul."

"No ma'am. I didn't know that, either." I sighed and looked at Gigi. "But I *do* know that the Reverend used scare tactics to get us to repent. Scared me shitless, preaching that the Vandals of Hell were loose in Whitecross, ready to grab me if I didn't turn my life over to Jesus."

"Pastor Abrams thought the more souls he could save, the greater his reward would be in Heaven."

"Anyway, Gigi, where is Daddy now?"

It was a question that hung stifled in the muggy evening air.

"I reckon whatever reward due Pastor Abrams, he ought to be getting it right about now." She fanned herself with her hat. "Whew, it's hot." She looked off into the distance, made a sudden twitch, and pointed past me. "Look there!" Electrified, she jabbed the air with her scepter. Five cucumber-shaped mammals, swirling in the tea-colored water below, peeped up at us with batting, inquisitive eyes.

Gigi always changed the subject when it came to Daddy, but this time she had a good excuse. I had mixed feelings about this moment that had stolen our conversation, but I'd waited for it all my life.

"Four adults and one baby." I took off my hat, wiped my forehead with the back of my hand.

"Yep and they migrated all the way from the Gulf upstream to feast on the algae in the Suwannee." She looked at me with the pride of a mother showing off her firstborn. "Aren't they the cutest things you ever saw?"

"Man alive. They look so . . . prehistoric."

Another quiet reverence fell over us. I slid my arm around Gigi's shoulder and looked down at her. As we shared our admiration for these nearly extinct mammals, I felt a tremendous stirring of heart and soul. Cocooned with the only link to the loved ones I'd lost, I gazed out at the distant twist of the Suwannee. I thought of Mama there, on Gigi's dock, in the favorite lounge chair she sat in when she watched the sunset over the water and the tune she hummed until I fell asleep in the warm cradle of her arms.

The silence of our wonder was broken only by the squishy sound of Voodoo Sally's bare feet crushing against the mushy wetlands. Gigi tilted her head in the direction of the sound as though it reminded her of something. I felt a strong undercurrent that she hadn't brought me here just to show off her beloved Suwannee and manatee.

"Son, there's something I got to confess . . ." She faltered. "I haven't been completely honest with you . . ." She studied my face.

"What?" I cleared my throat, waited.

There was another long hesitation. Then she cut it off. "Never mind."

"Are you sick?"

"Oh hell, no." She flapped her hand at me, then patted my shoulder reassuringly. "I'm healthier than a pig in shit. There's still a right smart you don't know about, and now's not the time."

"That's funny." I chuckled. "I was going to confess something, too, but I don't think it's time, either."

She nodded her head in a conciliatory manner, gently pushed against a loose strand of hair. "We butt heads a good bit on things. I 'spect we got a sight more talking to do before we see eye-to-eye."

"I suppose so."

Both of us were playing our cards close to our chests. We sparred with words that tested the strength of trust between us. I realized I might have to carry my secret to the grave. Part of me was saddened by that and another part was glad. She'd cared enough about what I thought to keep something from me and that made me feel equal to her.

Gigi chipped a chunk of limestone with the toe of her boot. It unearthed a rich, moist smell. "Did you know limestone is nothing but layers and layers of dead sea creatures and plants, one stacked on top of another for millions a' years?"

"No ma'am, I didn't." I mopped a trickle of sweat off my nose with a shirt sleeve.

She was completely dry. High cheekbones, chiseled nose, full lips—cracked from the summer sun—rounded the age-worn lines in her face. It was a youthful face whittled into a roadmap of crevices over the years.

"Yep. Nothing but fossils, pressed into hard rock by time." She squinted, then pointed at the limestone banks across the river. She used her other hand as a tent from the blinding sun. "I got a ton of respect for limestone. It's soft and lets running water eat holes in it, but that's what makes it strong. That's how it survives for so long."

"That doesn't make sense." I kicked at the limestone with my boot. "How can it be strong if it's soft?"

Gigi examined me with that appraising stare, her right eyebrow arched as if a question were nested inside her comment. "Some people got that same stamina when they let life's hard knocks roll over them. They got limestone gumption."

I jumped at the chance to change the subject to something that had been eating at *me*. "Speaking of hard knocks, why were you so hard on Gladys at the funeral? And what did Gladys mean when she said, 'We have to tell him what we did'?"

Gigi's eyes flew open like I'd slapped her. "That woman's got a big mouth is what I know. It's a private matter between her and me." The abruptness in her voice melted into concern behind her eyes.

"Why do your club sisters whisper and stare at me? Don't they know that's impolite?"

"They're star-struck." She let out a chuckle that morphed into a slow grunt.

"Star-struck?"

"They saw you on *Oprah*. I shouldn't have told them about it, but my pride got the best of me. Gladys checked out the book you wrote from the library, passed it around among the rest."

"Getting the Most out of Your Life?"

"Why, they acted like you were a motion picture star. They swooned at your photograph like a bunch of schoolgirls. Even discussed the book at some of our meetings. Recited their favorite lines from it, too." Gigi mimicked the schoolgirl voice of her sisterfriends: "The challenge before you is never greater than the power within you."

"Well, I'm flattered, but I sense something else."

She ignored my comment, looked beyond me toward the Suwannee. "This river's all the therapy I need. When my heart's heavy, I sit on these banks and let my troubles melt away."

"Yeah, there's calmness, a certainty to it anchored in time. On the other hand, change is inevitable; you can't stop progress."

"Progress? You want to see progress?" Her voice had a razor-sharp edge to it. "There, look at the scars on their backs!" As she pointed at the manatee, her eyes held a heavy sadness. "That *progress* was caused by motorboats. They've just about wiped these poor creatures out."

"And it took thirty-five years for me to see one."

She smiled and circled her arms around my neck. "I'm glad you finally did before they're all gone. You're officially a Pope now."

She conked my forehead with her scepter.

A hungry cormorant torpedoed the water, then disappeared for an instant before retrieving a bream that he carried to his mate who waited patiently on a willow limb. A green-necked heron stalked a bullfrog. I could smell the pungent algae in the river and feel the warm breeze against my face as it ruffled through the willow leaves.

For a good hour, we stood, arms around each other, watching the manatee swirl under puffy cumulus clouds that drifted aimlessly across the sky.

I could see why she felt something was being stolen from her. It wasn't just the land. It was the spirit of the Suwannee. The life she'd known—*her* life. Through her eyes it seemed that everyone had tried to steal her beloved Suwannee. If it wasn't outsiders moving in, it was one of her husbands.

Her longing stirred something deep inside me. I, too, had felt it as a boy. Frog gigging and gator hunting in the summer moonlight. Swinging high in the air from grapevines gnarled around giant live oaks. Swallowing hard, holding my breath, kerploping in the water. And exhaling after a safe landing. Floating down the Suwannee and Ichetucknee rivers in rubber inner tubes with playmates, each of us tied to the other so we wouldn't get separated.

My daddy had hijacked that precious life, a debt I intended to settle.

The sun began to sink behind the cypress trees. A light fog rolled in and gently covered the Suwannee. There was something loving and protective about this river. A steadiness that tomorrow everything would be all right.

But there was something unnerving about it, too. The Suwannee was always changing. Moving fast one day, slow the next. Dark black one season, shimmering gold another. Dropping in the summer, rising in the winter. Placid in the fall, raging in the spring.

I felt Voodoo Sally's pitchfork stare pierce the back of my neck again. I swung my head around. As she spun in circles, I was close enough to see the sides of her bare brown feet turn pink as they rustled the leaves. She chanted, "evol wanga obeah, evol wanga obeah." Then she stopped dead in her tracks, ogled us through tree limbs; her silver hair jutted a good five inches straight out on all sides.

Just as quickly as I had felt comforted, I started to feel unsettled.

As the sun dropped behind the trees, the hot July air took on a strange chill. A light wind fluttered the river birch. Everything felt so iffy—Gigi, the people in this small town, my future here.

It was a life still foreign to me.

Before I could fit into Whitecross's ways, I'd have to walk more confidently in my new boots.

The manatees were gone now. A family of deer grazed on the other side of the riverbank. An armadillo scuttled through the underbrush.

Gigi reached out her wrinkled scepter and beckoned me. "Let's go, son. The WPC's meeting at Gladys Nunn's tonight. I promised I'd make a squash casserole."

On the trek back to the car, my boots dug rhythmically into the wet sand and shoveled muck.

A voice in my head timed itself to my footsteps like a drumbeat, chanting, "evol wanga obeah, evol wanga obeah."

CHAPTER 6

When I pulled into my circular driveway later that evening, the *Charlotte Observer* and *Whitecross News* lay crisscrossed at my front door. It was as if my two worlds had collided against the cedar house in a bidding war, each vying to be on top. As I scooped the papers into my arms and pulled on the screen door, I noticed a strange-looking, red-cloth pouch swinging on the doorknob.

There had been others. With each sack, I had loosened the string at the mouth and examined the white powder inside. I had wondered about anthrax or cocaine. So I'd put one of the pouches in a box and dropped it off with Sylvia Wynn at the pharmacy. After sending it to her lab for testing, she informed me that it contained a harmless combination of ground rosebuds, a white bird feather, and maize kernels.

Somebody was trying to scare me off.

I absentmindedly tossed the pouch onto the kitchen countertop and tugged open the refrigerator door. The shelves were practically bare except for a dish with green mold that looked like a science experiment gone bad. I reached for the container of pimento cheese, slapped a sandwich together, and poured a glass of Merlot.

I stepped into the darkness of the den, soaking up the stillness, letting my eyes adjust to the shadows inside the rough-hewn cabin. I sank into the brown leather sofa, chomped on the sandwich, and washed it down with the red wine. My stare pierced the solid sheet of glass that wide-angled a magnificent view of the Suwannee, then studied the deer head mounted over the stone fireplace.

I thought about the tragedy that had drawn me back here from Charlotte, felt the tension rise in my chest, but couldn't stop it. Though I had visited Gigi in the years between high school and college, rejecting this way of life had been my only defense against the pain. I often referred to my family as rednecks, to Whitecross as Hicksville. After moving into my Charlotte loft, my private practice had taken off; book sales had provided a substantial income. I'd spent weekends in Atlanta and New York City, dining in the finest restaurants, sleeping in practically every world-class hotel on the planet. Anderson Cooper and Gloria Steinem had become long-distance friends.

But urban life had felt empty. I had tried to ignore the fact that Gigi was right: I had kept my head stuck in books and other people's problems. Work had become both a sanctuary and a prison, but years of therapy had helped me put the pieces together. Since childhood, I'd learned to keep my feelings caged to protect myself from being blindsided by another heartbreaking loss.

The answering machine blinked at me. I hopped up and hit the button for the first message. The edge in Chris's normally soft voice told me that somebody hadn't been taking their anti-depressant. As if to insulate my heart, I folded my arms over my chest.

"Brad, I've been thinking about what you said the other night. That you feel like you have a chain around your neck. I just wanted you to know that no one is putting a chain around your neck. I have *never* put a chain around your neck. This is just another ploy to push me away. All I wanted was to be part of your life, meet your family, be included in the lives of those who love you as much as I do. Obviously, that's not what you want, so don't bother calling me for a while, because I don't want to put any more chains around your neck." Click. Dial tone. Beep.

"That temper." I exhaled through my teeth, collapsed onto the cushion, put my feet up. I stared off into the night, picking at the leather seam on the sofa. "If Gigi knew Chris was Chinese-American, that would be it."

I wiped my hands across my face. I should've made myself clearer about the "chain thing." What I'd meant was that I'd felt caught between two people I love most, that getting them together had felt like a lost cause.

Chris had been the only person I'd felt safe enough with to allow my arrested feelings out on bail. We'd become so close that we completed each other's sentences. I'd never shown Gigi pictures of Chris, because I was certain she couldn't accept my relationship with an "Asian outsider." I'd always said Gigi had the "some-of-my-best-friends-are" syndrome. The fact that Betty-Jewel was local-born dwarfed the fact that she was Mexican-American. Quite frankly, I wasn't so sure Chris could tolerate Gigi's country-bumpkin style, either.

Though I felt like a cork bobbing in the water, if I didn't do something soon, I feared I might lose them both, and I knew I couldn't survive that kind of loss again.

I pushed the button on the answering machine for the second message. It was Gigi. "Son, I meant to tell you earlier that the Piggly Wiggly has boneless chicken on sale for a dollar-eighty-nine a pound. It wouldn't make good barbecue, but it's good for making chicken salad. I'm headed to Gladys Nunn's with the squash casserole. I hope you're eating right . . . Oh, I almost forgot. The mayor's office called. Said I'd been chosen White-cross Citizen of the Year for the WPC's preservation efforts, that the award would be conferred on me at Founder's Day. I feel like somebody died and made me Queen, but don't worry.

I'm not on crack. Ha, ha, ha . . . call me sometime." Click. Dial tone. Beep.

I toasted the air with my Merlot, looked down at my sandwich. "Oh yes, Dear Heart, I'm eating right." Then I made a second toast to the air. "And you can tell Gladys for me that she's better off without Big Jake." I knew the hell of living with a bully like Jake Nunn—a snake that fooled people into believing he was a pillar of the community.

Lifting my eyes toward the shimmering lights across the water, I studied Vasque Gaylord's place. His wooden deck curled like a python down the riverbank into the water. The river carried the sound of glasses clinking to the rhythm of clattering voices, the boom of Ricky Martin's "She Bangs." Laughter echoed from across the water where bodies brushed and men leaned against each other's hot flesh. Puffy smoke clouds drifted off into the late night air.

Flames jumped from Tiki torches. They seemed to pass so close to my face that I could almost feel the heat against my cheek, almost smell the smoke through the opened window. I felt the bone-weary memories of my boyhood sweep through me like a flash fire.

My stomach jackknifed.

Flames leapt into the black winter sky, engulfing the run-down, antebellum mansion that I'd lived in before boarding school. I was seven years old. Gigi had inherited the old estate from Grandpa Pope, had handed it down to my mama, Ada Lea.

Paralyzed by terror as the fire roared and swelled, Mama huddled me close. While neighbors worked frantically to retrieve household belongings from the raging inferno, I shuddered next to her. My cheek pressed against her hip, blood seeping from my brow.

"Johnny just went wild!" Mama cried hysterically.

She fell to her knees, wailing, her face against the ground. A fireman had told her that my five-year-old sister, Lydia, trapped inside her bedroom, had perished there.

I stroked Mama's hair, trying to comfort her.

Only minutes before, I had witnessed flames dancing up the living room wall, torched by my alcohol-crazed father. Angry muffled voices from the living room had stirred me. Breaking the peaceful silence of sleep, my bedroom door suddenly had burst open, harsh lights stabbing my eyes.

"I'm sick of you kids," Daddy had yelled. "Your mama never has time for me because of you sorry pieces of shit!"

He seized an old lantern—a prize I'd found in an abandoned house—and slung it at me, cutting a deep gash above my left brow. Confused, I clutched my blood-soaked forehead. He ripped my telephone out of the wall, marched into the living room, flung it into the fire.

When she saw me running behind him, gushing blood, Mama screamed for him to stop.

She swept me behind her like an angry wildcat, wielding a fire poker, hammering him twice in the nape of the neck. But he was too much for her. He grabbed her by the throat of the negligee and accused her of loving me more than him. Terrified, my attention was riveted on the melting telephone. That's the last I remember before we were outside.

The fire ebbed and flowed, engulfing the house. Flames exploded through the front door and windows, sprayed the night air with splintered wood and jagged glass. Fire soared through the ceiling, leaving skeletal roof beams sagging under the weight of charred debris. Columns of smoke billowed into the starry winter sky, leaving sparks and ash floating to the ground, visible, so the story goes, from miles away. By the time fire trucks had arrived, the house had been reduced to a steaming mound of soot and ash.

The memory of drunken outbursts had been stenciled in my brain: sounds of stomping feet into the bedroom closet, the shrieking of clothes hangers against the metal rod, and Daddy slamming clothes back against the wall to reach a rack of belts.

Not to spank us, but to beat us.

That place wasn't a home. It was a boxing ring where adults selected their weapons from an arsenal of knickknacks, appliances, and furniture, jousting in combat to see who could expel their misery first. A new lamp might've had a life of forty-eight hours. Kitchen knives, dishes, frying pans, mirrors, pictures off the wall, hairbrushes, even furniture—all were heaved, thrown, slung, and slammed during angry fights. Sweeping up shattered glass, plastic, or debris became my weekly ritual in second grade.

Somehow I always got caught in the crossfire, begging them to pipe down. I vaulted between Daddy's balled fist, bloodshot glares, and abrasive threats. He would strike wildly at me, whack me across the face, throw me against the wall. Then he'd return to his sport. Although I'd learned to sidestep his powerful swipes, my small frame was no match for his brute force. Though I was never able to protect Mama, she used her raised arms to shield her in an X pattern.

As the fights escalated, she caved in, protecting her classic beauty against the body blows and stomach punches with pathetic whimpers of, "Please, Johnny, anywhere but my face."

There were many trips to the hospital and the Whitecross Police Station. The police were called often at a concerned neighbor's request, but nothing was ever done. Daddy's brother was the sheriff.

I welcomed the break of morning and calm's descendance in the wee hours. I'd clean up messes and make sure things looked normal. A scrupulous eye, however, could discern clues from chipped glass figurines, dented furniture, holes in the wall.

After the fire, we were left with the charred remains of our lives: a few pieces of furniture, the family Bible, the clothes on our backs. And, of course, the trust fund from Grandpa Pope.

My last memory of Mama was standing side-by-side in front of the smoldering ruins looking up at her. She was cradling a giant green-velvet book that she'd grabbed from the bookshelf as she fled. I watched her stroke the golden letters Holy Bible *etched across the emerald book cover, and I worried what would become of us.*

I searched her face for answers. Daddy's knuckles had robbed her of her Ava Gardner good looks. Constant abuse had put its signature in dark circles around her eyes, deep lines across her face. Already, she had begun to walk with a cane. That's when it hit me: she didn't have any answers. There were none to be had.

Or so I thought at the time.

Soon after the fire, Mama sent me away against my wishes. It would be years before I'd discover it was for my own protection, that it had been her only answer. She'd explained it all in a letter to me right before Daddy beat her to death.

A letter I never received.

After I'd graduated from boarding school, Gigi had mentioned the contents of the letter to me in a phone call. She had said she'd looked high and low for it, finally decided that it had gotten swallowed up in the clutter of her house.

When I was down in the dumps, I'd try to remember as best I could what I'd been told Mama had said in the letter. The essence of it was that if she hadn't sent me away, he would've killed me, too, and she was right. After he murdered Mama, Daddy disappeared. I'd spent the rest of my childhood in boarding school without a family, except for Gigi, who had sent money but never visited.

My hatred for my daddy was born the night of the fire. It grew in magnitude after he murdered Mama. But it would be years as an adult in my own therapy before I'd realize the fervor of the rage that had possessed me.

A loud ring broke the spell. I lifted the portable phone with a trembling hand, then sank back into the sofa, amazed at how the sight of fire could still trigger me into my bleak past.

"Dr. Pope?" A voice on the other end asked.

I used my professional voice in case it was a client calling after hours. "Dr. Pope speaking."

"This is Myrtle Badger."

It was the busybody from the funeral whom Gigi had accused of looking down her nose at other people.

"We haven't had the pleasure of meeting, but I have a matter of utmost urgency to discuss with you."

She spoke in a high-pitched whine. At the funeral reception, I remembered thinking she looked like a hippopotamus—stocky set, round face, long droopy mouth, and fat eyes set high upon her forehead.

"What can I do for you, Mrs. Badger?"

"I don't know exactly how to put this, but it's about the Women's Preservation Club."

"I'm afraid you've reached the wrong Pope. You need to speak with my grandma, Gigi Pope."

"Doctor, there's bad blood between your grandmamma and me. I've tried talking with her but it's impossible."

There was a long pause, obviously to get a reaction. When I remained silent, she continued. "She's so hardheaded, I can't get a word in edgewise. I saw you at the funeral, tried to get your attention, but it looked like you had your hands full with her. I wanted to talk to you out of earshot of her anyway."

"About what?"

"Your grandmamma and the rest of her club sisters blackballed me from the WPC for no good reason. And after all my hard work on her husband, Gladys Nunn refused to open Big Jake's casket. They're trying to ruin my good name in the community. That's what."

"Ma'am, I don't have anything to do with the WPC."

"I know that, but I thought you could talk some sense into her."

"Mrs. Badger, I don't get in-between my grandma and her personal business."

"She said I was ineligible for membership because I was born

in Atlanta and had lived in Whitecross for only three years."
There was a grunt of disdain on the other end. "To top it off,
she said I was bad to dangle a participle. Now, does that sound
like a crazy woman to you or what?"

"Mrs. Badger, this is not my affair."

She pushed harder, her voice rising now. "There's something
strange about those women. The fact that they won't let me in."

"Hmm." I punctuated her comment with distance. It seemed
the more unyielding I was, the harder it became for her to hold
it together.

"I'm a Christian, damn it!" She snapped in a shrill tone.

I held the phone away from my ear, stared at it for a second,
and imagined her hand flying over her lips in a desperate attempt to herd the unholy word back into her mouth.

"Yes, I can see that you are." A long silence stretched between
us, broken only by the uncomfortable clearing of her throat.
"Mrs. Badger, are you still there?"

She finally spoke, her voice tightly guarded. "It's not my
nature to curse . . ." She stammered now, as she began to cover
her tracks. "It just goes to show you how upset they've made
me. What I meant to say was I'm a decent God-fearing Christian . . . that club's tarnishing my reputation . . . I was president
of the Virginia Highland's Garden Club. Why, I'm more of a
green thumb than Gigi Pope ever was. I was written up in the
garden section of the *Atlanta Constitution* for the camellias I
planted along Peachtree Street. The article said my Lady Clares
gave the streetscape an old-fashioned, Southern-to-the-core
feel."

"I'm sure you're very talented, but I can't help you with this.
Now, I really must go."

"Surely you can see why I'm so upset. You're not dealing
with just anybody. My good name's at stake, and I'm going to
get to the bottom of the WPC. I'll declare I've never seen a

group of women so glued together. It's just not normal."

My patience was thinning. "Mrs. Badger, don't you think you're making too much out of this?"

"Too much? They've made me a laughingstock blackballing me. My husband, Swayze, says I'm an outcast . . . I've got to prove . . ." Apparently realizing she'd revealed too much again, she began to whimper, choking on her tears. Between gasps of breath, she sniveled. "Dr. Pope, you're her grandson. Surely, you can put a good word in for me."

"As I just told you, Mrs. Badger, I don't interfere in my grandma's personal affairs."

Her tone sharpened. "Everybody in town knows your grand-mamma visits that evil Voodoo Sally. If you ask me, she's probably a devil worshipper, too."

"Hold on now." I sat upright, *evol wanga obeah! evol wanga obeah!* thumping in my head.

"I know for a fact that she's an atheist because she doesn't attend church." Her voice got higher and shriller. "That's why she won't let me join, isn't it? Because I'm a Christian and she's an atheist?"

After another dead silence, she continued. "I know one thing for sure. That floozy Jackie Priester was with a married man when he fell off a mountain ledge—Forney something or another. I read all about it in the paper. She and your grand-mamma are in some kind of evil coven, and I'm going to get to the bottom of it."

"Mrs. Badger, you can stop right there."

"What else could it be? They're all over Atlanta, devil worshippers *and* lesbians. That club has to be one or the other, and if you were any kind of Christian, you'd help me. But I can tell you're just like your grandmamma, all high and mighty like you're better than everybody else. Come to think of it, I haven't seen you at Sunday church service, either."

"Whoa. Whoa." I stood up.

"I don't know why I called you in the first place. Preacher Black warned the brethren of the likes of you. He says the devil masquerades as a normal person, that if you split the word *therapist* in half, it spells *the rapist.*"

"What kind of virulent crap?" I imagined her nostrils flaring with rage, felt the hair on the back of my neck standing at attention, as it became clear she was only interested in viper-tongued vengeance. "This conversation is over, Mrs. Badger."

"And you can just kiss THIS, and I don't mean my grocery list!" She slammed the phone in my ear.

I stared at the receiver in my tightly clenched hand, then shoved the phone on its cradle, my lips releasing a long puff of air.

I poured another glass of wine to wash down the gritty conversation and flopped back into the sofa. My hand swatted the *Charlotte Observer* and flipped open the *Whitecross News.* The glaring headlines seemed to jump off the page: "Phosphate Company Owner Dies from Fall on Hike." The article said that Forney Fowler, head of Triple Six Phosphate Company, knew the terrain well, but experience hadn't saved him. Authorities reported that Fowler, forty-two, of Starke, slipped while hiking the North Carolina Mountains and fell nearly 200 feet to his death from atop a ledge. He was accompanied by an unidentified female companion.

What was Jackie Priester doing in the mountains with this man?

My eyes leapt to a second article, "Campaign Underway for Town Council." It was accompanied by photos of candidates Betty-Jewel Iglesias, fifty-four-year-old realtor, and Swayze Badger, sixty-one-year-old developer—both sharing their favorite chili-bean recipes with voters.

When I looked up, the other side of the riverbank stole my attention again. I watched as a pontoon, lit in red and green from bow to stern, puttered away from Vasque Gaylord's house. The evening breeze carried the scent of marijuana. Two men passed a joint back and forth before flipping it into the water. Then they embraced, pressed their lips together. I sipped my wine, watching them strip naked, lock belly to belly, and dive into the water, yelping—poisoning the Suwannee with cigarette butts, empty beer containers, and unnatural sex.

At least that's how Gigi would see it.

It'd been a long, drawn-out day, and I was dog-tired. I gulped the last drop of wine, yawned and stretched wide like a lazy mutt. Then I felt my body melt into the softness of the leather sofa, felt it yearn for the taste of Chris's almond skin and my hands traveling over those long sleek curves.

The honky-tonk music of the Dixie Chicks skipped across the water. I drifted off to their haunting twang: "Tonight the Heartache's on Me."

In the middle of the night, still on the couch where I'd fallen asleep, I opened my eyes to the sound of a muffled voice. Off in a distant side of the room, a human form bobbed and weaved toward me. It shuffled up close. When I looked up, a gawking round face bent over me upside down. It hovered, wigwagging its head, waving a huge black leather hand.

I screamed bloody murder inside my skin, but my lips wouldn't work and sounds wouldn't come out of me. Trapped inside my body, I tried to wake myself but couldn't. I was soaking wet, pinching myself to see if I was awake or asleep. In the night, I had decided that I was awake, but it still felt like a dream. The rest blurred into tattered pieces in my mind, difficult to stitch together. And I drifted off again.

When I woke the next morning, I jumped off the couch trying to sort out the colliding thoughts from the night before. I'd decided that I *had* to have been dreaming.

But when I went to fetch the morning newspaper, my front door was ajar. A black leather glove lay by the threshold.

And another red pouch dangled from the doorknob.

CHAPTER 7

It had been a week since that creepy night—that ghostly figure and red pouch hanging on my door handle. It made me wonder if the old witch was up to something, trying to scare me again. Still spooked, everytime I closed my eyes, I saw Big Jake's bloated face, wondering if I'd played a role in his death. Under the opened sunroof of my Pathfinder and an immaculate Florida sky, I tore my attention from the nagging thoughts and savored the ripe air whipping through my hair, filling my lungs, and felt my spirits begin to lift. Being back home, enjoying life on the Suwannee was beginning to awaken a long-dormant feeling from my boyhood.

I relished the sweet smells of the countryside: the honey-suckle, freshly cut grass. I gloried in the beds of wild purple phlox that stretched along the roadside, rolled hay that dotted the horse and dairy farms like giant spools of thread. The local country-music station—which I'd tried at Gigi's arm-twisting—blared Reba McEntire.

I zipped past a produce stand with blood-red tomatoes and orange cantaloupes on my right. And an old geezer in straw hat and bib overalls peddled boiled peanuts on my left. A herd of Black Angus, crossing the road, ground me to a halt, blocked my path. For me, this simple life was where I belonged—the way locals lived close to the earth and kept a strong connection to the past, raising livestock for slaughter, growing their own vegetables. They tuned in to the heartbeat of the land, reading nature when it spoke to them, like when tree frogs barked, that meant rain. And you wouldn't find that tidbit on the weather channel or Wikipedia, either.

Sadly, Gigi was right: I'd come home to an uncomplicated way of life—as quiet, slow-paced, and meandering as the Suwannee itself—on the verge of extinction.

As I approached the town limits, a sign greeted me:

Welcome to Whitecross, Home of the Historic Suwannee River
Please Help Us Keep Our Town Clean and Green
                              —The Women's Preservation Club

To most Whitecross-bound motorists, the sign was just another blur on the road, but it had special meaning to me. It was flanked by a garden of red caladiums and fuchsia azaleas planted by the WPC.

My eyes zeroed in on the words at the bottom of the sign: *The Women's Preservation Club,* a reminder that I hadn't spoken to Gigi in a while. Between clients and trying to finish my new book, I'd been squeezed for time. I wanted to let her know about my phone conversation with Myrtle Badger.

I grabbed my cell and punched Gigi's number.

"Hello?"

"Morning, Gigi." Periodic static interfered with the reception. "What're you doing?"

"Folding laundry. What's up?"

"I had a close encounter of the Myrtle Badger kind."

"A what?"

"Myrtle Badger called me upset that you blackballed her. Says she's going to get to the bottom of the WPC."

"The only thing she's going to get to the bottom of is Preacher Black. Don't worry. I'll take care of her . . ." Her voice started to crackle and pop.

"I'm sure you will." More static crackled and popped. "We're breaking up. By the way, thanks for turning me on to Reba McEntire. She grows on you."

"Yep, she's my gal—the queen bee of home-grown . . ." A garbled answer.

"Gigi, we need to talk again . . . about Daddy."

"I can barely hear you, son. Speak up."

More static, Gigi's crackled voice and the connection started to break up again. How convenient for her that she couldn't hear me. I told her I'd call her later. We said our goodbyes, and I tossed my cell in the passenger's seat.

Off in the distance, I saw Free-Will Baptist Church, where Gigi and Mama had made me go to Sunday school when I was small. As I cruised in front of the church, I thought about all those times Preacher Abrams admonished us and spanked his ragged Bible. He'd hold it high in the air, warning the congregation of eternal damnation. Then, boom. He'd slam it hard against the lectern, and the congregation would gasp and shiver.

Even now, his voice echoed in my head. "There's only one thing between you and the undertaker, and that's the savin' grace of Jesus. Repent and wash yourself in the blood of Jesus Christ before the Vandals of Hell snatch you off the street."

As the memory moved in on me, it spun a thought: No wonder I got blindsided with bad dreams and dark moods from time to time . . . what with that crazy preacher, my alcoholic father, and Voodoo Sally.

Rough images, still sharp in my mind from that earlier time, rolled over me.

Sunday after Sunday, there I'd sit, stuffed between Mama and Gigi in the pew, waiting for the preacher to beat Jesus into me. To make time pass, I'd fold church bulletins into paper airplanes or daydream about cat fishing. I'd scratch a patch of poison ivy rash on my wrist or kick the pew in front of me until a grownup turned around and gave me a dirty look.

Preacher Abrams would rock on his heels, the balls of his feet. He'd leap off the floor, hands flung into the air, squeal in tongues. "Om a Sheeka Kabiah!"

In the front pews, church members would draw their bodies into themselves. His voice would break; he'd squall like a baby, begging us to come down front to the altar and save our souls. He'd snap open his white handkerchief, mop spittle from the corner of his lips. Then he'd walk among us looking for souls to save, pointing his index finger like an aimed rifle.

Powdered in sweet-smelling talcum, dressed in their Sunday finest, husbands and wives clenched hands. Other children my age stood motionless—wooden, like pieces of furniture, afraid one move would draw attention. They prayed, not for salvation, but for the preacher to overlook them just one more time.

One Sunday morning, I too prayed hard that Jesus would let me off the hook. "Dear Lord, I promise I'll be good. I won't cuss anymore. From now on, I'll put the offering money Gigi gave me in the collection plate and not spend it on candy. I promise I'll work on Daddy to stop drinking, take care of sister, and do my homework so Mama won't worry so much. But Dear Jesus, please let the preacher pick somebody else and leave me alone."

But the prayer didn't work. From the pulpit, Preacher Abrams aimed his lethal finger directly at me, called out a warning. "Being little don't get you off the hook, young feller!"

Then he descended from the pulpit, his eyes transfixed on me.

As he neared me, I swallowed hard. I sweated. I squirmed.

Unless I repented, I would be one of the lost sheep doomed to burn in hell.

His sweat-soaked arm coiled around my neck, choked me with the smell of perspiration and foul breath. He pulled hard on my shoulder, his pink fingers white on the edges as they pressed into my flesh. His words squeezed me like a vise, urged me down the aisle, up to the altar. I felt like a corralled sheep in the slaughterhouse. I sank my head low, eyes shut tight, feet glued to the wooden floor, hands cemented to the mahogany pew.

Frustrated by my stonewalling, he snapped in my ear, "Son, you still ain't accepted Jesus Christ. What's it gonna take?"

I shrugged, held my breath.

"You wanna burn in hell, son?"

I shook my head; my heart fluttered.

"Jesus don't give no guarantees just because you're little. If you wanna burn in hell with Voodoo Sally and all the other niggers and evil doers, then you go right ahead."

His arm loosened from my shoulder. Sensing other lost souls stealing his attention, I panicked. If I didn't do something quick, the Vandals of Hell would snatch me as soon as I walked out the church doors. I imagined falling into a flaming pit, Voodoo Sally's outstretched arms reaching up from the bottom to catch me in her evil embrace.

My hands broke loose from the pew. I hitched onto the preacher's shirt cuffs, a lifeline to Heaven that towed me down the aisle to the altar into the safe arms of Jesus. A picture of Jesus's face smiled back at me from Preacher Abrams's cuff links.

Quite frankly, the thought of eternal life never appealed to me, even as a boy. But it beat falling into the arms of Voodoo Sally, whom I'd begun to see as the Antichrist.

On the edge of town, a logging truck slowed me. As I crept my way into Whitecross, I inched past Whitecross Hardware and Glenda's Diner—featuring the best fried chicken, gulf seafood, and other "farm town" favorites. I continued on past Suwannee Dives and Outfitters, where experts led daily expeditions and taught the skill of cave diving and underwater cave exploration to the adventurous. I spent my days delving into the mental caverns of some of the locals, a sport much more fascinating than underground cave exploration. At least, I suspected that to be the case and one in which I could

---

participate from the safety of my office armchair.

My tires crunched on the blacktop parking lot of the yellow Victorian house that I'd rented at Fifteen Duval Street. I used the downstairs as an office and waiting room, the upstairs for storage. Pulling my Pathfinder into its usual space, I checked my watch. I had fifteen minutes before my appointment with Shirley Gilchrist, who had cornered me at the funeral reception.

Still sluggish from too much wine and a sleepless night, I trudged up the front steps of the old house. Even though the paint peeled in places and it needed a new roof, I'd rented it because of its charm: wrap-around porch, gingerbread trim, weathervane and high-arched roof. I'd hung eight big ferns from the porch eaves that wound around both sides of the house.

I rattled my keys until the correct one sprang up, unlocked the door, stepped inside the foyer. The sound of my clacking shoes on the shiny dark oak floors echoed off the thirteen-foot ceilings. The airy waiting room to the right was soaked with daylight from tall windows that sprinkled dots onto the Persian carpet. I flicked on two floor lamps in dark corners, arranged the magazines on the coffee table, walked back across the foyer to my office.

Stained-glass trim lined the tops of my office windows, spearing sprigs of yellows and greens against my wingback. Unburdened by logic or worry, I often flopped there and lost all sense of time. The office was a safe haven for me to practice my own brand of self-therapy—mindfulness meditation and daily reflections.

As I shrugged out of my backpack, it slid onto the file cabinet. I surveyed the room to make sure everything was in place. While fluffing the sofa pillows on the loveseat where my patients sat, I realized my thoughts were elsewhere. Something lurked beneath the surface of my mind.

Without warning, a faint memory from the previous night

seared through me. I dropped into the swivel chair behind my antique oak desk, pressed my fingers against my temples and rubbed. Hard. I tried to capture the blurry details from the fragmented thoughts that bled together. When I realized I couldn't tell if the memory was real or if I'd dreamt it, I collapsed my head into the cradle of my hands.

Shocked.

Was I having a mental breakdown? Or alcoholic blackouts? *I'll be damned if becoming an alcoholic is in the cards for me. I'll never be like my old man.*

The memory, as vague as it was, felt real to the bone, as real as the oak desk I was drumming my fingers on, as real as the drive I'd just made into the office. I scanned the knotty pine paneling. The wood grains began to take form, and I felt a quiver of recognition escape from below my awareness.

I'd awakened in the middle of the night on the couch where I'd passed out—again. I'd felt a cold stiff hand clamp down on my shoulder. When I jerked my eyes open, the eyeless apparition had twisted his jaw at me. Dressed in white suit, blue shirt, and white tie, he spoke through ruby lips and a ghoulish smile. What slipped out of him was a deep formless guttural sound, telling me that he'd returned to make me pay for what I'd done. His palms swept in the direction of his casket, offered me a place in the company of the Vandals of Hell.

Then he puckered his lips into a kiss and blew it at me.

I tried to cry out, but my scream was lodged in my throat.

I jolted myself awake, sat up on the edge of the couch, elbows on my knees, forefingers and thumbs forming a triangle. The dream had felt so real, but it had to have been a dream. Jake was dead and buried in the ground.

I sat in the stillness of my office, scratched my head. *Man, I must've really been wasted. Either that or . . .* The psychologist in me did a deep dive. *If I couldn't separate dreams from reality, what else couldn't I remember?*

Determined to fend off the pressing thought, I pushed it back with full throttle. I stood, busied myself. I cleaned off my desk, grabbed a manila folder from the file cabinet, scribbled the name of the next client, *Shirley Gilchrist,* at the top of the folder. But with unyielding force, the tsunami-of-a-thought flattened my resistance, crashed through my brain, floated to the top.

When I'd gotten to Suwannee Springs too late for the dive lesson with Big Jake, I'd seen his guideline tied to a tree. Nobody was around but me. I remembered thinking how easy it would be to use the knife from my dive bag to cut the line and nobody'd ever know.

Could my anger have driven me that far without me knowing it? That certainly was possible. Maybe the memory was simply the vague truth of what I'd done trying to resurface. Perhaps down deep, in a place unknown to me, I'd inherited Daddy's bad gene. In trying to redeem Gladys, was it possible that I had displaced my hatred for him onto Big Jake? Why not? After all, I'd worked with hospitalized patients who'd committed heinous crimes during bouts of temporary amnesia.

The more I considered it, the less crazy it seemed. My mouth went dry. My stomach gnawed in its pit. I stood, paced the spacious room, trying to pull it together. My heart and head raced each other. I unclenched my fists, loosened my tie, and rubbed both palms across my face.

Typical psychologist, I told myself, *I'm reading way too much into a drunken stupor. Kill somebody? That's absurd! I'm nothing like my daddy.*

The image of Gladys's milk cow eyes—large and brown— tugged at me, begged for help. I'd tried to walk that line, helping her get strong in the face of abuse. But had I gone too far?

In the final analysis, I blamed the psychobabble on too much alcohol and guilt—guilt that I was somehow responsible for not repairing Gladys's marriage before Big Jake's death. Then I thought of an old saying in psychologists' circles about Freud: "Sometimes a cigar is just a cigar." And I told myself, "Sometimes knotholes are just knotholes." My heart and head started to settle down at the finish line.

I flashed to Gladys at the funeral, remembered what she'd said about needing to tell me what they'd done. Then I thought of Shirley and Jackie, cornering me at the reception, insisting on seeing me right away, saying it had to do with Big Jake. And Gigi, dismissing the staring and whispering as star-struck sister-friends.

I chuckled at first until I thought about Myrtle Badger. She was right about one thing: the WPC *was* standoffish, but they weren't star-struck with her.

No. The sisterfriends were hiding something. The sudden rush for appointments from Shirley and Jackie had started around the time of Big Jake's murder.

A terrible fright gripped me.

Big Jake might've been dead and buried. But until I got to the bottom of his murder, he would continue to cloak my mind and heart like a funeral shroud.

The sisterfriends knew something about his death that I didn't.

And that *something* had steered them to me.

CHAPTER 8

"I despised Big Jake." Teary-eyed, a lump in her throat, Shirley Gilchrist had settled into my overstuffed sofa for a two-hour therapy session, facing me in my wingback. "I'm glad he's dead."

"You're glad?" My curiosity inched me forward.

"I was taught that it's wrong to speak ill of the dead." She sniffled and absentmindedly petted her oversized, artificial hair bun. "I guess 'glad' sounds awful bad to say out loud, about a dead man. Doesn't it, Dr. Pope?"

"Not if that's how you feel."

"Well, that's how I feel." She straightened her shoulders, lifted her chin. "He had it coming."

"So let's talk about what he did to make you feel that way."

She eyed me up and down. I was slouched in my chair, ankles crossed. She schooled me, starting at my feet. "Ladies sit pretty. Men sit strong. Uncross your ankles and sit up straight, Dr. Pope. Chairs were made to sit in, not sleep in." Then she lectured about the importance of never wearing white after Labor Day, keeping hands in laps at the dinner table, chewing with mouths closed.

I smiled but didn't adjust my position. The therapist in me didn't take Shirley's comments personally. I listened with an impartial ear as though I were entering an unfamiliar cave, watching, listening with heightened awareness. I didn't know where her diatribe was headed but knew that ultimately it would give me deeper insight into her.

She vehemently denounced women who broke the rules. "Ladies always cross right ankles over left, but some women get it backwards, a sign of bad breeding."

The tangent wasn't a complete waste of time. Her "propriety police" persona told me she feared loss of control. The fake bun anchored her fear, adding close to an extra half-foot to her height. It served as a monument to her stability—a pathetic, off-the-mark stab by a woman who lived by the books of Amy Vanderbilt, Martha Stewart, Emily Post—external roadmaps that hid her insecurities. Adhering to their standards of conduct proved she "was normal." The sad paradox was that the wobbly bun had become a destabilizing betrayal, which brought us to why she had such an intense dislike for Big Jake.

"When my bun got snared in the bread racks at the Piggly Wiggly, he made a public spectacle of me." She hugged a sofa pillow, rested her chin into it, scrolled her eyes up at me.

"Your bun got caught in the bread racks at the Piggly Wiggly?" It sounded so absurd that I had a hard time keeping a straight face. But I'd heard more outrageous things in therapy before.

Come to find out, she'd amplified the Piggly Wiggly story in her mind. To hear her tell it, you'd have thought she'd made the headlines of the *Whitecross News*. She'd bent down to administer her smell test on the fresh-baked breads. She inhaled the yeasty aromas and poked her finger against the grains. When she tried to erect herself, a piece of metal projecting from the bread racks hooked her bun, held her hostage.

"I had just stuffed my buggy with celery, potatoes, mayonnaise, pickles, and pimento—the ingredients for my Sunday potato salad. When I reached for the bread, it dawned on me I was caught. I thrashed about and pulled away from the bread rack. My bun stretched like an accordion opening its pleats."

"Why didn't you just remove the bun from your head?"

"Lord have mercy, Dr. Pope." She pawed at her bun. "That's the last thing I'd do."

"Why not?"

She put a stranglehold on the sofa pillow, picked up the Kleenex box and set it down, then scratched a spot on her arm.

"Shirley, why didn't you just unpin your bun?"

She hung her head to one side, spoke so softly I could barely hear her. "Because of my bald spot." Her eyes tried to meet mine but sagged under the weight of shame.

"Well, no wonder you were so upset," I said in a compassionate voice.

She raised her head, her mouth hanging open. She paused for a second, then continued. Tears made gullies in the makeup down her cheeks; hurt punctuated her voice. "The worst part was Big Jake's booming laugh, waving customers over like a circus barker, recruiting peeps at a freak show, giggling and sniggering at me."

"No wonder you despised him so."

With disbelief, she looked me directly in the eye, her lips curled into a half smile. "Checkers left their registers to gawk at me. All because of Big Jake. Shoppers, craning their necks for a peek, rammed one another."

"You must've been mortified."

"I was. I cried out, 'Somebody help me. Please!' And Big Jake mocked me, 'Call 911.'

"The clanging-metal ruckus of slamming carts drew the attention of Ibejean Martin. She knew what it was like to be held hostage in a public place. Ibejean told me to hold on, that they'd get me out of it. Then she summoned store manager, Earle Pearce, and patted my hand until he showed up. But it was cold comfort because Earle is shifty. He puts the good oranges underneath the bad ones and the outdated milk in front of the fresh. But I was in no position to be choosy. If I had to choose,

I'd certainly pick Earle over Big Jake."

Shirley went on to say how Earle consoled her. "Everything'll be all right now, Shirley. We're getting it." Then she said he did the unthinkable. He unhooked her bun, let it dangle from the bread racks, a public humiliation ten times worse than Big Jake's. She heard the snickering shift into gasps at the bald spot that shone through the wispy hairs on her scalp.

She said Big Jake hooted, slapped his knees, and yelled, "She's bald-headed." Then she plucked her bun, flattened it on her head, and balanced it with her right hand until her nerves calmed. Earle sat her down on a red plastic milk crate, gave her a to-go cup of water and a pack of bobby pins, saying, "On the house." Big Jake, Ibejean, and the small army of customers slowly wandered off, leaving Shirley weak and swimmy-headed.

Between long, slow sips of water, she told Earle that Big Jake was always making fun of her, that she'd like to take a crowbar to his head. She chewed on the edge of the Styrofoam cup. She assured Earle she wasn't crazy and had proof. She unzipped her pocketbook and showed him her competency papers from Doc Rogers. He read them: *To Whom It May Concern: Having examined and treated Shirley Floried Gilchrist, I hereby certify that she is of sound mind and competent to manage her own affairs.*

"There now, it's all over." Earle patted her shoulder.

But it wasn't over for Shirley. She headed straight for the hardware department, placed a hunting knife in her cart right beside her potato salad ingredients. In the check-out line, she explained to Earle that she needed a good sharp knife to cut up her potatoes. Pushing her squeaky buggy through the automatic sliding doors into the parking lot, she threw Earle a parting comment over her shoulder: "I'll get even with Jake Nunn if it's the last thing I do!"

"Did you get even with him?" I asked.

She ignored my question. "I try so hard to do what's right,

but . . ." Her shoulders sagged into the sofa cushions. "Big Jake and Myrtle Badger are like two peas in a pod."

"Myrtle Badger?"

"She goes around town telling folks I'm crazy, claimed I stole from her." She readjusted her posture, mashed her tilting bun to the center of her head.

"Why would Myrtle accuse you of stealing?"

"It's a long story. Myrtle had just moved into a new house, furnished with her grandmamma's antiques that she'd hauled down from Atlanta. They say she cheated her brothers and sisters out of their grandmamma's inheritance, got everything. Being neighborly and all, the sisterfriends threw her a welcome wagon party at her new house.

"Then they all surprised me by bringing out a birthday cake. Turned out, it was a double celebration—a welcome party for Myrtle and a birthday party for me. We both got gobs of stuff. After it was over, it took two Rubbermaids to haul out the trash. I brought a pasteboard box full of my own bowls for the punch and chip and dip and used it as a carrying box to pack up my gifts. I never thought anything more about it until two weeks later when the WPC met at my house. Myrtle had shanghaied us into interviewing her for membership."

Her voice dropped. She protected her words with a cupped palm at the side of her mouth, as if she thought somebody might be listening.

"Myrtle thought she was a shoo-in, but we were just pacifying her because she's mean as a rattlesnake when she doesn't get her way."

"Yeah, I've heard she's not shy about stepping on a few toes."

"According to the church rumor mill, Myrtle was pretty in her day. Back before exercise machines, her daddy used a rolling pin to shape her thighs. They say it helped her win Miss Atlanta and go to the Miss Georgia pageant in 1960-something."

I tried to reconcile in my mind the Myrtle I'd met with the image of Miss Georgia, but somehow it wouldn't compute. "Miss Georgia, huh?"

"Yes, and when she didn't win the title, she climbed on-stage during the pageant finals, yanked the crown off the winner's head, crumpled it, and kicked it across the floor. They say to this day she keeps a small golden shard of that crown tucked away in a jewelry box—that she's addicted to jewelry."

"So when she doesn't get her way, she makes people pay."

"Myrtle *always* gets her way. She was her daddy's favorite, and he spoiled her rotten. Growing up, she got whatever she wanted."

"So all that pampering has made her pretty pushy, huh?"

"Pushy." She pointed her finger at me, a signal I took to mean I was on target. "That rich boy she married from a bigwig Atlanta family, name of Swayze Badger, used to pamper her and give in to her just like her daddy did. Word around town is he lost interest in her when she gained weight and her supple skin turned to cottage cheese. All Swayze cared about was building strip malls and having pretty little one-night stands. When she wasn't the apple of his eye anymore, Myrtle started having an affair with Preacher Black for spite. The only reason Preacher Black sleeps with Myrtle is because he's half blind. The sisterfriends joke that if he could see what he was crawling on top of, it'd jolt his eyesight into twenty/twenty."

Shirley blushed, looked down at her lap, and hesitated for a few heartbeats. Then she straightened her shoulders, raised her chin, and continued. She said the sisterfriends met in her dining room and shot the breeze until Myrtle flounced through the door, infesting the mood like the sun went behind the clouds.

The women moved into the den. No sooner had Myrtle slammed into the sofa than her eyes bulged, mouth fell open. Myrtle clicked her ruby fingernails against Shirley's brand-new mahogany side table, twirled her big flashy opal ring—which Shirley believed to be another antique stolen from her grand-mamma. Then Myrtle started patting her foot real hard like she was agitated about something.

"I thought she had to pee," Shirley said. "I pointed her to the bathroom down the hall to the right, but Myrtle gave me one of her dirty looks."

Gigi asked Myrtle why she wanted to be a member, but Myrtle sat there dazed, staring at the coffee table. The sister-friends looked at each other, wondered if she'd been sniffing the furniture polish. Then all of a sudden Myrtle pushed to her feet, howling like a coyote. It scared Wilma-May and Gladys so bad they drew into themselves, gathered their dresses around their legs, dragged their pocketbooks into their chests. Myrtle pointed to a glass egg on Shirley's coffee table, one of the pres-ents somebody had given Shirley at the birthday party.

"That's my grandmommie's glass egg," Myrtle cried. "It's genuine crystal. And Shirley Gilchrist stole it from my house."

"What?" Shirley shrieked. Gasps echoed around the room.

"You flagrantly stole my glass egg." Myrtle turned on Shirley with a vengeance. "After I had a party for you at my own house. That glass egg was a remembrance from my poor departed grandmommie."

Crocodile teardrops poured down Myrtle's cheeks, leaving salty spots on Shirley's newly upholstered sofa. Shirley's Siamese, Racket, kept rubbing up against Myrtle, who elbowed him away. When Racket persisted, Myrtle smacked him on the head and cracked, "Get away, you smelly old thing."

"I wanted to tell her if she touched my cat again, I'd . . . why I'd . . ." Blushing, Shirley absentmindedly picked lint off the sofa. "Dr. Pope, you told me I could say anything that was on my mind in here. So I'm going to make myself tell you what I was thinking . . . even though I'm ashamed."

"Go ahead." I opened my arms wide, lifted them with complete abandon.

"I'd choke her so bad she'd think she was going down on Preacher Black." She looked down at the floor, her face the color of spaghetti sauce, then put an admonishing hand across her mouth like a little girl who'd said a bad word. "I just thought it, though, I didn't say it."

I cracked up.

"Isn't that awful, Dr. Pope?" She nudged her bun and looked surprised that I hadn't chastised her. "It's not very ladylike, is it?"

Heaving with laughter, I held my splitting stomach and popped my thigh with my notepad. But between chuckles, I gave a genuine head-nod and the words of approval she was seeking. "It's natural to have thoughts like that when you're pushed to your breaking point."

My comment seemed to ease her. Breathing a sigh of relief, she returned to her story. "That egg was in with the gifts that Betty-Jewel and Jackie packed up in my pasteboard carrying box. I never could figure out what the egg was for to begin with. So I just plopped it on the coffee table. Myrtle steam-rolled right over my explanation. Said that she didn't believe me or Betty-Jewel. She got downright hysterical, preaching at us that we'd broken the Ten Commandments, that we'd burn in hell along with all the other thieves and liars."

"I'm surprised my grandmamma didn't have a few choice words for her," I said.

"Oh, she did. Gigi stood up and jumped right on Myrtle, saying, 'Well then that settles it. I guess you don't want to be part of a pack of sinners, now do you?' "

"That sounds like her."

"Then Myrtle turned on me, calling me mental, saying I ought to be put in the loony bin in McClenny. I was so mad I pulled off one of my high heels and chased her around the room, threatening to kill her."

"That doesn't sound like you, Shirley."

"I was fit to be tied. She'd insulted my friends, abused Racket, and called me crazy. I told her I wasn't the crazy one and reached in my pocketbook and pulled out my competency papers that prove I'm not crazy. I said, 'I bet you don't have one of these!' "

"Do you carry those papers around with you?" I asked.

"Yep. I never know when I might need them."

"I'll bet Myrtle was sizzling," I said.

"Myrtle started shaking her finger at me, and I shook my papers back at her. I told her, 'I got proof I'm not crazy. Do you?' She acted calm and collected, like she was above the fray. She puffed up, strutted to the other side of the room, and declared, 'Normal people don't have to carry proof around with them. Only crazy people do that.'

"I drew back and slung my pulled-off shoe with all my might. But my bad aim clipped that glass egg from the coffee table and flipped it in the air. That egg crashed into the floor and broke into a million pieces. Myrtle threw both hands in the air and spun out of my house, yelping like a stepped-on puppy."

"That's quite a story," I said.

"Losing it like that has got me worried about myself, Dr. Pope. I didn't know that was in me. Doc Rogers said I wasn't crazy, but sometimes I wonder."

After fumbling around inside her pocketbook, she hunched toward me from the couch, brandishing yellow, dog-eared pages that she'd neatly tucked away. "Here are my papers if you don't believe me."

"You don't have to show me proof." I shooed them away. "You're not crazy."

"I'm not?" Her eyes widened and her shoulders loosened.

"So I *am* normal?"

"Shirley, *normal* is a cycle on a washing machine."

"Ha, I like that one, Dr. Pope." She burst out laughing, tilted her head. "Truth be told, every once in a while I do feel right jittery. My heart starts racing like it's about to jump out of my chest. Seems like ever since . . . Seems like it all started right after we . . ." Her fingertips flew to her lips, and she turned red again.

"Right after what?" My eyebrows arched in curiosity.

"I can't talk about that." She waved both palms wildly at me, not to go there. "If I go digging that up, you *will* have to haul me off to McClenny."

"You don't have to worry about McClenny, and you don't have to talk about anything you don't want to."

"I'm sorry for being such a big chicken." She sniffled, yanked a Kleenex, and blew into it two or three times.

"You're not chicken. I can tell this is hard for you." I laid down my notepad and arched forward, softening my voice. "When was the last time you had a complete physical?"

"I go to Doc Rogers once a year." She took a deep breath and exhaled. "He gave me a clean bill of health, except when I broke down in his office and couldn't stop crying, he ordered me to see you."

"It sounds like something has traumatized you."

"How can I hold my head up with dignity in proper society after what we did? After your grandmamma talked me into things?" She jerked another tissue and dabbed her pinched face. "I just wish I could forget about it! Dear Lord, p-l-e-a-s-e, p-l-e-a-s-e forgive me for what I did."

"Gigi talked you into something bad? Is that what you're saying?"

"Yes. Yes, that's what I'm saying." While holding a tissue against her nose with one hand, she motioned for me to stop with the other.

My insides rumbled from my stomach to my throat. Though I felt compelled to defend Gigi from something, I didn't know what I'd be defending her from. I realized I had to put it out of my mind and stay focused on Shirley, whose deep racking sobs were almost enough to shake the room. After boohooing for several minutes, she lifted her composed head, blew her nose, and limply folded her hands in her lap.

"I hope when everything comes out, Dr. Pope, that you'll find it in your heart to forgive me."

"Me forgive you? Sounds like you need to forgive yourself."

"I reckon so." She looked down and picked at her finger. "I reckon so."

"I'll put in a call to Doc Rogers and ask him to prescribe an antidepressant. He'll call it in to the Piggly Wiggly pharmacy, and it should fix those anxiety attacks."

"Anxiety attacks?" She nervously wove her fingers together and rested them on her stomach.

"Yes."

"Anxiety attacks." She had twisted the tear-soaked tissues into long soggy twine and discarded them in her lap. "But how can I face Sylvia Wynn? She already thinks I'm crazier than a June bug from that day in the bakery."

"Well, if it's any consolation, Sylvia takes an antidepressant herself."

"You mean to tell me Sylvia Wynn, Miss Perfect, takes nerve pills?" Shirley whirled her head around, her bun slanting to one side.

"Sylvia was never a client of mine. But one day when I was getting a prescription filled, she told me that if folks were concerned about taking medication that I could tell them that it had changed her life for the better."

"Well, I'll be. I always admired Sylvia Wynn, always said she had poise."

"Yes, she's a fine woman."

"My goodness gracious, who would've ever thought?" She pressed against her bun with both hands, nudging it to the center of her head. "My hair's so thin, it won't hold a pin."

"And when you're ready, we can talk about what upset you so much."

Her posture stiffened, voice stilted. "Your grandmamma was supposed to tell you."

I scooted straight up in my seat. "Tell me what?"

"It's not my place to say anymore." Then her mind drifted to the possibility of fitting in where she had felt unaccepted. "Why . . . Sylvia Wynn . . . I just can't believe it."

She clucked her tongue and shook her head. The Kleenex box was empty. She smashed it flat with her fist, folded it into a neat square, and flung it into the trash basket.

"Slam dunk." Her lips curled into a smile beneath red eyes that had swollen into tiny slits.

CHAPTER 9

"I decided to have sex with Forney Fowler the first time I laid eyes on him," Jackie Priester shamelessly announced after plunging into the sofa for our first therapy session.

I'd been hunkered behind my desk completing paper work when a deep throaty laugh from the waiting room announced her arrival. When I went out to welcome her, the heavy scent of Wild Musk had greeted me. I put out my hand, but she grabbed me in a bear hug, smothered me in her gargantuan breasts. I wasn't sure why she wanted to see me, but I knew right away that boundaries would be part of her therapy.

"How do you like my outfit?" Jackie strode into my office in a zebra-striped muumuu with gigantic yellow earrings and red toenails on orange flip-flops. Multiple gaudy stones adorned her fingers; trinkets wrapped her wrists. A jingle bell, tied around her left ankle—the kind of bell folks hung on their pets' necks to track their whereabouts—tinkled when she waddled to her seat.

"Very colorful." I had wanted to be both complimentary and honest at the same time.

She'd boasted that her trademark loose-fitting garments came from a marked-down bargain bin out front of Family Savers.

"Fifty cents for a pair of pink plastic shoes that I can slip on is too good to pass up," she'd told me, "even if they're two sizes too big. I just combed the sewing department for matching elastic, cut it to fit around my feet, and stretched it to hold the oversized shoes on my feet."

After she'd maneuvered herself onto the sofa, I wasted no time coming back to her jolting comment. "So what's this about you and Forney Fowler?"

"You know him?" She wiggled her wrist, jingling the metal bracelets up her arm.

"No, but the paper said he died from a fall."

"Thank God they didn't name me. I was right there with him, and Doodle doesn't know."

"Doodle's your husband, right?"

"Yes, I call him Do." She dropped her head back against the sofa pillows, stared at the ceiling. "I need to figure out why everything feels like it has to be stretched before it fits: my clothes, the refrigerator, even my marriage."

"In other words, you want to figure out how to fit into life instead of stretching life to fit you."

"You got a way with words, Dr. Brad." She lifted an impressed eyebrow. "When I turned forty, I thought my weight was caused by midlife stall, but I notice I eat when I'm upset. I got this new bikini bathing suit I'm trying to get into and hoped you could help."

"Maybe you're aiming too high to start," I said gently. I was concerned that she would expose herself to unnecessary ridicule. "Let's put the bikini idea on the back burner and begin with something a bit easier to get a jump-start. Like how you're using food as a mood elevator."

"Hmm. Mood elevator?" She kicked off her flip-flops. A toe ring winked at me. "Sounds like something you hitch a ride on. But food does calm me down. When I watch *Oprah,* she says I'm stuffing my feelings."

"Have you noticed when you have the urge to eat the most?"

"Speaking of." She raised her hand as if she'd read my mind. "Every once in a while I go to Britches for a drink. When I see them slim pretty women hanging all over them good-looking men, I feel about this big." She made a sign with a tiny space between two fingers. "By the way, have you noticed the light on the neon 'r' is burned out? I don't think that's an accident."

"I haven't been to Britches, but I wonder if feeling left out makes you want to binge."

"Makes me want to eat everything in sight."

"Do you think other women have something you don't?"

"They get taller and thinner. I get shorter and fatter." She let out a huge sigh. "But there was something about Forney Fowler that made all that go away. That's why I fell for him, and in the end he fell for me." She self-consciously heaved her large breasts upward. "Ha, just kidding, Doc."

The more Jackie talked, the more it became clear that she felt she didn't fit in anywhere. But before launching into her relationship with Forney Fowler, I needed more information about her husband, Doodle, whom she referred to as "a biddy man, short and bald-headed, who likes to spend money on me."

"Tell me about your marriage." I drew a stick figure in the corner of my notepad while she collected her thoughts.

She started with Doodle's proposal twelve years ago when he dragged her onto the football field before the half-time homecoming ceremony at Whitecross High School.

"We'd been dating and love making for three years and weren't getting any younger. It was high time for Doodle to pop the question, and I reckon he intended to do it in style. Unbeknownst to me, he'd pulled strings with his uncle, the school principal. But I didn't know anything about that. I had to put my hand over my mouth, because I couldn't stop giggling when he coaxed me onto the field.

"I panned the crowd for some kind of clue. I'd always dreamed of being homecoming queen, and my imagination started running away with me. Even though I'd dropped out of school in the eleventh grade and was thirty-seven at the time, I wondered if I *was* eligible. After all, I'd just completed my GED at Lake City Community College. I remember thinking, *Could it be? Could it be?* My eyes widened, and my neck stretched forward like a rubber band.

"With the microphone in one hand and my hand in the other, Doodle fell on one knee in front of a thousand spectators.

" 'Jackie, darlin',' he started.

" 'Huh?'

" 'Jackie, you're the love of my life. I wanna spend the rest of it with you.'

"After pledging his love, Doodle pulled out a diamond ring from his coat jacket. The crowd exploded with applause and wolf whistles. Then he stuck the microphone in my face, eager for my long-awaited answer.

" 'Honey, I ain't pregnant.' I reassured him, tugging on his coat sleeve, desperate to pull him up.

"The stands roared with laughter.

" 'Baby, I never said you was. I wanna know if you'll be my wife.'

" 'No way.' I rolled my eyes over the crowd, pleading for understanding. My lips faked a smile, but the strain in my voice felt like jagged glass. 'Get up honey. We can talk about this later.'

" 'I want an answer.' When Doodle refused to budge, I crouched down on one knee eye level with him.

" 'You asshole!' I blasted him, not knowing I was in range of the microphone. 'I told you last week I ain't through sowing my wild oats. Now get your bald-headed ass up!'

"A heavy hush had fallen over the stands. The loudspeaker's echo of 'bald-headed ass, ass, ass' washed across the stadium. Doodle finally gave in to my yanks and rose to his feet.

"Boos and hisses rained down on me as I ushered him off the

field. I was mortified, plum humiliated. I tried to redeem myself by throwing a parting word over my shoulder. 'It might happen one day, but I can't predict the future.'

"Then, the Whitecross High School marching band drowned me out. They high-stepped it onto the playing field tooting, 'Turn the Beat Around.'

"I stewed all the way home that night. 'I hope you're satisfied,' I told Doodle. 'You made me the laughingstock of Whitecross.' I was so mad that I vowed to never speak to him again. But he was persistent. When he'd call and say he had eyes only for me, I'd hang up on him.

"Then one day I read in the *Whitecross News* about a convict on death row in Raiford, claiming his innocence. I felt sorry for him. I sat down, wrote him a letter, and he wrote back. Before I knew it, I'd fallen head over heels in love. When he proposed by mail, I agreed to marry him. Why, it was the least I could do for a man who'd seen his last days—give him this one last thing before he died.

"But Doodle never gave up. He sent me flowers and candy. Called me every day for six months, even after learning about my courtship with the death-row inmate. I put off marrying the convict, hoping he'd get clemency, because I didn't want to be a widow-woman. After they electrocuted him, I guess it shocked me into my senses. That's when I caved in to Doodle's pressures for my hand in marriage.

"But I insisted on the whole nine yards: white wedding dress handmade from bargain-bin parachute material with a long train, a three-tiered wedding cake, and a wedding ceremony in the deli-bakery aisle of the Piggly Wiggly. That's where we met— when Doodle stocked the Holsum Bread racks and I worked in the dairy section.

"Gigi was matron of honor and the other WPC club sisters were bridesmaids. Several of Doodle's co-workers at the Holsum Bread factory in Mayo served as groomsmen. Your grandma paid for the metal fold-up chairs, decorations, and parking-lot reception tent and finger foods. But management didn't shut down the store. Customers kept pushing their carts into the wedding aisle in the middle of 'Here Comes the Bride.' It was a beautiful ceremony, though. Our exchange of vows took place under a white matrimonial arch in front of lighted candles on candelabras and a sign advertising a box of Deluxe Twinkies, a two-for-the-price-of-one bonus buy."

The newlyweds had settled down to a quiet but boring life—at least that's how Jackie described her marriage when I asked about it.

"Boring . . . boring," she sang in a shrill tone. "I'd like to be noticed once in a while for god sakes, but I'm invisible with Do. For a long time I busied myself with decorating our trailer from a dumpster on Highway 90, hoping that'd spice things up a bit."

She said she and Doodle had profited from the treasures she'd found ransacking through the rubbish. She had plucked a rickety armchair from the garbage, declaring she could find an arm to glue on it, a black-and-white TV set that needed fixing, and a twin bed and old mattress that she piled on top of her Pinto for safe transport home.

She was especially fond of the bamboo beads that covered each doorway in their trailer. On top of the TV, she'd proudly displayed a pair of wooden high-heel shoes that spelled *Sai Gon* when put side-by-side—a trophy from her brother's stint in Vietnam. She'd scattered whatnots around her trailer, along with plastic flowers and a frayed orange-and-brown crocheted throw that covered the Naugahyde settee.

"Do says our trailer looks like a Vietnamese whorehouse," Jackie said, "and I told him I'm just a sucker for doodads and he'd just have to get used to it."

Jackie and Doodle never had children but doted on their beloved Doohickey, an aging chocolate Chihuahua, who scrambled around on a broken leg with the aid of Popsicle sticks—prosthetics that penny-pinching Jackie had invented to save on vet bills. He ate all his meals under the bed covers. When squeezed in just the right spot, he would growl, "I love my mama." According to Jackie, Doodle had everything he wanted out of life: Jackie, a satellite dish, and a double wide. Jackie, on the other hand, wanted more.

"I always had Hollywood in my eyes, always dreamed of being a famous dancer. So I opened a dance school in what used to be the casket room of Bowen's funeral parlor before they moved into their fancy new building on Main Street. I called it Jackie's School of Buckshot Cloggers and Baton Twirlers."

"How's it doing?" I asked.

"We're still open, but sometimes them kids aggravate the dickens out of me. I spend half my time keeping order. They don't pay attention and can't twirl a baton worth a shit! At first things were slow, and I had to rob the penny jar to make ends meet. Then I finally got a job at Madge's Mess, and things picked up for a while. Until I got fired."

"Fired? For what?"

"Your grandmamma popped in on me one day at the shop to see how business was doing. The store was empty, not a soul in sight, and she thought we'd been robbed. She told me later that she'd checked the cash register and spied about fifty dollars in bills and change. Then she searched the store to see if I was out back. Nothing. When she trotted to the dressing room, she found me."

"Were you trying on clothes?"

"No. I was trying on Miguel, one of your grandmamma's field hands."

My eyes flew open. I was intrigued at how she continued to

speak about her infidelity without shame.

"I was braced against the viewing mirror with my fingers wound around two dressing hooks. Miguel was inside my muumuu. After giving me a good finger wagging, your grand-mamma fired me on the spot. Said I was too man hungry to keep my mind on business."

As Jackie continued talking about her mindless jobs, complacent husband, and extramarital affairs, I began to wonder if she were hitting on *me*. She'd tilt her head slightly to the right and then to the left, blinking her eyes at me. The stolen looks and furtive glances when I'd scan my notes. The way she pulled her muumuu above her knees and crossed and uncrossed her legs during the session. Not quick and offhandedly but legs spread wide—slow and deliberate like she was offering me a peep show—like Sharon Stone in *Basic Instinct* or Anne Bancroft in *The Graduate*.

At one point, she looked at me sideways, studied me longer than usual. "You're the spitting image of your daddy. You got his sassy, yellowish corn-silk hair and fair complexion."

"You know my daddy?" I sat forward on the edge of my chair.

"Just seen him once or twice, that's all." She grasped the top of her muumuu and drew it tight around her neck. "I didn't know him really, just knew *of* him."

"Have you seen him lately?" I cocked an eyebrow. "Do you know where he lives?"

A look of shock pinched her face. Her voice broke; she squirmed. "No, no. I don't know."

Adrenaline drenched me. I shuffled my legs. My palms pressed against my thighs, wiping away the moisture. It took everything in me to shove the thought away. But it would've been unethical to pump her for details for my personal gain. I exhaled through my teeth and started backpedaling, steering the conversation back to her. "Tell me what you've done to get a handle on your compulsive eating."

"I tried every diet under the sun, even had my stomach stapled—twice. After my first surgery, I'd raid the icebox in the middle of the night until my staples busted loose. After the second surgery, I had trouble resisting temptation. Did the same thing all over again."

"Have you discussed this with your family doctor?"

"Last time I went to Doc Rogers his nurse, Vera, said I weighed 257, up from 249, and that I was five-feet-nine, an inch shorter. I think she has bad arithmetic."

"I don't think Vera's math is the problem, Jackie."

The surgeries hadn't lasted, and the diets hadn't worked, either. Jackie wasn't food hungry; she was loved starved.

Hungry.

That was a good word for Jackie—an insatiable appetite for food, fun, flair, and fucking. She reminded me of a female version of the Bruce Springsteen hit, "Hungry Heart."

Jackie's hungry heart became more evident when I asked her about her childhood.

"I always felt like I wasn't good enough for my daddy." She shrugged. She couldn't understand why her father, who'd wanted a boy, never paid her attention. "One day in seventh grade I was sitting on the school steps with my legs open getting some air when I noticed a boy look up my dress. So I did it some more. I'd finally found a way to get noticed."

Her past explained the present—polka dots, floral prints, and rainbow-colored outfits that demanded, "Look at me." Through her loud attire and outlandish actions, she got the attention she craved.

"Jackie, can you see how eating and school-step flirtations have been unsatisfying substitutes for love?"

She looked down at the floor, studied it for a few seconds, then cocked her head at me. "You mean when I eat up attention from somebody like Forney Fowler, it's because I'm hungry for something else on the inside?"

"I'm beginning to think that's the draw you had to Forney. Tell me more about that relationship."

As Jackie described this man, whom she'd hoped would fill the empty spaces in her heart, the light flooded through a window behind her, splashing her hair with an orange glow.

"Big Do—that's what I call Doodle to separate him from Lil Do, which is what I call Doohickey, my dog. Anyway, Big Do started acting half-hearted about our marriage. He says to me, 'You done reached your peak, woman. You ain't gonna be able to do nothing else, so you might as well set your big-ass down here with me and Lil Do and watch TV and enjoy what we got.' I felt like Do—Big Do, that is—didn't believe in me anymore and that Lil Do probably didn't, either, and I didn't believe in myself. Bit by bit, things soured between Big Do and me. That night I ate a whole carton of Blue Bunny Chocolate Marble Crunch. When I pulled away, Big Do tried everything to win me over, even converted his eight-foot wide, galvanized cow trough into a swimming pool. We had fun skinny dipping, but it didn't change my feelings one bit."

After Jackie's jobs at the A&W and Madge's Mess fell through, the sisterfriends called a meeting of the WPC. Gladys got Big Jake to pull strings with his best friend, Forney Fowler, president of Triple Six Phosphate Company. Jackie got to kill two birds with one stone—get paid *and* keep an eye on Forney, who'd been put on the WPC's watch list. Within the week, Forney had hired Jackie as a receptionist.

"The first time I laid eyes on Forney, I felt combustion inside." Jackie started fanning herself with the HIPAA forms I'd given her to sign. "He mighta been a Yankee and talked funny. But the sound of his name, 'Forney,' made my toes curl inside my tennis shoes. Pretty soon, I became his personal assistant, which I thought was a promotion. He'd give me personal letters and packages to deliver to his high-society friends—handsome-smelling men in fancy suits with clean fingernails. Sometimes I'd drive clear to Gainesville to deliver packages. They'd give me boxes to bring back to Forney or Big Jake."

She stopped and looked at me. "Do you want me to keep going?"

I moved my palm forward and looked back down at my notes. "Yes, please."

"One day Forney had something on his mind. When I asked what was wrong, he said Triple Six had leaked seven thousand pounds of a chemical called HFA into the Suwannee with the plant's wastewater. He was more worried that the press might get wind of it than he was about the spill. A week later, when I asked him questions about it, he had a funny look on his face. Said I was nosey.

"Then about six months later he let it slip that he'd been dumping chemicals again after the EPA warning. He stopped mid-sentence, looked at me suspicious-like. That's when I thought he might be on to me. I started feeling stuck in the middle. I knew right then I had to let the WPC in on it."

"And did you tell the WPC?"

"Yes. Your grandmamma called the EPA and threatened to go to the media if they didn't take immediate action."

"I see. Go on, finish your story."

"Forney'd planned a long weekend for the two of us in the North Carolina Mountains. The morning we were leaving, news about Big Jake's murder was all over town. I figured Forney'd cancel the trip, being Jake's best friend and all. But he insisted on going, which made me feel even more special under the circumstances. I'd dreamed it'd be a romantic rendezvous. After Forney sweet-talked me into hiking up Rattlesnake Ridge, I figured we'd make passionate love behind the bushes. But with my frequent and sudden urges, the only thing that happened behind the bushes was a pit stop I took before we were halfway up the ridge.

"When we got to the top and sat down to cool off, I could feel the romance wearing off. I asked him why he invited me to come in the first place. After he told me I was a barrel of laughs, I translated that to mean he thought I was dumb enough to do anything he wanted. I told him to wipe his mouth, because there was a tiny speck of bullshit around his lips. Then I asked him what was in all those boxes I'd been delivering for him and Big Jake. He took a zip-lock bag filled with white powder out of his backpack, rubbed it on his gums, and snorted it. Then he told me to give it a try.

"I told him I didn't do drugs. He mocked me in a snotty voice, 'I don't do drugs. If it isn't Miz Goody-Two-Shoes.' His snarling scared me, so I scooted over and put a bigger space between us. Then his beady eyes narrowed on me, and he said, 'You know more about me than anybody—too much for your own damn good *and* for mine.' I told him if he didn't want me to know so much, why'd he tell me? He moved closer and said, 'You fat fucking slut. You called the EPA on me.' I stood up, shaking all over, and backed away. I started fast-walking back down the trail, and he ran after me. When I got close to a ledge, he rushed at me, both hands out, trying to push me over.

"Them dancing lessons of mine finally paid off. I did a quick pirouette. Forney skirted around me and wobbled on the edge, lost his balance. He slipped over the side but grabbed the roots of a pine tree, trying to pull up. When I ran over to help him, he latched on to one of my legs, still snarling at me, called me a bitch. When I jerked my leg back, he fell. I can still hear him yowling and the thump, thump, thump as he bounced against the rocky ledges. Then a loud splat when he hit the boulder below. I looked down and saw blood pooled under his head.

Next thing I remember, the police were driving me across the cattle guard in front of my trailer. After that, I vowed that nobody'd ever use me again."

She abruptly stopped talking, twisted her neck toward the window.

"What is it, Jackie?"

"I can't get that picture out of my mind. The blood oozing out of Forney's head. It brings back that time with the sister-friends when . . ." She faltered.

"Go on." My ears perked up.

"That time with the sisterfriends when we cut . . . it was terrible, but we had to . . ." She stopped short again, tugging at the hem of her muumuu, raising a darkly lined eyebrow at me. "I can't talk about that part. I took a oath not to."

"Okay . . ." I stammered, circled my temples with my fingertips. *What in God's name had these women done? What did she mean they'd cut something?*

Jackie'd been duped into trafficking cocaine. And at least two men—Forney Fowler and Sam Grimes—had died under the watchful eye of the WPC. It appeared that Big Jake had been involved in the drug trade as well.

I felt my heart go into free fall. With jaws clenched, I stood, paced the room, pulled my fingers against my chin.

"It's coincidental that Big Jake and Forney died so close together." I flopped into my wingback, leaned forward, rested my chin in my fist. "Don't you think?"

"Forney was breaking federal regulations dumping chemicals in the Suwannee. And he was in cahoots with Jake Nunn. The only reason the bastard got me that job was to run drugs for him. I can just see the two of them sniggering about me behind my back, like they could use me up and throw me away. Well, I reckon I showed them. They're gone, and I'm here."

Glint-eyed Jackie lifted a thin eyebrow, a gloating that unnerved me. Then she launched into the lyrics of that old Jim Croce song, "You Don't Mess Around With Jim." Instead of "Jim," she sang "Jackie."

I had to work hard to shake off my suspicions. Although Jackie had been alone with Forney when he fell, the police had cleared her. I had to stay focused on helping her get the most mileage out of her romantic romps, so she could see her pattern of self-sabotage.

"Jackie, do you realize you've been choosing men you couldn't have?"

"Huh? How come?"

"One man was behind bars on death row. The other was a married migrant worker, moving from town to town with his family. Forney Fowler used you while keeping you at arm's length. The man who worships you, waits for you with open arms is Doodle. But you've walked *away* from the man you *can* have and *toward* men you *cannot* have."

"I never thought about it that way." Jackie picked at a loose thread in the sofa. "I reckon I always thought deep down if a man loved me as much as Big Do, he must not be worth two cents."

"It's like the old lady searching for her glasses when they're on her nose the whole time."

"When I hear you say it, it's plain as day. I already had a man that worshipped me—a tenderhearted man that humbled himself on his knees in front of a crowd, asking me to marry him. Even after I turned him down, he kept on loving me anyway."

She paused. Then, without warning, she sprang out of her seat, clapping her hands, jumping up and down. The floor shook as she bunny-hopped around the room, the ankle bell tinkling wildly. I laughed and felt her joy so much that, uncharacteristic of me, I, too, bounced out of my chair, high-fived her, whirled around. Breathless, we dropped back into our seats. She dabbed her forehead and caught her running makeup in a tissue. She took a deep breath and threw her head backwards against the sofa cushions.

"My thinking's been wrong-side-out. You've helped me see I *am* worth something, that I don't have to sink low anymore for love."

"You hadn't been used to real love before Doodle, so you were pushing it away."

The session ending, she stood, laid something on my desk.

"It's a slab of pie. The rhubarb's from my garden. I picked the strawberries at Odom's Strawberry Patch, made it from scratch."

"Thank you, Jackie."

"You're welcome. And thank you, Dr. Brad. I feel like I've already shed ten pounds!"

Before leaving the session, Jackie decided to buy a George Foreman and membership to *Curves* in Lake City. She said she realized her dance school couldn't get off the ground until she lost enough to get herself off the ground.

After Jackie's therapy session, I caught myself straightening things on my desk that didn't need straightening. I was spooked by whatever the closed-mouthed sisterhood had done, even though I didn't know what it was.

Until now, people had always trusted me with their secrets, but the club sisters carefully guarded theirs. On the surface they were open books, but on the inside they were as confusing as the limestone corridors that snaked beneath my feet.

I felt the shiver of suspicion, unleashed in my head, move through my shoulders and chest. *What were Gigi and her sister-friends really planting around town?*

Camellias or corpses?
And I was determined to find out.

CHAPTER 10

Rain clouds lifted after a drenching downpour, unveiling a bruised magenta sky and a loafer's-glory afternoon. After deciding to take the day off, I launched my yellow Carolina in front of my cabin and kayaked the Suwannee. I paddled toward Gigi's, a good five miles along the winding river's edge. I had to find out what she and her sisterfriends were up to. Three men had died on their watch. I needed proof that my thinking was all wrong, that my imagination was running away with me.

As my kayak glided through the water, I took in the nearly soundless beauty of the landscape, teeming with life. Creeping resurrection ferns unfolded in the tops of live oaks. A mild breeze swept the Sabal palms, nudging pungent river smells of breeding fish and yellow jasmine my way. Beards of Spanish moss, dangling in sweet gums along the shore, skimmed the water's surface. I was captured by sounds of fish kerploping and a strutting alabaster-colored egret with its long stick-like neck, lugging mouthfuls of fish for dinner. A flock of brown-and-ivory checkered limpkins, swirling near the riverbank, resembled broad strokes on an artist's palate.

I stopped here and there to slosh the water, traipse the pristine-white sandy beaches. I hunted for Indian relics and fossils, discovered several arrowheads and what looked like an ancient hand ax. I felt like I was six again. While trudging the sandbars, I picked purple figs and wild southern grapes known as muscadines and scuppernongs and savored their tangy tastes.

It reminded me of the many boyhood hunts with Gigi, picking berries and fruits, making preserves from whole figs and thin lemon slices and from the grape hulls and their simmered-out pulp.

When I rounded the bend a quarter of a mile from Gigi's, I spied her dock sprawling down the side of the riverbank, fanning out like a hand over the Suwannee. Spirals of smoke singeing the trees near Gigi's double wide meant she was cooking on a barbecue grill. Good. I hadn't eaten all day and was starving. I cruised up beside Gigi's dock, glided underneath it, and tied my boat to one of the pilings.

As I disembarked, I heard the sounds of voices and froze, bracing myself against the cross ties to keep my balance. The wooden platform rumbled with heavy footsteps descending the boardwalk onto the dock. The timbers moaned and swayed gently until the tongue-clatter, feet-shuffling, and smack-smack of sandals, and flip-flops were directly overhead.

I spread-eagled on my back across the kayak, water sloshing the boat side to side. I could see the club sisters without them seeing me through a peephole, worn into the wooden slats over time. When I looked up, I could see slices of the women dressed in tank tops, T-shirts, and cutoffs, slouched in aluminum beach chairs above me.

They propped their feet against the wooden railing, chattered about gaining weight, medical problems, and menopause, creaking the wooden floorboards of the deck when they gestured to make a point. There were several conversations at once.

Betty-Jewel was complimenting Shirley on her new hairdo. "You look younger without the bun. I like the way Bernice backcombed your hair over the bald spot."

"Why, bless your heart," Shirley said. "It's easier to take care of, too."

Jackie was telling Wilma-May how much she loved Doodle.

"Just yesterday, I realized how happy I was taking care of him, even when I'm washing the skid marks out of his Jockey shorts. Big Do said he'd seen me smile for the first time in he didn't know how long. And Lil Do ain't as depressed as he used to be. He's eating his meals outside the bedcovers and playing some."

"The Lord has really blessed you," Wilma-May said.

"In more ways than one." Jackie dropped her voice. "I tried out some new sexual techniques on Big Do the other night. He has become a hunka hunka burning love. We started reading a book called *Hot Monogamy* by some Dr. Love. It turned him into a sexual monster. Have you heard of the squirrel procedure?"

"Lord have mercy, no!" Wilma-May screeched. "But can I borrow the book and show it to Walter? He could use some of that information."

"Maybe you should go to Dr. Brad for sex therapy. He really helped me."

"Dear Sweet Jesus. A sex therapist? Why, I can't even begin to imagine it."

I grabbed my head with both hands and thought. *Dear Sweet Jesus, neither can I.*

As Jackie croaked with that deep throaty laugh, the sounds of giggling and slapping hands against flesh boomeranged off the water. I could hear Gigi flipping burgers on the barbecue grill on the bank above them. The beef hissed over open flames. Grease smacked hot coals. Hickory-flavored smoke signals lifted skyward, carrying whiffs of their tantalizing, taunting smell.

My stomach growled, but the guilt for eavesdropping dwarfed the hunger pangs. Though I hadn't planned it this way, it was perfect timing because Gigi was hosting the WPC meeting. After what I'd already heard, I thought it unwise to show myself. Then as the conversations turned from idle chitchat to serious revelations, I was glad I hadn't.

"How are the graves coming, Betty-Jewel?" Gladys asked. "Aren't you heading that up?"

"Real good, thanks to Lick . . . I mean Rufus." In my mind's eye, I imagined Betty-Jewel pushing her glasses up her nose, the way she usually did to make a point. "He's a pro. We couldn't have dug that deep without him."

Then Jackie chimed in. "This whole thing sucks. I don't like killing or anything to do with dead people—even though I know we had to do it to protect ourselves."

"It gives me the heebie-jeebies standing out in the middle of nowhere over a dead body with a shovel," Shirley said. "Thank heavens for my nerve pills."

"So how many graves have we got so far?" Gladys asked.

"Three at last count, and there's more to come." Betty-Jewel made a snort-like sound. I could barely see her rubbing her finger under her nose. "But we have to be careful. I did some checking. It's a third-degree felony to possess a used coffin or gravestone. Florida law's even stiffer for possession of body parts and dead bodies."

"Nobody'll question *us*," Gladys said. "We have special dispensation because the WPC's an official organization."

I wiped my arm across my mouth, absorbing moisture that hung above my upper lip.

My ears were burning. They talked about disposing of bodies as casually as they'd plan a reunion under the churchyard shade trees.

Apparently, Gigi'd left her chef post. I could hear her bounding down the steps to the dock. I squinched through the peephole, saw Thump, her pet gray cockatiel, perched on her shoulder. I barely made out Gigi's slouchy T-shirt, one I'd seen a hundred times before, which read, *I'm Not A Bitch. I'm THE BITCH! And I'm MISS BITCH to you!*

"Would you girls like some cheese to go with your whine?"

Gigi asked. "I could hear you complaining all the way up the bank."

I had Jackie in my line of sight. She popped a Busch Light, winced at the bitter hops as she chugged it down. "We're bitching about that Confederate grave project we got ourselves into with that federal money."

I clamped my hand over my forehead and blew a huge sigh of relief, biting my lip for intruding on their privacy. It was too late to turn back now, so I hung on.

"You might as well stop your bellyaching." Gigi stroked Thump's feathers. "Finding those Civil War graves and preserving them will be our biggest achievement yet. I plan to announce it in my Founder's Day speech."

"I don't know about ya'll, but right now my biggest achievement is doing some serious eating." Through the peephole, I could barely make out Jackie patting her stomach against a splashy, caution-light orange bathing suit. Not a bikini but a full-piece that said her sense of taste might've improved, but her flair for color hadn't.

"I left Lick taking up the burgers," Gigi said. "Let's eat."

"You mean Rufus." Gladys jumped out of her chair in a dither, causing it to fall behind her in a thunderous clang, her eyes searching the riverbank. "Is he here?"

"He just got here." Gigi's voice resonated concern. "Calm yourself down, Sisterfriend."

"Rufus." Gladys ignored Gigi, yelled toward the trailer, waved her hand. "Hey, sweetheart."

"Sweetheart?" I murmured under my breath. Big Jake had been much younger, too. Obviously, Gladys had a penchant for younger men and strays, Lick being the perfect combination. But Gladys a cougar? It wouldn't compute.

"Hey," Lick hollered. He must have appeared at the edge of the slope and looked down on the women.

"We'll be up in a minute, Rufus," Gladys bellowed.

"You don't have a clutch between your head and mouth, Sisterfriend," Gigi fumed. "Sound carries on this river. You want the whole town to hear?"

"I'm not stuffing my feelings anymore," Gladys snipped. "I had enough of that with Big."

"You have to lay low with Lick until the investigation's over," Gigi said. "You know how news travels in Whitecross. Everybody'd love to pin Big Jake's death on that boy, just because he's not right."

Gladys's tone was pulverizing. "I love Rufus and want to be with him."

Gigi held steady. "A connection between you and Lick right now will throw suspicion on the whole WPC. One thing leads to another, and we all go to jail."

"The W-P-C." Gladys mimicked the letters in a mocking fashion. "What about me?"

"You've been through a right smart." Gigi spoke softly now. "You can be with him in due time. But you have to wait until the dust settles around Big Jake."

"First Big, now you, telling me how to live my life." Gladys bent down to retrieve her fallen chair, then slammed it into its upright position. "I want my life back. I'm tired of you running it. Or *ruining* it."

"Big Jake's the one that put us in this tight spot, not me," Gigi said. "Now we have to stick together. If the law starts asking questions, we're up shit's creek."

"He came between Rufus and me when he was alive. Now he's doing it from the grave."

"We don't have to worry about Big Jake anymore," Gigi said.

"No, but we have to worry about Myrtle pushing to get in the WPC." Gladys flopped into the chair. "And Ibejean wanting to know why we didn't let her back in after she missed that one meeting twenty-some years ago."

"If we let them in, we couldn't even talk amongst ourselves," Gigi snapped. "They'd find out everything."

"Speaking of finding out, did you tell your grandson?" I could see Gladys cross her legs.

"Mind your own business." Gigi flapped a dismissive palm at Gladys.

"What?" Gladys sounded incredulous as she stood up again and faced Gigi. "This *is* my business. You pulled me into it." She extended her arm indicating the other women, her voice cracking. "You drug all of us into it. You made murderers out of us. That makes it my business—all our business. And your grandson's got a right to know."

I almost fell out of the kayak. This was not about some long-dead Confederate soldier, that's for sure. This was about Big Jake's murder.

"She's right, Gigi," Jackie said. "I almost let it slip out in counseling."

"I told you the day of the funeral that I *will* tell Brad, when the time's right."

While Gigi and Gladys continued squabbling, I heard an outburst of tongue clucking, sounds of aluminum clanking, boards creaking. The other sisterfriends were squirming in their chairs.

"You keep dragging it out because you're afraid he'll disown you." Gladys said. "And you'll die all alone in jail."

"I'm an expert at being alone, Sisterfriend." Gigi growled. "Truth be told, if he knew about the killing, he'd be an automatic accomplice. If you tell him in counseling, he's legal-bound to go to the law and report us. And I don't want my grand young'un pulled into this mess. He's been stuck in the middle of stuff that's none of his doings all his life."

My heart catapulted into my throat. My hands trembled.

What in the world had I come back home to?

"But it's okay for us to be stuck in it?" I squinted into the peephole, saw Gladys turn her palms up to match the sarcasm in her voice. "You sawed like you were cutting up a chicken for Sunday dinner, then asked us to help. I still can't get that picture out of my mind. His arms spread wide open. His eyes all bugged out."

"Gladys Nunn, I did what I had to," Gigi said. "He was coming after my grandson. He would've gotten him, and you know it."

So that's what Gladys had tried to warn me about in our last session? I was so startled that I lurched forward, lost my balance, and flipped the kayak back and forth a few times. I stabilized the boat, held my breath. The sisterfriends went on with their conversation, talking over the splashing sounds.

"You're only thinking of yourself. What about me and Rufus? I should've told Dr. Pope at the funeral, like I had a mind to do."

"You do, and I'll knock you side winding." Gigi was sizzling, and I could've sworn she'd balled up her fist.

"My 'Give a Damn' is on the blink." Gladys shouted as she pointed her finger. "Now, I'm telling you for the last time. Either you tell him what we did, or I will."

Through the splintered slats, I could see slivers of Gigi coaxing Thump from her shoulder onto her scepter. She handed him over to Shirley, as if she were squaring off for body contact. The wooden platform bent and groaned as the other sisterfriends clucked and scrambled toward the twosome. The scuffle caused a speck of dust to sift through the wooden slats and fall into my eye.

"Stop it!" I heard a loud thud as Betty-Jewel leapt between Gladys and Gigi. "Both of you."

I could barely make out Betty-Jewel pulling Gigi by her elbow to the other side of the deck. Gigi leaned against a wooden post and shot Gladys a dirty look.

"I'd better not hear of anybody talking about this outside of here." Gigi aimed her scepter at each woman as she spoke. "Remember, God gave you *two* ears and *one* mouth for a reason."

I had a direct bead on Gladys. She stared through the slatted deck into the water, her forefinger mashed against her teeth. I thought she was looking straight at me until she stood when Gigi announced, "All right, let's eat before it gets cold."

Gladys and the other sisterfriends clomped up the plank stairway and hauled drinks and piled-high food back down. Since I didn't hear Lick's voice, I assumed he was eating alone under the sprawling, hundred-year-old live oak near the grill.

I felt so bad I wanted to lie down, a luxury kayaks don't afford. So I sat and waited, my body aching, stomach sick with hunger pangs. I closed my eyes using concentration techniques I'd learned in meditation.

The wooden deck slumped suddenly under the weight of the women. They jumped up and down at the flap-flap of a homemade river craft, piloted by an eighty-year-old local who came by once in the morning, once in late afternoon. Aloft on a bicycle rigged to a set of pontoons, the old man waved vigorously at the women. His pedals powered a waterwheel type device that slapped the river, giving the contraption propulsion.

"He gets a ten," cried Gigi.

"Get the paper plates and pass them around," ordered Wilma-May.

For the next twenty minutes, the women sat shoulder to shoulder, laughing and clapping as though there was no tension among them. They impersonated Olympic judges, each with a set of paper plates, numbered one through ten in Magic Marker. When river craft floated by, they raised a plate with a number on it, giving high marks to environmental-friendly craft. Kayaks, canoes, pontoons, and small fishing boats got nines and tens. High-powered motorboats or loud ski-doos received zeros or one-half's. Reactions from passersby ranged from high fives and hysterical laughter to the finger. The women interspersed their gabbing with bites of burgers, swigs of sweet iced tea and beer, and Little Debbie Cakes.

I glimpsed Gigi—mustard on her lip, jaws bulging with food—putting her food down on the dock, then clambering up the wooden staircase. My discomfort was beginning to over-power me. I was getting hungrier and wilting from the sun, which had fallen low in the sky, aiming directly in my face. I had sweated so much my tank top was stuck to my back, and the no-see-ums were nipping my ears. I made a hard swipe at the pesky bugs, landed a loud smack on my chest, causing the kayak to flop and swash the water.

"What was that?" Gigi asked, as she bounded down the wooden steps.

I cocked my eye over the peephole. She had stopped dead in her tracks.

"What?" asked Betty-Jewel.

"I heard a splashing sound," Gigi said.

"Me too," said Wilma-May. "Where was it coming from?"

"Hard to tell," said Gigi, "sounded like under the dock."

The activity above me freeze-framed into a silent lull, a long tomblike silence. I lay on my back, heavy and stiff like a corpse, holding my breath. I succumbed to the bugs, yielding up my warm flesh as a blood feast, hell-bent on remaining still. The buzzing of mosquitoes and flies sounded as if they had microphones strapped to their wings, amplifying the quiet.

After several minutes, Jackie broke the stillness. "Probably just a sturgeon smacking the water."

"Guess so." Gigi trotted to her lawn chair. As she leaned back, I heard the sound of something slap between her knees. I gingerly peeked through the thin wooden opening and spied the green-velvet Bible on Gigi's lap—the one Mama had saved from the fire.

Gigi opened the Good Book to the front, served up a reminder to her club sisters. "Each of you took a solemn oath of restitution for what we did." Then she scribbled something in the Book, saying, "I'm adding another name to the watch list."

"That means it's time to do another drawing," Wilma-May said.

"You got it." Gigi hollered up the bank to Lick. "Son, bring me that wide-mouthed Mason jar on the bar in the kitchen."

I could hear the pounding of Lick's feet as he lumbered down the steps, the contents clattering inside the canning jar. In my head, I imagined he dutifully passed the jar to Gigi and ambled back up to his perch under the oak tree. Then I heard the jangle of beans against glass as Gigi shook the jar to get attention.

"Okay, listen up." Her voice dropped to a whisper. "You know the drill. I got five white navy beans and one black bean in this jar. You close your eyes, draw a bean, and the one who gets the black bean is next to take a turn."

"Let me go first and get it over with." Gladys stuck her fingers inside the jar. "Whew, I'm off the hook this time."

Shirley dipped her fingers into the jar next. She looked down at the bean with a blank stare, saying nothing.

"I'll go." Jackie reached inside the jar then flashed a peek at her palm.

I had a pinhole view of Betty-Jewel, raising her hand to go next. She pulled her fingers out of the jar, opened her palm. "Looks like it's my turn." Betty-Jewel gazed at the sisterfriends over black-rimmed glasses, then rose to her feet.

The other women stood, circled up, and simultaneously raised their drinks.

I was able to spy Gigi standing in the middle of the circle lift-

ing her Styrofoam cup high in the air. "Sisterfriends forever!"
She toasted the WPC's solidarity.

"Sisterfriends forever!" They chanted in unison.

The cadence of their collected voices mingling with the clicking of plastic against aluminum had an eerie cultish tone that
chilled me. Then a malevolent silence, filled only with the
sounds of chirping birds, cloaked the sisterfriends as they put
down their drinks and linked hands.

I heard Thump flutter on Shirley's shoulder, saw her place
the bird on her finger, return him to Gigi. The women stomped
back up the steps of the dock, leaving a heavy stillness above
me.

Up the bank, I heard the twittering of gold finches. They
scrambled for feed scattered on the ground from a birdfeeder
stocked outside Gigi's kitchen window. The door of the mobile
home slammed. The gravel driveway popped and crunched
underneath car engines that roared off into the distance.

Inside I felt a shiver as my feelings for the sisterfriends began
to sour into the clabbered taste of fear.

CHAPTER 11

Instead of relaxing me, the lazy cruise down the Suwannee had unnerved me. I felt a cold weight in my stomach, my body tightening. With Gigi as ringleader, fronting as a preservation club, the WPC was nothing more than a geriatric Mafia. What if Myrtle was right—that the WPC *was* some kind of coven?

I paddled in the direction of my cabin, shoulders listless and hunched with the burden of worry. Turtles basked in the last sunrays of the day on fallen logs that had collapsed in rotten pieces along the shoreline. A donkey, used by local cattlemen to fend off coyotes, brayed in the distance. Unleashed by the earlier storm, water lettuce and hyacinth floated downstream. Barely visible off to my right was the head of a gator, jaws popping together like a door slamming, tail wallowing in circles, flapping the water.

A perfectly rounded sun glowed the shade of blood. It dropped like a red ball behind the trees, filtering sunbeams, casting thin slices of light across a choppy current.

My mind began to drift with the ripples, rushing thoughts swallowing me. *Had coming back to Whitecross been a mistake? Was I floating through life looking through the rearview mirror?*

Although I had a deep appreciation for life here, I was beginning to realize that yearning for my lost boyhood had caused me to idealize Whitecross with an innocence it couldn't live up to—an innocence that had blinded me to the truth. As the saying goes "Nostalgia is a seductive liar."

Growing up, I'd learned to love my life here and to fear it, too. The hungry underwater caves had swallowed more than one of the locals alive. I thought about the many chilly nights as a boy huddled around crackling campfires listening to tales of cave divers drowning in the twisted, turning underwater caverns, stretching miles beneath the earth. My heart thudding, I'd listened to river dwellers as they spun terrifying yarns, their shadows bent like ghosts against the white Florida sand.

Stories of lost cavers running out of air, stabbing each other with knives to steal a last breath from their partner's tank. Tales of corpses wrapped in tangled guidelines, entombed like mummies, arms tightly pinned against their stiff bodies. Stories of bodies so bloated that rescue teams had to pry them out of narrow passageways. And of goodbye messages hastily carved in limestone walls during a final dying breath. As a boy, I never knew which parts of the stories were made up, but one thing was certain: Big Jake's death wasn't a yarn.

It was real. It was murder.

And Gigi and her sisterfriends had killed him.

I had been a silent accomplice, standing in the wings, encouraging Gladys to take charge of her life. And take charge she did.

The laps of water, slapping against the kayak, took the form of a casket standing upright. Inside the coffin, an eyeless corpse dressed in white suit, blue shirt, and white tie wagged a finger, his condemnation ringing in my ears.

"All of this could have been prevented, Brad Pope. If it hadn't been for you, I wouldn't be stuck inside this goddamned box. You filled the old biddies' minds with shit that put me here. You might as well have cut the rope right along with them, you son-of-a-bitch! Before it's over with, you're gonna pay. You're gonna join me in hell for what you did."

I tried to shove the thoughts away, but the echo of Preacher

Abrams's voice won out. "The only way to rid yourself of eternal damnation is to be born again in the blood of Jesus Christ. The Vandals of Hell will be waitin' for you when you get home. Then you'll go straight to hell and burn for eternity. What you gonna do about it, boy?"

Preacher Abrams's chant, "Om a Sheeka Kabiah" began to morph into "evol wanga obeah, evol wanga obeah."

I smacked my forehead, tried to clear the haunting memories, and kept paddling upstream. A squadron of fireflies glimmered against the dark-purplish sky, triggering flashbacks of Alvin Dukes, who used to lead lightning bug safaris on warm summer nights. We'd snatch the elusive bugs in our small fists, chunk them in mayonnaise and pickle jars with punched holes in the lids so they could breathe. Then we'd dangle the jars in front of us like lanterns, our path lit by spasmodic bursts of light, guiding us through the dark jungle to the Suwannee's edge.

One night we romped farther into the woods than usual. A clump of four dirt-faced, scabby-kneed boys plopped into the middle of a clearing. The moon was full. Echoes of night owls stalked us. We sat cross-legged in a circle, darkness shrouding us, moonlight falling on our excited faces. We turned our eyelids inside out, exposed the tender pink tissue underneath. We scared each other with tales of cave divers drowning deep under the ground where we sat.

Alvin told us that this was the exact same spot where he stumbled into a meeting of Voodoo Sally and the Vandals of Hell. He said they were a circle of beings without faces, varying in size and shape— beings that the wild-eyed, frizzy-haired witch sent out to do her evil deeds.

Alvin opened his jar, pulled out one of the flashing bugs, pinched off its rear-end. "You can't never tell a soul what we see and do here."

When Alvin used his spit to paste the bug's backside on his ring finger, I gulped in amazement as it kept on flashing.

"Now you do it," he demanded, his eyes inspecting each face to see if one among us was yellow. *"The rings mark our promise not to tell about this place. They're our only protection against the witch."*

That was all it took to get the rest of us to reach into our jars, rip the lightning bugs in half, and glue the flashers on the tops of our fingers with spit. Standing in the middle of the circle, Alvin spun his finger in spirals, creating swirls of circles and figure eights against the backdrop of the dark, moaning cypress trees. I stuck another flasher in the center of my forehead for a third eye—like I'd read in geography class that they did in India—to give me extra protection.

The four of us danced in the splinters of moonbeams spilling onto the forest floor, waving our fingers, proclaiming our bond, our might. It was a light show of spectacular proportions until suddenly, a chill parachuted over us. Our hands dripping in "diamonds," we froze in motionless silence. We waited. Watched. Rolled our eyes at one another. Wondered what was happening. The only movement was the erratic flashers adorning our hands and faces, like neon signs winking along a dark, empty street. A faint rustling of the palm fronds from behind made me tremble.

"It's just a hoot owl flapping or armadillo rooting around." I boldly waved my lit finger, applying my newfound strength. The silence got heavier, then the river birch jittered from the breeze off the water.

"That ain't no critter." Alvin stuttered in a broken voice. *"It's Voodoo Sally!"*

Twigs snapped all around us. Limbs bent, and the bushes shook in a convulsive rhythm. From behind palm fronds, whites of large wild eyes darted back and forth, then seemed to swoop at us.

We launched our small bodies into the blackness, tore back through the underbrush and briers, jumping over fallen logs and tangled limbs, flapping our ringed hands against our ears to smite the wicked curse Voodoo Sally had put on us.

The abandoned open-faced jars freed the remaining lightning bugs *from their glass prisons. And we, too, were freed once more from the grasp of the wild-haired witch's spell.*

As I continued upstream, I realized that my imagination had run away with me again. Silly, childish memories. Why did they still hold such power over me? Did all my training as a therapist count for nothing? I was intelligent enough to know there's no such thing as black magic and evil spells. The eerie conversations on the dock had triggered the scary flashbacks. With a compassionate but curious eye, I began to separate the frightening boyhood recollections from the WPC's strange goings-on.

A slew of questions were piling up, and Gigi had withheld answers to all of them—the WPC's sinister secrets, their role in Big Jake's death, and the whereabouts of my daddy. As soon as I got home, I would call and invite her to grab a bite at Glenda's Diner.

I was determined to make her talk, no matter what it took.

I swiped at a sweat bead above my eye. I was almost back to my cabin.

Exhausted. Starving.

A family of black cypress trees formed a line down each side of the river, standing guard in the shadows of their beloved Suwannee: Grownups with fingers on their hips, hands dangling by their sides, gnarled arms reaching upwards toward the darkened sky. Smaller offspring, cradled steadily by the careful arms of their protectors, clutched the big ones' knees. All of them gawked at me, watched my every move, warned me.

An ominous foreboding.

Another red pouch of white powder, swinging from my doorknob, welcomed me home.

Boyhood fears clawed at my heart again.

Were the Vandals of Hell waiting for me inside?

CHAPTER 12

Doubling as cashier and hostess, Glenda sat at the front door greeting customers with a buttermilk lilt. "Hey, honey. Y'all seat yourself. Hope you enjoy it."

The dimly lit restaurant was dark and drab inside. The pine-paneled walls and rough-hewn, wooden tables and benches were brightened by the background music of Loretta Lynn and Glenda's colorful personality. When she rang the cash register, Glenda made what could only be considered a racist remark.

Although some customers laughed, I didn't think it was funny. Prejudice was one thing about Whitecross that had never appealed to me. But there was a joke on Glenda around town, too: "If it's got gravy on it, she's trying to pull a fast one on you."

A mound of homemade biscuits, golden fried chicken, macaroni and cheese, fluffy mashed potatoes, and mixed green salads rested upon a resplendent buffet. We piled our plates high, and sat at a table off in the corner. Gigi was wearing jeans and a T-shirt with the words, *I like you; I'll kill you last*, printed on the front.

I was mortified. "Where'd you get that shirt?"

As we bent into a wooden booth, I could see it in her face. I knew she'd done it. She and her gang of sisters had killed Big Jake for the way he'd treated Gladys, the way he'd treated all of them, like second-class citizens. Plus, Jake was so much like Daddy that it was Gigi's way to avenge Mama's murder. I could see every bit of it reflected in the blue sparkle of her eyes. I couldn't believe I'd not put it all together before now.

"My secondhand shop." She pinched the T-shirt, looked down at the letters, as if she didn't realize what she had on. "How come?"

"Because it's . . ."

"Oops, there's Smiley," she bleated before I could get it out. She fiddled with her newly dyed red hair and preened herself, running her palms down her curvy hips. "And he's headed this way. He's been trying to get me to go out with him."

"Who?" I was annoyed at her adolescent flirtations. I wondered what was bothering her enough to command a new hair color.

"Mayor Hoyle Bishop." Gigi dropped her voice. "He's the one I wanted you to meet at the funeral receiving. They nicknamed him Smiley. He's got the cutest little permanent smile plastered across his face, even when he's upset."

I turned around and checked him out. A congenial glad-handler, he was a thick-haired, grizzled seventyish man with a pleasant disposition. Sure enough his bloated but handsome face broadcast a billboard smile as he hand-shook and politicked a path to our table.

"Hey Gigi, I like your new hairdo."

"Thank you, Smiley. I call it Reba red." She patted her fiery tresses.

"How you been doin'?" he asked.

"Fine, fine, Smiley." Gigi batted her downcast eyes, coyly braided the paper napkin in her lap. Looking up, she introduced us in a formal manner uncharacteristic of her. "Smiley, I want you to meet my grandson, Dr. Brad Pope. Brad, Mayor Hoyle Bishop."

"Pleased to meet you, sir." I stood and extended my hand.

"Same here, Brad." He shook my hand, hinged his thumbs in

the lapels of his blue seersucker suit, and started working on me. "Heard good things about you and the practice you started up. Looks like you got to Whitecross just in the nick of time, just as we started havin' all the problems."

"Well, sir, I guess there's two ways to look at it. Either it was good timing or I brought the bad luck with me." I let out a self-deprecating laugh. Gigi rolled her eyes but didn't crack a smile.

"Suppose so. Yes siree, suppose so." He chuckled and slapped me on the back. Then, without the slightest fade of his eternal smile, he added, "Guess you heard they're treatin' Big Jake's death as a homicide. Just found out from Bobby-Cy they're DNA-testin' a glove found at the crime scene."

There was something behind the mayor's thousand-watt smile, a cleverness, a relentless cunning. The way he looked at me, hesitating when he mentioned Big Jake, made me wonder if he knew I was at Suwannee Springs around the time of the murder. I caught myself popping my knuckles and stopped, but Gigi was jumpy enough for both of us.

"Lord have mercy." She squirmed worse than a porcupine in a balloon factory. "Who'd do such a thing?"

Gigi's charade made me more irritated with her.

"Your guess is as good as mine," Smiley said. "Anyway, Gigi, you put any more thought into the dance Friday night? Be mighty pleased to have you as my cloggin' partner."

"Matter-of-fact, Smiley," I said, "she was just saying she was looking forward to going clogging with you Friday night."

Gigi's mouth looked like it was about to drop to the floor.

"It's all settled then. I'll pick you up at seven sharp." He looked at his watch and smiled. "I gotta scoot to a town council meeting." He winked at me, shook my hand again, then turned on his heels.

"Okay, see you Friday." As Gigi arched her head, the shock of flaming-red hair touched her shoulders. Her eyes followed

Smiley, glad-handing his way back through the lunch crowd. Then she turned back to me. "Bradford Henry Pope, for crying out loud. Since when do you speak for me? Don't I have a mouth?"

"Nobody in town would dispute that, Gigi. Just giving you a taste of your own medicine."

"Now who's interfering with whose love life? You're doing what you accused me of doing with Christine." Gigi sank her teeth into a chicken leg and tore the meat away from the bone with a vengeance, chewing hard and fast as if she couldn't get it down fast enough. "Speaking of interfering with people's love life, son, you won't believe what happened."

"What?" My annoyance with her caused me to avoid her eyes. I surveyed the mounted wild boar heads, the taxidermied blue gill and bass that had been yanked from the Suwannee and nailed on the walls.

"After you called me about Myrtle on your cellular telephone, I was fit to be tied. So I high-tailed it over to Bowen's Funeral Home, where Myrtle gets the corpses all duded up. But she was nowhere in sight. They said things were slow, that she'd gone over to the church to help Pastor Black fix Sunday's bulletin. So I sashayed my ass over to the church."

"What about your policy? Funerals only?"

"I busted my policy, but it was worth it." She wigwagged her head. "The more I think about it, though, maybe I didn't bust my policy because it was a funeral in a way. At least, it's something I buried for good. I paraded into that sanctuary. There wasn't a soul around. I went to the back of the church and tried the office door, but it was locked. So I figured they must've finished up and gone home. Then I heard the awfulest racket coming from behind me, like somebody was dying— dreadful grunting and groaning sounds from the multipurpose room beside the church office."

"Multipurpose room?" I speared the fried chicken, swallowed a bite, and licked my fingers.

"More of a makeshift health room where they reproduce and assemble the church bulletin. Took you in there and put you on a cot one time when you had a bellyache during Sunday service. You couldn't have been more than four or five. Anyway, I tried that door, and it swung open. Guess who was on that cot?"

"Who?" I dabbed at the macaroni and cheese with my fork.

"Myrtle Badger."

"Was she sick?"

"Sick?" Gigi hooted. "She looked like one helluva healthy woman to me. And she was reproducing all right, but it wasn't the church bulletin. Guess who was on top of her?"

"On top of her?" My half-interest had sprouted into full-blown curiosity. I looked up from my plate. "Who?"

"Pastor Black, stark naked, pumping away, his eyes rolled every which-a-way. Myrtle's humongous topaz ring was flopping up and down, showering the light around the room like a beacon atop a lighthouse. I pulled out that cellular telephone you gave me and snapped their picture."

"Are you making this up?" At this point I couldn't believe much of anything she said.

"Cross my heart and hope to die." She dried the chicken grease off her hands with a napkin, reached in her purse, and fished out a snapshot. "Look here. I printed it off."

I glanced at the photograph. "Wow," was as much as I could muster. The mingling of droopy pale flesh made my stomach turn. I handed the picture back.

"They both jumped around, howling and hollering, jerking on their drawers like they'd been bitten by a rattler. 'Woman,' I said, 'If you have something to say, you come to me instead of bothering my grandson.' I do believe I saw the devil in her eyes blazing back at me. After they hopped in their clothes, they sniffed, put on airs like nothing ever happened. I wasn't going to let them get away with that. Halfway out the door, I told her, 'As far as you telling my grandson you'll get to the bottom of me and the WPC, I saw the only thing you're going to get to the bottom of. And that's Pastor Black.' Then, bam. I slammed the door."

"Let's talk about something else. This conversation is ruining my appetite."

"Well, I don't think we'll be hearing any more from Myrtle about getting to the bottom of anything. It makes me madder than a wet hen, her calling you, dragging you into the middle of my business."

I shrugged, waving her concern away with my hand. "Ah, it's no big deal."

"Reminds me of when you were a boy. When your mama and daddy pulled you into the midst of their goings-on." The laughter that had brightened her face drained into a pale overcast. "That was no place for a child. You were always such a sweet innocent little boy. Why, I remember the day you were born. You were slap beautiful. Everybody said so. 'What a beautiful baby,' they said. Even Doc Rogers, after delivering hundreds of babies, said so. Those sassy golden locks of yours still shine like fresh-cut hay."

She reached across the table and mussed my hair with her fingers.

"Stop it." I nudged her hand away. "You're getting grease in my hair."

"Nobody'll notice." She beamed. "You got your daddy's thick blond mane and your mama's good looks." She paused, examined my face. Then in an afterthought, she added, "But you got my stubborn disposition."

My voice sagged with exasperation. "I'm nothing like you."

An awkward silence welled up between us. After a few

heartbeats, Gigi broke it. "What's wrong, son? You've got your ass on your shoulders like an old bull ant."

"I don't know what you mean." I peeled my eyes away from her, glanced down at crumbs of food that littered the concrete floor.

"Hell, yes you do. Now what is it, Tug-a-Love?"

"Don't call me that stupid name." The edge to my voice didn't go unnoticed.

Gigi twitched, turned pale as if she'd been sucker punched. Her smile rescinded into a crack, the blue sparkle in her pupils deadened to black, her eyes narrowed. Her voice was steady, deliberate.

"What's wrong, Brad?" She cleared her throat, waited for an answer. "Come on, what is it?"

"I know what you did." I kept my voice down so customers wouldn't hear.

"And just exactly what did I do?" She spoke matter-of-factly, fingered Mama's golden heart locket that hung around her neck.

"I know you and your 'sister*freaks*' killed Big Jake and a bunch of other people."

She dropped her head halfway; her eyes rolled up at me, chest pressed forward. "Come again?"

"I hear you're pretty good at cutting, so cut the innocent act."

She tilted her body further over the table toward me. "Brad, what the hell are you talking about?"

"I heard the WPC's entire conversation last Saturday—Gladys talking about you cutting Big Jake's rope, you forcing her to cover it up and not tell me."

"What?" She sounded astonished. "You didn't hear any such thing. You weren't even there Saturday . . . unless somebody tape recorded . . . wait a minute. Has Gladys been blabbing to you?"

"I *was* there, in my kayak, underneath the dock. I heard everything. So don't give me any more of your bullshit."

She bammed the table with her fist. "Bradford Henry Pope, you little sneak." When heads turned our way, she softened her voice. "What're you doing snooping in my personal business?"

"You're not going to turn the tables on me like you usually do, making me the guilty one. I accidentally overheard you confess to Big Jake's murder."

"Accidentally, my hind foot." She looked around the tables, dropped her voice. "And if you think you heard me confessing to killing Big Jake, you're crazier than a bed bug." She looked at me sideways. "Son, have you lost your mind? What's gotten into you?"

"Let me put it to you this way. A watch list is one thing, but instructing your so-called sisterfriends to kill people . . . my God, Gigi. What are you thinking? That's . . . that's insane." My face and neck felt swollen, blood-red.

"I always knew you got a mighty creative imagination, but this takes the cake." Her jaw hung half open.

"I heard it with my own ears. Gladys said you made murderers out of all of them."

"You've got it all turned around." She bammed her fist again.

"You and your 'sister*freaks*' cut Big Jake's guideline, didn't you? Because he was coming after me. You said so. I heard you."

"Listen to you. What a thing to say. If the sisterfriends knew you called them that and accused them of such a thing, why, every blessed one of them'd have a coronary."

"What about those other men that died?" I asked. "It's mighty funny that one of your club sisters was in the vicinity every time."

"Son, you've been watching too many *Murder She Wrote* reruns." She tapped the table lightly with her scepter, underscoring her words. "It's like Sally says, 'Evil carries the seeds of its own destruction.' "

Hearing Gigi quote that old witch made my eyes roll involuntarily. "You mean to sit here and tell me that you and your sisterfriends didn't have anything to do with Big Jake's death?"

"That's exactly what I mean." She cackled. "Lord have mercy. Wait until I tell them about this. They're gonna have a conniption fit, and you're going to have a pile of old dead women on your hands."

I exhaled my exasperation through my teeth. There was no way to tell if she was leveling with me.

"Next time you want to know something, just ask me. You don't have to go snooping."

"I've asked you until I'm blue in the face. And you keep me in the dark."

"What do you want to know?" She burrowed both elbows on the table, her palms cupping her jaws.

"For one thing, I want to know what you were talking about on the dock."

"Forget it. That subject's off-limits."

"You said all I had to do was ask. I'm asking."

I'd never seen her so skittish. She looked off, bit her bottom lip. "I gotta go pee." She rose halfway up, plopped back down, flung her napkin into her plate. "No. Hell no, I don't have to go to the ladies' room. Okay, the whole thing's about your daddy . . ." She trailed off.

"And? Keep going."

"I'd planned to tell you that day on the Suwannee with the manatee, but I couldn't get it out. The timing was off . . ." She faltered.

Both of us had put our forks down now, rested our elbows on the table, gazed into each other's faces. Then she lowered her eyes, arranged and rearranged her knife and fork.

I gently covered her hands to hold them still. "So you know where he is. You know I want to face the son-of-a-bitch."

Unable to look me in the face, she stared off. "Things were just beginning to settle down between us." She fidgeted, pulled her hands free, swished the gold locket against its chain. "I don't want to ruin it."

"Gigi, if you know where he is, tell me." I probed her face, squeezed her harder now.

"I know where he is."

"Then where?"

"He's right where I put him."

"Where *you* put him?"

"Son, you misunderstood all along." She narrowed her eyes. "Big Jake and your daddy were like two peas in a pod, but I never killed Jake Nunn. I killed your daddy." She smacked both palms on the table, flipping her fork and knife into cartwheels. "There now, I got it out." She started fanning herself with her wrinkled napkin.

"You what?" I sprang up, banging my knee under the table, sloshing sweet tea over the rim of my glass. My eyes swept the room for safe landing. Finding none, they fell back on Gigi. "You did what?"

Gigi looked around the tables at the curious onlookers who'd stopped mid-bite to listen. She nodded at them, motioned for me to settle down. As I slid slowly back into the booth, she spoke under her breath. "Johnny was coming after you. I did it to save you—and me. That's why we started the WPC, to pay back for the wrong we did."

"We? Who's we?"

"The sisterfriends helped me."

"Helped you? Kill him?" I let out a bolt of air; my body went limp. The whole thing sounded so unbelievable. Was this the same grandma who had great reverence for life and preservation? The same grandma I'd remembered as a boy who'd stop snapping pole beans on the back porch, pull her head out of the oven from a blackberry cobbler to appreciate a crayon-swirled sunset? And her sisterfriends? Sure, they squabbled among themselves like Lucy and Ethel, folding their arms and patting their feet. But murder? It wouldn't sink in.

"I know this is a lot to take at one time, son." She reached across the table for my hand.

I pulled it back.

"You're damn straight it is." The anger rose from my chest to my throat, played there. I thought for a second that it might gag me, but I was able to speak through it. I took a deep breath and asked with resignation, "So what'd the fucker do this time?"

I knew that whatever it was, it must've been huge to involve the church ladies.

"I want to tell you what happened—but not here."

"Where then?"

"I put your daddy in a place where he's doing some good for once in his life. Let's go, I'll take you there." She stood up, threw a tip on the table, and mumbled, "Gladys was right. You have a right to know."

"Where're we going?"

She had already trotted up to the cash register, handed Glenda a twenty, and instructed her to keep the change.

CHAPTER 13

We elbowed our way through the lunch crowd into the parking lot where Lick sat on a bench eating an orange. Gigi petted the purple bandana that wrapped his hair and sang out, "How you doing, Lick?"

"Fine, Miss Gigi." He flashed a sheepish grin, spitting orange seeds into his hand.

After we hopped into Gigi's old pink clunker, she made a light stab at the heavy mood. "Takes a lickin' and keeps on kickin'." Then she stared straight ahead, her mouth set in a grave line. As she drove, she gripped the steering wheel tightly with her left hand, clicked her pink-chipped nails with her right.

"Your daddy skipped town when he found out your mama was pregnant with you and he wasn't around to make you his namesake. The only reason he came back at all was because he had gotten another woman pregnant and had run out of money. By that time, Ada Lea had already birthed you, given you the Pope name. Your daddy didn't marry her until after you were born."

"I never knew that." Tightness squeezed my chest; dread paled my face.

"That was the one good he did for you. And that was by accident because you got the Pope family name instead of his."

"I want you to tell me everything. I need to know *everything*."

"Okay, son." With hesitation dawdling in her eyes, she took a deep breath, pushed through it, and continued.

"Not long after Johnny'd burned the house down, Ada Lea sent you off to boarding school. About a month or so after that, I got a call from the police. They said Johnny'd come home drunk from being out all night. Ada Lea had packed her bags. Said she was through with him, that she was leaving. Johnny flew into a drunken rage, beat her with her cane. Bashed her head in so hard, she died right there on the spot. Then Johnny disappeared into thin air. The Whitecross Police claimed they were looking for him, but they didn't do a damn thing to find him. Said Ada Lea musta provoked him.

"Two years later a banging on my trailer door woke me at three in the morning. I remember looking at the clock, wondered who in the world could be calling that time of night. I was alone, between husbands, scared half to death. I grabbed my double barrel, leaned it against the couch. When I swung the door open, there he stood: red-eyed Johnny Devillers—three sheets to the wind, smelling of Ancient Age, slurring his words, swaying side to side.

" 'Johnny, the law's looking for you,' I told him.

" 'I don't give a shit, and I didn't come here to listen to your goddamn bitchin'.' He snarled at me. 'I came here to find my boy.'

"I said, 'Well he's not here.'

"He didn't know you were at the boy's school in Asheville. When I wouldn't tell him where you were, he butted his chest up against me, barged inside the trailer.

" 'Okay, you old slut.' He yelled, grabbed both my arms. 'You know where my boy is, and I got legal rights on him. I'm gonna lay claim to what's rightly mine.'

"I told him, 'He's not yours.' Then, he body-slammed me, threw me off balance, caused me to stumble backwards. As I latched on to the door frame to steady myself, I hollered back at him. 'Your seed created him, but that's as far as it went. He's not anything like you. He's not a piece of property you can claim squatter's rights on.'

"For every step I took backwards, he took one forwards until I dropped into the La-Z-Boy. He towered over me, glared through bloodshot eyes. 'Fuck, you're turnin' him into a sissy. I'm gonna make a man outa him. I'm bringin' him back to help out around my place, to learn to hunt and rope a steer, to get some toughness in him.'

" 'He's not your slave property,' I told him.

"He glued his hands on both sides of the chair, stuck his boozy face in mine, and sneered, 'You think you can run everybody's life don't you, old biddy? Well, you ain't gonna run mine.'

"I pushed up against his chest with both hands. He loosened his grip, and I ran to the phone. He caught me by the arm, jerked the phone cord out of the socket, slung the phone against the wall. Then he balled up his fist, smashed me in the face with all his might, hurled me onto the settee where the shotgun was leaning.

"He said, 'Now, you tell me where he is or I'm . . .' "

Gigi stopped cold, eyed me, and made a funny face. "Son, I don't feel right telling you this part."

I put on my game face. "I'm a psychologist. I've heard it all. I can handle it." I rolled my palm forward, gesturing for her to continue, but inside I felt a volcano brewing.

"Okay, so . . . so . . . he said, 'You tell me where he is or I'm gonna teach you a lesson.' He looked down at his fly, cupped the bulge in his jeans. 'I always wondered what it'd be like to fuck a buckin' bronco.'

"He unzipped his pants and staggered backwards, giving me just enough time to grab the shotgun. Blood spouted out of my nose. My blood-soaked fingers were slippery on the trigger. I was shaking so hard my aim was bad. He came at me, knocked the gun out of my hands, and seized me by the hair on my head. Then he wrestled me to the floor, slammed his stinking body on top of me, and pressed his hard mouth against my lips. I could hardly breathe, and he was too heavy for me to get out from under. On a low shelf within my reach, an old Mason jar that I'd used for storing navy beans caught my attention."

For a brief second, Gigi took her eyes off the road and checked me out. "You okay?"

"Fine," I lied. "I'm fine." I was slumped in my seat, my jaw sealed, hands resting into fists on my knees.

Her eyes returned to the road, she to her story.

"It's funny the things you think about to take your mind off dying. In the flutter of snatching that Mason jar, I noticed one black bean peeking out from amongst all those white navy beans. I remember thinking, just like it was yesterday. *I'm not going to live long enough to get that black bean out of there.*

"I conked him hard over the head. He fell off of me. I clambered for the shotgun. He pulled up, wobbled toward me. My fingers slipped on the trigger again. I wiped the blood down my jeans, took good aim, and nailed him right between the eyes. It pitched him against the Old Gold Cigarette sign over my TV set.

"Then everything went into slow motion. I watched Johnny slide down the wall, slump on the floor. Most of his head was gone, and it seemed like it took him forever to die. His body started a violent twitching and jerking. When his fingers stopped fluttering, I knew he was done for. I dropped the shotgun, ran to the bathroom, trembling all over. I collapsed on the settee, threw my head back with a cold wash rag on my nose to stop the bleeding, and just fell apart. I sat and I sat and I fretted, not knowing what to do. When I picked up the Mason jar to wipe off the blood, I saw that one black bean amongst all those navy beans. It hit me that there was only one person I could call on who'd understand. And that was the woman you kids used to call Voodoo Sally. She'd been dealing with evil all her life, and she'd know exactly what to do.

"Sally was sick in bed with a fever, but she knew something was up as soon as I crumpled onto the side of her mattress. She said, 'Child, what's ailin' you? And what happened to your nose?' She cupped my chin, turned it side to side saying, 'You all swole up.'

"I confessed to her that I'd done something awful. I told her the whole story, broke down, cried my eyes out, and dropped my head in her lap, not caring if I caught the fever. Sweat beads had collected on Sally's forehead. She was weak, but that didn't stop her from comforting me.

" 'Child, you didn't go lookin' for this. It came lookin' for you. You ain't done wrong by protectin' yourself. What happened, happened. You can't change that. Now you got to turn it inside out and make good out of it. That's limestone gumption. Um hmm. You have to take what you got and make the best of it. All bad contains some good. Now, expel the bad, drain off the good and make it work for you.'

" 'How?' I asked her.

" 'That's for you to figure out—that's how you get your gumption.'

"I felt stronger after leaving Sally's that night. She'd helped me find a speck of hope and strength."

I stared through the windshield at storefronts zipping by, down at white lines in the middle of the road in front of us. Gigi tumbled a look in my direction, taking my trauma pulse. She must've noticed my head, too heavy to hold itself up on its own, fall like dead weight into my hands.

"How you doing, son?"

"This is so fucked up." I tried to push away the booming *evol wanga obeah, evol wanga obeah.* "My crazy daddy killed my mama and sister, tried to rape you. Then you go to a witch doctor for advice. How fucked up is that?"

"Sally's not a witch doctor." She slowed the car down, reached her hand toward me. "Want me to pull over?"

"No. Keep going." I'd tried to give her my strong, confident therapist face again. But she could see straight through it. She knew me inside out.

"You sure?" She wrinkled her brow.

"Yeah, finish your story." Inhaling deeply, I flipped my hand forward.

"When I got back from Sally's, it was almost daylight. Johnny lay in the middle of the floor where I'd left him, stiff and gray like a mannequin. I stood over him, looked down, felt contempt rise up in me. I remember thinking, 'You good-for-nothing parasite, you never did anything but suck off all the good in life, contaminate what's pure. You never gave to anybody. All you did was take.' "

"So, then what'd you do?"

"I thought about what Sally'd said. A light bulb went off in my head. I decided to turn the bad deed into something good. From then on, I was going to make Johnny give back for all the pain he'd caused. So the sisterfriends and me put him where he'd do some good."

"Where?"

She stepped on the gas. I felt the car accelerate.

Her chipped nails, clicking the steering wheel, kept time to my rapid heartbeat.

"You'll see."

CHAPTER 14

The car's fast pace slowed to a crawl. We arrived near the outskirts of town at the greeting sign that I had admired so often.

Welcome to Whitecross, Home of the Historic Suwannee River
Please Help Us Keep Our Town Clean and Green
—The Women's Preservation Club

Gigi screeched to a halt. "This is it."

I scratched my head, looked around. "The welcome garden?"

"Yep, the bastard's finally doing some good. Some of the richest soil I ever saw."

"Uh huh." My jaw rigid, I could barely speak.

When she stepped out of the car, she motioned for me to get out. Stunned, I sat still, rage clawing in my stomach. She rested her hands on the roof of the car, hunched her head inside the opened window. The pain in her face showed as she pointed to a willow bent and swayed by the same delicate breeze that lifted wisps of her red hair. "The sisterfriends and me planted that weeping willow in honor of your mama."

I slammed my fist against the dashboard. A sharp pain shot up my arm from the force of the thrust. But my rage deadened it. "The fucker took everything from us. Why didn't you report him to the police?"

"The Whitecross Police? They were a big fat help." She opened the door and slid back into the driver's seat. "They were as crooked as a snake." She let out a soulful sigh, rubbed my back. "After Johnny killed Ada Lea, the law closed the case, told him to lay low. I was so put out with them *and* with Pastor Abrams. He hid Johnny so he could save his soul. After that, I started questioning religion, but I kept on going to church. Johnny had disappeared for nearly two years until he showed up that night at my place."

"But what you did was *clearly* self-defense."

"We're talking the eighties. If you were a woman back then in Whitecross, there was no such thing as self-defense against a man. Plus, Johnny was *clearly* a decorated war hero, wounded in Vietnam with a purple heart, *clearly* a good-looking charmer. Not to mention the Devillers's dynasty: Johnny's brother, Ronny, was *clearly* the sheriff."

"Sounds like the story of Big Jake all over again."

She nodded. "Years before Ada Lea's death, she and I went down to the police station to report your daddy for raping her. They laughed in our faces. Said there's no such thing as a husband raping his wife. If I'd reported the shooting, the law would've turned it into a trumped-up charge against *me*."

I shook my head. "He was a sorry excuse for a father." I put my arm around her neck. "Thank God for you."

"You want to hear the rest?" The hesitation in her voice had a protective ring.

"Can't say I want to, but I need to."

We climbed out of the car and sat on the stone border of the garden. The tree frogs deafened us with their relentless barking. That meant rain. A brisk breeze brushed my face, raised the ends of Gigi's red curls as she continued.

"I plunked down at the kitchen table, not knowing what to do. It didn't sink in at the time that I was in shock. When I looked down, the names and phone numbers of the church circle jumped off the paper. There were eight members back then, including myself, plus Betty-Jewel, Wilma-May, Gladys, Shirley, Jackie, Ibejean Martin, and Talithia Abrams. I was active in church and was having the circle meeting at my house late that Sunday afternoon. Ibejean missed because she was visiting her sister in Plant City. Talithia was in the hospital dying of cancer.

"At our circle meetings, we'd always talked about personal problems, quoted scripture, and prayed for one another. We'd vowed to stand together through thick and thin. Thick and thin was one thing, but expecting them to stand by my side through murder was a whole nother ballgame. We all believed in the Commandments, that Thou shalt not kill.

"I met them at the trailer door. My back was pressed up against the metal frame. I still remember that cool metal door against my back. Oh, how it soothed me.

"Betty-Jewel looked over the top of her glasses. When she saw my face, she drew in a quick breath, said, 'What on earth?'

"When she saw the blood on my clothes, Wilma-May cried out, 'Dear sweet Jesus.' Then she stuttered, 'What happened to you, Gigi?'

"My throat closed. Took me a second before I could speak. 'I never asked a single one of you for nothing before,' I told them, 'but I'm asking for all the help I can get now.'

" 'Bless your heart,' Shirley said, 'What's wrong?'

"The sisterfriends got under both arms and lifted me back inside. After they saw the covered-up lump in the middle of the floor, I said, 'Brace yourselves.' Then I pulled back the blanket. Johnny's arm stuck straight up like a tree stump.

"Wilma-May fell on her knees and howled, 'Dear Heavenly Father.'

"It sent a quake through the group. The sisterfriends went into a tizzy, eyes popping open and mouths hanging loose. They gasped and shrieked and clutched on to one another. They walked around in circles, clucked their tongues. Shirley started shivering like she had the chills, saying she'd never seen a dead person outside of a coffin before.

"I told them I'd understand if they didn't want to get mixed up in this mess. They pushed me down on the settee. Said after all I'd done for them, they didn't even have to think twice about it. They started naming this, that, and the other. Like when I helped get Wilma-May into AA after her drinking and shoplifting got out of control. She said I saved her life. And Betty-Jewel recalled how I'd helped pay for an immigration lawyer to get her sister here from Mexico. They went on and on.

"But the sisterfriends knew what a lowlife Johnny was. And they knew how corrupt the police force was, too. By that time, the police had already ruled Ada Lea's death accidental. A domestic dispute, they'd called it. Humph! Every single one of the sisterfriends had been wronged by the Whitecross Police in one way or another. They didn't have a drop of respect for the law in this town.

"We decided that working together as a team to get rid of the body was the only way. The sisterfriends changed into some old clothes that I was fixing to take to Goodwill. We waited until sundown. Jackie and me tugged Johnny through the door by his feet. I'll never forget that sound, his head banging down the aluminum steps like a lead ball as we pulled him into the yard.

"We dragged him down to the dock, cut off his fingertips with a hacksaw, and knocked his teeth out with a hammer so nobody could identify him. Blood was seeping everywhere. We threw the bloody pieces of teeth and fingertips into the Suwannee. I had an old chainsaw at the time. We revved it up, cut him apart limb from limb, just like a frying chicken."

When the shudder of horror widened my eyes, Gigi paused, looked at me with concern. "You okay?"

"Why'd you cut him up?" I asked, pushing down the acid rising in my throat.

"Had to. He was too heavy to carry in one piece. We didn't want folks to see us lifting a body. Plus, we knew we weren't strong enough to dig a deep enough hole. So the plan was to scatter his body parts around the garden in a bunch of shallow graves."

"Okay," I nodded. "Keep going."

"Gladys and Betty-Jewel wrapped the body parts in some old blankets, stuffed them in Hefty plastic garbage bags. Wilma-May and Shirley kept a lookout for surprise visitors, then stuffed the black plastic bags into the trunk of the Eldorado I'd just bought.

"When we'd finished, we were soaked in blood. I had a bunch of oversized dress shirts from one of my ex's that each of them put on to hide the blood stains. We hauled the body parts off from my house in the trunk of my car.

"By the time we got to the outskirts of town, it was nightfall. But we carried plenty of flashlights, so we could see to dig. Most townsfolk were at Sunday evening worship service. The folks driving by honked and waved, thinking we were the church circle doing our normal planting. That was the first official project of the WPC. It took all six of us to carry Johnny's parts from the car to the garden. After he'd got back from Vietnam, he'd had a hip replacement. That one side of him was heavier than the other.

"We scattered his severed head, hands, arms, legs, feet, and torso in shallow graves. Shoveled dirt back on top, packed them as tight as we could. Then, all of a sudden, a stiff hand wrapped in black plastic sprang up through the dirt."

Gigi stopped talking, turned to me. Despite the morbid nature of her story, both of us released a chuckle of comic relief, then she continued.

"Wilma-May shrieked, took off running. Shirley fell on her

knees, held her chest like she was having a heart attack. I rammed the hand with a shovel, jammed it deeper into the sandy soil, and planted a small-at-the-time willow on top of it.

"Once we got back to my house later that night, everybody took showers, changed back into their church clothes. When the full jolt of what we'd done hit us—that we'd broke the law and committed a mortal sin—Wilma-May and Shirley went to pieces. They wailed and cried, flailed their arms, and flung themselves onto the settee. Betty-Jewel grabbed Shirley, and Jackie held Wilma-May until the two of them simmered down. Gladys was as quiet as a church mouse, staring off into space at the blood smeared on the Old Gold Cigarette sign."

As I listened to Gigi, I wondered if that was when Gladys had started thinking about killing Big Jake, not from my therapy. Even though it was a long time ago, Jake had already started abusing her by that time.

"That Old Gold sign has seen a lot in its lifetime, hasn't it?" I said.

Gigi nodded and pressed on. "After everybody's nerves settled, we circled up, joined hands, and prayed for redemption. Then we swore to never speak about that night to a soul, vowing to take care of each other from then on.

"I told the sisterfriends, when I thought I was dying, the thing that stuck out was that one black bean inside the Mason jar with all those navy beans. They agreed that it was a sign that the black bean was out of place and had to go. Just like Johnny was a speck of bad amongst the good folks he'd hurt. The more we talked, the more we realized that it was ordained for us to pay back for what we'd done by ridding the town of its black specks.

"So we started a watch list of folks threatening Whitecross's way of life, started the practice of passing the jar around. The one drawing the black bean took a name on the watch list, so we could report lawbreakers to the authorities. We called ourselves watchdogs and made our mission to protect and preserve Whitecross's way of life.

"When you go through something as disturbing as that, it has a way of binding you together. As time went on, we became more like sisters than just friends. The sisterfriends were the only family I had, except for you, Tug-a-Love. And you were in boarding school. Soon after that night, I left the church. Instead of the church circle, the sisterfriends and me threw ourselves into the Women's Preservation Club to redeem ourselves from the sin we'd committed."

I swabbed my fingers over my eyes, feeling queasy, but saying nothing.

"I give credit to your so-called Voodoo Sally. Bless her dear soul for giving me the notion of turning the bad inside out to make good out of it. Her and that old Mason jar put me on the path to redemption. It's the only way I could've got through it."

I heard the crackle of leaves, the rustling of branches coming from a clump of hydrangea bushes behind us. I jerked my head around. "What was that?"

"The wind's picking up. Looks like we're in for a big storm."

She stood from the stone wall, ambled to the trunk of her car, and lugged a shovel over to the willow tree. She compressed the soil around the plantings with the back of it. Under bright sunshine, pellets of rain smacked the dirt, spreading its sweet smell into the summer air.

"Look." She raised her arms to the heavens. "The devil's beating his wife."

From the time I was a boy, I'd heard old-timers use that expression when the sun shone while it rained. As I watched her work the soil, it hit me why a group of women as different as day and night had stuck so closely together. The grizzly horror of that night in 1983 had thrown them into a sisterhood that had stabilized the aftershocks.

Their benevolent bond salved their private pains and emboldened them. Gigi was their pontiff, they her cardinals. And I'd become their confessional—an outlet for the group sin they'd committed and the secrets that scabbed their transgression.

It was understandable why the WPC had sealed themselves off instead of coming forward to a corrupt legal system that had failed them time and time again. As far as I was concerned, the case was closed. But Gigi's revelations made me even more suspicious of the club. Had they changed from watchdogs to vigilantes? And what did they know about Big Jake's murder?

A lightning bolt zigzagged toward us; thunder rumbled the ground. The sky darkened. With my elbows dug into my knees, I braced my head in my hands, stared at the ground. A praying mantis hobbled for cover. When I looked up, the rain began to hammer the earth. The willow tree bent double.

Drenched, her hair falling into stringy red strands, Gigi packed the sand around the flowers and trees like she was soothing a newborn to sleep.

"There now," she said in a lullaby voice. "It's only natural that Johnny be here."

She spun her head in my direction, shot me a long, fixed stare. "Johnny got what was coming to him. And so did Big Jake."

CHAPTER 15

We scrambled to the car. Beneath the sound of raindrops thumping the roof, the radio crooned Willie Nelson's "Always On my Mind." Gigi pulled two towels from the back seat, threw one at me, and dabbed herself with the other. The shudder of relief freed my mind from the stab of Gigi's story, and my love for her warmed me on the inside. I couldn't bear to think about the private pain she'd carried all these years, just so she wouldn't burden me.

I rolled my shoulders, looked at her. "Gigi, why didn't you tell me before now?"

"I tried to, son, so many times." She patted my hand and held it. "But I couldn't bring myself to dash your hopes of settling things with your daddy. I thought if I kept it in the past where it belonged, you'd eventually drop it. The sisterfriends were on pins and needles when they'd run into you, because they feel guilty for their part. The way they see it, we put away the life that gave you life. As for me, I was afraid you'd wash your hands of your old grandmamma once you found out."

I kissed her hand. "That'll never happen."

When the hate for my daddy rose up in me again, I exhaled its force in a huge sigh. It hit me that Johnny'd been a sperm donor, not a father—a relationship that had been counterfeit from the beginning. Gigi'd been the one who had nurtured and protected me. With Willie Nelson humming in the background, I turned a page that night. I eliminated the word *Daddy* from my vocabulary—a label I would never apply again. Knowing that Gigi had put him in his rightful place helped me bury Johnny Devillers along with my rage. Something lifted, and I felt free of him for good.

Gigi goosed the engine. As we pulled away from the welcome garden, I could have sworn I saw a figure moving in the bushes. But I dismissed the thought, assumed my imagination was running away with me because Gigi's story had creeped me out.

We headed back to Glenda's. The mellow music of Patsy Cline's "Walking After Midnight" was broken by an announcement from broadcaster, Vasque Gaylord:

We interrupt our musical program to bring you this important weather update. The national hurricane center reports that Tropical Storm Eduardo could be upgraded to a hurricane by nightfall. Doppler radar shows Eduardo picking up wind speed over the Gulf with maximum sustained winds of sixty-five miles per hour. Whitecross and the surrounding area remain under a hurricane watch until midnight tonight. Stay tuned to WHCS 99.5 for further information.

"I've never been in a hurricane before," I said.

"Sonny boy, you better come home with me. This could be a rough one. The weather report this morning said if this storm stays over warm water, it could be worse than Katrina." She looked at me through concern.

"Thanks Gigi, but I'm a big boy. I can take care of myself."

"You sure?"

"Positive." I blinked and smiled at her. "You've always protected me, haven't you? You saved me from that monster, just like Mama did. I'll always be indebted to you."

"And I'll always be indebted to you, son, for helping my sisterfriends."

I glowed. That was the first time she'd given me a vote of confidence, at least out loud and to my face.

"But you said you didn't believe in psychology."

"I don't for me. I have my own brand." She rocked her right palm back and forth. "But it seems like it's been helping them. Sally'd say it's giving them their limestone gumption."

"Limestone gumption?" I wrapped my tongue around the words.

"Johnny was like Big Jake, weak inside. He stole strength from running over good-hearted people and helpless animals, forcing things instead of letting them flow naturally. Limestone gumption gives you strong insides to let life's hard slaps roll over you. Kind of like the limestone under the Suwannee that survives by letting the river cut through it.

"Sally always said, 'Don't push the Suwannee; it flows by itself.' "

I shivered off the thought of the old witch and looked at Gigi with admiration. "You kept your end of the deal."

She looked puzzled. "Deal?"

"Bringing me to Johnny. Now it's my turn to bring Chris to you on Founder's Day."

"You mean I'll finally get to meet her?" Unsuccessful at holding back the tears, she fluttered her moist eyes, patted her chest. I stretched across the car seat, pecked her on the cheek. "Why son, what a wonderful surprise." She pulled the car to the side of the road, threw her arms around my neck. Swiping at her eyes with the towel, she let out a little screech. "We'll have a big party at my place, a special party for the whole push of sister-friends to meet her."

"Nah, Gigi. Keep it simple, please." My voice went up. "There are things about Chris you don't know. I want the two of you to get acquainted first, before the WPC . . . Just maybe the three of us to start. Okay? Promise?"

"I promise to keep it simple."

Gigi was a lot of things, but simple wasn't one of them. As she pulled the pink clunker into Glenda's parking lot, it occurred to me that Gigi's secret was out, but mine was still underground. After our talk about limestone gumption, I decided to let nature take its course with Gigi and Chris from here on out.

But I couldn't let go of the lingering thought in the back of my mind: that Gigi and her sisterfriends were still not telling me everything about Big Jake's murder.

And if they didn't kill him, then who did?

CHAPTER 16

I swung by my office and spent the rest of the afternoon on paperwork. As dark fell and rain slugged my office window, I thought it wise to head home. By the time I pulled into my driveway, the dashboard digital clock blinked seven-thirty. The howling wind had picked up, propping my screen door open, bending palms and live oaks, making them sound agitated as they roared and whined.

As I sprinted to the porch, rain beat me hard. I scooted a few potted plants into the house, tugged my kayak and barbeque grill into a storage shed. And by the time I'd gotten inside, rain had soaked my clothes through to the skin. Too exhausted to take a shower, I peeled off the wet clothes, crawled into bed with a good book, and snapped on the radio.

A weather report was in progress: *Although Eduardo remains a tropical storm, a hurricane watch is in effect for Whitecross and the surrounding area. Our AccuWeather radar is tracking Eduardo's path as he picks up speed over the Gulf and heads toward north central Florida with the potential to be a category three hurricane by landfall, bringing a wind speed of 115 miles per hour, gusting to 140 miles per hour. We urge everyone to take cover. Now we resume our regularly scheduled program.*

The weather was relentless. Wind hammered the small cabin with a vengeance, whipping water from the Suwannee against the pier, whisking it into the air, splashing it against the sliding-glass doors. An aluminum fold-up chair clattered against the porch; wind chimes jangled an angry tune. The whirring wind, rounding the corners of the house, gave me the creepy feeling that something wicked was coming to take me.

While shadows of trees shimmied on my bedroom wall, bits of debris and tree limbs slammed against the house. At one point, I thought I saw a face pressed against the windowpane, fingers scratching on the glass. But it was the branches of a tree limb. With so much clamor, there was no way I'd be able to concentrate on my reading.

I slipped on my cutoffs and an old T-shirt, grabbed a Tsing-tao beer from the fridge, and plunged into the leather sofa. It was hard to tell how much water on the plate glass was rain, how much was blown from the river.

The screen door behind me rattled, startling me. When I jerked my head around, I noticed the doorknob turn ever so slightly. *Damn, can the wind do that?* I bounced up, raced to the door, and yanked it open. Another red pouch dangled from the doorknob. Off in the night, a rain-coated figure moved fast on foot.

"Goddamn you!" I screamed into the black. "Leave me the fuck alone!"

It was time to put a stop to this shit. Another sleepless night wondering who the prowler was, wasn't an option. After frantically pulling on my boots, I grabbed a flashlight by the door, launched myself off the porch into the wet night. I didn't care if I got waterlogged. All I cared about was apprehending this nuisance.

I hoofed it through the woods, tripping over untied shoelaces, raindrops stinging my eyes. The ghostly form fast-walked deeper and deeper into the forest. All I could make out was a dark raincoat and hat. The phantom moved like a man, fast and jerky, hands held high for balance against the slippery leaves. I'd remembered Lick Skillet had a habit of showing up on Gladys's porch, but the body was too short and round to be Lick. Or Voodoo Sally, for that matter—she would have been my first guess about the figure's identity. The figure stopped and turned, saw me, and took off, moving faster.

Without taking time to tie my shoelaces, I picked up my pace, sprinting now. I hobbled through the brush, moving deeper into the woods. When I hurdle-jumped a fallen log blocking my path, it snagged my shoelaces, tripped me hard to the ground, knocking the breath out of me. I lifted my head, noticed the gashes and bloody scratches that the thickets and sharp tree limbs had tattooed up and down my legs. I hurled my body off the ground, flying faster now, letting loose all the fury inside me. I protected my face from the slicing briars and brambles by thrashing back at them, using my fists as a machete.

Numb from the cuts, I felt nothing but anger, nothing but determination.

After rounding another twist in the Suwannee, I stopped dead in my tracks. Through whirling leaves and smacking rain, the darkly cloaked figure stood on top of a tree stump, staring at me. Mesmerized, I lingered. Like an apparition, it seemed to beckon me further, to silently lure me to follow. Then it slowly turned, leapt unsteadily to the ground, disappeared into a curl in the riverbank. I jogged behind it and rounded the bend into a clearing that led to a long stretch of land and an old shack set back from the banks of the Suwannee.

Breathing hard, hands on my hips, I turned in circles kicking the sand. "Shit, I should've known." It was Voodoo Sally's place. A door slammed, and I gritted my teeth. "Damn that woman!"

The old witch had taunted me since second grade. When I was a boy, she'd appear out of nowhere, scare my friends and me half to death. One time Alvin Dukes and I trampled the outside of empty Sun Drop cans so they'd stick to the heels of our shoes. We clanked along the street, played in the DDT fog behind a mosquito truck. We pretended that we were pilots flying airplanes through the clouds. Our fists were radios that we talked back and forth through.

Then like a magical poof in the mist, Voodoo Sally appeared. She reached toward us with her huge brown hands like an apparition. We could see the whites of her eyes and those piercing green specks as she chanted, "evol wanga obeah, evol wanga obeah." She didn't look *at* us like normal. She looked *through* us like she was trying to take something from inside us.

"It's the witch," Alvin hollered, and we took off, never looking back.

Running scared, out of breath, we scrambled up the back porch steps where Gigi sat shelling lima beans.

"What in tarnation are you young'uns talking about?" Gigi sat her shelling aside and rubbed our backs.

"Voodoo Sally tried to put a spell on us!" I squawked.

"She tried to grab us!" Alvin choked on his words. "Tried to put a hex on us!"

"Hogwash. That woman's just protecting you young'uns. How many times have I told you not to play in that stuff? That bug spray's poison."

Gigi's reassurance didn't stick then or now. Although I wasn't buying it, I was embarrassed I couldn't shrug off the childhood fear with logic. I even thought about turning back, but I was tired of those fucking intrusive, red pouches. I jogged up to an old wooden fence, rotten from age. A lopsided gate attached by a single hinge leaned into the white sand. When I tugged hard on the reluctant gate, it ploughed a mound of sand as it jerked open. A single banana tree stood on one side of the front yard. On the other side, snakes of smoke swirled from an old iron kettle perched over rain-doused, smoldering coals. The overflowing black kettle contained a long wooden stick, clothes floating around inside.

Boyhood memories flooded my mind—flashes of Alvin Dukes, a couple of friends and me there on a full moon. We'd see that old kettle and claim it was witches' brew. It was a rite of passage to take turns to run through the gate, sprint around the house once and back out the gate without the old hag putting a curse on us.

As I approached the small, unpainted clapboard shack, my heart's beating seemed to match the wind's wild pace. The inside of the windows appeared to be covered with aluminum foil, framing a dim illumination. Some people in these parts believed that tin foil plastered over windows kept the devil out.

A rain barrel backed up against the steps. An old rusty oval "Esso" gas sign had been nailed to the outside porch wall. An old corn broom, probably used for sweeping the yard, stood in one corner of the porch; a sleepy hound dog curled against the rain in the other. The mutt raised his head, peered at me with disinterest, and drooped his jaws back onto his paw.

When I crossed the porch, loose boards creaked beneath my feet. I banged on the door, raced back down the steps into the yard. In the long delay, I could hear a faint scraping and banging from the back of the house. As the footsteps got louder, I felt like Jack waiting for the giant to appear at the top of the beanstalk. Once the door slowly cracked open, a dark face with large green eyes peeped through the slit.

"What you want?" A soft voice asked.

"I think you know." My hands balled into fists. "I want to talk to you."

The sluggish door croaked as it opened wide, revealing Voodoo Sally, barefoot in the doorway. A quivering light from inside cast a shadow against the wall behind her, making her look larger than life. Her eyes were wide and glassy, and she wore a gold ring in her nose.

"Listen, you old sorcerer, I'm not six anymore. So you can stop your mumbo jumbo."

"Sorcerer? Mumbo jumbo?" She stared a hole into me.

"All that hocus-pocus stuff you've been hanging on my doorknob. The evil spells you cast on people. The spinning and spewing the day you followed Gigi and me along the Suwannee."

She gave me a toothy smile, called me by name. "Mister Brad, you bein' silly. I haven't seen you since you was a little ole thing. Won't you come inside out of this mess?"

I winced from rain pelting me in the face, raised my elbow into a tent above my head, and looked up at her. Wary of her sly tricks, I dared not take my eyes off the old witch. There was no telling what she might do.

"I didn't come here to socialize. You've been hanging pouches of crap on my doorknob." I started to stutter like a schoolboy. "Some kinda . . . uh . . . I don't know . . . some kinda weird white powdered stuff." Then I gestured toward her with my hand. "You know you did."

"Why don't you come on in out of the wet, son? We need to talk."

"Hell no, I won't." When I stepped backwards, a tree limb crashed behind me, propelling me forward again.

"You gettin' joshed about by this bad weather." She snickered at first. Then, apparently having noticed my scratches, she looked me up and down and frowned. "Looks like that jungle ate you up, Mister Brad. Now, why don't you come on in and let me tend to your cuts?"

"No way." I shook my head in defiance.

"Suit yourself." She started to close the door. "Goodnight, then."

"Wait." My cry was muted by the howling wind. "I want you

to stay off my property, stay away from me."

"I was just tryin' to help you, boy." Sprays of rain had begun to sweep onto the porch, inside the doorway, spotting her yellow blousy shirt. She used one hand to cover herself from the rain, the other to tuck her brown upside-down skirt between her legs.

"Voodoo Sally, you've tried to scare me with your hoodoo crap since I was little."

"Scarin' you? Hoodoo crap?" Her huge emerald eyes examined me. "I just been tryin' to protect you, son."

"Protect me? Ha, that's a joke. Why would I need *your* protection?"

"There are things you don't know bout. But if you don't want to know, there's nothin' I can do bout that."

Grimacing from the wetness, she started to swing the door shut again.

"Wait!" I cried. She left the door ajar. "I'm a grown man. Do I look like I need protecting?" I had swallowed so much rain I started choking and coughing. Bits of debris were pelting me in the face.

"I reckon you do right now, uh huh." She chuckled.

"Well, I don't."

"Mister Brad, why don't you come in before you catch your death. You look like you could stand some chamomile tea."

"What I could stand is for you to leave me alone."

"I didn't mean no harm. I'll do that from now on, but you been in danger and don't even know it. So you take good care of yourself."

The door moaned in objection as it clicked shut. I scrambled up the steps onto the porch to get a reprieve from the drowning rain. The old hound dog stretched and yawned, stared at me as if to say, "Well, are you yellow or what?" It reminded me of Alvin Dukes's dares.

"What are you looking at?" I directed my comments to the mutt, but he looked blank.

My curiosity was starting to get the better of me, *What had I been in danger from?* After all, she wasn't going to chop my head off, al-Qaeda style. If she hadn't killed Gigi by now, she wasn't going to make witches brew out of *me*. I could feel myself caving in.

I knocked on the door again. When she opened it, I asked, "So what's this about my being in danger?"

"Come on in."

"I'm just fine right here."

"Suit yourself. This belongs to you." She handed me a yellowish ragged envelope. "It's high time you had it, but don't let it get wet. You'll want to save it."

She clicked the door shut again. I leaned my head against her front door, my back to the rain to protect the contents of the frayed envelope. I slit it open with my finger.

The ink had faded with age. It was a copy of a handwritten letter from Mama, the one Gigi had misplaced.

April 16, 1980
Dear Bradford,

I miss you terribly. Even though you've only been in Asheville for a month, it feels like an eternity. I don't want to alarm you, but I had to write this letter because I'm afraid I might never see you again. But then, you know me, I'm probably overreacting to things like I usually do. Still, if something should happen to me, I want you to know how much I love you, so much so that I had to let you go. You are too young to understand this now, but someday when you are grown, I hope you will know that I sent you away to have the chance that Lydia never had.

It softens my grief of not having you close to me to know that you are out of harm's way, away from the dangers all of us have endured.

Your father is a sick man. He has threatened time and again to take you from me. He claims I never gave him the love I gave to you and Lydia. But I am confident you will be safe in Asheville, and Mama has promised to take care of you if anything happens to me.

Brad, I hope we can be together again soon. When you read this letter, if it was not meant to be, I may be nothing more than a faint memory. If that is the case, I want you to always remember how much I love you. And even though I cannot hold you in my arms in this moment, I will hold you close in my heart forever.

All My love,
Mama

P.S. I'm giving a copy of this letter to Sally Cutter in case something happens to the original. She is a wonderful woman and has always helped me when I needed her.

I held the letter close to my heart and sobbed, tears fighting the rain for space in my eyes. The hound dog, as if trying to comfort me, ambled over and began licking my boots. With my back slumped against the door, I slid down into a squat and gave him a tight hug. As I leaned forward to stroke his back, he licked my salty tears.

Then the door swung open behind me, and a tender voice said, "Now how's bout that chamomile tea?"

CHAPTER 17

Without a word, I turned and followed the old woman, her large, bare feet shuffling as she ushered me into her home. It had a warm, cozy feeling. The ceiling was made of pressed tin. Pale blue paint peeled off the walls in sheets like shedding skin. Copies of the *Whitecross News*, yellowed from age, had been jammed into crevices of the walls for extra insulation.

She put a teapot on top of the stove to boil. A wet brown hat and raincoat hung on a hook, dripping a puddle on the floor. Wooden shelves of glass containers lined the walls. I ran my fingers across her many canning jars, apothecaries full of herbs: chamomile for relaxation, peppermint to soothe the stomach, blue cohosh to bring on labor, slippery elm to soothe a sore throat, skullcap for . . .

"Sit here." As she directed me to a torn brown sofa next to a lit kerosene heater, a small mouse skittered out from the glass herb jars. "I know it looks cluttered, but I live by the notion that a body's house ought to be a safe landin' place."

I sat on the edge of my seat, self-consciously tracing the curling cracks through the wooden armrest, much like the underground caves twisting beneath us. A wide mirror hung above an armchair across the room in front of me. A handmade sign above my head read *evol. She can't even spell,* I thought. *Why would Mama put her confidence in a woman who prescribes evil?*

The old woman placed an oversized towel around my shoulders, dabbed at the cuts on my arms. I pulled the towel tight, shrugged off her touch, swabbed at my bleeding legs. She plunked into the armchair opposite me.

When my eyes slid over her, I could see that she had been unscathed by the sticker bushes. Of course, she'd grown up on the riverbanks, known the clear paths like the back of her hand. She could move through the thorns and thickets faster than a teenager without getting snagged, barefoot no less.

Before speaking, I swiped the last hint of tears away with the back of my hand. "A fire this time of year?"

"To keep the damp at bay." She ran her hands through her frizzy hair, stared through the slits of her eyes.

I stared back at her. "I want to know why you're stalking me."

The oil lamp on the side table flickered a yellow glow, bathing her face, illuminating her smooth caramel skin. Her teeth were pearly white, perfectly straight. In a flash that came and went, I had the strangest thought that she was actually quite beautiful. Then the pupils of her emerald green eyes descended on me.

"I got a bone to pick with you, too, Mister Brad."

"You do?" My voice cracked.

The wind howled and slashed at the house, whirling leaves into shadows against the covered windows.

"How come you call me names like 'Voodoo Sally' and 'Ole Witch'?"

Taken back by the question, I paused at first before answering. "That's what everybody calls you."

"How would you like it if I called you 'the head shrinker' or 'the rapist,' like Myrtle Badger does?"

I bristled. "How'd you know about that?"

"Cause she's sayin' it all over town."

"Myrtle Badger's an ignorant woman."

"*She's* ignorant? Well, how bout that?" She let out a confident laugh, shaking her head from side to side. "Um, um, um. Well, Mister Brad, for your information, I don't make witches brew or cast spells on people."

"Who do you think you're kidding? You spread evil voodoo everywhere you go. The whole town knows that."

"Son, you all mixed up."

"Wait a minute. You wear a ring in your nose, spin in circles, and spew those weird sounds like . . . like . . . *evol, wangy oprah* . . . whatever the heck that means." I pointed above my head. "That sign hanging there says it all."

"It's *evol wanga obeah*. It means *Love is the strongest medicine*. By the way, your grandmamma told me you told her your sweetheart sometimes wears a nose ring. Is that right?"

"That's different."

"Oh, is it?" Her head bobbed in my direction. "You might *think* it's different. For your information, I'm not a witch, and I don't practice hoodoo or black magic. My first name's not Voodoo, and my last name's not Sally. I got a name just like you do, young man."

Thunderstruck, I felt as if *I were* shrinking. "But that's all I ever knew you as."

"How do you think that makes me feel? Nothin's worse for a black woman than bein' called Aunt Jemima or Ole Witch." She lifted herself up, repositioned her body, and backhanded a speck of lint off her skirt. "You supposed to be an educated man. Callin' me names like voodoo and witch make you sound like Myrtle Badger, like you drunk an extra cup of stupid, too."

Her green eyes held my gaze. I felt a defensive wave wash over me. "I'm nothing like *that* woman."

"Let me tell you bout *that* woman." She cackled, shook her head, prefaced her remarks with, "Um, um, um. *That* woman's somethin' else."

"One time Myrtle's pregnant daughter came down from

Atlanta for a weekend visit. It was a Saturday night. Myrtle and Swayze left her alone at their house. Her water broke, and the baby started to come. Doc Rogers was out of town, so the daughter shouted for the next-door neighbor to get help. The baby was comin' fast, and it was too late to drive all the way to Lake City General Hospital, so they sent for me.

"I'd just caught the baby and finished tyin' off the cord when Myrtle crept through the front door. She saw me comin' out of the bedroom to wash up, threw her hands up screamin', 'What you doin' in my house, voodoo nigger woman?'

"She musta noticed blood smudged on my hands, down my apron. She squealed louder than a slaughtered pig. Her pocketbook went flyin' across the room. She started runnin' around in circles, croakin', 'Dear Heavenly Jesus, save me! You're tryin' to take my grandbaby for devil worship! Get out of my house!'

"I begged her to at least let me call LaKeshia, my oldest daughter. I was so weary from the birthin' and needed to get off my feet. But she wouldn't let me use the phone. So I left, trekked the backstreets in the dark, avoidin' streetlights and public places, fearin' if townsfolk saw me they'd blame me for somebody else's killin'. What an awful night that was. Accusin' me of voodoo and devil worship. Um, um, um."

"After all you did, that's the thanks you got?" I said.

"The thanks I got was savin' that baby and its mama. And that was a-plenty for me."

A shade lifted from over my heart. "I didn't mean any harm. 'Voodoo Sally' is what all the kids called you since I was little. I was always afraid of you."

"Afraid of me? What did I ever do to you?"

"You were always scaring me, twirling around in circles, speaking in tongues."

"Great day in the mornin'." Her eyes widened. As she

chuckled, she rubbed the tops of her legs. "Lord have mercy."

"What?" I wondered what amused her.

"When folks get upset by what they see in somebody else, they lookin' through somethin' in their own selves." She dropped her voice and said softly, "If they hate me, it's their own hate. If they belittle me, the belittlement is inside them. Mister Brad, if you afraid on the inside, you'll see everythin' in your life dressed up in fear."

"I'm not afraid of anything." I popped my knuckles.

She waggled her hand back and forth. "Don't do that, son. It's a nervous habit, bad for the joints."

I wove my fingers together in my lap.

"You're a grown man, as you rightly say . . . smart, too. And I'm just an old woman, trying to help people. If you're scared of me, you're scared of life."

"I didn't come here to be psychoanalyzed. I just want you to stop leaving those weird bags at my house." My defensiveness raised me to my feet. The mirror above her head caught my gaze. When I looked into it, it reflected the sign hanging above my head as *love*, not *evol*.

"Everythin's reflection," she said, "Everythin'. Folks are done in by their own ways."

I eased my body back into the sofa. While her words sank in, I reached down to tie my shoelaces. Everything was backwards. She wasn't promoting evil; she was promoting love, which made me ask her, "How'd you know my mama?"

The teapot whistled. The floor squeaked as she stepped to the kitchen. I was beginning to feel something shift inside me. As she handed me a cup of hot tea, I looked up at her and said, "Thank you."

"All right." She dropped back into the chair, rubbed both legs. "Ooh. I'm gettin' stiff as a board from the damp."

A clap of thunder caused me to flinch. The rain hammered

the metal roof.

"Your mama and me were of like minds." As she spoke of Mama, she had a catch in her throat, a hint of lingering sadness. "She was a true believer."

"In what?"

"I've been a medicine woman all my life. Your mama came to me for help. When you were a baby, bout six months old, you got a rash over your body. Doc Rogers put you on antibiotics. It caused a thrush in your mouth. Your mama was fit to be tied, and she called on me. I talked that thrush right out of your mouth."

"You talked it out?" The lines in my forehead rose with skepticism.

"Uh huh, sure did. I know as much bout gettin' rid of warts, preventin' markin's and deliverin' babies as you do shrinkin' folks' heads. And I been doin' it twice as long as you. Matter-of-fact, I caught you."

I blew against the hot tea, staring at her over the rim of my cup, my body tightening from her accusation. "Caught me doing what?"

"I midwifed you."

"What?"

"Sure enough did. Doc Rogers and your grandmamma asked me to come over and help catch you when you came out. They didn't ever tell you that? I knew you ever since you first come into the world."

She was with Gigi and Mama when I was born? "You helped birth me?"

"Son, I been watchin' out for you since day one. I'd try to get you out of that poison mosquito spray, and you'd run away squealin'. You had such a hard childhood with your daddy and all. When you were up north, your mama used to hide out here with me after that drunk-ass Johnny'd beat up on her."

I was starting to see the old woman in a different light. She was the real deal. Between sips of tea, I glanced down and peeked at the last part of Mama's letter, which hadn't completely sunk in: *P.S. I'm giving a copy of this letter to Sally Cutter in case something happens to the original. She is a wonderful woman and has always helped me out when I needed her.*

Mama wouldn't have put me in the hands of somebody she didn't trust. I started to feel my misunderstanding of the old woman fall away. In its place, I felt a connection to Mama through her. Rain on the metal roof sounded like golf balls, hammering me for how close-minded I'd been.

"But what about those cloth pouches you put on my door?"

"I been keepin' up with you all these years through your grandmamma. Heard you were comin' back and wanted to make sure you safe this time around, like I promised your mama. Those wangas keep Plait-eye at bay."

"Wangas? Plait-eye?"

"Plait-eye . . . evil spirits. Those pouches are wangas, magic potions that protect you from Plait-eye. Tonight it was the storm. Before that, Big Jake."

"Big Jake?"

"Mister Brad, Big Jake was comin' after you for interferin' with his wife."

"But I was trying to help her."

"Not the way *he* saw it. You were helpin' her get strong, and he was losing his grip. He made her stop comin' to see you. But he's been took care of, so no need to worry bout him now."

Been took care of. I thought that was an odd way of putting it. "With all due respect, I don't believe in evil spirits."

"Jake Nunn was a spirit killer. He trampled on folks' hearts. Squished all the good out. Wangas turn evil around into love. That's what that sign above your head stands for."

I glanced up at the words again. "So Big Jake was going to

get me. And you believe that little red pouch—that wanga—saved me?"

"Mister Brad, my medicine works just as good as yours whether you believe it or not. And I can prove it."

"You can? How?"

"I can take that wart off your hand."

She had a keen eye. I had a wart on the side of my left hand that I hadn't been able to get rid of. I fought the scoffing sound in the back of my throat until it settled into inquisitiveness. "Really?"

She went into the kitchen and brought out a cut onion. With lakes of tenderness in her eyes, she rubbed it on the wart. "Now, I'll put this onion in a brown paper sack. When you get home, put it on top of the kitchen cabinet. Don't look at that onion for two weeks until it dries up. When that onion is dried up, that wart'll be gone."

I rolled my skeptical eyes while at the same time respecting her beliefs. "Will do." Then, a question popped into my head. "There's one thing I still don't understand. Big Jake is dead. Why do you keep hanging potions, I mean wangas, on my door?"

"To keep you safe from accusations. Bobby-Cy dropped by yesterday afternoon. Arrested Lick for questionin' in Jake's murder. Said Myrtle pointed the finger at Lick. Said she pointed her finger at you, too."

"Me?" I shot off the sofa. "What?"

"Said Myrtle Badger put you at the crime scene at the time of Big Jake's murder."

"Truth is, I was, but . . ."

"Tsk, tsk, tsk." She shook her head. "Mystery to me how much that Myrtle knows bout other people's business."

"Yeah, it is." My eyes searched the floor, trying to make sense out of things.

"Finger-pointers like Myrtle, safeguardin' right and wrong,

are the ones you have to watch out for. Because as long as they point at somebody else, the attention's off them."

"I was supposed to meet Big Jake for a dive lesson that day, but I got there too late."

"Good thing you did. Or you wouldn't be sittin' here right now."

"What do you mean?"

"Gladys told me the only reason he wanted to take you divin' was to do you in. Said Jake shrugged his shoulders, told her accidents happen in the caves all the time."

Dumbfounded and speechless, I slid back into the chair. Our eyes met in a silent understanding that stretched between us for a long moment.

The rain had slowed to a gentle cadence. A tree branch fell on the tin roof. She stood, shuffled to the door, and peered out at the wet landscape.

"The storm musta blowed right on by. Looks like it's clearin' up."

"I guess I'd better hit the road, then."

Paper bag in hand, I thanked her for her hospitality. As I started down the steps, I turned, looked up at her. "So, what *do* I call you?"

"By my nickname, Sally. Or my real name, Serena Angeles, Serena Angeles Cutter. Just not Voodoo Sally."

"Serena Angeles? That's a pretty name. Please call me Brad, not *Mister* Brad." I laid the paper bag down and took her hand in mine, sealing a heartfelt appreciation. "Thank you, Sally. For everything."

"Okay, Brad." She started to turn, hesitated, and then raised her finger. "Oh, just a minute." She disappeared into her kitchen for a few seconds and returned with a large serrated knife. "Use this to hack the briars, so they don't eat you up."

I thanked her again, and we said our goodbyes. The hound

dog gave my boots a few parting licks, tottered over to his corner of the porch, and curled into a circle, grunting as he flopped into a comfortable position.

As I made my way back to the cabin, raindrops pooled in leaves high in the trees pecked me on the head. The woods were so swollen with life that my senses had to work overtime. Muted scents of yellow honeysuckle and Confederate jasmine perfumed the air; a fleet of lightning bugs dotted the sky. I marched to the lonesome night sounds of whippoorwills, the sleepy tu-whit-tu-whoo of a hoot owl, and a train tooting drowsily off somewhere in the distance.

My thoughts kept coming back to this simple woman with a simple name, Serena Angeles, a woman with a big heart, doing good things for others. Of course, she was right. It wasn't *her* that I feared; it was the fearful lens that I had looked at her through, learned as a boy from the outlook of others. That realization conquered something inside, and I felt a peace settle over me.

Though the ground was mushy, I felt more confident in my Whitecross Hardware boots. I wasn't worried about Plait-eye anymore. I stomped *over* tricky groundcover and tangled roots instead of getting snagged *under* them.

But underneath the Willie Nelson tune that I was humming, I felt my stomach flip-flop. From what Sally had said, I'd become a murder suspect.

Through the slight struggle of my anguished breath, I felt the stranglehold that Big Jake still had on me as though he were breathing on the back of my neck. I stopped and looked behind me. Nothing was there, but I could feel his vengeful reach from far beyond the grave.

CHAPTER 18

A little over two weeks later, I heard Gigi's screen door slam around noon. I'd been cat fishing off her dock for the last few hours. The crickets had started a ruckus. A family of otters splashed near the dock where I'd cast my line.

I glanced down at my wrist, and it hit me. The wart on the side of my hand was completely gone. I smiled, shook my head. *Maybe there was something to old Plait-eye after all.* Although I had wanted to tell Gigi about my visit with Sally, a little voice in my head had told me to wait and see what the wart did before swallowing Sally's story hook, line, and sinker.

Gigi yelled at me from the bank above the dock. "Brad, the pink clunker died on me in town. Bobby-Cy had it towed to the body shop and drove me home."

"What happened to *takes a lickin' and keeps on kickin'*?" I hollered over my shoulder. "I figured it was on its last leg."

"Where's your manners? Why don't you come up and say hello to Bobby-Cy. I got to go inside for something."

"No problem. Be right up."

My bare feet were dangling off the dock. I laid down my fishing pole and scrambled tender-footed up the bank. Bobby-Cy sat on the hood of his Dodge King Cab truck, cleaning his teeth with a toothpick, staring at me with a crooked smile. He reminded me of a pouty Tim McGraw, peeping from below the brim of the sheriff's hat pulled low on his face. Handsome and thirty-something in gray uniform, he reached my six-foot-two height as he stood to greet me. For some reason, I felt immediately intimidated by his thorny gaze.

"Howdy-do, Brad." He smacked his lips, politely tipped his hat, and skimmed his fingers over his thick, straw-colored hair. Clenching the toothpick at the side of his mouth, he put out his hand to shake mine. "Name's Abbott. Bobby-Cy Abbott."

"Brad Pope. Pleased to meet you." I gave him a firm handshake. "My grandma has told me a lot of good things about you."

"Thank you, kindly. Sorry we had to meet under these circumstances."

"You mean the car breaking down? Yeah, it's a pain in the ass, but I appreciate you giving Gigi a hand."

"Not that." As he inspected my face, he hooked his thumbs in the belt loops of his uniform. "Just had a long talk with your grandmamma. Been meanin' to see if I could have a word with you, too, Doc."

"A word with me?" I asked. "Now?"

"Not now. Too busy gettin' ready for Founder's Day. But later."

"You mean you want to set up an appointment to see me at my office?"

"I mean a word *with* you, not *from* you." His tone had a sharp edge to it. His hard-fixed stare hinted of a no-nonsense sternness. "I'm afraid you the one that's gonna need the help, not me. We talkin' legal business, not counselin' business. We talkin' serious business."

"Oh, I see." Even though I'd known it was only a matter of time before I'd have to face this, I felt the sudden speed of my heartbeat. I took a deep breath, tilted my chin. "Can you tell me what this is about?" I sounded more distant, more formal, now.

"It's about Big Jake's murder."

"I don't know anything about that."

He went from folksy to professional without skipping a beat, speaking out of one side of his mouth. "My source tells me you do. I got an eyewitness that saw you at the scene of the murder."

"Well, but that was . . . I was supposed to go diving with him, but . . ." My tongue had caught the stammers and my explanation was in tatters.

"I don't have time to go into that now. There's more, lots more, that you're gonna need to explain."

"You see, Sheriff, it's very simple . . ."

"You can call me Bobby-Cy like everybody else."

"Bobby-Cy, it's really very simple . . ."

"And save it for later. I really do gotta go."

"Well sure." I fumbled in my wallet for a business card. "Here's my phone number. Give me a shout. I'll be glad to discuss this with you anytime."

While flipping the card back and forth between his slender fingers, he threw me a piercing gaze that unnerved me. But I refused to flinch. Instead, I broadened my smile. Then he thumped the card hard and slid it into his shirt pocket. "Let's see, today's Wednesday. Your grandmamma says you're headin' over to Jacksonville tomorrow to pick up your girlfriend."

"That's right, tomorrow afternoon."

"Jacksonville airport, huh?" He looked at the ground, rubbing his chin. "Tell you what, swing by my office tomorrow at noon before you leave, and we can talk private." Then he looked up at me. "You're not thinking about leaving the state are you?"

"Of course not."

"Good; see that you don't."

I felt the jitters in my stomach. Besides me being at the murder scene, I wondered what else there was. *"Lots more," he'd said. But what more could there be?*

The screen door slammed.

"Son, I got a hair appointment at Bernice's Hairport and Bobby-Cy's going t'other direction. Can you take me?" Gigi strutted up to the truck.

"Sure. No problem."

I covered my concern with my old game face, a veil of confidence. And I thought to myself, *What a fucking joke. I wouldn't know confidence right now if it bit me in the ass. Gigi'd say "The cobbler's children have no shoes." I'd say I feel like a fucking hypocrite.*

"Excuse me, then." Bobby-Cy lifted his hat again. "Gotta be goin'. Lots to do before the big day."

We shook hands goodbye. The faint smell of tobacco followed him as he delivered a hard fist to the hood of his truck, swaggered around to the driver's side door. I was taken aback by his silent authority, transfixed on the pistol holster flopping against his hip.

I looked at Gigi, who avoided eye contact with me. There was a weird undercurrent from her. Something was up, but I didn't have a clue what it was. She smiled, waved goodbye to the sheriff.

Bobby-Cy revved his engine, tipped his hat, slung gravel as he sped away. Right hand on the steering wheel, left elbow propped out the window, his crooked smile and steely eyes sized me up through the rearview mirror.

It was a look that both confused me and chilled my spine.

CHAPTER 19

On the drive to the beauty parlor, neither of us mentioned Bobby-Cy. I don't know why Gigi didn't bring it up. But after what she'd gone through with killing and burying Johnny, I didn't want to burden her. I'd get things straightened out with Bobby-Cy, then I'd explain about the accusations leveled at me.

What I had wanted to tell her about was my visit with Sally. But the conversation with Bobby-Cy had blown my enthusiasm over Sally's magic. Plus, I couldn't get a word in edgewise. Gigi had launched into nonstop Myrtle bashing.

"I just got off the phone with Wilma-May," Gigi said. "She's working today. Said Myrtle's on the books at Bernice's right after me. Plus, get a load of this. They threw Lick in jail, all because Myrtle Badger claimed she saw him at Suwannee Springs around the time of Big Jake's drowning. Can you believe the trouble that blabbermouth has caused?"

"She's a pain in the ass, all right . . ." I trailed off, falling into introspection, my thoughts half present as I watched the white lines in the road. The other half wondered what else Bobby-Cy had on me. Gigi's words came from far off. It was a time when I'd needed to think—a time when I'd wished she spoke with fewer commas and more periods.

Gigi must have mistaken my silence for discomfort about being around so many women. She seemed to want to put me at ease, spouting off about Vasque Gaylord. "Vasque can hold his own with us girls. He always joins in the gossip, gets his hair styled and dyed, right with us. We've accepted him as one of our own."

"That's nice," I said, my eyes still focused on the blacktop, my thoughts somewhere else.

But when she said, "Don't worry. You'll feel right at home too," I looked at her with dismay.

We pulled in the parking lot of Bernice's Hairport, a squat shoebox of a building. The sign had a drawing of a huge airplane with *Bernice's* on one wing and *Hairport* on the other. As we glided through the double doors, sure enough, Vasque sat under the hair dryer, flipping through the *National Enquirer.* He threw up his hand, and Bernice waved with a comb from across the room where she was teasing hair.

The whining-guitar music of Tammy Wynette and George Jones hummed in the background, just below the frenetic yakking of patrons and the sputtering of hairspray and chemical fumes that permeated the air. I took a seat out of the way of traffic near Bernice's chair and flipped through outdated pages of *People.*

All five chairs under the roaring dryers were stuffed with beautified hopefuls. A hodgepodge of cut hair—golden, gray, and black, and thin, thick, wiry, and silky—amassed like mountains in the four corners of the room. The blue cement-block walls, peppered with artificial flower arrangements in sconces, boasted photographs of runway models and the latest hairstyles.

The low-ceilinged room accommodated three beautician stations—Bernice, the owner, and her two assistants, Wilma-May Church and Daisy-Flo. Gigi called them the three amigos, each with a specialty that complemented the others. She said Bernice—whose double-knee replacement made it hard for her to get around and left her with a slight limp that got worse from standing on concrete slab all day—specialized in coloring. Daisy-Flo—who wore an orange toboggan to conceal her perpetual bad hair days—was an expert in cutting and styling. Wilma-May—who prided herself in rolling and perms—bragged it was her nimble fingers (the same God-given talent that made her such a good page-turner at church) that made her the best and fastest hair roller of the three.

After Gigi's roots had begun to show white, she had decided it was time for another coloring. But since her idol, Reba McEntire, would be the grand marshal of the Founder's Day parade, she would keep the fire-engine red and just get a touch-up job.

I could have dropped Gigi off and come back for her, but I had nothing else to do. Besides, I thought it'd be entertaining to watch and listen. I'd spent a small fortune training to become a good listener. That's what I did now—listened. Or Gigi might say snooped, while Bernice went on for a good twenty minutes, applying color along with the gossip.

"Did you hear about poor Edna Black?" Bernice nodded, her eyes pointing out the preacher's wife who had two round bald spots on each side of her head.

"Afraid not," Gigi said. "How come?"

"She came in here about a month ago and said she wanted a makeover—somethin' that would make her look younger. So we wove two hair extensions into her hair and braided them. When she left here, she was so excited. She thought she looked like Bo Derek in that movie *10*." I had to read Bernice's lips when her voice dropped to a low whisper. "To tell you the truth, she looked more like Jesse Ventura in pigtails."

"Oh mercy." Gigi squawked, shaming Bernice with her shaking scepter.

"But that's not the worst of it. Edna was at the carnival in Mayo last week and got the braids caught in one of those rides. She was on the Sky Diver, that Ferris wheel–type ride where you sit in a metal cage and it flips you over and over while the wheel goes around. Well, her braids got caught in the cage. It ripped two bald spots in her head."

"Ouch!" Gigi crouched, grabbed her head with her scepter, as if to console her scalp. "Mercy me, that hurts just hearing about it."

"Nat . . . nat . . . nat," sputtered Bernice, smacking Gigi's hand away from the red dye she was applying. Bernice caught the run-off liquid in a wet blue towel at the back of Gigi's neck and continued her story. "I'm gonna use the same technique to cover Edna's bald spots that I used on Shirley when I removed her bun. I think she'll look fine for Founder's Day."

"Edna looks like she's fell off. I wonder why she started losing weight and gussying up?"

"I think she's tryin' to win her man back," Bernice said. "Word is that when Myrtle broke off the affair, Preacher Black rededicated his life to Jesus. When he dropped Edna off this mornin', he opened the car door for her. They strolled in together holdin' hands like high-school sweethearts. He's settin' up shop outside, takin' advantage of today's business for the church's bake sale. Now that Myrtle's out of the picture, maybe they'll have more rainbows."

"Speak of the devil." Gigi concealed her comment behind a walled hand, but I was close enough that I could hear.

Myrtle promenaded into the reception area, cradling her Bible, holding her head high, her nylons swishing between her thighs. "I need a shampoo and a set. I refuse to let a soul touch my hair except Bernice."

"Gigi is in the chair now," Daisy-Flo said. "One customer is ahead of you, but I can start you with a shampoo."

"That's fine." Myrtle shot Gigi a disapproving look. "Just make sure you sanitize the chair for cooties before I get in it."

Unamused, Gigi kept a bead on Myrtle while Daisy-Flo

escorted her to the sink. After Daisy-Flo leaned her back for a hair wash, Myrtle went off on nonstop chatter. "Swayze says the only reason I come to Bernice's Hairport is to hear the latest gossip. I told him if you tell it once, it's Christian gossip. If you tell it more than once, it's a sin. Speaking of which, I reckon you heard they throwed that retarded boy in jail for Big Jake's murder. Poor Jake's hardly cold in the ground and his widow is already robbing the cradle with that dimwit."

Upon hearing Myrtle's rant, Gigi held her tongue, but her hooded eyes glared across the room at the gossipmonger.

"What would she want with a retarded boy?" asked Daisy-Flo.

Myrtle rolled her eyes up. "What do you think? She can train a man like she wants for once in her life." Her cackling made the fat on her arms and stomach roll like Jell-O.

Daisy-Flo sniffed at Myrtle. "What's that good-smellin' stuff you got on?"

"It's called *Arousal,* my husband's favorite." Myrtle was practically yelling so that everyone could hear.

"Sounds like the horny bitch is sweet on her husband again," Gigi said.

Bernice nodded. "You mean you haven't heard? Swayze's buildin' Myrtle a Southern-style mansion out on the Whitecross Lake City highway."

"Get out of town." Gigi raised her eyebrows. "I thought she loved her old house."

"She had to sell. It all started when she got wind that her next-door-neighbor's house was under contract with a black family. She got so upset that she put her house on the market, and it sold in two hours. Then her neighbor's contract fell through. Myrtle was fit to be tied, but it was too late. She couldn't get out of her contract to sell. Rumor has it that she threatened to leave Swayze if he didn't come through. And come through he did. Big time."

"Serves her right," Gigi said.

"He can afford a mansion now that he's in the last stages of closin' that multimillion-dollar deal for a theme park, right here in Whitecross."

"Say again?" Gigi snapped her head around. "You saying Swayze Badger is in cahoots with developers? Smells like high noon at the sewage plant."

"Sit still." Bernice smacked Gigi's shoulder. "They're sayin' it'll bring buckets of money to the town, boost the economy and raise our standard of livin'. Myrtle's been braggin' to everybody that she's gonna be a millionaire. As soon as Swayze struck that deal, she dumped Preacher Black."

Gigi's body jerked with agitation. "Lord have mercy. Just what we need, more sprawl. A deal like that'll draw a snake of stores, gas stations, and motels. We'll be just another cookie-cutter exit off some interstate going Lord knows where."

"Rumor has it they'll have showboats runnin' up and down the Suwannee with gamblin' and a supper club with dancehall girls."

When Bernice went to get a Coke out of the drink machine, Wilma-May meandered away from her post, threw a wave at me, and put her mouth against Gigi's ear. She mumbled loud enough for me to hear, "I was working on Edna and Sylvia. They want to know why we won't let them in the WPC. And Ibejean wants to know why we won't let her back in after all these years. They're madder than wet hens and joined up with Myrtle, claiming we blackballed them."

"If we let them in, we wouldn't be able to talk openly amongst ourselves. One of you would surely let you-know-what slip out. Just say that our club's full up. If they got a problem with that, tell them to see me."

"Okie-dokie." Wilma-May shot me a toothless smile and crept

back to rolling Ibejean Martin's hair, finishing it off by covering it with a hairnet and mumbling Gigi's message. Ibejean, grizzled and stooped, narrowed her resentful eyes on Gigi.

"Okay, you're ready for the dryer, Gigi." Bernice grimaced as she walked up. "Vasque, it's time to switch with Gigi. I'll finish you up. Then I gotta get off my feet for a few minutes. My knees are actin' up again."

Gigi took Vasque's seat under the dryer between Sylvia and Edna. Neither of the women acknowledged Gigi, who broke the ice. "So, Edna, I hope you enjoyed the chicken and dumplings I sent you."

"They were fine." Edna, eyes glued on her cross-stitching, refused to look up.

After an awkward silence, Gigi asked, "Sylvia, how's everything over at the pharmacy?"

"Fine," was Sylvia's only response while she held her downward glare at *Country-Western Life*.

"Fine. Everything's fine. Well, I'd sure as hell hate to see it when they're not fine." Gigi's swearing caused Edna to twitch. Flipping the dryer backwards off her head, Gigi grumbled, "I know you girls are upset with me about something Myrtle told you. Whatever it is, it's a damn lie."

"Such crude, un-Christian talk." Edna sniffed, reached in her purse for a tissue, and blew her nose. "Myrtle's right. You talk like a heathen. She also said that club you started is a sinful cult. Seems to me she's got you pegged—you and your grandson."

"What's my grandson got to do with it?" Gigi asked.

I blanched at the comment, looked up from the magazine, and slung it on the table.

Sylvia bobbed her head around and sneered at me. Then she glared at Gigi, answering through her deep smoker's voice. "Myrtle says she saw Dr. Pope at Suwannee Springs at the same time Big Jake was murdered. Says he was there for one reason and one reason only—to kill Big Jake. And you have the nerve to blackball *me* from a club?" Her nicotine-stained fingers plundered her handbag. Then she popped a cigarette into her mouth and lit it.

At first, I thought I couldn't just sit there and say nothing, but that's exactly what I did. I didn't want to get sucked into a silly squabble over club membership. I knew that Gigi was tough enough to handle herself. Plus, I didn't have to defend myself because I hadn't done anything wrong.

But Gigi wasn't as calm. When she saw Sylvia's bag, it triggered a cry. "My pocketbook! Where's my pocketbook?" She plowed around the dried-up, ripped plastic seat covers and underneath her chair. "Brad, have you seen it?"

"You didn't have it when you sat down," I said.

"Dang it," Gigi said, "I'm getting so forgetful I'd lose my head if it wasn't connected."

Edna stiffened under the umbrella of Gigi's swearing. Sylvia exhaled clouds of cigarette smoke without offering to help.

"I always carry it over my right arm. I had it when I walked in the front door. Then I got waylaid when I got money from my change purse to put in the Jerry Lewis Muscular Dystrophy jar at the front desk."

Gigi flew to the reception desk, a towel swaddling her neck, her blue smock lifting in the flutter. Daisy-Flo was counting greenbacks.

"I heard you frettin' about your pocketbook." Daisy-Flo pulled the bag from underneath the counter. "I was just fixin' to bring it to you after I finished countin'."

"Thank goodness." Gigi looped her handbag over her shoulder, flapped her hand over her heart two or three times. "Much obliged, Daisy-Flo."

"You'll have to thank Myrtle."

"Myrtle?" Gigi wiped a trickle of red dye running down her forehead with the towel.

"Uh huh, she had the same chair you did when I washed her hair. She found your bag under the sink, rifled through it a couple a times, saw it belonged to you, and stuck it underneath the counter for safekeepin'."

"Safekeeping my ass." Gigi sneered.

"She's such a good Christian woman," Daisy-Flo said.

Gigi looked over at me, mouthing under her breath, "Yep, and shit sparkles if you sprinkle glitter on it." Then, she smiled at Daisy-Flo and said, "Much obliged anyway."

Gigi padded back towards the hair dryer, fumbled around inside her pocketbook. She plopped on a bench in the waiting area, turned her pocketbook upside down, dumping the contents into a pile onto the cracked, concrete floor.

"What's wrong, Gigi?" Bernice limped by her and plunked tips into a Hav-A-Tampa cigar box.

"Oh, nothing. Just trying to find something." Gigi sighed, looked glumly at Bernice. "But I can tell those knees of yours are putting up a fuss."

Bernice smiled, snapped gum, and hobbled back to her station. Gigi marched over and whispered in my ear. "Myrtle stole the picture of her and Pastor Black screwing. And I accidentally erased it from my cellular phone."

I panned the room, my eyes landing on Myrtle. She sat on Bernice's throne beaming a broad smile, taunting. "Whatcha looking for, Gigi?"

Without hesitation, Gigi snipped, "That picture you stole out of my purse . . . the one of you and Preacher Black getting it on at the church. I wonder if there's anybody in Whitecross who has broken as many of the Ten Commandments as you have."

Eyes leapt from magazine pages; hands flipped hair dryers slightly backward so every word could be heard.

"You're makin' that up." Myrtle chomped on an apple, giggled smugly. "Honey, you don't even have enough fingers to count the Ten Commandments on, much less Bible-learning to know what they are." Myrtle gave the salon a once-over, as if recruiting support for her mockery of Gigi.

Gigi waltzed toward Myrtle, her voice booming. "I got enough fingers to count your sins on." Gigi rapped her scepter against her palm for the count. "You stole from me. You coveted and lied. And you mastered adultery a long time ago . . ."

At the exact moment the word *adultery* boomed like a war whoop from Gigi's lips, Myrtle sank her teeth deep into the apple, making a loud crunching sound. Then she released her mouth from the apple and exploded. "I'm a Christian, damn it. That's more than I can say for you."

"I hear stock in Resilient condoms nose-dived since you stopped helping Preacher Black with the church bulletin."

A loud hush fell over the beauty parlor, except for the faint background twang of Tammy Wynette's "Stand By Your Man." Eyes downcast, Edna blushed, remained silent underneath the hair dryer. I straightened my body, stretching the tension in my arms, and gazed over Edna's shoulder at the words on her cross-stitching, *God Bless Our Home*.

Then I checked out Myrtle from across the room. Her bottom lip began to quiver. She jumped out of her seat, gulped the remainder of the apple lodged in her throat, and unloaded. "Goddamn you, Gigi Pope!" With that she flung her Bible, clipping Gigi in the side.

Gasps ricocheted off the walls. Jaws dropped. Bernice made the sign of the cross over her chest. Wilma-May caressed a cross dangling from a silver chain around her neck and shuddered, "Dear sweet Jesus."

Myrtle slapped her palm over her mouth, her eyes wild-wide with shock. In a gurgling sound, she tried to suck the mutinied words back into her mouth, but it was too late. Another sin had sped off the tip of her tongue. Gigi, having fired the last shot, let her hands settle on her hips, as though she were blowing into the barrel of a gun.

"Now look what you made me do." Myrtle realized that she'd plowed up a snake. "You'll burn in hell for making me take the Lord's name in vain."

"So now I'm responsible for *your* sins?" Gigi said.

"You'll pay for this. You *and* your grandson." Myrtle whirled her body in my direction, jabbing her forefinger at me. "Murderer!"

The lightning-fast jolt of her words made me jerk with a startled intake of air, almost jump out of my skin. I could feel protruding eyes from around the room, the beet-red flooding into my cheeks. But I sat quietly rubbing the back of my neck. This was Gigi's battle, not mine.

Gigi threw her head back, pretending to chuckle. "Well, if you were at Suwannee Springs when Big Jake was murdered, then that makes you as much a suspect as my grandson. For all we know you broke another Commandment and are trying to hide it—like you've been hiding your new Escalade in your garage so you won't have to tithe your fair share."

For the first time, Edna jerked her head up.

"For your information, I've been cleared by Bobby-Cy. Sounds like you're jealous of me because I got something you don't." Myrtle grabbed her pocketbook, swiped her Bible off the floor. Then she looked back at Gigi, her voice shaking. "The whole town knows you never could keep a man. Makes me think there's more missing to you than that finger of yours."

With wet, disheveled hair, Myrtle flounced to the front door, her blue smock lifting in the flurry.

"I hear *your* nickname in school was Easy Rider." Gigi zinged Myrtle as she slammed the door on her way out. Through the window, I saw Myrtle, handbag looped over her shoulder, blue smock flapping as she stomped the ground hard.

"Okay, show's over." Bernice rattled in bar-room-brawl fashion. "Everybody back to your places."

After a long, thick silence, the cloud of tension that hovered over the beauty parlor was broken by the sounds of clamoring hair dryers and patron gabble. I breathed a sigh of relief as Gigi slid back in her chair at Bernice's station.

After finishing with her, Bernice pressed both hands on the back of Gigi's shoulders. "Now don't you let her get to you, honey. You're a dead ringer for Reba McEntire. You break a leg when you get up on that stage to give your speech. You hear me?"

"Much obliged, Bernice." Gigi crumpled a hundred-dollar bill into Bernice's palm.

"Gigi, that's too much."

"No, it's not enough for the hard work you do. Besides, I know you don't have insurance. Those knee surgery bills mount up."

Bernice pocketed the tip, smoothed her fingers down the front of her pants, and shot Gigi a heartwarming grin. Gigi thanked Bernice, said her goodbyes, but she didn't have a smile to give back. Her mouth sagged, and her mood seemed to plunge under the weight of Myrtle's allegations.

I, too, was keenly aware of the sideways glances and cool distance of the patrons as we shoved the door open and stepped into the blinding light of the parking lot.

CHAPTER 20

Preacher Black had set up a booth in Bernice's parking lot to collect money for the church bake sale. The fold-up table was filled with cakes of every variety—pineapple upside-down cake, German chocolate, fresh-baked coconut, and pound cake, dripping with orange-vanilla icing. From behind the wooden table, the preacher leaned forward on propped fists; his eyes whirled, and he frowned in pain. A reddish burn in the shape of an iron was seared over his right ear and cheek.

"Why, Preacher Black," I said neighborly-like. "What'd you do to your face?"

"Well, you see, I heard the phone ringin' off the hook this mornin' and accidentally answered the iron. Unbeknownst to me, Edna had set the phone by the iron when she was pressin' her outfit for today."

"For crying out loud." Gigi winced; her eyes crept away from his face, fixated on the baked goods. "I hope you're going to be okay."

"Doc Rogers looked at it this mornin' and shot me two thumbs up. Gave me some ointment to go on it, said it was a good thing the iron had shut down a bit or it coulda been permanent."

Gigi changed the subject. "Those sure are some handsome cakes you got there."

"You can thank Myrtle Badger for that. She headed up the bake sale this year."

"Oh," was Gigi's only comment. But when she shot a dirty look at the cakes, that said it all. "I might as well be going."

"Come on, Gigi," I whispered. "Like Bernice said, don't let her get under your skin. You're bigger than that."

My eyes had narrowed on a small handmade sign that read, *Proceeds to help pay for Reverend Ollis Black's eye surgery.* When I nodded toward it, she stopped dead in her tracks.

She swallowed her pride, making an audible gulp before she spoke. "You're right, son. On second thought, Pastor Black, I need two cakes for my celebration party. Let me have the red velvet and the apple stack."

"Okay, Gigi."

Gigi hesitated. "By the way, Pastor, who made those two cakes?"

I assumed she was double checking to make sure she didn't buy anything that was Myrtle made."

"Let's see, now. Vasque made the red velvet and Edna the apple stack."

"Okay, then." Gigi handed him two fifties. "Keep the change. I haven't been to church in I don't know how long. I figure I owe at least that much."

"Why Gigi, that's right generous of you." Preacher Black cupped his hand at a corner of his mouth, mumbled out of the side of it. "I owe you an apology. I been meanin' to tell you that I was feelin' mighty bad about what you seen in the church workroom that day. I ain't been with Myrtle since then. I asked my wife and the Lord for forgiveness. They both did. So if it's the same to you, I'd just as soon forget what happened and let bygones be bygones."

"Just as well." Gigi kicked the white sand with her tennis shoe, winked at him. "Myrtle stole the picture back anyway."

I could tell Gigi was beginning to feel sorry for the man and didn't want to cause him any more hardships than he already had. Plus, she had bigger fish to fry.

As we walked to the car, I slid on my sunglasses and put my arm around Gigi, who stared at the ground, sullen. When I reached for the door handle, my eyes descended on a sheet of white paper clamped under the windshield wipers.

"An advertisement." I jerked the piece of paper off the window, started to wad it up.

"What is it?" Gigi asked as she rounded the passenger side and bent into the front seat.

I pulled off my shades, stared at the hastily scribbled words in bright red lipstick, THE RAPIST KILLER. I leaned my back against the car door and sighed. "Take a look." I sailed the paper through the opened window into Gigi's lap.

"My gracious. What in the name of . . . ?"

I slipped beneath the steering wheel, looked at her. "And on Bowen's Funeral Home stationery, no less. That can only be one person."

Gigi rolled her eyes then glared out the car window. "It'll all blow over."

On the drive home, her stone silence and set face said that she hadn't really believed things would blow over. When she finally spoke, she turned her head away from me, stared out the window. "There's something I wasn't going to tell you, but you might as well hear it from me first."

"What's that?"

"When Bobby-Cy brought me home, we drove past the welcome garden. A back-hoe was digging it up. Said he got a tip that a dead body was buried there."

"What?" I twirled my head in her direction.

"I wasn't going to tell you, but I didn't want you hearing about it the way I just found out you were at Jake's crime scene."

"I'm sorry, Gigi. I was going to tell you, but with all you've had on your mind I didn't want to throw more problems on the pile."

"No matter. I knew you were planning to meet Big Jake that afternoon." She shrugged.

I double-blinked. "You did?"

"Gladys called me the morning of the dive. Told me Jake had made mention of it . . . said she was worried what he might do. But after you got such a late start, I figured you'd call it off."

I slipped my sunglasses down my nose and peeked over the frames at her. "I was late thanks to you and your sisterfriends. But I went on anyway hoping to make it on time."

Gigi nodded her head.

Another silence pushed up between us. Gigi looked like someone who was silently beating her head against a brick wall.

As I drove, the deafening quiet made it hard for me to ignore my churning stomach, my heart tugging downward in my chest.

CHAPTER 21

Later that evening, I sat at Gigi's kitchen table, scarfing down beef tips over rice, noting Gigi's grimace as she hung up the phone.

"That was Wilma-May. She said business has been off because of Myrtle's lips flapping all over town. Said everybody wants Daisy-Flo or Bernice."

I drummed my fingers on the table. "Man alive, that Loose Lip Looney *is* a troublemaker." I put my fork down, propped my elbows on the table, wove my fingers together. "Gigi, what if they find out about Johnny?"

She eyed me suspiciously from across the room where she leaned against the kitchen counter sipping a mug of herbal tea. "What if they find out about Big Jake?"

"What's that supposed to mean?" She stared out the window. Her face sagged from the weight of worry. "Gigi, you okay?"

"Yeah, I'm fine . . ." As her voice trailed off, she put down her mug and began sweeping the floor with urgent strokes.

I could tell her mind was far away. I watched her through a blur of my own swimming thoughts.

I wondered where all the crap with Johnny and Big Jake would lead.

My life had been frenetic in Charlotte but nothing like this. Though I should've never agreed to dive with Big Jake, the thought of going back to Charlotte never occurred to me. Even the gut-wrenching problems I faced here beat the meaningless life I'd left behind.

These problems were real. For some odd reason, I felt more alive than ever.

No. Going back wasn't an option. I would stick this out.

The whole deal with Big Jake was just one big, fucking misunderstanding.

After a long silence of sweeping, Gigi absentmindedly leaned the broom against the kitchen counter next to the Mason jar with one black bean and five navy beans inside. Then she started scrubbing the countertops. After another short stretch, she stopped mid-swipe and looked up, as if she'd had an epiphany. "That's it. I got a plan."

"A plan? For what?"

She slapped a box of Arm & Hammer onto the windowsill above the kitchen sink. "My fountain of youth that Sally told me about. That woman's been a life saver. I put a smidgen of it in just about everything to speak of, even the beef tips. The baking soda made me think of Sally and what she'd do."

"Yeah, I remember as a boy you swore by it. You used to mix it with water and lime juice to make exfoliate, toothpaste, even bath soak."

I went back to eating. It dawned on me that I hadn't told Gigi about my visit with Sally. I spoke with my mouth full. "Speaking of Sally, now I realize what a life saver she's been for me, too." I chuckled.

I felt Gigi's eyes on me as she resumed wiping down the Formica. "I don't know what *I* would've done without her."

"Me neither."

She scrubbed the countertops in slow motion, studied my expression. "Since when did you become best buds with Sally?"

"She took that wart off my hand, gave me Mama's letter."

"Say what?" With dishrag in hand, she paused, beamed at me, and wigwagged her head in amazement. "She had a copy of the one I lost?"

"Sure did."

"Your mama'd be so proud." She carried her mug over, slid in the chair across from me, then pinched off a piece of beef and popped it into her mouth. "How is it?"

"Hits the spot!" I shot her two thumbs up.

"The baking soda made me think of what Sally would do to get us . . . *you* out of this mess."

"What mess? I'm not in any mess."

She rolled her accusing eyes at me. "You can stop the pretend."

"What pretend?" I turned my palms up.

"Son, I told you my secret, and I think I've figured out yours." A heavy concern drooped her eyes as she observed me over the rim of her mug.

"Oh really?" I raised my eyebrows. "Don't tell me you think that I . . ."

"Can't put much creed in what Myrtle Badger says. But *you* admit you were at the crime scene at the time of the murder. That means while Big Jake was diving in the caves, you were up at the springhead where the rope was tied."

"That's right. He'd already gone . . ."

"You always said Big Jake reminded you of your daddy." She slapped her palms against the table and stood. "You don't have to say another word." She patted my shoulder, scuttled toward her bedroom.

I called after her. "If you think I killed Big Jake, then you *are* strung out on crack!" When she kept going, I shook my head.

I heard her paw through the bottom drawer of her chifferobe. She hauled a large emerald-colored book into the kitchen and plopped it on the table beside me.

The faded green-velvet cover had a brass filigree family crest and a brass clasp that clipped on the side. The gold-leaf letters spelled out the words *Holy Bible*. The Good Book had been passed down all the way from Great-Great-Grandpa Henry Pope to Gigi and on to Mama. It was one of the few things Mama had saved from the house fire.

Gigi plucked a small key from a hook on the side of her kitchen cabinet and used it to unlock the book. The pages had yellowed from age, had a heavy musty odor. A bookmark made the book flop open to a chapter of the Bible that obviously had received a lot of attention. It was Ecclesiastes chapter three: verses one through eight. The Bible verses had been underlined in black ink. Gigi ran her fingers over the lines, slowly underscored them with her wrinkled scepter, and softly mouthed the words:

To every thing there is a season, and a time to every purpose under the heaven: A time to be born, and a time to die; a time to plant, and a time to pluck up that which is planted; A time to kill, and a time to heal; a time to break down, and a time to build up.

As she read the scripture, "Turn! Turn! Turn!" by the Byrds pranced in my head. Bugs popping against the window screen punctuated the verses. Then she looked up at me. "Son, there's a time for everything. A title to kill and a time to heal."

She flipped the Book to the front page where the births and deaths of family members had been recorded all the way back to Great-Great-Grandpa Pope. Then she slapped to the back inside cover where she and the WPC had started a watch list, each name written at a different time in a different color of ink.

From across the table, I noticed she had scrawled *Myrtle Badger* in the list of names underneath Big Jake's. As the Book flipped shut, I blinked when the pages made a loud smack and a puff of air brushed my eyes.

She put the key in the lock, turned it, placed it back on its hook. With her hand on top of the cover, she pensively thumped the Bible with her scepter, fingered the raised golden letters beneath her palm. She peered over the kitchen sink through the window, past the chinaberry tree to the Suwannee where silver moonlight glimmered against the water.

Then she gazed into my eyes and sighed. "There now, I know what you did."

"You don't know any such thing . . ."

She pressed her scepter against my lips. "I've been in your shoes and I understand. Causing somebody to die changes you forever." She glanced out the window again and back at me. "When Bobby-Cy brought me home after my car broke down, he said he needed to have a serious talk with you. Now, I know why."

"No, you don't." Her suspicion seared a hot scar through me. "Listen damn it! I was at Suwannee Springs for a dive lesson, but I did *not* kill Big Jake."

She brushed my lips with her scepter again. "You don't ever have to speak it. The shame makes it hard to admit. Now's a time to heal, a time to build up." She patted my hand again. This time I felt the sandpaper roughness of her palms. "Myrtle won't get away with this. I got a plan. Now, I gotta call Betty-Jewel." As she rose from the table, she squeezed my shoulder, headed toward the telephone. "Don't worry. Everything's going to be okay."

But *everything* wasn't okay. Gigi was so hardheaded. If she didn't believe I was innocent, then who would? It felt like *everything* was collapsing around me.

I put my head in the cradle of my hands, stared at the floor, jerked a fistful of hair.

The townspeople began to shun the WPC members and me. Businesses came to a standstill. Customers at Madge's Mess dried up. Parents withdrew their children from Jackie's School of Buckshot Cloggers and Baton Twirlers. Betty-Jewel lost campaign volunteers who had helped her in a bid for town council. My office phone rang with cancellations.

Word had spread like wildfire from the beauty parlor to the Hurry Hut, to Whitecross Savings Bank, over to Glenda's Diner. Folks thought something wasn't quite right about the Women's Preservation Club. There was something odd about those six women, their secret club, and that new psychologist in town.

CHAPTER 22

I could see my bleary reflection, hear the click of my loafers echo on the polished floor leading to Bobby-Cy's office. The hallway smelled of floor wax, musty documents, and the slight scent of disinfectant. A bank of vending machines and two automated newspaper stands lined the institutional-green walls. One contained the *Whitecross News,* the other the *Gainesville Sun.* The headlines of the *Whitecross News* hooked my attention: "Another Civil War in Whitecross," accompanied by split-screen photographs of Gigi and Myrtle. I bought a copy, folded it under my arm.

After I passed the men's and women's restrooms at the end of the hall, I came to a sign marked, *Sheriff's Office, Bobby-Cy Abbott, Sheriff.* As I opened the main door, a flutter of anxiety rose in my belly. The empty reception desk allowed me to walk up to his office door, which was standing ajar. I leaned in the doorway for a second before he saw me.

His office reflected his personality—simple, open, and to the point. He was tilted back in a swivel chair, arms folded behind his head. His legs were propped up on a desk piled high with papers that zigzagged like a mountain range. A dangling metal chain pinged off-and-on against a ceiling fan that made a faint purring sound and gently lifted the corners of the stacked paper work. A half-eaten sandwich rested on wax paper.

The dismal green walls were bare, except for peeling paint and photographs of former Governor Jeb Bush and Mayor Smiley Bishop, hanging side-by-side behind Bobby-Cy's desk. The Florida state flag, stuck in a tarnished flag stand, was jammed in one corner.

The only light came from a dimly lit fluorescent fixture overhead, a computer blinking off to the side, and wooden Venetian blinds that shot slender threads of sunlight across his desk. Yellow-stained water pipes snaked up one wall, across the ceiling, and dropped into a squatty partitioned toilet on the opposite end.

I rapped on the door frame. He peeped at me from underneath his sheriff's hat, pulled low on his face. After a long, hard look, he hopped to his feet, pointed to a seat in front of his desk.

"Take a load off." He looked befuddled. "It's a hell of a mess out there today, wouldn't you say?"

I nodded, swiped at the sweat that beaded at my temples. "It's a scorcher. Traffic's bad too. Folks are getting ready for Saturday."

"Yes siree. It's a humdinger." He thrust a box of facial tissue in my direction.

I jerked a handful and mopped my face. "Thanks."

Before I could sink into the leather chair, he blurted, "I guess you know your grandmamma's in a shitload of trouble? And so are you."

As I plunked down, he gently pushed the door closed and returned to a propped-up position behind his desk. The chair squeaked as he leaned back.

"What kind of trouble?" I asked, thinking *I'm royally fucked.*

I wiped another drop of sweat from my brow and wondered if he could hear my pulse quicken, my heart thudder. But I struggled to stay calm.

"Myrtle Badger's been snooping for the last couple of weeks. She's made some mighty serious claims against your grandmamma's club. Made some claims against you, too. And she's bringin' them to the town meetin' this Saturday."

"Yeah, I know all about the accusations." I self-consciously jerked at my socks.

"Said she couldn't figure out how the WPC growed such vibrant . . . verdant . . . some fuckin'-fancy *v*-word flowers. Anyhoe, she was checkin' out the soil at the welcome garden when you and your grandmamma drove up. Said she hid out behind some hydrangea bushes. Overheard Gigi tellin' you the whole story of how the WPC planted a dead body there."

After I feigned a chuckle, I thought, *I knew I'd seen somebody in the bushes that night,* but I said, "She's got a pretty wild imagination. Sounds like an episode from *CSI.*"

"Maybe not." His jaw tightened. As he spoke, he flipped his uniform-gray tie over and examined the underside. "It's my duty to investigate all reports. I haveta say I came up with some mighty interestin' results."

"And?" I held my breath.

"I called in an investigator from the state medical examiner's office in Tallahassee. He brought in a backhoe, excavated some bones at the site."

"Probably was some animal . . ."

From one side of his mouth, his thundering voice trampled over mine. "The medical examiner said the body musta been in the ground between twenty and thirty years. Said the man was likely between thirty-five and forty based on the maturity of the bones he examined in the lab. Most of the bones necessary to reliably determine ethnic origin were either crushed or not found."

"That's odd." I swallowed hard.

"Cut the bullshit." He pushed his hat back. His brows met in the middle. His close-set eyes cornered me. "Come clean with me, and we'll get this over real fast. You know it wasn't a coincidence. You know exactly what happened. So do I."

I felt like I was diving without a safety line. I sat in stunned silence.

The replay of Gigi's voice boomed in my head: *I had an old chainsaw. We revved it up. Cut him apart limb from limb, just like a frying chicken. The sisterfriends and me planted that weeping willow in honor of your mama. The bastard's finally doing something good. Some of the richest soil I ever saw.*

Bobby-Cy stared me down, fiddled with a pencil on his desk for a few minutes. He didn't sound mad; he sounded more like he wanted to cut to the chase, to get on with it.

He lowered his feet from the desk again, leaned over it on his elbows. "Can't say that I've ever seen a case like this in White-cross." He fished a piece of paper from under the towering stacks of documents, looked down, grunted as he studied his notes. "There was a plastic bag containin' bones from a left leg, a lower right leg, a left foot, a skull, and part of a pelvic bone." Then he examined my face. "The report came back from Tallahassee inconclusive. They had a skull with no teeth, so they couldn't use dental records to identify the corpse. From what I can tell, they were lookin' for bones and overlooked the artificial hip. As far as the State's concerned, this is a cold case."

He pitched the paper aside.

"What's this all got to do with me?"

"Everything." He turned a laser-beam gaze on me.

The thought flicked across my mind: *He knows! Shit, He knows!* I shoved it away.

"I did some extra checkin' on my own. Went back to the site, dug around, found that artificial hip. It got me to thinkin'. A local man, name of Johnny Devillers, had a hip replacement after he got back from Vietnam. He'd been missin' about the same amount of time that that body'd been in the ground.

"I checked with the VA hospital in Gainesville, where he had hip replacement surgery. That artificial hip? His. The serial number on the metal hip matched up with the number recorded in Johnny Devillers's medical records."

I dropped my head. "Then I guess you know he was my daddy."

"Oh, I know a hellava lot more than that. I know your grand-mamma killed him."

I jerked my head up. "Holy shit! It was self-defense, Bobby-Cy. I'll do anything to keep her from going to jail."

"She confessed. Told me the whole story when her car broke down and I took her home. Said you knew all about it, too, which technically makes you and the rest of her club members accomplices to murder."

"I don't give a shit about me." I exhaled loudly, rubbed the back of my neck. "I just don't want anything to happen to her. Surely you're not going to lock her up, are you? An old woman, that long ago, self-defense . . ."

"Don't get your bowels in an uproar. I know it was self-defense. She's not goin' anywhere as long as she keeps her mouth shut. I instructed her not to talk to anybody about this coming to my attention, includin' you. Has she? Anythin' at all?"

"Absolutely nothing." *So that's the undercurrent I'd felt from Gigi. Bobby-Cy had warned her not to tip me off.*

"So where does that leave me?" I cocked my head, felt my chest tighten.

"I said hold your horses. I know Johnny Devillers was your daddy." He looked up from the papers on his desk and studied me. "He was mine, too."

"Your what?"

"My daddy."

"What?" I launched myself out of the seat. "Are you playing me?"

"Hate to be a buzz-killer, but you and me are blood-kin."

I inspected his face, tried to stitch my thoughts together, then noticed the resemblance between us and it clicked. *He's my fucking half-brother!*

"I'll be damned!" The disbelief in my eyes searched the room for safe landing.

He motioned for me to sit back down. "Hell, she did all of us a favor."

"What do you mean?" I eased into the chair, crossed my legs.

"Did you know about the time Johnny disappeared after he got your mama pregnant with you?"

"I heard about it."

"He was living with my mama durin' that time until he found out she was pregnant with me. Then, the asshole did the same thing to my mama—left her and went back to yours. Before he left, he beat Mama within an inch of her life, sayin' he didn't want more kids, that the ones he had were trouble enough. Then he vanished."

"He beat my mama, too, killed her in the end."

"Oh yeah, I know all about that. The old-timers tried to keep it hush-hush around here over the years. The officers still talk about it amongst themselves, about how the sheriff before me—Ronny, Johnny's brother—covered it up." Bobby-Cy slid his hat back off his forehead. His hard stare covered the pain in his face. "After I was born, Mama didn't have any money, so she started cleanin' houses. I was little when she couldn't make ends meet. She went off to find Johnny, never came back. So my grandparents raised me. After I was grown, Granny told me Johnny had choked Mama to death. I swore if I ever found him, I'd make him pay. Gigi just beat me to the punch. I figure keepin' this quiet is the best revenge we have. What's good for the goose . . . if you get my drift?"

"I read you loud and clear." I felt relief wash over me. "But what about Myrtle Badger?"

"I'm not gonna give her *my* findin's, but I can't stop what she'll say about the State's." Cross-armed, he tilted back in his squeaky chair and swiveled. "But there's another matter I gotta discuss with you."

"What's that?"

"Jake Nunn. Myrtle puts you at the scene of the murder. What do you have to say about that?"

I sucked in a deep breath before I replied. "I was. I mean he'd offered me a dive lesson, but I got there too late. He'd gone without me."

"Is that all you gotta say about it?" His steel-jawed stare gripped me. "You lied to me once already, tellin' me you didn't know your grandmamma killed Johnny. Twice is one too many."

"Well I . . . I . . ."

"You have the right to a lawyer before you say anything else."

"No that's okay." I waved the offer away. "Truth be told, I *did* think about killing Big Jake so he couldn't hurt anyone else."

"You thought about it and did what?" He straightened his body, jotted notes.

I swiped my face with the facial tissue and matched his hard cold eyes. "Big Jake cast a long shadow, and I saw Johnny Devillers in it. They used to say Elvis shot up TVs in hotels when he'd see somebody on screen that reminded him of a person who'd hurt him in real life. In the blink of an eye, that's what happened when I saw Big Jake's guideline. I'll admit that for a split second I thought about cutting it, but I knew it was my anger talking, not me. And I didn't want to live with that on my conscience. So I picked up my gear and headed home."

"I guarantee you one thing; this town won't rest until it finds Big Jake's murderer." He aimed his pencil at me. "And that somebody's goin' down."

I shifted my body, wrung one hand over the other. "Well, I

didn't do it."

"You sure about that?" He flipped his pencil in the air; his eyes penetrated me.

"Yes, I'm sure. A voice in my head tore at me, wanted to real bad. But I didn't kill him."

"Hmm." He shook his head, tilted it, then let out a small laugh as he glared through the wooden blinds. "To tell you the truth, I wanted to kill the son-of-a-bitch myself. You're right. I never thought about it 'til you mentioned it, but Big Jake *was* another Johnny Devillers in disguise. Problem is, the other boys on the force thought he hung the moon, and somebody's gonna fry for his murder. Mighty glad to hear it won't be you, though."

He stood. As he reached out his hand, he shot me a crooked smile. "Wouldn't want my big brother goin' off to prison before I got to know him."

"Same here." I shook his hand, smiled back.

"Your grandmamma's a renegade. I like that about her. When I took her home, we had a long talk. She cracked me up, thankin' me sayin' what you and me have in common is that I'm an abbot and you're a pope. And you can't do much better than that."

"Yeah, she's a piece of work, all right." I laughed, then paused. "We should have a drink sometime and catch up. You ever go to Britches?"

"You mean Bitches? Nah. I'm in Alcoholics Anonymous. Haven't had a drop in going on twelve years."

"Good for you, man."

As I neared the door, he stopped me. "Say Brad, you ever go fishin' down at Hatchbend?"

"No, but I hear the catfish bite real good there."

"Maybe we could drop a line there sometime."

"I'd like that." I grabbed the door handle.

"Oh, and one more thing." He looked down, shuffled through

the papers on his desk, and sighed. "I got a search warrant. Since you were at the murder scene, I'll need to poke around your place while you're in Jacksonville. No big deal."

"Be my guest. I have nothing to hide." My words sounded hollow and forced—even to me.

"And I'll need to do a DNA test on you, buddy." His eyebrows dipped as he spoke.

I opened the door and looked over my shoulder at him. "No problem. Just give me a holler when you're ready."

I nodded and closed the door behind me.

My hurried strides pounded the hallway racing my thumping heartbeat. I would barely make the two-hour drive in time to meet Chris's flight.

It was all too much—the tension with Chris, questions about Johnny's murder, and now suspicions that I'd killed Big Jake.

As I stepped back into the sweltering heat, I rubbed the sweat from the back of my neck. I hopped in my car, flicked on the air conditioner full blast, and headed east to Jacksonville, my back to the scalding sun.

It was hot.

Damn hot.

Chapter 23

"Exclusive Club on Downhill Skids," screamed the headlines of the *Whitecross News,* sprawled open-faced on the floor of the Jacksonville Comfort Inn. Underneath the headline, bold print raised the question, "Theme Park Coming to Town?"

After reading and digesting the news story with Chris, I had paced across the newsprint countless times during the sleepless night. The reality of what I faced had snapped at me with each step I'd taken over the bold dark letters.

Like a slow leak in a tire, the credibility of the Women's Preservation Club is going flat. A small group of Whitecross citizens has charged that the exclusive club has not lived up to community standards. We contacted Myrtle Badger, part-time employee at Bowen's Funeral Home, who claimed that the club is a cover for unthinkable crimes and is illegally barring new members: "Some of the members have shady reputations and questionable ethics," Mrs. Badger was quoted as saying.

Several other candidates, who were rejected from club membership, petitioned Mayor Smiley Bishop on Wednesday to rescind the award proclamation to the club's founder, Gigi Pope, who is scheduled to receive the honor on Founder's Day. When contacted by this reporter, Ms. Pope and other members of the Women's Preservation Club refused comment, saying only that they would be vindicated on Founder's Day.

The mayor refused to rescind the honor but compromised with the feuding parties by granting Mrs. Badger time on the podium at

215

Saturday's town hall meeting to present her side. When questioned about the specifics of her allegations, Mrs. Badger refused further comment, saying only, "I will expose this club for what it is at the town hall meeting." The town council said they would also consider a proposal for more sidewalks and a plan for creating jobs with a multimillion-dollar theme park.

A photo of Myrtle posing like a movie star accompanied the article. Ruby fingernails grazed her cheek; her humongous fire topaz dazzler corralled the light into a large white flash. In the article, Myrtle had made no mention of a dead body or allegations of murder. I imagined she was saving that for the town hall meeting as her crowning glory.

During the ride from the airport to the hotel, a thick tension had howled loudly between Chris and me. Though we had a lot of catching up to do, we had ridden in silence, miles apart in dead conversation. Once we got to the hotel, a discussion of the newspaper's cover story had diverted us from talking about *us*.

We were exhausted from the delayed US Airways flight 5210 that had landed in Jacksonville from Charlotte at 11:30 the night before. We had fallen asleep watching CNN's late-night rerun of Piers Morgan interviewing Gigi's idol, Reba McEntire. Before we fell asleep, Chris, dismayed over my fascination with Reba and her music, had raised a circumspect eyebrow at my interest in country music, saying, "You're different."

That was the only comment that hinted of problems in our relationship.

After Chris had fallen asleep, I had watched the rise and fall of breath beside me. Then, I quietly flipped through the paper scanning for news of Big Jake's murder. I blew a sigh of relief when I read a small article on the back page. It'd been over a month and still no charges in the ongoing homicide investigation into Jake Nunn's death, although several persons of interest were being interviewed. There was no mention of the discovery of bones at the welcome garden. True to his word, Bobby-Cy had kept that part quiet.

The rain made a tappity-tap, tappity-tap sound against the windowsill of the motel room, briefly lulling me away from the worry that tugged at my slumber.

But nothing could have deepened my sleep.

The world outside the motel room was up and stirring, hustling and bustling in that loud frenzied way all cities do after a few cups of morning coffee. The uneasy night of agitated body flopping had finally passed. The neon numbers on the bedside clock blinked nine a.m.

I looked over at Chris, naked beside me, eyes closed, savoring the last few drops of sleep. Our legs brushed ever so lightly at uncomfortable points of contact, lingering briefly before pulling away. A Taoist ankle tattoo—a circle split in half by a black-and-white swirl, symbolizing harmony—peeked up at me. My eyes traveled the length of Chris's long, sleek body and almond-colored skin, toned from head to toe with rippled muscles—the result of dedicated workouts. Thin brows framed heavy-lidded eyes underneath raven-black hair styled in a buzz cut.

I stroked the face of the one I loved and remarked, "Boy, you need a shave." A dark stubble had sprouted on his chiseled jaw and chin. His chest moved lightly up and down. His breathing, it seemed, was synchronized to the pestering thoughts that waltzed in my head. *We had two strikes against us: we were a same-sex couple and Chris was Asian. How would that set with Gigi and her outsider phobia? How would it set with my new life? I was becoming a small-town boy again and liked it. But could Chris hang with life in the boonies? And could they hang with us?*

I've never been a fence sitter, and I don't like uncertainty. My soul had been searching, and half of me had found a home; the other half wouldn't rest until I could piece together where Chris fit. I rubbed the sleep from my eyes and lamely tried to lighten the conversation. "Chris Cross comes to Whitecross."

"Please, Brad." Chris yawned and stretched. "Spare me the Don Rickles one-liners, the fart jokes, and any other ploy you plan to pull out of your bag of tricks to avoid talking about us."

With the Mamas and Papas's "Words of Love" thumping in my head, I realized worn-out phrases and longing gazes wouldn't fix the widening gap between us. "My, we're testy this morning," I said. "Which side of the bed do you plan to get up on?"

"I'm being asked a sarcastic question . . ." Chris sat up, hugged his knees to his chest, and hooked my gaze. ". . . by a man who constantly gives me mixed signals, saying he loves me and wants to be with me, then excludes me from his life. And you have the nerve to say that I'm putting a chain around your neck? So excuse me if I sound cranky."

"I need coffee. A big cup of coffee." I swung my feet around and sat up on the side of the bed. "This whole thing is so complicated. Let's face it; we're not your everyday run-of-the-mill couple. I do love you and want to spend my life with you, but we've got two big problems standing in the way."

"Just two?" He batted those roasted-black eyes at me.

"Yeah, and I don't know which is bigger—the fact that you're Chinese or that you're a man."

"It's not a problem for me. I've been an Asian man for thirty-two years and have been pretty happy most of my life."

"I know you're comfortable in your skin. I've always liked that about you, but this is Whitecross, not Atlanta or New York City."

"Brad, I'm comfortable with myself because I'm the same wherever I go, whether it's Whitecross or Hong Kong."

"Don't you think I know that?" There was a hint of irritation in my voice. I felt like he was saying, *Mr. Hotshot Know-It-All, not able to practice what he preaches. What about the power within you, Brad?* I was probably reading way too much into it, but the edge was there nonetheless.

"Listen here." He pulled my chin toward his face, "You've been too involved in your work and other people's lives. We've talked about this before; sometimes you seem unwilling to deal with your own."

"Damn it, that's not true—not anymore." I twisted away, grabbed my pillow, and punched it. "People in Whitecross don't think like you and me. It's a life based on tradition, and the WPC is trying to preserve that tradition."

"So what does that have to do with you and me?" He traced the line of my bare shoulder with a finger.

"In case you haven't noticed, we're not exactly textbook tradition."

"Why didn't you tell your grandmother the truth to begin with? Why did you tell her I was a woman?"

"She decided that on her own. I guess because of your name . . . and the fact that you're a flight attendant. She decides everything on her own."

"With a little help from you, maybe? Sounds like you led her on."

"Maybe I did, a little, but I never referred to you as a 'she.' When Gigi gets a thought in her head, there's no changing it. She's expecting to see a Caucasian woman. She referred to you as 'Christine, her future granddaughter-in-law.' "

As he scrubbed the sleep from his eyes, he chuckled, then tightened his lips. "So why didn't you correct her? If you let her believe something that was untrue, you might as well have lied to her—a lie of omission. What's up with that?"

I paused. "I feel like I'm caught in the middle. I don't want to lose either of you."

"You won't lose me, if you don't push me away, dumb ass." He teasingly mopped my hair. "I want the same thing you do—

for us to have a life together." He put his hands on top of mine, pressing them firmly but affectionately against the mattress. "If *you* don't fuck it up. Is that asking too much?"

"Of course not." *Funny, he made it all sound so simple.*

He squeezed my hands, hopped off the bed, and scurried into the bathroom. I heard the shower spraying against the glass door. By the time I threw on a baggy Carolina Panthers jersey and made a pot of coffee, a nagging doubt overtook me.

"But Gigi and her friends are sort of weird." I yelled into the bathroom. "I wonder if you know what you're getting into."

"Listen, babe." Chris shouted above the gushing water. "If they can handle our weird, I can handle theirs."

The shower door slammed. Chris hopped out and cracked the bathroom door. A bolt of hot steamy mist seeped through the opening, layering my face with moisture.

"They're endearing," I said, "but I'm talking, really *strange.*"

"What's so strange about a bunch of elderly women forming a garden club and keeping another bunch of old fuddy-duddies out?"

I raised a reprimanding hand above my head as Chris emerged from the bathroom, tying a white terry-cloth bathrobe around his waist. "Hold it," I said. His perky wet hair stood at attention. I took my first sip of coffee, threw Chris a few words of caution. "Don't *ever* use the term 'garden club' with Gigi. The WPC takes their preservation efforts very seriously."

"Excuse me. Preservation club." He sat beside me on the bed.

"It's a long story, but they share a special bond around something that happened twenty-some years ago, a bond so tight that outsiders can't penetrate it."

"Must've been pretty intense to tie people together for that long."

"They confide everything in each other. They do most things

together. Newcomers don't have a snowball's chance in hell because they're so close-knit." I pointed to the newspaper scattered across the carpet. "Their bond has become a problem to reckon with. Small towns don't take kindly to excluding people. That's big-city stuff."

"News flash." Chris whipped his head around. "We big-city folks don't take kindly to being excluded, either."

"Okay. I give up." I raised both palms as if I had a gun in my back. "You've made your point."

"Now, you've got my curiosity up." He rolled his eyes up into his head. "Let's see, that would've been the eighties. What could've been such a big deal back then that bound the women together?"

I set my coffee mug on the side table, ignored his question, and peeled off my clothes for a shower. Chris snapped me with a towel as I rounded the bed for the bathroom.

As I lathered my body, the warm water spattered against my face. Thank God Chris wanted to meet Gigi and was willing to accept the outcome. He had even defended her by accusing me of lying to her. What more could I ask? I didn't want to put up more barriers than necessary, so I avoided the question like a cottonmouth.

I was afraid it would've been too much for him to handle. As far as he knew, the article was just a jealous small-town squabble over club membership. I wanted to leave it that way, so as not to taint Whitecross's image before we'd even arrived. And there was absolutely no way I'd bring up the controversy over Johnny's bones or Big Jake's murder. We had our own problems to work out. And if things went well, Chris had planned to stay in Whitecross indefinitely.

When I came out of the bathroom, Chris was in bed propped up on his elbow finishing off the last sips of coffee. I toweled off and jerked on my shorts. "Let's get moving. We have a two-hour drive."

Unlike Gigi, Chris rarely pressed me. He just shrugged and got dressed.

And I breathed a temporary sigh of relief.

CHAPTER 24

After a bite at a local restaurant, we packed the car, swung by Starbucks, and headed for Whitecross. Although I didn't have a clue how Chris and Gigi would react to each other, I played the worse-case scenario of their first meeting over and over in my head. Plus, I remembered Gigi's comment about a plan "to get us . . . *me* out of this mess."

My heart gave a stabbing lurch.

As I drove farther, asphalt parking decks and concrete high-rises gave way to fields of sweeping green grass, palm trees, an expansive blue sky. The further we traveled from the gridlock and fast pace, the more settled I felt.

In the short time I'd been back in Whitecross, I'd re-discovered a whole side of me. Gigi had helped me tap into the old me—the me that feels at home inside his skin.

She'd even told folks that I was right handy.

She had shown me how to use a chainsaw, a pickax, and a mattock to chisel away soil and roots around my A-frame so we could plant bottlebrush and caladiums. Up before sunrise, she had taken me on expeditions to dig for night crawlers that we'd used as bait to catch catfish. We'd hiked to the banks of the Suwannee, hauled empty gallon buckets, a ten-pound iron rod, and a wooden stake that Gigi called a stob. On her knees, she'd slam the stob into the soil, rub the iron across the top, and make a rhythmic vibration that lured colonies of writhing worms out of the earth.

She'd taught me the skill of bricklaying, and we'd built a walkway in front of my cabin, lined it with limestone from the Suwannee. We'd dug a ditch and buried drain pipes that bled storm water from drenching north Florida rains into a bed of blazing fuchsia azaleas. Even when the heat swooned around us and our sweat drew fleets of orbiting gnats, we were soothed by fertile smells of earth and the symphony of wildlife abundant on the ground, in the shrubs, trees, and water.

I looked over at Chris, watched him as he gazed out the window. "I'm finding something in Whitecross," I said.

He searched my face. "Yeah? What's that?"

"I'm not exactly sure, but I feel at peace there."

"Like I said before, I can tell you've changed. You seem more settled. Have you had some kind of spell cast on you or something?" He threw his head to one side and laughed.

The tires made a steady hum as we sped over a steel expansion bridge with looming metal overhangs. Through the sun roof, I saw bolts in the bridge's arches flashing overhead like silver bullets. Dappled below us, the glassy Suwannee mirrored green billowing trees with thick, puffy branches intertwined against a white sandy shoreline.

"Pick your feet up," I teased.

"Why?"

"There's an old saying when you cross the Suwannee, you're supposed to pick your feet up for good luck. If you don't, you'll never get married."

"Shit, if getting married is considered good luck, I think I'll leave my feet on the floorboard, if it's just the same to you."

We hooted over the whiny sound of tires against the steel bridge. A train trestle off to the right matched the length of the bridge. It was as if it raced us, disappearing behind lush green vegetation once we hit solid highway again. A crayon-colored sky, scribbled like a child's painting, welcomed us at the end of the bridge as we entered Suwannee County.

Out of the corner of my eye, I could see Chris, mouth agog, eyes absorbing the beauty of the landscape. "It's so tropical here. It reminds me of a Caribbean island."

"I thought you'd like it." I reveled with delight.

A handmade sign, nailed to a roadside stand, spelled out *Sweet Corn.* I wheeled up beside the crates of green shucks and paid the white-haired, suspendered man two dollars for a dozen ears.

"Where you from?" His bottom lip protruded with a wad of chew.

"Whitecross."

"Whitecross?" He examined my face as if to question my answer. He spit a splash of brown liquid that splattered into a white sandy ball and rolled by a pile of corn husks.

Unable to claim Whitecross with full confidence, I recanted, "Charlotte."

"Oh." He looked satisfied. "Well then, have a good visit." Wiping his mouth with the back of his hand, he shuffled back behind the bins of corn and waved us off.

Tubing rental shacks were strung along the road to Whitecross. Towers of black inner tubes and yellow rubber rafts were stacked out front for tubing the pristine waters of the Ichetucknee River. I flipped on the radio and got the Whitecross station, broadcasting Thelma's Gospel Hour, sponsored by Margie's Produce Stand.

Despite its key-lime sweetness and home-baked freshness, Whitecross had taught me that it had its dark side, too, just like big cities. I thought about the innocent-looking church ladies, jabbering in public about the next bake sale or Sunday's church bulletin, branding people who are different as "outsiders," shunning them behind closed doors. As we neared town, I was struck by the contradiction of friendly farm folk, doddering along in their pickups, throwing up their hands at us, shotguns stuck firmly in gun racks behind their heads.

"Why are all these people waving at you?" Chris asked. "You must know everybody in the county."

"I don't know any of them. It's just the way here."

"You could get murdered waving at the wrong person in Charlotte."

My jaw stiffened at the word "murdered." A squadron of Florida Reds—grasshoppers as big as humming birds—swarmed the air, feasting from crop to crop, splattering into the windshield and headlights of my Nissan.

When I turned on the windshield wipers to wash pieces of the insects away, the dismembered body parts smeared across the windshield. Gigi's panicked voice reverberated in my head. *We cut off his fingertips with a hacksaw and knocked his teeth out with a hammer so nobody could identify him. We threw the bloody pieces into the Suwannee . . . We scattered his severed head, hands, arms, legs, feet, and torso in shallow graves.*

An image of Big Jake—ghoulish smile, oozing holes where eyes had been eaten away—burst before me on the hood of the car; his palms swept in the direction of his coffin. Gigi's voice echoed again in tattered pieces. *You always said Big Jake reminded you of your daddy . . . There now, I know what you did. You don't ever have to speak it. Causing somebody to die changes you forever. I've been in your shoes, and I understand.*

I looked over at Chris. He had jerked his baseball cap over his eyes and slunk down in the seat, hoping to steal a few more z's before arriving in Whitecross. I couldn't bring myself to tell him that I was accused of a homicide.

From the roadside, a weathered wooden sign, loosely nailed to a tree, waggled at me, *Repent: Final Warning.*

My grip tightened on the wheel; my foot pressed harder on the accelerator. It felt as if the Starbucks double latte surged through my veins faster than my speedy Pathfinder hugged the road.

We hit the outskirts of town. That now-dubious green sign greeted us.

> *Welcome to Whitecross, Home of the Historic Suwannee River*
> *Please Help Us Keep Our Town Clean and Green*
> *—The Women's Preservation Club*

Once flanked by beds of pristine camellias and azaleas, the welcome sign was flanked now by mounds of excavated dirt and a rusted, dust-covered backhoe. Mama's weeping willow leaned sideways, uprooted by the heavy machinery.

As my eyes fell on the site, my stomach did a slow roll into my throat.

CHAPTER 25

After a few hours of showing Chris around town and strolling along the Suwannee, we dropped our bags off at my place. By the time we got to Gigi's, it was almost dark. When we squeaked to a stop in her driveway, it was jammed with cars. It looked like every light in the house was on. I glanced at the lonely double-wide trailer plopped in the middle of nowhere, hard-edged and stark against the soft, swaying pines and velvety flow of the Suwannee.

Silhouettes of shadowed figures, hands held high waving the air, moved against the pulled shades of the den.

"Looks like someone's having a party," Chris said.

"Holy shit." I recognized the cars—it was the WPC. I turned off the engine, slid the keys out of the ignition. "Seems like every time I come here, something's going on. I told her not to . . ."

"What?" Chris turned his palms up.

"Never mind. Let's get out."

Chris opened the door, stretched his long legs; I stretched my arms. The air smelled green. As we mounted the steps, a horned owl swooped us.

"What the hell was that?" Chris ducked his head.

The sight of a flyswatter hanging on a nail outside Gigi's front door made me blush. I didn't want Chris to think Gigi's was a haven for flies, but he was a green thumb. He seemed more interested in the purple petals of the cast-iron plant that grew in a cloisonné pot in a shady corner of the trailer porch. Then he examined the fragrant moon flowers that twined around a wooden trellis on either side of the front door.

I rapped lightly. Chris pointed at a furry caterpillar inching a path up one of the green leaves and then to the gutter on the house where a writing spider had woven a tangled web with zigzags that looked like handwriting.

"Don't say our names or let the spider see your teeth," I warned, "because if you do, it'll write your name and you'll die. That's what my daddy—uh, Johnny—used to tell us as kids."

"Probably to keep you quiet."

"Well, it worked."

And in some strange way, it worked now, too. A dog barked off in the distance. The walls of the mobile home were paper thin. We could hear the low rumble of voices over the constant hum of insects in the bushes.

"Sounds like they're chanting," Chris said.

"Or praying." I stuffed my hands in the pockets of my shorts, bounced the toe of my Teva against the porch post.

The crescendo of voices rose and fell in a strange incantation. A few more mumbles and mutters. The noise of scraping chairs, scurrying feet, shuffling belongings.

They had adjourned.

I knocked on the door again. After a minute or two, it swung open. The whiff of home-cooked food soaked us. Gigi stood in the doorway, her cockatiel, Thump, flapping on her shoulder. Her hair had been gathered and pinned at the back. She wore lipstick and makeup. Clad in a shirt-waist dress with dangly cow earrings, she had dressed up on Chris's account. Obviously, this meeting was important to her, too, and she wanted to make an impression. She looked demure, as sweet and innocent as a preacher's wife. I handed her the plastic bag of sweet corn.

"Oooh, thank you, son. You know how I love fresh corn. Where's Christine?" She said in a meowing voice. Her eyes darted back and forth between Chris and me. Then she rose up on tiptoes, looked over our shoulders.

"Gigi, this *is* Chris." My right palm glided toward him.

"Oh." Gigi chuckled. "There for a second I thought you were a boy." Her smile tightened as she eyeballed his face, studied his soft features. "That cap threw me for a minute."

"Hello, Mrs. Pope." Chris slid his cap off, revealing his crew cut. "I'm pleased to meet you." They shook hands. He folded his arms across the green letters of his athletic jersey that spelled *University of North Carolina at Charlotte.*

"Call me Gigi. All the gals are cropping their hair off nowadays. Guess that's the new style." She absentmindedly fingered the back of her twisted hairdo as if she might be thinking of giving it a whack, too.

Spinning his cap backwards on his head, he said, "But I *am* a man."

Gigi's face went blank. She squared herself toward Chris, looked into his eyes, scanned his sleek figure. "Holy Moses." She squinted, cupped her palm over her mouth. "I'm so confused I don't know whether to scratch my watch or wind my ass."

"Gigi!" I chided.

The three of us broke into laughter. Our squeals layered the muggy night air with a light frosting.

"So you're not a girl?" she said.

"No, Gigi, he's not a girl," I interjected.

With uncomprehending eyes, she searched Chris's face, then mine. "We're letting the bugs out. Ya'll come on in."

She put her arm around Chris's shoulder, ushered him into the den. She pointed her slim scepter in my direction. It was a nonverbal order; she expected me to close the door. And it was a silent reprimand for not leveling with her.

Gigi had never been one for surprises.

"We don't want to interrupt your meeting," Chris said.

"Oh, don't worry about that. We already adjourned. The girls are in the kitchen having refreshments." She rubbernecked in my direction and glared. "Won't they be surprised?" Then, she turned back to Chris and asked, "Want some strawberry punch?"

"No thanks," replied Chris. "We had Starbucks just outside of Jacksonville."

"Had what?" She handed me the bird and motioned for me to put him back in his cage, while she and Chris settled on the settee in the den.

"Coffee." Chris smiled warmly at Gigi.

"Oh." Gigi sat erect, her neck thrust slightly forward with ankles properly crossed right over left. Shirley must have given her a crash course on etiquette just for the occasion. "I made some swamp cabbage, acre peas, and a hoecake."

"Thanks, but we grabbed a bite in Jacksonville," Chris said.

"Got persimmon pudding for dessert. Had one cold snap last year that made the persimmons just right for cooking. What about it?"

"Umm, now you're talking." Chris made a little bounce before melting back into the cushy settee.

"Okay, as soon as the girls leave," I heard Gigi say as I padded off to her bedroom where she kept the bird cage.

I stood transfixed between a soft spill of sunset through the slatted wooden shudders and the patina cage into which the bird eagerly flitted. My eyes swept the room. The wide-mouth Mason jar, containing five navy beans and one black bean, rested innocent-looking on Gigi's nightstand. A light breeze from the open window made the sheer curtains quiver. *Save the Suwannee* bumper stickers were strewn onto the floor, the words smudged with benign footprints.

When I returned to the den, I heard the sounds of clanging kitchen pots co-mingled with scurrying feet and muffled voices of the sisterfriends. Gigi stared at me with a leer that gagged a smile, making her lips wiggle.

"Bradford Henry Pope." She swished my mother's golden-heart locket that hung around her neck. "How come you told me Chris was a girl?"

"I didn't, Gigi. You drew that conclusion on your own." I plopped beside her on the couch.

"Humph, with your help."

"You lied through your teeth," Chris said.

"Now, don't the two of you go ganging up on me. I'll admit I did lead you on, Gigi."

Still twisting the locket, she pointed at me with her free finger. "Well that means if you're a man and Chris is a man. That means . . ." As she waved her free hand in front of her lips, a smile flirted on the lines of her mouth.

"We're a couple." I felt a rumble of discomfort in opening up to Gigi about my love life. But after the secrets she'd withheld from me, I also felt a small revenge that she was on the receiving end, though I was confused by her arrested smile, which prompted me to ask, "What is it?"

Gigi eyed me with a loving, full-bodied smile that spread across her wrinkled face. It was as if she saw directly into my soul. She clasped my hands in hers and leaned into me. "Son, I always knew. I knew and loved you anyway since you were a little thing." Her eyes swelled with tears. "It never mattered to me then. It don't matter now."

My mind staggered for a heartbeat. I almost gasped. "You knew ever since I was a boy?" My eyes flitted between Chris and her.

"Mamas and grandmammas *always* know. Even if they don't

know that they know, they *know*."

"And you never said anything?"

"It wasn't for *me* to say. It was for *you* to say."

She bent closer, whispered in my ear. "You can always tell me the truth. *About anything*. It will set you free."

I took that to mean that she thought I'd killed Big Jake and could accept that, too.

"You know how I feel about liars and hypocrites. Don't ever lie to me again, son."

I dropped my voice and coded a message back to her, "I'm not lying, Gigi." Twirling Chris's ring around my finger, I paused and spoke in my normal tone. "I tried to tell you about Chris and me the day we saw the manatee, but it just wouldn't come out."

"I understand," she said. "You might recall I had a similar problem."

Chris looked puzzled; his dark eyes glimmered, skimmed back and forth over Gigi and me.

"Yeah, so . . . Gigi . . ." I stammered, still feeling awkward about the subject matter. "Does that mean you're okay with this? I mean with Chris . . . with us?"

"Okay that you ride sidesaddle?"

Chris and I looked at each other and cackled before he said, "I've never heard it put quite that way."

Gigi looked at me, her eyes filled with sadness. "Your great Uncle Ranlo, my oldest brother, never married. Back then people called Ranlo 'funny.' I didn't see anything funny about it, and it wasn't funny to Ranlo, either, the way they teased and taunted him. I never heard him laughing about it. Always had a soft spot in my heart for him. When two folks love each other, it doesn't matter to me who they are." Gigi threw her arms around both our necks and gave us a bear hug.

I shook my head. "So that's why you told me about Vasque

Gaylord when I took you to the beauty parlor? To put me at ease?"

"I've always tried to make you as comfortable as I was with it, until I realized that that was your job, not mine. Oh, yeah, when you were little, I tried to toughen you up at first. Then I caught on that you weren't like most boys, that it was unnatural for me to change what was natural for you."

Chris had been listening intently and seemed eager to know more. "What was he like as a child?"

I groaned.

She squeezed my hands, smiled through teardrops that pooled like lakes in her eyes. "Never could tell a Phillips screwdriver from a socket wrench, a carburetor from a battery. But he knew Faberge from Chanel, Barbra Streisand from Liza Minnelli, knitting from crochet. There always was a special softness about him. When he was little, I used to think I had to protect him from life. Not anymore. He's bulletproof, now. He's got what we call limestone gumption down here."

She wiped her eyes with the back of her hand and turned back to Chris. "So you're a Chinaman?"

"Gigi?" My admonishing voice went up a few octaves.

"Hush up." She turned her back on me and cupped Chris's hands, making no bones about her curiosities. But I sensed her question was more a test of Chris's resilience than a fact-finding mission.

"My parents immigrated here from China. I was born in Seattle." When Chris held steady, I realized he could handle her.

"Always had great respect for the Chinese. Hard workers; smart, too." She delivered him a few love pats on the knees and stood. She straightened her dress, ran her fingers down both hips. "We've got a sight more to talk about. Been looking forward to this night for a long time."

Chris and I rose to our feet, too. "But what about your sister-friends?" I raised my eyebrows and nodded toward the kitchen.

"We spent the whole afternoon talking about it in the WPC meeting. They weren't born yesterday. You know what Shirley said?"

"What?" I asked.

"She said, 'Normal is a cycle on a washing machine.' Now, I wonder where she got that?" Gigi winked and elbowed me in the ribs.

"I'll be damned." I said.

A wry smile cracked her lips, and in an afterthought, she said, "Oh, by the way, Tug-a-Love, next time you don't want somebody to know Chris is a man, tell him when he mails you a letter, to leave off the name, 'Christopher' on the outside of the envelope."

"What?" My mouth fell open. I rubbed the back of my neck. "How'd you know?"

"Remember when you first moved back to town before you had a place of your own, and your mail was forwarded to my address? Well, a day or so after Big Jake's funeral, two letters addressed to you with a return address from Christopher Cross on US Airways envelopes ended up in my mailbox. I guess they slipped through the system. I dropped them off in your mail slot but figured you never noticed."

"Why didn't you let on?"

"I was going by your playbook, son, waiting to see how you wanted it to play out. It was your call."

Chris turned his palms up again, shrugged, pursed his lips. "What'd I tell you?"

I shook my head in half-disbelief. From the kitchen, the sounds of muffled giggles and scraping chairs caused Gigi to change the subject.

"We better get a move on. The sisterfriends will be leaving

pretty soon, and I want them to meet Chris before they go. They're being polite, holding up in the kitchen, so we can get acquainted."

"We need to get on over to my place and get settled," I said. "It's been a long day."

"Go now, and I'll put you on my watch list," Gigi said, half serious, half teasing. She motioned her palm downward, searched Chris's face for an answer. "Stay and we can shoot the breeze over swamp cabbage and persimmon pudding."

"I'd love to," Chris said.

"Good." Gigi clapped her hands once and vanished into the kitchen.

"I'm so freaked out." I threw my arms out, unfurled my body onto the settee in a backward spread-eagle. "I should've known. Nothing gets past Gigi."

"Relax, Brad." Chris tumbled beside me. He threw his arms around me, pecked me on the lips. He tasted of wintergreen. "I really like Gigi. She's bossy but amusing and sweet as can be."

"You have no idea what you're getting us into."

CHAPTER 26

Gigi was gone a good five minutes. We could hear her mumbling in the kitchen and the sharp hiss of her whispering sisterfriends.

Chris browsed the room. He fingered a spindle-spooled whatnot shelf, loaded with souvenirs from Great Uncle Ranlo's trip to Bali. He fumbled through family picture frames on a side table adjacent to the couch, plucked a photo of me at five, wearing chaps, cowboy hat, and boots and sitting on a pony. Another picture of my young mother, holding me in her arms, caught his attention. He lifted it for closer inspection.

"I was no more than two in that one."

"She's the spitting image of Ava Gardner."

"That's what everybody says."

"She was beautiful, so were you." He glanced back and forth between the photograph and me. "You still are."

When I reached out and grasped his hand, I felt a bolt of love connecting me to him through Mama's picture. He leaned over, planted a lingering kiss on my lips. At that moment, a flurry of high-pitched screeches and a collective gasp pierced our ears. With Chris's lips still glued to mine, the sisterfriends stood motionless just inside the cracked kitchen door. They gawked at us like that family of cypress trees that lined the Suwannee.

We broke it off. I looked down for a second, then caught my breath. After a long stretch of silence, I smiled, speaking over the awkwardness that hung in the room. "Hello ladies."

Hellos and throat-clearings resounded from the sisterfriends.

Then, Gigi ordered, "Okay, let's go." She herded her sister-friends into the den like a border collie and arranged them into a semicircle in front of the settee where we sat.

Gigi's eyes landed on the photograph in Chris's hand. She made a quick swish of her locket and cleared her throat. "He went from crawl to run. Skipped right over walking and never stopped since." She scooched into the settee between Chris and me. As she flopped her arm around my shoulder, a faint lavender fragrance wafted over me.

"Here we go again." I groaned and massaged my forehead. "Gigi, don't start with the childhood stories . . ."

"Every Sunday his mama'd press a twenty-five-cent offering money in his palm. It was gone before he got halfway down the street. He'd spend it on bubble gum and candy at the country store. When the collection plate came around, he'd mash his fingers in it, pretending he was depositing that twenty-five cents."

"You knew about that?"

"Course I knew." The blue sparkles in her eyes did a brilliant dance. "And he hasn't changed a bit. You still can't turn your back on him."

"Is there anything you don't know about me?"

"Not much." As she pushed to her feet, she grunted, then strutted to the front of the room where her sisterfriends whispered and fidgeted among themselves.

I wondered if she was sending another double message. So I sent her one, just in case. "You're one to talk. Who used to make brownies for Alvin Dukes and me and sneak castor oil in them?"

"Castor oil's good for you."

"Not in brownies." I made a hacking sound in the back of my throat. "That was the nastiest tasting stuff."

The club sisters cackled among themselves—cardboard-like

in their stance—as if they were ready to perform their first school play, their lines carefully written and rehearsed, ready to take direction from their off-stage teacher.

"He always was so tenderhearted." Gigi scanned the matronly lineup of sisters. "He used to bring home insects with broken wings, frogs with hopping problems and nurse them back to health. I knew one day he'd end up a doctor or preacher, one or the other."

"Okay, enough about me, Gigi." Though there was nothing in her eyes but love, the focus on my childhood made me uneasy. "Let's get on with the introductions."

I put my hand over my mouth and muttered to Chris. "Being with the WPC is a little like being in church for the first time. You never know what's coming next."

Chris nodded, reared back in his seat, locked his hands behind his head. A curious grin lit his face, tickled, I think, that he was welcomed with such enthusiasm.

Gigi introduced her sisterfriends one by one.

Jackie stepped forward first. Her ankle made a ding-a-ling sound. She clicked a quick soft-shoe, stumbled briefly, flipped her palms upward in a flashy finish. Giant hair rollers made of empty toilet paper cylinders bigger than Florida Reds were planted in her head, primping her for Founder's Day.

"Guess what, Dr. Brad? I made the dean's list in my sewing and cake decorating classes. The teacher said my roses and swirls were the best she'd ever seen."

"Jackie, that's so cool." I gave her two thumbs up. "Eat your heart out, Martha Stewart."

Jackie squeezed her shoulders together at the compliment and ding-a-linged to Chris. She threw her arms around him, suffocated him in her colossal breasts. It caused his fingers to unlock, his arms to fall helplessly onto the sofa. "Welcome to Whitecross, honey." She pulled her head back, examined his face, then directed a comment at me. "You got you some eye candy right here."

I leaned forward, planted my elbows on my knees, and checked Chris out. His mouth fell open and he blushed. "Pleased to meet you," he said.

The sisterfriends twisted their heads, twittered among themselves, and swished their shoulders. "I declare, Jackie." Betty-Jewel shuddered, rolling her eyes back in her head. "Where's your manners?"

"Don't be such a buzz-killer." Jackie dismissed her club sisters with a flop of the hand, glared at Betty-Jewel. "Especially you, Miz Goody Two Shoes." Then she looked back at Chris. "They're just a bunch of party poopers. Just remember, whatever happens in Whitecross stays in Whitecross." Jackie cocked an eyebrow, turned, and ding-a-linged back in place, glowering at Betty-Jewel.

Wilma-May stepped out from the line, pointed at her opened mouth, proudly flashing her new dentures. "What do you think, Dr. Pope? Pretty hot, huh?"

"Wilma-May, you look like a new woman." I said.

She beamed at Chris. "You got pretty teeth, too. Are they yours or store bought?"

"They're all mine." Chris narrowed his eyes. An imperceptible smile cracked his lips. "So far."

"Well, I want you to know that we're not a bunch of prudes, as some of my sisterfriends may have you think." She made a face at Betty-Jewel. "My daughter wanted to put me in the senior center to play bingo and make baskets from Popsicle sticks. The arthritis in my hands wouldn't let me do that. Besides, I told her it was boring. I've always enjoyed getting drunk and going shoplifting." Betty-Jewel grabbed at Wilma-May's arm, tried to pull her back in line, but Wilma-May twisted from her hold. "But thanks to my sisterfriends, I've mended my ways."

Gigi rolled her eyes. "Next?"

"Anyhow, here's a little welcome present for you." She handed Chris a plastic Jesus nightlight and slid backward in line with slow mopey steps. "If you need more, you can buy them at the Family Savers."

"Thank you." As Chris stared at his opened palm where the slight-weight plastic Jesus lay in state, a warm smile parted his lips. I wondered what his die-hard Buddhist mind was thinking.

Gigi shook her head and introduced Gladys, who clomped forward.

"Nice to meet you, Gladys," Chris said.

"Likewise. Welcome to Whitecross." She shifted her weight from one foot to the other. She looked over at Gigi, as though she had her toes curled around the end of a diving board, about to jump into deep water for the first time. "You might've heard that there was a murder here about a month ago . . ." She hesitated. "That was my husband. Crime is unusual in these parts. Whitecross is mostly a safe place."

I shifted in my chair. A mild unrest stirred among the sister-friends. Chris hiked his puzzled eyes at me. "No ma'am, I didn't know anything about that. I'm so sorry for your loss."

Gladys flapped her hand at him. "Oh, it wasn't a loss. It was a gain."

When Chris raised his eyebrows and shot me another confused look, I rolled my shoulders.

"Anyhow, things are pretty dead around here most of the time," Gladys continued. "Every once in a while something big *does* happen like last week a black lady got bit by a baby rattler, curled up in the mustard greens at Margie's Produce Stand."

As he wove his fingers behind his head again, Chris blanched. And Gladys clomped back in place.

Betty-Jewel was next. Sweat beads slipped her black-rimmed glasses ever so slowly down her nose. She shoved them back with her middle finger and welcomed us in Spanish. "Bienvenido a Whitecross, Chris. Don't worry. For the most part, Whitecross is pretty friendly toward minorities."

"Gracias, Betty-Jewel." Chris, fluent in three languages, responded in Spanish. "Gusto en conocerlo."

The club sisters nodded their heads, fluttered among themselves like a covey of nestlings. Betty-Jewel extended a handshake to Chris, then stepped back in line.

Chris suppressed a yawn, obviously tired after the long journey. I respected these women and could tell he liked them, too. Neither of us wanted to come off as rude.

Shirley stood stiffly erect, hands cupped, and stepped center stage. "I put my competency papers away, Dr. Pope."

"You did?" I asked.

"Normal people don't need to carry around proof that they're normal." She raised her nose in a dignified air, pursed her lips, turned to Chris. "Only crazy people do that, so I put my papers away . . . for the time being."

Chris cut his eyes at me. Aping Steve Martin, he quipped, "Okay, but I'm a wild and crazy guy, and I like wild and crazy people."

"You do?" Shirley's smile broadened. "Do you carry a set of papers, too?"

"No. But if you ask me, a normal life is a boring life." He pondered his thoughts for a second. "I'm glad you're not crazy, but even if you were, I think I'd like you anyway."

"Well now, I like your philosophy, Chris." Shirley's jaw drooped, ever so slightly. "Not only are you a handsome man, you're mannered, too. I can tell you come from good stock."

When Gigi placed her hand on Shirley's shoulder, she stepped back in line. Then Gigi brushed her palms together and took over the helm. "Okay, sisterfriends, I'll see you tomorrow."

The women crowded around Chris and me, hugged our necks, and offered final goodbyes. Within a few minutes, the club sisters, jabbering among themselves, had gathered their belongings. As they scrambled out the door, a profound stillness squeezed through the narrow opening. Even the crickets had ceased their racket. Gigi stood on the porch clapping her hands twice as if dismissing them for recess. "You know the plan. We'll snatch victory from the jaws of defeat."

Although I wondered what her plan was, I said nothing. But it must have been a good one because if the WPC was worried about what they were facing at the town hall meeting, they didn't show it. I plunged into the sofa beside Chris, soaking up how the house stretched and breathed as silence settled over us. I was mildly shell-shocked that the sisterfriends didn't flip out over my relationship with Chris. They'd treated us like an ordinary couple. The more I thought about their own history as misfits, plus the terrible group secret they'd carried, I figured they knew what it was like to be different and how important it was to fit in.

Gigi, Chris, and I lingered in the kitchen where Gigi never skimped on food. Fresh-picked eggplant and tomatoes from her garden soaked on one side of the sink. Lettuce and snap beans drained in a colander on the other. Split-open watermelon, reposed on a plastic Piggly Wiggly shopping bag, draining onto the kitchen counter.

I insisted that Chris sample the local delicacies he'd never heard of, much less tasted. Out of the corner of my eye, I could see Gigi watching intently as I showed him how to sop hoecake in the pot liquor made from the swamp cabbage juice. I popped a piece of sappy hoecake into his mouth. He bent hunchback over the cooking pot, juice running out of the corners of his mouth.

"Oh, my goodness." His black eyes snapped a bluish color; his skin flushed with pleasure. "That may be the best stuff I've ever tasted in my whole life."

"So good it makes your tongue want to slap your brains out." Gigi gave a hard nod of approval and wiped down the kitchen table. I put the vegetables and cooked food away, and Chris and I washed dishes.

"We make a pretty good threesome," Gigi said. Then something outside the window stole her attention. "Those lightning bugs look like fireworks exploding over the river."

The three of us stood close together staring over the sink through the slightly cracked window. We inhaled the sweet smell of night-blooming jessamine.

"They're mating signals," Chris said, "caused by nitric oxide."

"That's right," Gigi cocked her head at Chris, obviously impressed by his knowledge of nature. "It's the same chemical that controls heartbeat and memory in people."

"Whoa, that's enough." I threw up my hands in protest. "The science takes away the romance. Next thing I know you'll be telling me the sun doesn't set, that it's caused by the rotation of the earth."

"Shh, listen." Chris interrupted me. "It's a Chuck-will's-widow."

"Nah, that's a whippoorwill," I said.

"No," Gigi corrected me. "Chris's right. It's a Chuck-will's-widow. Sounds like a whippoorwill, but the whippoorwill lives a tad further north."

"Yeah, from Georgia on up into Canada," Chris said.

"I yield to the experts." I was thrilled that the two of them were hitting it off.

"Don't matter a bit what the sound, sight, or smell is."

Sandwiched between Chris and me, Gigi threw her arms around our waists. "What matters is that you let the nighttime music soothe your soul, bring you peace."

"That's a pretty tall order, given the problem we have to face tomorrow," I said.

"Not to worry, Tug-a-Love." She squeezed my love handles. "Besides, it's not a problem. It's a situation. You can't do anything about a problem, but you can fix a situation. And I got a plan."

Plan or not, there was something roaming around inside me that the night sounds didn't console. Myrtle had overheard Gigi telling me about shooting and burying Johnny. And she had spread rumors that I'd killed Big Jake. Bobby-Cy had said that Myrtle was bringing her own findings to the town meeting. That made me wonder what kind of rancor she had up her sleeve.

So far, Myrtle had done a good job of discrediting the sister-friends and me.

Despite Gigi's confidence, I felt mine rupturing.

After the hubbub at Bernice's Hairport, from my perspective, it felt like we were about to walk into a buzz saw.

CHAPTER 27

In mid-August, Whitecross is always hot and sticky. This Founder's Day was no exception. People came from miles around to attend the annual parade and craft fair.

Gigi, Chris, and I wormed a path through the jungle of sunburned bodies, sweaty tank tops, and cutoffs. Gigi toted a green JanSport backpack on her right shoulder that jangled with something inside. Chris and I loped a few steps behind.

Without warning, Gigi stopped dead in her tracks. She had spotted Gladys and Lick walking hand-in-hand, townsfolk looking them up and down and backing away. Though Lick's shirttail hung out of the back of his pants, he had a haircut, shave, and wore clean clothes.

"I can't believe that woman," Gigi huffed. "She won't listen to reason." As Gladys and Lick approached us, Gigi softened. "We wondered where you were, Sisterfriend."

"They let Rufus out late last night." Gladys held her head high. "Bobby-Cy said that Rufus wasn't a DNA match, that they had a suspect. So I moved him into my place."

Something seared through me. "Who do they think did it?"

Gigi cut her eyes at me, said nothing. But her lifted eyebrow spoke volumes.

"He didn't say," Gladys replied. "Just that they had an airtight case against somebody, that charges would be filed soon."

I was relieved to hear that I was off the hook. But as Gigi directed her comments to Gladys, she shot me a look of agitation. "Dad-gum it, parading Lick around is going to throw a kink in my plan." Gigi let out a long sigh, looked at Lick's combed hair and clean face, then relented, "Oh, all right, come on with us anyway."

The five of us tromped onward to the parade route, arriving at city hall where Bobby-Cy Abbott sat on a bench smoking a cigarette.

"Howdy-do, Gigi." Bobby-Cy stood, smacked his lips, and politely tipped his hat. "Lookin' forward to your speech today."

"Hey, Bobby-Cy. We were supposed to meet our sisterfriends. Have you seen them?"

"Can't say as I have." He pulled his hat low on his face; his eyes settled on me. "Howdy, Brad. Good to see you again."

"What do you say, Bobby-Cy?" I gave him a firm handshake and introduced him to Chris.

"Pleased to meet you, Chris." His eyes flicked back and forth between Chris and me.

"I hear you have a suspect in the Big Jake murder case," I said.

He lifted his hat and scratched his head, looked me directly in the eyes. "Yep. We'll make an arrest in the next day or two." After taking a final drag on his cigarette, he flipped it with his middle finger into a long arc, skidding it into the sand. "I gotta talk to you, Brother Boy."

"I hope it's about cat fishing," I said.

"I wish it was." Bobby-Cy turned away, lifted his hat again. "Excuse me, ladies. Gotta get to work now. Enjoy the jamboree."

Chris elbowed me, leaned his head in, and whispered. "What the hell's up with that 'Brother Boy thing'? And what century is he stuck in with the hat tipping?"

"He's a bit old-fashioned, but he's a stand-up guy. I'll explain later."

Bobby-Cy swaggered into the distance, and Chris shot me a

baffled eye. Then, true to form, he shrugged. Our attention was snatched away when Gigi spotted her sisterfriends. "There they are." Gigi aimed her scepter at several people on Main Street where traffic had stopped in preparation for the parade. She pointed out Shirley, Wilma-May, and Betty-Jewel, tromping toward us.

When we converged with the three women into a larger group, I felt a little like the pied piper. We meandered through a lane of accusing faces, drawing ogle eyes from the locals. After the *Whitecross News* article, Gigi's popularity in town had continued to unspool, and I was guilty by association.

As we continued our trek to the parade site, it dawned on me that somebody was missing. "Where's Jackie?" I asked.

"Shoot." Gigi said. "That woman won't listen to anything I say, either. She's determined to have her school marching today come hell or high water."

"What school?" I asked. "I thought it'd gone to pot."

"She's trying to piece it together with some of the field hand's young'uns, dressing them up, parading them in place of the ones that withdrew. Students or no students, she's not going to miss her day of glory. This is her chance to strut her stuff."

Gigi continued to part the crowd like Moses parted the waters. We trooped behind her to the square at Duval and Main, where the parade would stop and perform. Once the parade was over, festivities would move to the fairgrounds of the VFW and last long into the night.

After sitting and fidgeting for twenty minutes, we craned our necks in the direction of the parade route. For their part, the club sisters acted like a bunch of rowdy teenagers, loose from a parental grip for the first time. They stood, pushed, shuffled their feet.

"What's taking them so long?" Gigi snorted.

Gladys, Shirley, and Wilma-May restlessly elbowed one

another, competing for a place in front of the line as first spotter. Betty-Jewel busied herself keeping order and instructing them to behave.

The crowd swelled from the sidewalk and spilled onto Main Street. Bobby-Cy sauntered by and nudged spectators back to the curb. "Let's keep a path clear," he ordered out of the side of his mouth. He singled me out of the crowd with a suspicious once-over. His knitted brows and clenched jaw made him look angry.

After much impatience, we heard the faint sound of a drumbeat. Chris exulted, "Here it comes!"

"Here it comes!" Lick echoed, eyes blinking, arms flopping in excitement.

As the drumbeat got louder, the crowd snaked into the street peering and clapping. Shirley shaded her eyes with her hand, pointed in the direction of the sound. "There they come."

"There they come." Lick twitched his body, sprang up and down at the knees.

At first barely visible, the American flag curled in the breeze. A single drum pounded in the distance and got louder and louder as it approached.

We could see the American and Florida state flags flapping in the wind, held from below by the American Legion and National Guardsmen, leading the parade with drums. At first sight of the American flag streaming on high, spectators stood, hands over their hearts.

Sirens blasted. Blue lights flashed. The Whitecross Police followed the drummers on three motorcycles in front of Shriners with *Red Fez* scribbled across the front of their red turbans, dangly gold tassels cascading down the side. They drove miniature cars that spun around in the street, red and orange flags attached to their antennae. Ambulances, fire trucks, and the rescue squad puttered by. Florida state troopers, decked in tan and gold uniforms, straddled their motorcycles.

Mayor Hoyle "Smiley" Bishop rode in back of a black Dodge Dakota sport truck. He slung shiny gold-blue-and-green necklaces at the crowd as fast as he could pull them out of a cardboard box. The truck paused at the square. Smiley stood to give the kickoff speech for the eighty-second Annual Whitecross Founder's Day. He squinched his face from the sun and scraped his teeth across his bottom lip. He waved vigorously at the spectators. Then he fastened his thumbs in his belt loops and spoke in a deep-throated tone:

"Founder's Day is a celebration of our forefathers who settled this great town and made it what it is today. Founded in 1924, Founder's Day is a showcase of country music and dancin' and singin' passed down from our Scots-Irish and German ancestors who brought their own brand of cloggin', fiddle playin,' and ballads that date back to the Middle Ages."

Smiley's low-hanging belly, well stocked with biscuits and gravy, bounced over his wide belt as he shouted. "We, the descendants of Whitecross's forefathers, are proud of our heritage. We still use their traditions in our daily lives to rock a baby to sleep, call the cows home, or to tear ourselves away from everyday stress. Founder's Day is a remembrance of everything we hold sacred, the bedrock of our lives. Lest we not forget, let the parade begin."

"Yoo-hoo." Gigi yelled and waved. She tried to grab Smiley's attention, but his car lurched forward before she nabbed his eye. Either that or he'd ignored her for political reasons. It was hard to tell which.

Gigi looked disappointed but not defeated. Her eyes caught on Little Miss Suwannee Valley, five-year-old Darcella Gaylord, perched on the sun roof of a Pontiac Trans Am. Dressed in period costumes, Founder's Day Granny and Pappy bumped along in a horse and buggy behind her.

Most of the bands were anemic, except for the Whitecross "Shark Attack" High School Marching Band, dressed in aqua-and-white uniforms. They strutted to the tune of "Way Down Upon the Suwannee River." Behind them, Miss Founder's Day, Bokaye Mercer, and her royal court rode on the first float, practicing their white-gloved, queen waves on the townspeople who lined both sides of the street. The wind picked up, whirled the beauty queens' hair over their faces, hiding their Southern-belle charm.

Model-T horns blowing "Yahooga" grabbed the crowd's attention as did the Sons of Confederate Veterans waving the Confederate flag from a float pulled by a tractor. A four-wheeler chugged along behind them with a sign that read *Mayo's Bait, Tackle, and Pecan Cracking: 239-4718*. The Triple C Riding Club clop-clopped on horses, covered in Indian blankets. Ibejean Martin's nine-year-old grandson, Brandon, brought up the rear. He fervently shoveled up horse droppings and bounced the crowd to their feet with chuckles and applause.

"Isn't that Brandon plum adorable?" gushed Gigi. Then she frowned at the sight rolling along behind him. "Heaven sakes, I thought it was the horse shit that stunk, but it's Myrtle Badger."

Myrtle, Ibejean Martin, and Edna Black were squeezed onto the back of a pink 1956 Thunderbird convertible with a Continental kit on the rear bumper. A sign on the door read, *Daughters of the Confederacy*. Each of them waved a tiny Confederate flag on a wooden stick.

The club sisters clucked their tongues, shook their heads. Chris and I looked at each other. We had to chuckle at Myrtle's short stout legs, flying-buttress hips, and cream-puff cheeks. At the exact moment Myrtle raised her hand in our direction to wave, Gigi pretended to scratch her nose with her scepter.

When Myrtle saw Gigi flipping the finger, she gave a passing sneer, mouthed the word "bitch," and stuck her haughty nose in the air. Then she turned her head toward the other side of the street, throwing a vigorous wave to admirers.

"The Bible says, 'Love thine enemies.' " Wilma-May sniffled and wiped her eyes with the sleeve of her blouse. "We oughta be praying for Myrtle, not judging her."

"What's wrong, Wilma-May?" I asked.

"Ibejean fired me as her page-turner for the Glory Bees's new CD. She replaced me with Myrtle Badger. And that woman has never page-turned a day in her life."

"It'll be their loss, not yours." Gigi wound her arm around Wilma-May's neck. "Myrtle don't hold a candle to you."

Another high-school band drowned out the club sisters. They were followed by the president of Lake City Community College in a red Corvette convertible. Silver-haired Senator Jasper Horn rode in back of a green Ford pickup. Then came the "hut, two, three, four" of the ROTC, who proudly carried the American flag. The crowd jumped to its feet again, hands over hearts at the sight of the flag.

A smattering of clowns, children with painted faces, and Scottish bagpipers filed by. Miss River Reunion rode in a horse-drawn carriage, followed by the Future Farmers of America and a medley of walking Florida oranges, pineapples, and strawberries.

Next in the procession was Jackie, pulling out all the stops, stacked on top of clogging shoes, clicking and clacking toward us in a pink tutu with a floppy bow in her hair. Like a Rockette, she hoofed it up, pushing a red Piggly Wiggly grocery cart. Doohickey was propped in the child's seat, all dolled up in color-coordinated tutu and red bow. The basket was full of play pretties and chew toys to keep Doohickey entertained.

She had cajoled Miguel and Sergio, another one of Gigi's field hands, into carrying a large white banner inscribed in red letters, *Jackie's School of Buckshot Cloggers and Baton Twirlers*. It featured only three snappy small fries, children of field hands, who clogged and tapped their little feet up the street. Jackie had talked her frowning husband, Doodle, into the ultimate exhibition of love for her: putting on a tutu, clogging along with the strange bedfellows, and carrying a boom box that pumped out, "Shake It Up Baby."

We cheered for Jackie and gave Doodle wolf whistles of approval for going to the ends of the earth for his wife. A few hecklers booed and jeered, but their attention was quickly stolen by the final attraction idling along behind Jackie.

Decked out in blue jeans, Western denim blouse with rhinestone pockets, fringe down the arms, and cowgirl boots, the Grand Marshal of the parade, Reba McEntire, sat on back of a blue Ford Mustang convertible, the same color as her deep azure eyes. Wisps of her crimson shortcut hair gently lifted in the breeze. Her perky smile and frisky hand-wagging warmed the hearts of the spectators who gave her a rousing reception along the parade route.

As Reba's car rolled by, a recording of her hit song, "Rumor Has It", blasted from a CD inside the car. Gigi and her sister-friends threw their palms in the air and bowed as if she were the Queen of Sheba.

"Thank ya'll," Reba hollered in her fried-okra drawl, waving her hands off.

The WPC laughed and elbowed each other. Gigi pulled a hunk of her red hair declaring, "Look here. My hair's the spitting image of yours."

Reba flashed her trademark smile and gave Gigi two thumbs up. Gigi put two fingers to her lips, blew air through them in a cat whistle, and punched her fist skyward.

"Gigi, I've never seen you bow to anybody before," I said.

"And Tug-a-Love . . ." she breathed excitedly, resting her

arm on my shoulder, "you won't ever again. She's my idol."

"How'd the little town of Whitecross manage to book such a big star as Reba McEntire?" Chris asked.

"Smiley's got connections," Gigi said proudly. I watched Gigi's eyes follow Reba's Mustang as it puttered into the distance. The crowd dribbled into the street, shuffling us forward.

I turned to find Chris but instead locked eyes with Bobby-Cy, leaning against a wooden post in front of Whitecross Hardware, sucking on a dangling cigarette. His steel glare trailed us as we headed toward the VFW, where we'd partake of fried fish and chicken, cakes, pies and homemade ice cream.

I couldn't figure out why Bobby-Cy wanted to talk to me again. And I wondered what Gigi was toting around in her bag of tricks that she thought would neutralize the town's disfavor.

When I nodded and waved, Bobby-Cy arced his cigarette in the air, skidded it into the sand toward me. Then he pulled his hat over his eyes, hooked his thumbs in the belt loops of his uniform, and rested the back of his head against the post.

The small hairs on my neck prickled up, and I felt a rumble of trepidation.

All I could do was roll my shoulders and wonder, *Now what?*

CHAPTER 28

Handmade crafts. Music. Singing and dancing.

For the remainder of the day, we were entertained by The Prairie Trio from Live Oak: Teeny-Weenie, Teensy-Weensy, and Tiny-Winy—seventy-five-year-old, tap-dancing triplets. The four-feet-five-inch red-heads were dolled up in matching sequined outfits of red, white, and blue. They had us dancing between bites of pie and ice cream. Special attractions included a rodeo, barnyard petting zoo, tractor pull, balloon-blowing goat, lamb-jumping contest, and McCullers's Racing Pigs.

The circus-like atmosphere left Chris open-mouthed. His eyes were so wide they looked as if they'd been pried open with a crowbar. We spent an hour perusing the country handicrafts, food, and agricultural exhibits.

Sylvia Wynn exhibited stained-glass windows constructed from pieces of old Mason jars, plus candle holders made from blue upside-down telephone pole insulators. Earle Pearce manned a booth of homemade willow rocking chairs and hand-painted saw blades. Sandy Nelson peddled decorative gourds and wall hangings of dried flowers shellacked onto chopping blocks. Bernice Rankin proudly displayed note holders made from clothespins and stuffed dolls sewn from fiber-filled socks with Magic Marker smiles. Vera the nurse sat in a fold-up chair surrounded by multicolored, hand-woven crocheted lap blankets.

Vasque Gaylord broadcast his popular radio show before a

purple banner that read: *WHCS 99.5 AM Radio: Go to bed, and get up with us.* On the side, he sold canned Mayhaw jelly, bread and butter pickles, Vidalia-onion relish, and maple syrup pie.

"We want to send out a special 'get well' to Pastor Ollis Black, who couldn't be here with us today," Vasque squealed into his microphone. "Preacher Black, if you're a-listenin', we wish you a speedy recovery."

"For crying out loud, Vasque," Gigi said as he went to commercial. "What on earth happened to Pastor Black this time?"

"He's been in the hospital in Lake City. He was eatin' pizza pie and reached for the parmesan. But, accordin' to Edna, he grabbed a can of Zip disinfectant powder, sprinkled it all over the top. He told her it was the best pizza pie she'd ever made. He'd already eaten three pieces and started wheezin' before she realized what he'd done."

"Mercy me," cried Wilma-May, "is he gonna be all right?"

"Yep, he's fine. Doctors pumped his stomach, said he might not be so lucky next time. So they decided to go ahead with eye surgery."

"That poor man." Gigi reached down, took a Founder's Day schedule of events brochure off Vasque's display table, and fanned herself with it. "It's a miracle he's still kicking after all the close calls."

"He never loses his faith." Vasque leaned on his fists against the display table, the sun mirroring off his shiny, dyed-black hair. "He's an inspiration."

"I guess so." Gigi shot a devilish grin at Chris and me. After we walked out of earshot, she balled up her fist and muttered into it, "It's wrongdoing coming back on him. He's getting his comeuppance. Plain and simple."

We snickered among ourselves, tramped through the sweet-smelling sawdust until we reached Founder's Village. Exhibitors in period costumes sold their wares and demonstrated pioneer skills—spinning, rope-making, weaving, chair-caning, molasses-making, corn-shucking, shelling, apple-butter-making, horse-shoeing, blacksmithing, beekeeping, and woodcarving—traditions that would have been lost if it wasn't for the locals' desire to keep them alive. Several operating steam engines and other antique farm machinery were on display, along with area quilts and a hands-on quilting demonstration.

Gigi's backpack jingled as we made our way to the stage. Sounds of an accordion, fiddle, and washboard pounded through the loudspeaker. By the time we reached the front of the stage, Jackie had changed into shorts and a tight T-shirt that read, *I wish these were brains.* She shimmied her shoulders to the music; her mammoth breasts swung wildly like two wrecking balls.

"Somebody could get killed if they got too close to you, Sisterfriend," Gigi teased.

"Just shaking what my mama gave me, my weapons of mass destruction." Jackie giggled and stretched her lips into a zero. Then she squinched her eyes into slits and shook her hips at us.

I spied Ibejean and Edna, shoulders tightened, shaking their heads at us, arms folded into a cradle, as if nursing contempt close to their chests. To the outside world we must have looked carefree, a sharp contrast to the consternation I felt inside—a consternation that came thundering home when I looked up and saw Myrtle stepping on stage with a contemptuous squint. On the podium she placed something, revenge maybe, in a daunting, brown leather satchel.

She straightened her diamond necklace with her fingers, using the other hand as a tarp against the sun. She scrinched her eyes in our direction, anger dripping off her, and snarled at our jubilance, eager to make us pay a price for it.

I thought about what Gigi had said and wondered, *Is this a*

problem or a situation?
We were about to find out.

CHAPTER 29

Nestled in a grove of hundred-year-old live oaks, the cedar-shake gazebo stood wide and cone-shaped, dappled with green moss. Bales of hay and a draped American flag served as set decorations for the five town council members who faced the audience on one end of the stage. At the opposite end, Myrtle delivered Mayor Smiley Bishop a two-cheek kiss and plopped down on his right side. Gigi had already seated herself on his left. Long wooden benches stuffed with spectators stretched away from the stage underneath five-feet-thick tree trunks, limbs shrouded in Spanish moss. The packed assembly buzzed with anticipation.

As Gigi's honored guests, Chris and I had front-row seats. The remainder of front-row seats had been reserved for the town manager, head of the zoning board, Sheriff Bobby-Cy Abbott, and other town officials. Gigi had nabbed reserved seats on the second row for her sisterfriends.

It was strange watching Myrtle, Smiley, and Gigi together in a clump, waiting to be introduced by master of ceremonies Vasque Gaylord, who stood in front of the podium. Myrtle seemed to be basking in the glow of whatever she had on us. Everything about her had that blow-dried, perfectly manicured look, not a hair out of place. Her diamond necklace winked at the crowd; her ring sparkled like a strobe light.

Gigi ignored Myrtle, worked the crowd. She looked down into the audience, waving at familiar faces, reaching over the stage to pass out bumper stickers that read, *Sprawl Stops Here.* She shook hands with folks who would speak to her. For those who iced her, she had a smile over steel.

I turned around. Gladys and Lick sat directly behind me on the second row, exchanging looks like they'd done at Big Jake's funeral. Only this time their hands were locked in solidarity. Vasque introduced Smiley, who had been schmoozing the crowd. As he approached the microphone, he waved, looking smooth and handsome in a paisley tie and sports coat.

After a quick rustling of notes, Smiley extolled Gigi.

"It's common, when people think of environmental protection, to focus on city government's role—buyin' park land and enactin' and enforcin' laws against pollution. Those duties are critical in protectin' resources and ensurin' clean air to breathe and pure water to drink. But as our honored guest has demonstrated, private works have a role as well. Without her generosity and leadership, this region and the State of Florida would be immeasurably poorer."

Gigi stood, brushed her hands down the front of her blue pants suit, and ran her fingers over both hips, adding a final touch before being introduced. She took a long deep breath, pressed a palm against the back of her hair still pinned into a French twist. Then she made a nervous swish of the gold-heart locket around her neck.

I was nervous for her. The lyrics of Sonny and Cher's "The Beat Goes On" thudded in my head. Smiley continued his introduction. "Gigi Pope's fingerprints can be found on most of Whitecross's civic, cultural, and health-care institutions . . ."

"Her fingerprints can be found on a lot more than that." Myrtle's voice torpedoed him from behind, causing a flurry of jabber and tense shuffling among the spectators.

Clearly flustered, Smiley rotated his neck toward her. "Mrs. Badger, please. Let me finish. You'll have a chance to speak when it's your turn."

Myrtle frowned as Smiley turned back to the microphone. "As I was sayin', a lot of people give money, but few people give time, energy, *and* financial resources to charitable causes. Gigi Pope has carried on the legacy of her grandfather, Henry Pope, who founded this great town in 1886. If he were here today, he'd be proud of his granddaughter and the unselfish contributions she's made to Whitecross. Gigi Pope always shies away from takin' credit for her good work. But there's not a soul here today who hasn't benefited from her generosity. Ladies and gentlemen, please give it up for this year's recipient of Whitecross's Citizen of the Year, Gigi Pope."

Gigi strutted downstage. Her face glowed as she stepped in front of the mic. Smiley shook her hand and gave her a peck on the cheek. Gigi clasped her hands in front while he placed a gold commendation medal around her neck.

She adjusted the microphone, spoke into it like a pro.

"Mr. Mayor, honored council members, town leaders, fellow citizens of Whitecross. As you know my roots go back a long way in this beloved town. This is the greatest honor I've ever received, and I'm very touched. Because I love this town so much, I am equally concerned for its survival. I want to talk to you today about crime. Crime against innocent people, children, yes and even animals . . ."

"You speaking for it or against it?" From behind, Myrtle pulled at her skirt, jerked at the collar of her blouse.

Low, heavy murmurs rumbled through the crowd. A grim-looking Gigi wrinkled her brow, drew her lips into a tight line, then continued to speak.

"The Women's Preservation Club has dedicated itself to preservation, not only of the natural beauty around us but prevention of environmental and human crimes—crimes that are fast destroying our way of life as we know it in Whitecross.

Environmental crimes include deforestation, pollution of our drinking water, overbuilding, and what I call 'uglification.' We don't want the animals we hold dear to lose their habitats and breeding corridors. We don't want our air and water to be degraded. It's still safe here to walk alone at night or to sleep with doors unlocked, a major difference between Whitecross and big cities. But strip malls, more subdivisions, and any notion of a theme park will change all that and cut the very soul from the land we so dearly love . . ."

"Wait just a minute!" Myrtle jumped to her feet, stabbed her finger at Gigi. "You're using your acceptance speech as political maneuvering against our theme park proposal!"

"Sit down, Mrs. Badger." Smiley's husky voice cut in. "You'll have a spot on the agenda for rebuttal, but you gotta wait your turn. Now, sit down."

Myrtle flopped back into her chair and quieted herself, but you could see rage ballooning in her body.

"I accept this medal with appreciation and humility." Gigi fiddled with the microphone. "But all of us still have a lot of work to do. I urge you to join with me and the WPC to fight the crimes and the criminals robbing us of our future, our children's futures, and our grandchildren's futures. No developments and no theme park in Whitecross."

Weak applause sprinkled with scattered boos and catcalls.

Smiley approached the microphone, bleating, "Come on now, you can do better than that. Put your hands together for Gigi Pope's hard work. On account of her, the Florida State Park Service is gonna create a seventy-eight-acre nature preserve keepin' an intact wooded tract on the outskirts of Whitecross that backs up to the Suwannee."

After Gigi took her seat, the applause, still anemic, stretched an octave or two higher through the grove of trees. Myrtle stomped to the side of the podium, itching to get to the microphone, and patted an impatient foot. After Smiley introduced her as a concerned citizen and employee of Bowen's Funeral Home, she whispered something in his ear. He murmured back to her, then spoke into the microphone, directing his comments to the audience.

"Sorry, Mrs. Badger, I stand corrected. Her correct job title is mortuary cosmetologist." Smiley cleared his throat. "Anyhow, ladies and gentlemen, please give a warm welcome to Mrs. Myrtle Badger, who has prepared a ten-minute rebuttal."

As Myrtle approached the podium where she had plunked the satchel, a piercing whistle caused me to twist my neck around. Myrtle's husband, Swayze, who'd been sitting on the row behind me, gave her a standing ovation.

"Mr. Mayor, council members, honored . . ." As she spoke into the microphone, it screeched. She smacked it—like she'd smacked Shirley's Siamese—and it screeched even more. "What's wrong with this thing?" She clicked her nails against it. When it didn't work, she whacked it hard.

Smiley adjusted the height of the microphone. Vasque whirled a few knobs on the sound equipment, which seemed to clear the static.

"Try it now," Vasque shouted.

"Mr. Mayor . . ." Myrtle cleared her throat. "Mr. Mayor, council members, honored guests, and citizens of Whitecross, I've been to the edge and back." She pulled away from the microphone and paused as if she were expecting thunderous applause. When there was only the dim whirring of the mic above the dead silence, she continued.

"I have decided to dispense with my argument for a theme park because it's a no-brainer that we need the income in this town. Instead, I'd like to take a few minutes to reveal what the WPC, better known as the Women's Preservation *Cult,* has been up to. The WPC has dedicated itself to crime all right—their own crimes."

The contents of the satchel made a loud thunk as she dumped the contents onto the lectern. A glint of spite in her eye, Myrtle continued. "Mr. Mayor, you were right about one thing. Gigi Pope's fingerprints are on everything in this town, including the dead people."

Mumbles rippled across the gathering.

"I consider it my civic duty to inform my fellow citizens that these plastic bones before me represent real human bones that were exhumed at the WPC's planting site at the town welcome sign. I overheard Gigi Pope bragging to her grandson that she had masterminded the murder. I'm calling for a full investigation and have already alerted Bobby-Cy, who called in the state medical examiner."

Myrtle's accusations provoked another flutter of jeers.

Smiley's face paled, his perpetual smile turned upside down. Chris caught me scratching the back of my neck and furtively pinned my hand down by my side.

"Hold on," Smiley said as he nudged in front of Myrtle to get to the microphone. "This is a serious charge, you're makin' here. What about it, Bobby-Cy?"

Bobby-Cy stood, shouted from below the stage at the top of his lungs so that he could be heard. "The team from the medical examiner's office closed the case, because they couldn't identify the body. Damn-dest thing. There was no teeth. Right now, we're doin' preliminary work until we get somethin' concrete. I don't know if we ever will."

"Closed the case?" Myrtle said. "What about those bones?"

"Finding a bunch of bones at the welcome site don't mean the WPC committed a crime," Bobby-Cy said. "You gotta have more evidence than that."

"I'll bet you anything," Smiley said, "that those bones belong to some of our Confederate War dead. Olustee, just a mile down the road, was a major battlefield durin' the Civil War. And the archives at the Whitecross library documents twenty unmarked graves in and around Whitecross believed to be those of Confederate soldiers. As part of their preservation efforts, the WPC has been tryin' to find those graves and place bronze markers at the gravesites in honor of the Civil War veterans." Then he turned to Gigi for confirmation. "Right, Gigi?"

"That's right, Mayor." Gigi stood and approached the microphone. "Fact is, the town received federal funds to earmark Confederate graves and battlegrounds in our area before they fall prey to malls, subdivisions, and theme parks." Gigi threw Myrtle a smirk. "The WPC went before the town board of commissioners to request funds to install twelve-by-twenty-four-inch flat bronze markers at each grave site."

"What about it, Bobby-Cy?" Smiley asked again.

"This is a worthwhile project the WPC has undertaken." Bobby-Cy shrugged. "I'm not a gamblin' man, but I'll bet you my sheriff's badge that those are bones of the war dead."

"There then, that settles it," Smiley proclaimed.

Bobby-Cy caught me looking up at him. He shrugged his shoulders again, as if to say he wasn't lying. After all, Johnny did serve a stint in Vietnam.

Myrtle squinched her face in a defeated look. "But . . ."

"Thank you, Bobby-Cy," said Smiley. "And thank you, Mrs. Badger."

"Hold on, Mayor." Myrtle held up five fingers. "I've still got five more minutes."

"Okay, five minutes."

"Thank you, your honor." She threw Smiley a phony half-grin and turned back to the microphone, this time jabbing for the kill. "I believe it's my God-given duty to divulge the internal goings-on of this cult. I want to prove to you beyond a shadow of a doubt that they've been up to no good."

A roar of jeers and jabbering reverberated through the crowd.

"Hold on; let me finish." Myrtle raised both palms, as though she couldn't wait to start badmouthing. "Bobby-Cy, get out your handcuffs; we're talking murder one here. Let me go down the line and bullet a few facts for you about this cult. First off, Jackie Priester was with the owner of Triple Six Phosphate Company when he was killed. And for those of you who don't know the sign of the beast, its triple six—666. Second of all, Gladys Nunn nursed a man who died in her care at the VA hospital. You can say that's coincidence, and some of you will, but then there's the matter of Jake Nunn's horrible death. I was driving by Suwannee Springs at the time of the murder and saw Brad Pope reaching down toward Big Jake's guideline. I'm positive he had a knife in his hand. And I might add that he lives on a section of the river known as Devil's Elbow."

I snapped my head up, flinched from a jolt of adrenaline, and felt my body go numb. Chris, incredulous and wide-eyed, tilted his head, elbowed me, and murmured, "What the . . . ?" I shook my head, said nothing, and focused on staying calm.

But my silence didn't quiet Myrtle's rising voice. "Before Big Jake was put in the ground his widow-woman, Gladys Nunn, started sleeping with that retarded boy, Lick. Even though the boy's elevator don't go to the top floor, she's taking advantage of him because she can't get a man her own age."

The crowd stirred. Roaming eyes. Muffled sounds.

Wilma-May bounced to her feet, cupping her mouth, "Gladys Nunn's my friend. And she's an honest, respectable woman."

Myrtle looked down at Wilma-May, came back at her in a fury. "I'd say you were lying through your teeth, if you had any."

"For your information," Wilma-May roared back, "I just bought a brand-new set." She pointed at her wide-opened mouth.

Shirley stood, yelling to the audience, shaking her finger at Myrtle. "The next thing she'll claim is that the WPC is hiding weapons of mass destruction."

A volley of laughter echoed across the spectators.

"You better hold on to your crazy papers, honey. You gonna need them where you're going," Myrtle declared. "I'm on a mission to clean up this town."

"Now hold on just a minute here." A voice boomed from the back row. When I craned my neck around, Doc Rogers was sucking on a stogie, wiggling it back and forth between his teeth, jerking at his scruffy white beard. "I've heard just about all I can take! Clean up the town? Seems to me like you're dirtyin' it up with your pack of lies."

"How dare you accuse me of lying." Myrtle stiffened, narrowed her eyes on the doctor, then played with her necklace. "I don't tell lies; I'm a Christian."

"Let's just say you've got your facts wrong, then." The more she had talked, the redder Doc Rogers's face got, and the veins in his neck swelled. He took a long draw on his cigar before he spoke, made smoke rings. The pause seemed to help him steady his voice. "It saddens me to see a member of this community stand in front of its citizens and besmirch the reputation of one of Whitecross's finest. I delivered Lick near on twenty years ago at home. His real name is Rufus. Big Jake was his papa, leastways in name, even though he wanted to get rid of that boy from the get-go. How'd you feel if you were dumped by your own papa? And this fine upstanding woman you accusin' of havin' an affair with this young man is finally takin' her own son back in, somethin' Big Jake wouldn't let her to do when he was alive."

Shock waves blasted through the crowd. Myrtle looked stunned, too; her hand jettisoned to her mouth. Thunderstruck, I turned around, combed the sea of faces. Edna and Ibejean clamped their hands over their mouths, faced each other in disbelief.

I put my palm on top of Gladys's hand. "Why didn't you tell me?"

"I was sworn to secrecy. If I'd said anything, Big would've killed me. Besides, I was afraid you wouldn't think much of a woman who'd turn away her own flesh and blood . . ."

"You don't have to say another word." I squeezed her hand.

Doc Rogers launched into a cross-examination of Myrtle. "So, Mrs. Badger, can you provide proof of the other egregious claims you've made here today against some of Whitecross's finest citizens?"

"I'll take over from here." Gigi wedged herself between Myrtle and the podium, bumping Myrtle out of the way. "When somebody points a finger at everybody else, they have three pointing back at them. Myrtle Badger has done a good job of cleaning *out* this town instead of cleaning it *up.*"

"What's she talking about?" Myrtle braced her fists against her hips, her muted voice barely picked up by the microphone.

"Robbing the departed of their keepsakes." When Gigi turned her green backpack upside down, a treasure trove of jewelry clanked against the wooden podium. "There, that's what I'm talking about."

"You got my piece of crown from the beauty pageant." Myrtle shook her finger; her lidded eyes blazed, nostrils flared. "How'd you get that?"

"This watch is one of a kind." Gigi held up a gold watch. "Has Japanese writing on it. Korman Martin got it overseas during the war—the one that Ibejean *thought* she'd buried him with."

Ibejean shrieked from the back of the crowd, bolted to her feet. "That's my husband's watch! He loved that watch." She crumbled into Edna Black's arms, bawling.

"You broke into my house and stole . . ." Myrtle blurted before she realized that she'd given herself away. Then she tried to redeem herself. "That's breaking and entering."

"And what about this antique piece?" Gigi held up a cameo broach.

"Dear Sweet Lord," Edna Black wailed. "That was my mama's. She was buried with it." While still trying to console Ibejean, Edna threw her hands over her face, suddenly overtaken by her own grief. "It belonged to Mama's mama, my grand-mamma."

Myrtle faked a smile. "I collected that jewelry. I was gonna return it to the rightful owners, just never got around to it."

"It's been two years since Mama died," Edna cried. "How long does it take?"

"And what about this?" Gigi dangled a large ring in front of her.

Gladys shouted. "That's Big's ring. They gave it to him when he made All-American!"

"Well . . ." Myrtle stammered, her eyes wide with panic, "they didn't have use for jewelry where they were going; they've got all the treasures they need in Heaven . . ."

"You're not gonna have any use for it where you're goin' neither." Bobby-Cy had walked up to the side of the stage, mounted the steps.

Myrtle slowly backed away from the sheriff and scuttled in circles. "I'll put an extra five in the church plate on Sunday for backsliding. I'll return every piece of it to the rightful owners."

"You're under arrest for larceny." As Myrtle scuffled against the sheriff's massive grip, he handcuffed her wrists behind her back, read her her Miranda rights. "You have the right to remain silent . . ."

Swayze Badger sprang to his feet. "Hold on, Sheriff. Where are you taking my wife?"

Myrtle's eyes landed on her husband. "Shut up, Swayze. I wouldn't be in this fix if it wasn't for you. I never wanted to move to this hick town in the first place."

Swayze directed his comments to Bobby-Cy. "Sheriff, I swear I never knew anything about her stealing problem. Maybe you can straighten her out."

Myrtle exploded. "Whose side are you on, dumb-ass?" Then she airlifted her attention to Bobby-Cy. "Aren't you gonna arrest Gigi for breaking and entering? What do I have to do for redemption? Send me to rehab. I promise I'll turn my life around. The Bible says forgive seventy times seven."

"That'll be up to the judge," Bobby-Cy said.

"Just you wait until the second coming, Bobby-Cy Abbott. When that trumpet sounds and Jesus comes floating down from the sky, he'll take care of you." Then her fiery eyes landed on Gigi. "You *and* Lucifer's imp. You'll both burn in hell for this."

Bobby-Cy nudged Myrtle down the stairs. Her hair drooped in her eyes like wilted grass. At the bottom of the stairs, she became emotionally unhinged, howling at the top of her lungs, breaking loose from Bobby-Cy's grip, whirling in circles. She hurled herself into the sawdust, flipped and flopped like one of those catfish I'd yanked from the Suwannee.

Bobby-Cy reached down under her armpits. He gently lifted her to her feet; his face was set, stern, and unemotional. "Get up, Badger, and stop actin' like a damn fool." She was covered in sawdust. It had stuck to the makeup on her eyes, nose, and mouth. I noticed that Myrtle's blinding humongous ring had lost its sparkle. Covered in sawdust, its urgent light had retreated into itself and dulled.

Town officials adjourned and deliberated on the theme park proposal for a good twenty minutes. When they reconvened, Smiley announced that they had rejected the theme park proposal. They had passed a town ordinance restricting development within a ten-mile radius of Whitecross. Smiley said it was the WPC's hard work that inspired them to preserve the soul of the town.

During intermission, while Reba's band was setting up to play, the crowd trickled out of the grove. Chris and I joined Smiley, Gigi, and Gladys at the side of the stage. Rufus stayed in his seat, saving spaces for the concert.

"Who'd ever thought I'd be a warm-up for Reba McEntire." Gigi swallowed hard.

Chris and I gave Gigi a congratulatory hug. "I'm so proud of you," I said.

Smiley locked his arm around Gigi and pulled her against his side. "Gigi, how'd you come by all this?"

"Myrtle always had a reputation for swindling her own blood-kin. Then after Gladys viewed Big Jake and said his ring was missing, I started putting two-and-two together."

Gladys spoke up. "The viewing was so emotional, I figured I'd just misplaced it."

"I still don't understand how Myrtle got her hands on all that other jewelry without the families knowing it," Smiley said.

Gladys piped up. "According to my son, who digs graves for Bowen's, Myrtle was always the last to leave the cemetery. Said she'd open the casket to say a little prayer over the departed."

Chris rolled his eyes. "Oh man, give me a break."

"It all came together for me at the last WPC cookout," Gigi said. "When Rufus was grilling the burgers, he droned on about how Myrtle lingered over the opened casket after everybody had left the graveyard, claiming she wanted to make sure the departed were presentable before they met their Maker. That's when I knew right off that she'd been fleecing the dead bodies. We added her to our watch list that same day, and Betty-Jewel drew the turn. Then when Bernice told me Myrtle's house was up for sale, I called Betty-Jewel, and we decided to take a look-see."

Smiley rocked on the balls of his feet, arm still glued to Gigi. "I suppose that Betty-Jewel, being a realtor and all, had access to the lockbox?"

"That's right. Even though the house was already sold, I had a hunch about the missing jewelry," Gigi said. "When we toured the bedroom, I noticed Myrtle's jewelry box wide open. Big Jake's All-American ring—the one Gladys buried him with—was lying out in plain sight. We rifled through the jewelry box and found the rest."

"Makes you wonder if old Myrtle might've had something to do with Big Jake's murder." Smiley looked at us for our reactions.

"I don't know about that." Gigi crossed her arms. "But I can tell you one thing, dead folks are the only people she could get along with because they don't talk back."

Between chuckles, Smiley said, "That's for sure."

Gigi's eyes drifted to me. She pulled a small box out of the pocket of her pants suit, opened it, handed it to me. "Here son, this belongs to you."

"Mama's ring?" I slipped the ring out of the box and closed my palm around it. When I opened my arms, Gigi fell into them. I put my lips against her ear and whispered through a catch in my throat. "Thank you. I love you."

Chris embraced Gigi. She squeezed back. After a round of hugs, Chris and I descended the side of the stage, Gigi leaning against Smiley, his arm hanging around her neck, his lips split open into a wide grin. Gladys stood with her finger against her teeth looking down at Rufus, making sure he was okay.

We had just walked out of earshot of the threesome when I saw Betty-Jewel scurry up the stairs of the stage, frantically waving her arms, Shirley, Jackie, and Wilma-May in tow. Betty-

Jewel mashed her glasses up her nose and moaned. She seized Gigi by the shoulders, mumbled something, then motioned with her hands. Gigi began sobbing, clutched both sides of her head, and buried her face in Smiley's chest. The sisterfriends circled around her, clucking their tongues. Beneath a stream of applause and Reba McEntire's velvety voice echoing through the microphone, I tore after Gigi as fast as my legs would carry me. Chris flew behind me.

Betty-Jewel's wild-eyed gaze met us halfway. "It's Sally! She dropped dead this afternoon! They found her lying on the banks of the Suwannee. Your grandmamma's taking it awful hard."

CHAPTER 30

After a day of tubing down the Ichetucknee River, Chris and I had had a long, leisurely dinner on the waterfront. Though he'd never met Sally, I'd spoken affectionately of her over dinner, telling him how much she'd meant to me. On the way home from the restaurant, the sweet smell of honeysuckle breezed through the opened car window. The digital clock on the dashboard showed almost eight o'clock. The shock of Myrtle's stinging allegations linking me to Big Jake's murder hung unspoken in the warm night air.

Until Chris finally spoke. "Brad, are you in some kind of trouble?"

"Nah. It'll all blow over."

"I want to know what's going on. What will blow over?"

"I'll tell you later." I kept my eyes on the road. The serene five-hour float down the river hadn't eased the tension from the town meeting or the sting of Sally's death. I was downhearted, and Chris knew it. When he shrugged and gazed out the window, I got the sense that he didn't want to add insult to injury.

I'd spoken with Gigi by cell phone. With the help of Lick and her sisterfriends, she had spent most of Sunday replanting the welcome garden with camellias and knock-out roses. In honor of Mama and Sally, they'd put in two new willow trees, one on each side of the welcome sign. I thought about how the willow trees symbolized Sally's close relationship with Mama. It wasn't just Sally that I mourned; it was also the loss of a living link to Mama and my past—a link severed forever.

I thought about what I often advised clients when they were going through a rough patch: *An ending is a beginning in disguise. When you say goodbye to one thing, you're saying hello to something else.* My own advice didn't console me, though. I didn't know about Bobby-Cy, but I didn't relish the idea of being linked through our old man, even though having a half-brother was a new beginning. I only hoped Bobby-Cy would see it that way.

We drove by stately old Victorian homes with lush green manicured lawns. Once we crossed over the railroad tracks, the houses got smaller, more run-down. Mobile homes dotted the landscape. When we passed Madge's Mess, I frowned.

Chris noticed. "What's wrong?"

"I was thinking about Gigi and what she's going through right now."

"Oh." He squeezed my hand.

I realized how fortunate I was. I didn't have to worry about money even if my practice dried up. Gigi's father had squandered the family fortune, except for a trust fund set aside for my mama, his only grandchild. After her death, Mama'd left it to me. It sent me through school. The royalty money from my book sales supplemented the trust.

"I have to say that I was dead wrong about one thing." Chris shook his head and showed his perfectly straight white teeth behind a smile.

I turned toward him. "What's that?"

"For a small town, Whitecross has a lot of action. Shit, I just got here and already there's talk of a homicide, slander, larceny, and a sudden death. Makes you wonder what's coming next."

I nodded, exchanging glances with Chris amid another long uncomfortable silence that had fallen between us.

Bryan E. Robinson

★ ★ ★ ★ ★

As we pulled into my driveway, a light mist hung over the Suwannee behind the simple cabin that looked as if it had been swallowed by the dark. It seemed emptier, quieter than usual. It was lit only by bright moonbeams that streamed through the trees, casting shiny fingers across the roofline onto the porch.

I turned off the ignition, stared at the small house, reflected on how I loved the place. The cabin sat backward; the front door faced the river. The back kitchen door faced the sandy road and circular drive. A privet hedge, which Gigi and I had planted, crowded up against both ends of the porch.

When I stepped out of the car, I felt my shoes sink into the soft white sand. A soggy breeze carried the damp scent of the river. Arm-in-arm, Chris and I ambled up the walkway, another project with Gigi. We climbed the steps through daggers of moonlight jutting across the porch.

I froze when I saw the screen door propped open, the front door ajar.

"That's weird." Chris paused too; his arms dropped against his hips.

I stuck my head through the opening. The refrigerator door hung open, spilling a ribbon of light across knives, spoons, and forks that had been dumped from kitchen drawers, strewn over the floor. I reached for the light switch inside by the door, flipped it on. We stepped into the kitchen. It had been ransacked, left in complete disarray. A vinegary smell floated above the faint odor of warm food. Cabinet doors stood half-shut. Plastic containers and pots and pans littered countertops. I scanned the den. It looked as if the entire house had been torn apart.

"Shit, we've been robbed!" Chris cried.

"Probably looking for drugs."

"I told you we should've locked up." Chris stormed through

the den into the bedroom. "Oh, my God! Brad, come look at this."

As I tore through the den, I noticed sofa cushions tossed onto the floor, side table drawers turned upside down. Emptied. I stepped into the bedroom where clothes, jerked from the closet, cluttered the room.

Chris held his wallet in the palm of his hand, his lips flat-lined. "I can't believe this. They pulled off the mattress and dumped the contents of my briefcase. They left my laptop and wallet with a hundred-dollar bill and two twenties on top of the nightstand."

I glided my palms across my face. "This wasn't the work of burglars, Chris."

"You got that right, Brother Boy." The looming voice from behind caused me to jerk.

"Damn, Bobby-Cy, you scared the shit out of me! What the hell are you doing here?"

Bobby-Cy stood in the doorway. He shifted his weight, leaned against the doorjamb, tipped his hat in his customary manner. Then he crossed one leg over the other, hooked his thumbs in his belt loops, and eyeballed me up and down. "I'll ask the questions from here on out."

"What the fuck are you talking about?" I faced him, hands tightly clenched into fists.

There was no mistaking the alarm in Chris's voice. "Brad, what's going on?"

Bobby-Cy hiked his eyes at Chris. "He's in a shitload of trouble." Then his knitted eyebrows scrunched up, fell back in my direction, hard eyes penetrating me. "You lied."

"What?" My body surged with electricity. "Is this a joke?"

"Humph. We found a glove that matches the one from the crime scene, lying out in plain sight on your kitchen counter."

"I found that glove on the floor in my doorway. I have no

idea where it came from or how it got there."

His flat face and terse tone left little doubt of what he thought of my explanation. "Yeah, seems to me you might be a lot more like *your* daddy than I thought."

"What the fuck is going on, Bobby-Cy?" My voice quivered.

"We found the knife that cut Big Jake's rope in your kitchen drawer, too."

"What?" A tectonic shift rocked my insides. "That's impossible."

"Tell that to the forensics lab. They did a rush job on the knife and found rope fibers in the blade matchin' the fibers in Big Jake's guideline."

Chris dropped onto the box springs. "For fuck's sake, Brad. What have you done?"

Bobby-Cy looked at me. "There's no easy way to say this." As he pulled out a piece of paper, the words *under arrest* slipped through one side of his mouth. "You have the right to remain silent. Anything you say can and will be used against you in a court of law. You have the right to have an attorney present during questionin' . . ."

A bolt of horror ripped through me. "Wait, this is a big misunderstanding!"

He ignored my plea. "Put your hands behind your back." As he moved toward me, his voice was as calm and steady as his hands. I heard a loud click and felt the tight clench of cold handcuffs around my wrists.

"If you cannot afford an attorney, one will be appointed for you. Do you understand these rights?"

"Yes." I panted. I heaved. I clenched my teeth. "But you've got the wrong guy. Somebody set me up."

"You must think I'm a goddamned idiot." As he frisked me, his eyes dilated, face reddened, voice spiked. "You move down here with your slick city ways and think we're a bunch of dumb-ass rednecks. Don't fuck with me, Brad. I'll roast your ass."

"Jesus fucking Christ, I swear I did not kill Big Jake!"

He confiscated my wallet and car keys. "You can keep your cell phone until we get to the jail."

My eyes searched the carpet, trying to make sense out of what was happening. At first Bobby-Cy's anger had smeared my nose in my own words. Then, for an instant, his face softened, voice cracked, disheartened. "I thought I'd found a big brother I could look up to." Then he took on a calloused tone again. "Man, this has been one big cluster fuck. Two arrests in one week."

It seemed he was holding disappointment at arm's length, as if crusting his feelings would help him carry out his duties. It reminded me of *me*—the way I'd dealt with heartbreak my whole life. On the other hand, perhaps the psychologist in me was simply diving too deeply, projecting my own personal longing.

In the end, it didn't matter. He had marginalized me as if I were a common criminal. Just another day's work. The fact that he associated me in his head with Myrtle Badger made me want to puke.

I pushed aside my own wishful thinking, looked down at Chris. "I'm so sorry."

Chris stood—tall, strong, calm—and squeezed my shoulder. "Where's your cell? I'll call Gigi."

"It's in my right pocket." I trembled.

Chris's hand dove into my pocket, hooking my cell, his eyes swirling with a blend of concern and confusion "Don't worry. We'll get you out."

Bobby-Cy's eyebrows hunched together. Then they fell into a straight line. It was a look that said, *Oh, now I get it.*

"I'd hoped I wouldn't have to do this, Brother Boy." His voice seemed to carry a tinge of regret.

Or was it wishful thinking again? It was hard to tell.

I saw Chris push speed dial, his back to me as he disappeared into the bathroom, slamming the door. Bobby-Cy's massive hand wound around my biceps, swept me through the front door. When we stepped into the moonlight, his gigantic shadow did a wicked dance alongside us down the walkway to the police cruiser. He pushed firmly but gently down on my head, arching my body into the back seat.

No flashing lights. No newspaper hyenas. No crowds or big-city hullabaloo.

Inside the patrol car, the seats were grungy. It smelled of sweat and cigarette butts.

I suddenly felt dirty myself.

It was eerily quiet—quiet enough for me to hear my own banging heartbeat inside my chest, the roaring thoughts in my head. *I can't believe this is happening. Maybe I'm having trouble telling the difference between a dream and reality again. God, I hope I'm dreaming.*

As the patrol car pulled away, I angled my head back at Chris, standing on the porch, phone at his ear, mouthing something, waving me away.

I blew out a bolt of air between my lips.

We hit a bump in the road. Bobby-Cy grunted.

This was no dream.

It had the sour taste and the one-two-stomach-punch of stark, cold reality.

CHAPTER 31

Morning light, stretching through the boxy wire-mesh window, scattered a checkerboard design across the grimy floor of the jail cell. I lay on the bed, hands behind my head, examining the scuff marks streaked on the drab, mustard-colored walls. It occurred to me that that alone would be enough to drive someone criminally insane. Before the hard-slamming metal doors had snatched my freedom, I had been strip-searched and fingerprinted the previous evening.

I'd never been behind bars, had never even seen a jail cell except on TV shows like *Boston Legal* and *Law and Order*. On screen, you couldn't smell the stagnant commode stench mixed with the heavy aroma of Pine-Sol or feel the stone-hard bed that squeaked every time I turned during the night. When I had dozed, the drunk in the cell beside me yelled obscenities or rattled the bars to his cage. I had finally given up on sleep; my head staggered with drowsy thoughts that I'd tried to stitch together.

At first I had felt like a fish swimming upstream. But then I remembered a passage from my book: "The challenge before you is never greater than the power within you." It brought me a sense of peace and clarity. As the misery began to evaporate, everything began to crystallize. I had an aha moment. If I were a religious man, I'd say it was God speaking to me.

When the revelation crashed down on me, my eyes had flashed open. I sat straight up on the side of the hard, squeaky bed. It started with a snort, then a snicker bubbled up inside me—a bubble of relief, more of a cathartic understanding than one of joy. Then I lost it, an uncontrollable crescendo of delirious laughter. I held my stomach and hooted. I wiped my hands over my face, exhaled a huge sigh of relief. The glove, the knife containing the rope fibers, the patient who caused me to miss my dive lesson with Big Jake, even the motive had aligned in one big harmonic convergence. I couldn't believe I hadn't seen it.

Without a shadow of a doubt, I knew who'd murdered Big Jake. But I had to get the proof before I could tell. My credibility had been compromised. Any attempt by me to identify the murderer would be viewed with skepticism, as a desperate stab to get myself off the hook. I had threaded the needle. Before revealing what I knew, I would have to sew everything up.

Bobby-Cy appeared outside my jail cell, rattling keys, rolling his tongue around inside his cheek, as if he'd just had breakfast.

"Heard you howling. Sleep okay?" His tone sounded genuine.

My response was more on the sarcastic side. "Like a baby."

He opened the cell door, leaving it ajar, plopped down on the bed in front of me. "We gotta talk."

I swung my socked feet off the bed onto the floor. "What's up?"

"Your grandmamma and Chris are bailin' you out. Smiley helped them retain a lawyer."

"Oh man, that's great news." I stood, eyes searching the bare cellblock walls. "Where are they?"

"In my office." He took off his hat, scanned the floor. He swiped at his blond hair, motioned for me to sit back down.

I slumped onto the bed and looked at him. "What is it?"

He sounded sincere. "Now, you know that you don't have to talk to me. But your fingerprints are all over that kitchen knife with rope fibers from Big Jake's guideline. They're DNA-testin' the tissue samples you threw in my trash can last week."

"Tissue samples?"

"The tissues you used the day you were sweating bullets in my office. Forensics said the results should be back from Tallahassee tomorrow. If there's a DNA match with the glove from the crime scene, you're dead meat."

"Yeah, the vultures are already circling." I rubbed my neck and matched his eyes. "I know what I'm up against."

"I want to help you, if I can. I'm gonna give you one last chance to level with me. You say you have an alibi. I need the name of the patient who caused you to miss the dive lesson with Big Jake."

I leaned forward, rested my elbows on my knees, stared him down. "Why would you want to help me? You're the one who threw me in this shithole."

"I got a job to do . . . Hell, I don't know . . ." He snaked his head as if that would help him push out the words. "Shit, you're the only blood-kin I got left. For some reason, I'm wonderin' if maybe you *were* framed. But I gotta confirm your alibi before I'm willin' to gamble on you."

"First, I have a question for you. Have you seen Wilma-May Church at your AA meetings lately?"

"AA stands for Alcoholics *Anonymous*. We don't blab."

"Yeah, I know. I'm bound by ethics, too. Anonymity has us both hog-tied."

"You're speakin' code, Brother Boy. Are you sayin' it *was* Wilma-May?"

"I didn't say that."

"Okay, forewarned is forearmed." He threw up his hands; his face hardened as he stood. "If you're not goin' to tell me, then there's nothin' else I can do."

I rubbed my palms together and thought for a shadow of a second. "Tell you what, if you're willing to take a gamble on me, I'm willing to risk losing my license instead of frying for a crime I didn't commit. I'll answer your question, if you'll answer mine."

"Okay, shoot."

"When was the last time you saw Wilma-May at an AA meeting?"

As he sat back down, his brows furrowed. "We belong to the same AA home group in Lake City. Saw her at a meetin' one night last week. Why?"

"Has she fallen off the wagon recently?"

"That's two questions. You don't get but one."

"Answer me, goddamn it. How long has she been sober?"

Startled by my forcefulness, he quickly complied. "She led the meetin' last week. Picked up a blue chip. She's been clean for ten fuckin' years! What the hell are you drivin' at?"

I could feel the smile cracking my lips apart. "I knew it."

"What?"

"On the afternoon of the dive lesson, I was in the middle of throwing my dive gear in the back of my car when Gigi and her sisterfriends showed up unannounced. They had Wilma-May in tow. Said she'd relapsed, that church elders had caught her drunk, stealing from the collection plate. They pleaded with me to postpone my dive lesson and lead an intervention to get her into rehab. So I did."

He took off his hat, scratched his head. I could see the genuineness in his eyes as he spoke. "That's a little too coincidental, don't you think? That the WPC would have an emergency right when you were meetin' up with Big Jake for a dive? And then he ends up murdered? I might not be a psychologist, but even I know you don't intervene on somebody with a recovery program as strong as Wilma-May's. You've been had, Brother Boy."

"I know that now. When I started thinking back on it in the

middle of the night, I realized what a dumb-shit I'd been. After about a half an hour, Wilma-May still had refused to go for treatment. And the sisterfriends had dropped the whole matter as if it hadn't been a problem to begin with. 'Maybe we overreacted,' Betty-Jewel said. Then Gigi piped up with, 'Well, let's just let sleeping dogs lie.' I should've known, but I dismissed it, too, because I was itching to go diving and was already late for the lesson. The sisterfriends left my office with Gigi saying, 'Sorry you had to miss your dive lesson. Maybe you can go another time.' "

"You're not suggestin' that Wilma-May or the club sisters . . ."

"Oh, hell no. Gladys knew Big Jake was coming after me. She called Gigi the morning of the dive to tell her. They were just holding me there to keep me out of harm's way. Somebody else cut the line."

"So whoever that was framed you, huh?"

I stood. "I don't want to say anymore right now. I just want to get out of here."

"Okay, but remember, I'll be watchin' over your shoulder and verifyin' that story with Wilma-May and your grand-mamma. One more lie and you're back in the slammer."

"I know, I know. You have a job to do."

"All right, then. Let's go into my office and get your belon-gin's, and you're a free man . . . at least for now."

"Thank you." I bit down on the phrase *free man* as if it was a piece of homemade key-lime pie.

When I walked into Bobby-Cy's office, Gigi and Chris threw their arms around me.

"Son, you all right?" Gigi's scratchy voice sounded as if she'd been wounded to the core. She looked haggard. Thin. Ashen. Her disheveled hair, flat face, puffy eyes made her look ten years older than her seventy-three years.

Chris looked tired, too. The skin around his eyes loose and darkened. He was still in last night's clothes, his speech sluggish. "Gigi and I . . . up all night talking . . . she told me about you and Big Jake . . . I had no idea you'd been going through . . ."

"Well, she told *you* more than she told *me*." The hard edge in my voice said it all—that I'd figured out that Wilma-May's intervention had been a farce.

Gigi stared off sheepishly into space, saying only, "Just trying to do what I thought was right, son."

I wrapped my arms around them, pulled them into either side of me. I had my psychologist face on. And it was real.

Through a genuine smile, I reassured Chris as much as I could. "Don't worry."

"Don't worry?" He smoothed his hand over his hair, shrugged. "You're jailed for murder, and you tell me not to worry?"

Gigi shot me a quizzical look, her voice drawn. "What're you gonna do now?"

With a hard squeeze, I looked her squarely in the eyes. "This is not a problem. It's a situation. Remember? You can't do anything about a problem, but you can fix a situation."

Chris and Gigi eyed each other and then glanced back at me. Before they could get a word out, I said, "And I have a plan."

CHAPTER 32

Inside the church a huge wooden cross hung above the altar. Underneath the cross, Sally was laid out in an open coffin of metallic-blue aluminum, lined on the inside with quilted white satin. Her hands were crossed over her purple-laced dress, her stunning gray hair swept back; a smile of contentment lit her face.

Pink roses and a myriad of flower arrangements lined the aisles and adorned the altar. Antioch Baptist Church was not Sally's church. Sally didn't go to church, but her children did. It was their wish that the funeral be held here. I expect it wouldn't matter much to Sally one way or another. The pews were only half full, but it was still fifteen minutes before the service. I had come early because I had wanted to pay my last respects to her alone.

I stared into the casket. The solemn organ music unearthed a swell of boyhood memories, rivulets of tears tumbling down my cheeks. I thought about all the times Alvin Dukes and I had fled from Sally, choking on our own breath. I remembered when Alvin took me to dig up his dead sister whom he insisted was still alive. One night we dragged shovels to the old cemetery, found an empty grave that he claimed was hers. When he saw the empty hole, the freshly dugsoil piled to one side, he squealed, "Voodoo Sally beat us to it. The witch has already got her!" And we lit out of the graveyard, heaving the shovels into the air behind us. Later, I found out Alvin didn't even have a sister, much less a dead one. That grave had been dug for a funeral the next day.

I spied the flowers that Chris and I had sent, placed in a wire stand beside the casket. A purple sash crossed the Lilies of the Valley with the words *evol wanga obeah* silk-screened into it. I reflected on what those words meant: *Love is the strongest medicine*. I thought about all those times Preacher Abrams had tried to *scare the bad out of me* and *beat the love of Jesus into me*. And all those times Sally had tried to *draw the love out of me* and *scare the bad away from me*.

Sally had helped me see how backward life can be. She'd turned the whole idea of good and bad around. Evil resides in those who've had it beaten into them; love resides in us naturally. Just as limestone surrenders to the Suwannee without resistance, folks overcome hardships by accepting what they can't control and changing what they can. That's where real strength comes from.

I thought of Mama, Gigi, even Johnny and how central Sally had been to my life without my realizing it. She had helped Mama bring me into the world. While I was away at school, she had ministered to Gigi, protected Mama from Johnny. She had earned a special place in my heart.

Without warning, a strong hand from behind clamped down on my shoulder. My heart tilted. I jerked my head around.

"Hey sport, how ya doin'?" It was Bobby-Cy.

"Okay, what's up?" I noticed how handsome he looked in a brown sports coat and blue-and-yellow striped tie instead of his usual sheriff's uniform.

With a somber look in his eyes, he nodded toward a quiet corner of the church. I followed him. "Got the forensics report back from Tallahassee this mornin'."

I stuck my index finger inside my shirt collar, pulled on it hard, loosened the scratchy material from my neck. "And?

What'd it say?"

"I think *you* know, Brother Boy."

"Know what?"

"That you're innocent. The fingerprints and DNA on the knife matched yours. That makes sense because you used it. But the DNA inside the glove didn't match up. Looks like you *were* framed after all."

"No, I *wasn't* framed. After I left jail, I did some digging, and I can tell you without a doubt who the murderer is."

"Oh yeah?" His voice had a skeptical ring to it. "So who's our man?"

Before I could answer, up walked Alvin Dukes, whom I hadn't seen since I was a boy. "You're a sight for sore eyes, Brad." He slapped me on the back, pumped my hand like there was no tomorrow. "I was hopin' you'd be here."

Though I didn't want to pull out of my conversation with Bobby-Cy, Alvin didn't give me much choice. He wound his arm around my shoulder, detoured me aside to reminisce. Remember the time when we did this and that, he said, retracing a volume of memories. Dressed in a blue suit, white shirt, and red tie, he looked like the banker he'd become. After telling me he lived over in Jasper and was president of Florida Safety Bank, he pulled at his chin. "Remember that time me and you went to the Alimar and saw that scary movie? What was the name of it?"

"*The Shining* with Jack Nicholson," I said.

"That's it." He hitched his belt up above his potbelly. "Every time I eat Raisinets and popcorn, I think of Jack Nicholson stalkin' through that house with an ax."

"Yeah, and on the way home we had to walk by a cemetery. We both pretended to be so brave."

"Talk about whistlin' past the graveyard." He snickered, straightened his tie.

"Yeah and then you said, 'I wonder what Voodoo Sally's doing tonight?' We both took off running to beat the band."

He looked over at the coffin. "We had a lot of fun with that old witch, didn't we?"

"Old witch?" I looked over at Sally.

Shame seared through my heart for the many times I, too, had demonized her. She'd spent her life taking care of others, particularly me. Even in the mosquito mist, she'd only wanted to protect Alvin and me. It was the rest of us who had made her into something wicked—a fear we carried inside ourselves, put there by our own upbringing.

"Brad? You all right?" He whistled under his breath.

My eyes fell back on him. "She wasn't a witch, Alvin. She was a good-hearted woman. This town had her all wrong. We were pretty hard on her."

"Eh, we were kids." A sharp edge in his voice rejected an acceptance of the true Sally. With a flip of the hand, he continued down memory lane. "Remember the time—"

I interrupted him. "I got to know Sally for the loving woman she really was."

"Loving woman?" Alvin chuckled, reined his neck in like an accordion, then inspected my face as if I was half crazy. "You shitin' me? She was a witch doctor. Everybody knew that."

"Then why are you here?"

"Old times' sake. To see you, have a few laughs, make sure the old witch is really dead." He rocked back on his heels, jiggling loose change in his pockets; his lips slithered into a shit-eating grin.

I recoiled. I felt a distance between us wider than the Everglades. "Excuse me, Alvin. It's good seeing you, but I need to have a word with my brother."

"Brother?" He looked astonished. "I never knew you had . . ."

I had walked away before he could finish, left him tugging at the pants that had fallen below his belly. The disappointment that rose up in me was salved by that old reminder, "Nostalgia is a seductive liar."

The sanctuary was beginning to fill up. The choir had started to sing old-timey spirituals.

Heading to sit with Bobby-Cy, I recognized the tune of "There is a Balm in Gilead." I passed Preacher Black walking in the door with wife, Edna. After motioning for her to go ahead and save him a seat, he shook my hand. Since his eyes had been straightened, he looked much younger. For some reason, he was philosophical, appealing to the therapist in me.

"It's funny how I can see clearer since my eye operation," he said, "not just my eyesight, but my insight, too."

I braced my hand on his shoulder, looked at him sideways. "Preacher Black, that's the best sermon you ever delivered."

He smiled with appreciation, and we parted ways. I had to climb over a few people to sandwich myself in the walnut pew between Chris and Bobby-Cy. They had already grabbed a place beside the two lovebirds, Gigi and Smiley Bishop, who were holding hands.

After Chris steadied my arm to help me over knees and feet, I whispered in Bobby-Cy's ear. "You're not going to believe this."

"Try me," he said, speaking under his breath.

I kept my voice down, too. "At first, I wondered if it might've been Myrtle Badger. Big Jake rejected her advances, made fun of her. Plus, she was hell on wheels when she didn't get her way. But it wasn't Myrtle. She didn't have a real motive."

"I could've told you that. That's old news. Is that all you got?"

"Just wait." I lifted my hand. "Willard McCullers had a motive, though, because he was always stuck in Big Jake's shadow."

"Yep, but he had an alibi. I checked him out right at the start."

"Right. Then it dawned on me when I was in jail that . . ."

Bobby-Cy rolled his eyes, poked me in the ribs, lowered his voice. "Will you stop the cat-and-mouse shit." When I hesitated, his voice went up a few octaves over the church music. "Just tell me."

Necks craned. Heads turned our way.

Gigi leaned forward and glared at us through tears. When she made a slashing motion against her throat with her knobby scepter, I noticed a diamond engagement ring on her finger. I'd have to wait until after the service to finish my conversation with Bobby-Cy.

I shook my head from side to side and smiled. Gigi shushed me for a change, and I had the upper hand with Bobby-Cy. After the traumatic arrest and night in jail, a tiny part of me enjoyed the idea of keeping him in the dark. And I was confident enough in my own innocence that I could afford to do that.

The minister had begun the service with the apt theme of "Reap What You Sow," his voice loud and steady. "Life is not lost by dying." His words resounded through the little chapel. "Life is lost by not living fully. Serena Angeles Cutter, our beloved Sally, lived her life to the fullest."

LaKeshia, Sally's hollow-eyed daughter, turned around and gaped at me from the front row several times during the service. I didn't know what was up with her, but it caused me to self-consciously gaze down at the funeral memorial that I unwadded from my suit pocket. The front of the memorial had a drawing of an opened Bible resting in front of a cross. Below the drawing were the words: *Homegoing for Serena Angeles Cutter 1931–2012: Interment in Antioch Cemetery.*

After the brief sermon, Gigi, LaKeshia, and several family members eulogized Sally. I panned the congregation, reflecting on how, in one way or another, Sally had brought all of us together. After the discovery of Johnny's bones and the Founder's Day debacle, Bobby-Cy had cleared Gigi and her sisterfriends. And the WPC opened up club membership to Edna, Ibejean, and Sylvia. Instead of sitting together in a clump, the sisterfriends had broken away from the herd, spread out over the sanctuary.

Ibejean sat between Wilma-May and Betty-Jewel. Even though she mashed her glasses back on her nose several times, Betty-Jewel didn't yawn once. In fact, I saw her wipe away a tear or two. Now that Swayze had lost his credibility with the town, Betty-Jewel was a shoo-in for the vacant town council seat.

Instead of staring down at the floor, Gladys sat in a front pew with son, Rufus, and held her head up, dabbing her eyes. With Doodle nuzzled by her side, Jackie huddled quietly in back of the church, apparently content with husband and career now that her dance school had started to take off again.

Shirley—who sat with her daughter and Sylvia Wynn—seemed more interested in gabbing with her new friend than in primping makeup and hair. Gigi had told me that Shirley and Sylvia planned to start a local support group for people on anxiety medication. Gigi had finally found a respectable man she could trust, a man who would take care of *her* for a change.

As for me, sitting with my new brother, my life partner, a beloved grandma, and a thousand-watt smiling, soon-to-be step-granddad made me realize how Whitecross had stretched me into finding a real life for myself.

After the eulogies, the choir led with the hymn, "Swing Low, Sweet Chariot," and the congregation followed.

We stood and sang, clapped blissfully, swung and swayed back and forth. Then a tambourine chimed in, built the jubilance into a foot-stomping crescendo. At first, I thought that the floor would collapse and the walls would burst open. But they didn't. Everybody smiled, laughed, rejoiced, just the way Sally would've wanted it.

As we filed out of the sanctuary, I bumped into Wilma-May coming down the church steps.

"Well, hello, good doctor," she said. "Wasn't that a beautiful service?"

"Yes it was. And you look fetching in that apricot-colored dress."

"You ain't no slouch yourself." With a mischievous glint in her eye, she put her hand over her mouth and spoke softly through it. "I got this dress shoplifting years ago. When I got sober, I made amends, went back and paid for it."

My eyebrows shot up, and I couldn't resist asking her. "So I understand you've stopped shoplifting, but how are you doing with the drinking since my intervention with you?"

She blushed, lifted her head into a wide arc to make sure no one was listening. Then she stammered. "Bobby-Cy . . . he asked me about that . . . Shoot, I knew we couldn't pull the wool over your eyes. I haven't had a drop in years. I'm sorry I misled you, doctor. After Gladys told the WPC what Big Jake was up to, I had to go along with the sisterfriends. We couldn't afford to have more blood on our hands, especially yours."

"I understand." I nodded. "Appreciate your concern."

"By the way, doctor, would you autograph my copy of your book?" She thrust the copy in my direction.

"Be happy to." I signed the book and continued down the steps.

"Oh, by the way." She tugged at my coat sleeve. "After what happened on Founder's Day, Ibejean hired me back to page-turn for her and the Glory Bees." She smacked her palms together. "I can't wait."

I smiled. "Make sure I get an autographed copy of the CD when it comes out."

"You bet your sweet behind I will."

As she descended the steps, the book poked out from under her arm. My eye caught the words, *Property of Whitecross Public Library* imprinted on the spine. I chuckled, thinking, *At least she's still sober.*

I shook my head and breezed across the churchyard to my car where I retrieved a purple-velvet box. A color palette of magenta and red tinged a rainbow across the August sky, a memento from a short thunderstorm that brewed during the funeral service. Fast-moving, puffy clouds hung so low I felt like I could almost touch them.

Then I joined Chris, Bobby-Cy, Smiley, and Gigi under a huge shade tree. We watched Sally's casket roll down the steps and slide into the white hearse. LaKeshia, who'd been eyeing me during the service, broke away from her family, walked up to me. She handed me a sealed, cantaloupe-colored envelope.

"I found this in Mama's personal things." She flicked at her Diana Ross hair, stared through me. "It's addressed to you."

"Thank you." I saw the same lakes of beauty in her large emerald eyes that I'd seen in Sally's. "Sorry about your mama. She was a wonderful woman. We'll miss her."

A smiling LaKeshia turned and walked away. She looked back over her shoulder at me as she climbed into the black limo that would carry her and two sisters to the graveyard. As the car whined into the distance, her eyes followed me from the back window until she disappeared behind a hazy steam rising from the pavement. Her gaze had reminded me of how Sally used to look *inside* of me instead of *at* me.

I ripped the envelop open and slipped out two pieces of folded paper. One appeared to be some kind of scribbling. I read it first:

If you can't surrender to life's hard knocks, you're like the limestone arguing with the Suwannee. When a river comes up to a stone, do you think the stone spends all its time trying to push the water back? No siree. The limestone yields as the Suwannee encompasses it and becomes one with the rushing water. The Suwannee carves the limestone into shapes and images, and it becomes a feature of the river. In time, the limestone becomes a smooth, well-polished cavern. And the strength of its true character is revealed. That's limestone gumption.

The second sheet was a thoughtful handwritten letter addressed to me:

Dear Brad:

By the time you read this letter, I will be passed on to the next life. They say the truth sets you free. I'm writing this to set us both free. I had to hold to the promise I made to your mama to keep you safe. Like I told you, Big Jake was coming after you, son.

After what Gladys told me and after I overheard him bragging in the Piggly Wiggly that you wouldn't make it to Founder's Day, I had to do something. I couldn't stand idly by and let him squash one more human spirit. I was afraid you would want to go after him too. I wasn't just protecting you from him, but you from yourself. We all killed Big Jake. We killed him in our hearts a million times. The only difference is I cut the rope.

I'm putting this letter in my safe keepins box with my important papers for my daughters to pass on to you after I'm gone. I always thought of you as the son I never had. I hope you will understand and find it in your heart to forgive me.

> *Love,*
> *Serena Angeles Cutter*

My heart skittered into my throat, then into my stomach before settling back into my chest. *Forgive you?* I thought. *Can you forgive me?*

I felt a strange unburdening, relief that something was

complete, an inner peace that I hadn't felt before.

Bobby-Cy had been trying to read over my shoulder. I blocked his view by pulling the letter into my chest. When I had finished reading it, I pulled him aside from the others and handed it over to him. "This is what you've been looking for. It proves my innocence."

His eyes skimmed the letter. "Well, I be damned, so that's our man, huh? Serena Angeles Cutter, a.k.a. Voodoo Sally." He cocked his head at me. "How'd you know, Brother Boy?"

"That night in jail I couldn't sleep, so I started thinking back about a nightmare I'd had that seemed more than real. An apparition was standing over me, waving its black leather hand, staring down at me. The next day I found a red pouch on my door handle and a single leather glove on the floor. It was Sally. She must've worn the glove to cut through the woods and dropped it in the den."

"What the hell was she wavin' over your face?"

"Sally had her own brand of medicine that keeps people safe. Probably some kind of incantation."

His eyebrows dipped. "Incantation? That's some weird shit. No wonder folks called her a witch."

"Maybe not, Bobby-Cy. Believe it or not, some of it works."

"So that was part of her protection plan she mentions in the letter?" He scratched his head. "How about the kitchen knife?"

"Since I hadn't seen the knife you took, I figured it *was* one of mine. Until that night in jail, it hadn't occurred to me that it was the knife Sally had given me. After she'd been leaving pouches on my doorknob, I trailed her home one night. Had it out with her. I was cut up pretty bad by the woods. Before I left her house, she gave me a serrated knife. Naturally, you found my fingerprints and DNA on it because I used it to hack the briars and sticker bushes. When I got home, I left it on the kitchen counter. Never thought any more about it."

"So the glove and knife both belonged to Sally?"

"That's right. After I got out of jail, I went back to her house, rifled through her kitchen drawers, and found this." I handed Bobby-Cy the purple box. "It's a set of matching serrated knives like the one she gave me. There are six knife slots, one of which is empty. When you test the glove, I guarantee you'll find a DNA match with Sally."

"Damn, for somebody who was tryin' to protect you, she got you into a shitload of trouble."

"It's one of those paradoxes. In a way it's one of the best things that's ever happened to me. In a strange sort of way, it strengthened me."

Bobby-Cy looked puzzled. "That's a head scratcher. I'll have to think on that one."

"Always said Sally was a life saver—in more ways than one." Gigi had walked up behind us, obviously had overheard our conversation. Her eyes crinkled as she winked at me. "Glad that's all settled. Now who's gonna join Smiley and me for lunch at Glenda's?"

"I'm game," Bobby-Cy said. "My stomach was growlin' through the whole service."

"I could eat a horse," Chris said.

"We'll meet you there." Gigi threaded her hand through Smiley's open arm, headed toward the church parking lot.

After agreeing to drive, I looked at Chris and Bobby-Cy. "Ready to roll?"

Bobby-Cy slapped his arm around my left shoulder and Chris my right. The three of us ambled to my car. A hound dog poked his head out of the cracked window from the back seat. When we opened the car doors, he welcomed us with a deep-throated bark.

Bobby-Cy stiffened, stepped back. "Whose dog is that?"

"It's okay," I said. "He's an old friend."

Chris climbed in back, put his arm around the dog. Bobby-Cy slipped in the front passenger's seat. While I started the engine, Bobby-Cy checked out the dog. "What's his name?"

"I named him Gumption," I said. "When I went back to Sally's to inspect that set of knives, he moseyed over and licked my boots. He'd lost a lot of weight. Looked like nobody'd been feeding him. He lay on his back, stuck his feet in the air, looked up at me. I scratched his belly, and that was all it took, so I brought him home."

Bobby-Cy reached in back and rubbed the mutt's head. "Hey there, Gumption. How ya doin', boy?"

On the drive to Glenda's, we passed the *Welcome to Whitecross* sign. I thought about the first time I had seen it on the drive into town and how proud I'd felt when I read the words, *The Women's Preservation Club*. This time I felt pride, too, but I noticed something different about the sign. A barely visible bronze plaque swung at the bottom, brushing the tops of pink camellias and red knock-out roses. I pulled to the side of the road, so we could read it. *Here Lies One of Our War Dead Who Fought for His Country.*

It wasn't the Confederate dead. But it would satisfy Whitecross's need to know whose bones had been reburied on that site, at least as long as Bobby-Cy was sheriff. Johnny received anonymous credit for his tour of Vietnam, Gigi and her sister-friends got off the hook, and I connected with a brother I never knew I had.

When he saw the plaque, Bobby-Cy shot me one of his crooked smiles. Chris leaned forward from the back seat, put his chin on the front headrest. "Those are some of the most exquisite flowers I've ever seen." He rolled down the window. "Umm, and that sweet smell. Wonder what they used for fertilizer?"

I twisted my head toward Chris and grinned. "It's an old

family secret."

I swapped glances with Bobby-Cy but not before bursting out laughing. Then he fisted me on the arm like a little brother would. I found life's irony amusing, and for that reason alone, I trusted the smile that lingered on my lips. Whitecross had taken from me *and* had given back: a half-brother, loving grandma, and life partner.

In that moment, I envisioned my life stretched before me and trusted that the future would be okay. I thought again about the adage, "An ending is a beginning in disguise," and realized that's where we start from.

I also realized I'd found my beginning back in a place where once I'd thought my life had ended.

And my heart did a little soft-shoe.

THE WOMEN'S PRESERVATION CLUB RECIPES

"Murder is always a mistake . . . One should never do anything that one cannot talk about after dinner." Oscar Wilde, *The Picture of Dorian Gray*

GIGI'S MERCENARY MESS OF CHICKEN AND DUMPLINGS

(To die for)

4 chicken breasts or 6 chicken thighs or a mixture of each (dark meat adds more flavor than white)
6 cups water
6–8 chicken bouillon cubes or more to taste
1 tbsp. coarse ground black pepper
1 heaping tbsp. vegetable shortening
1 1/2 cups self-rising flour

Cook chicken in water and bouillon cubes and pepper until tender. Cool chicken and take meat off bone. Save seasoned water. Let water simmer and add de-boned chicken to the water. Mix shortening and flour together into a ball. Roll out into flat round dough as thin or thick as you like. Cut dough into thin strips. Add to simmering broth one at a time. You may use spoon or move dough around but **don't stir.** Stirring will cause the dough to break. Cook until dough is done to taste. Serves 6–8.

WILMA-MAY'S WHACKY BEAN SALAD
(It'll save your soul)

1 (14.05 oz.) can cut green beans
1 (14.05 oz.) can French-style green beans
1 (14.05 oz.) can red kidney beans
1 (14.05 oz.) can whole kernel shoe-peg corn
1 large jar pimento, chopped
1 cup celery, chopped
1 cup onions, chopped
1 bell pepper, chopped
1 cup apple cider vinegar
1/2 cup sugar (or honey)
1/2 cup vegetable oil
1 tsp. ground black pepper
1/4 tsp. oregano

Drain beans, corn, and pimento and mix together. Add celery, onions, and bell pepper. Heat vinegar, sugar, oil, black pepper, and oregano to boil and let cool to room temperature. Pour over beans. Refrigerate and serve cold. Serves 16–18.

GLADYS'S MANGLED MEATLOAF

(You'll kill for a bite of this)

1 large onion, chopped
1 package fresh mushrooms, chopped
2 lbs. hamburger meat
1 lb. country sausage (Gladys uses the hot flavor)
1 can tomato puree
1/2 cup ketchup
1 1/2 cups seasoned croutons (to bind meat together)
Salt and pepper to taste

Sauté chopped onions and mushrooms until done. Mangle hamburger and sausage together, along with the tomato puree and ketchup. Add croutons and salt and pepper to taste. Mix the mangled meat and sautéed onions and mushrooms together. Form mangled mixture into a loaf. Place on greased-slotted broiling pan. Put topping of ketchup on top of loaf. Cover top with aluminum foil. Bake 1 1/2–2 hours until done at 350 degrees. Take foil off for the last 30 minutes of cooking time. Serves 8–10.

GIGI'S SQUISHY SQUASH CASSEROLE

(You'll feel like you've died and gone to Heaven)

4–6 lbs. yellow squash
1 extra large Vidalia or Texas Sweet onion
6–8 chicken bouillon cubes
1 tbsp. coarse ground black pepper
1–1 1/2 cups seasoned bread crumbs
4 eggs
1/2 cup of sweet milk (whole milk)
1 block extra sharp cheddar cheese, cubed

Cook squash and chopped onions in enough water to cover, along with the chicken bouillon and pepper until tender (about 20–25 minutes). Let cool. Blend in seasoned bread crumbs. Add 4 beaten eggs and the 1/2 cup of milk. Cube cheese and add to mixture, mixing well. Pour mixture into greased 9 × 12 casserole dish or larger if needed. Bake at 375 degrees until golden brown for 30 to 45 minutes. Stays hot for an hour if covered. Serves 8–12.

BETTY-JEWEL'S TURKEY CHILI RECIPE

(It'll sway your vote)

1 tsp. olive oil
1 onion, finely chopped
2 cloves garlic, minced
1 green bell pepper, chopped
1 red bell pepper, chopped
2 tsp. chili powder
3/4 tsp. oregano
3/4 tsp. ground cumin
3/4 tsp. coriander
4 lbs. lean ground turkey
3 (15 oz.) cans diced tomatoes, drained
1 (8 oz.) can tomato sauce
1 (8 oz.) can tomato paste
1/2 tsp. salt
2 tbsp. ground black pepper
2 (15 oz.) cans red kidney beans, drained and rinsed
Grated cheese or sour cream, as needed for garnish

In a large skillet, heat oil over medium heat. Add onions and garlic, sauté for 5 minutes. Stir in bell peppers and sauté another 5 minutes or until all vegetables are soft. Add in the chili powder, oregano, cumin, and coriander. Stir to combine and cook for 1 minute. Add turkey and sauté for 3 minutes, or until meat is no longer pink. Put all ingredients into crock pot. Add diced tomatoes, tomato sauce and tomato paste, salt, and pepper. Gently stir in kidney beans. Cook on low all day, stirring occasionally. Serve with grated cheese or sour cream on top. Serves a congregation.

SHIRLEY'S KNIFE-BLADE POTATO SALAD
(It'll sharpen your taste buds)

10–14 large red potatoes
1 tbsp. salt
1/2 to 1 cup chopped celery
1/2 cup sweet pickle cubes
1/2 cup mayonnaise (or to taste)
1 tbsp. dill weed
1 medium-sized jar diced pimento
Pepper to taste
1–2 tbsp. prepared yellow mustard (optional)

Make sure your knife is good and sharp. Cut potatoes into cubes with peeling left on. Cook with salt in enough water to cover—until slightly soft. Drain and cool for at least 30 minutes. Add celery, pickle cubes, mayonnaise, dill weed, pimento, and more salt and pepper to taste. Yellow mustard to taste. Serves 10–12.

JACKIE'S BLOOD-RED STRAWBERRY-RHUBARB PIE

(So easy there's no blood, sweat, or tears)

3 stalks rhubarb (sliced)
1 cup water
1/2 to 1 cup sugar
6 tsp. cornstarch
4 heaping tbsp. strawberry Jell-O
1 pt. blood-red strawberries (sliced)
1 pie shell browned in the oven
Whipped cream or vanilla ice cream

Cook sliced rhubarb in water until tender. Add sugar, cornstarch, Jell-O. Cook until absorbed. Add sliced strawberries. Mix well. Pour mixture into prepared pie shell. Refrigerate until cool. Add whipped cream or vanilla ice cream to top.

LICK'S (I MEAN RUFUS'S) HICKORY-SMOKED HAMBURGERS

(It'll help you bury your problems)

1 onion
1 tbsp. garlic
4–6 tbsp. olive oil
Salt and pepper to taste
2 lbs. ground beef (chuck)
Charcoal for grill
Hickory chips, soaked

Sauté onion and garlic in olive oil until soft. Add mixture with salt and pepper to ground chuck. Mix well. Make patties to desired size. Heat charcoal for 20–30 minutes. Soak hickory chips in hot water for 30 minutes. Add soaked hickory chips to charcoal. Place chips on each side of grill to avoid flaming. Cook until medium-well. Serves 6–8.

GLENDA'S PULLING-A-FAST-ONE FRIED CHICKEN

(Glenda doesn't put gravy on it, so you can't get duped with this recipe)

1 (3 lb.) frying chicken cut in pieces
3 cups buttermilk
Salt and pepper to taste
3 cups self-rising flour
4–6 cups vegetable oil

Soak chicken in buttermilk in large bowl for 4–6 hours in refrigerator. Drain chicken in colander. Salt and pepper each piece of chicken. Dredge chicken in flour, covering all areas of chicken. Place floured chicken on plate. Pour oil in large skillet, allowing it to become hot at 350 degrees. Add each piece of chicken slowly. Cook until golden brown and tender. Serves 8–10.

Recipes

VASQUE GAYLORD'S RED-VELVET CAKE

(You'll want to broadcast this to all your friends)

1 cup minus 1 tbsp. butter
1 3/4 cup sugar
2 eggs
1 tsp. vanilla
1 tbsp. cocoa
1 tbsp. vinegar
1/2 tsp. salt
1 1/2 tsp. baking soda
2 1/2 cups all-purpose flour
1 cup buttermilk
1 oz. red food coloring

Cream butter and sugar; add eggs and vanilla. Beat well. Make a paste from cocoa and vinegar; add to butter mixture. Sift salt, soda, and flour. Add to mixture alternately with buttermilk and food coloring. Bake in 2 9-inch prepared layer pans. Bake in 375 degree oven 20–25 minutes.

Frosting: 3/4 cup sweet milk, 1 cup coconut, 2 tbsp. flour, 1/2 cup chopped nuts, 3/4 cup butter, 1 tsp. vanilla, 3/4 cup sugar. Cook milk and flour until thick; set aside and cool completely. Mix sugar and butter and beat until fluffy. Add cooled mixture, coconut, nuts, and vanilla. Spread on cooled cake layers.

Brad's Key Lime Pie

(When you bite down on this, it'll set you free)

4 eggs, separated
1 can sweetened condensed milk (14 oz. size)
1 tbsp. butter
Grated rind of 1 lime
1/2 cup fresh-squeezed lime juice
Baked 9-inch pie shell
3 tsp. sugar
1/2 tsp. cream of tartar

Preheat oven to 350 degrees. Beat yolks in a bowl until thick. Add condensed milk, butter, and lime rind and beat until well blended. Gradually add lime juice, mixing well until the custard has thickened. Pour custard in baked pie shell.

Beat egg whites until light and frothy. Slowly add sugar and cream of tartar, beating constantly until stiff. Spread meringue topping on the custard. Bake about 15 minutes or until golden brown. Cool.

GIGI'S SWAMP CABBAGE POT LIQUOR RECIPE

(So good your tongue will want to slap your brains out)
True swamp cabbage comes *only* from the palmetto palm, which grows locally in Florida. But variations can be made with regular cabbage heads or hearts of palm.

3 slices of fat back or bacon
2 tbsp. butter
1/4 cup brown sugar
1 tbsp. salt
1/2 tbsp. freshly ground black pepper
1 large onion
1 tsp. roasted garlic
2 heads freshly cut chopped swamp cabbage (palmetto palm)

In a large frying pan, fry the fat back or bacon over medium heat. Reserve drippings. Combine bacon or fat back drippings with butter, sugar, salt, and black pepper. Heat until butter and sugar are melted. Add onion and roasted garlic. Sauté until onions are translucent. Fill a 6-quart pot 1/2 full of water and bring to a boil. Add swamp cabbage and other ingredients, including fried meat and drippings in the pot. Continue to boil for 10 to 15 minutes, until the cabbage is tender. Serves an army.

DISCUSSION QUESTIONS FOR READING GROUPS

1. The author, Bryan Robinson, begins *Limestone Gumption* with this quote from Voodoo Sally: "If you can't surrender to life's hard knocks, you're like the limestone arguing with the Suwannee. When a river comes up to a stone, do you think the stone spends all its time trying to push the water back? No siree. The limestone yields as the Suwannee encompasses it and becomes one with the rushing water. The Suwannee carves the limestone into shapes and images, and it becomes a feature of the river. In time, the limestone becomes a smooth, well-polished cavern. And the strength of its true character is revealed. That's Limestone Gumption." What do you think Sally means by "Limestone Gumption"? What does it have to do with the way we live our lives? How do you see it threaded throughout the story? Do you have your limestone gumption?

2. In the beginning of the novel with the murder of Big Jake, what do you immediately learn about the book's protagonist? What do you learn about the book's antagonist?

3. Why are Gigi and her sisterfriends kindred spirits? Why do they move in a herd, clinging to one another? What liberates them from the herd but still keeps them connected for life?

4. What does Brad's early experience with religion have to do with his reactions to the two murders in Whitecross? Why does

Brad risk diving with Big Jake when he knows the violent man is already upset with him? Would you take such a risk in that situation?

5. Throughout the novel, you notice that many of the characters, perhaps even your favorite ones, profile people who are different from them. How many characters can you name who were profiled and who profiled others? Which characters learned from their mistakes and which ones didn't?

6. What parallels do you see between the prejudice and profiling in this story and real-life events in today's society? What can be learned from the dangers of profiling others? Have you ever been profiled? If not, what do you think it's like?

7. In some ways, *Limestone Gumption* is a story about the age-old battle between good and evil, hypocrisy and authenticity, greed and generosity, and ego and spirituality. Even some of the characters' names portray where they fall on the spectrum. What is it about some of the characters that would cause you to put them in one category versus another?

8. How are Brad and Myrtle similar? What happens in the book to make them dissimilar? Have you ever had a rude awakening that turned your perspective on something upside down?

9. What is your reaction when the true nature of Brad and Chris's relationship is revealed? How do you feel about your reaction? Is any aspect of your reaction reminiscent of one you've had in real life?

10. Who is your favorite character in the book? Why? What does your choice reflect about your personality?

11. Voodoo Sally says that life is an illusion—that things are not what they appear to be on the surface: "Evol" is "Love" spelled backwards. What are some of the beliefs you formed from the story that turned out to be the opposite of what you originally thought? Is there a takeaway for you that you can apply to your own life?

12. How does spirituality play a part in Gigi's life? What happens that causes her to struggle with religion? How do you reconcile the fact that Gigi washes her hands of the church, yet she is generous, loving, and caring with those who are less fortunate?

13. How are Brad and Grandma Gigi similar? Different? In which ways do they challenge each other? Is any aspect of their relationship reminiscent of one you've had in your personal life?

14. Gigi refers to the other members of the Women's Preservation Club as "sisterfriends." Why do you think that term means more to her than just "friend" or "sister"? Have you had that type of relationship with another person?

15. Do you think Gigi is wrong to cover up the murder she committed? Why or why not? What would you do in that situation?

16. Why does Voodoo Sally continue to help the very people who stack the cards against her? What do you think of Sally's actions? Have you ever known anyone like her?

17. How is Big Jake similar to Johnny Devillers? What are your impressions of these men? What are their roles in the story?

18. When Gigi meets Chris for the first time, what do you think of her reaction when she discovers the nature of Brad's relationship with Chris? What do you think it's like for Brad when he discovers that Gigi knew about his secret all along?

19. What is your reaction when Bobby-Cy discloses to Brad that they are brothers? How does their relationship flip-flop after Brad is jailed for murder? What actions does Brad take to create that reversal?

20. What do the relationships between Brad and Chris, Bobby-Cy and Brad, and Gladys and Lick all have in common?

21. At Voodoo Sally's funeral, how does Brad's conversation with his boyhood pal, Alvin Dukes, give you a glimpse into Brad's personality?

22. What do you think Brad is searching for at the beginning of the novel that he discovers in the final pages of the book?

23. How would this book have been different had it been told from someone else's point of view—for instance, that of Myrtle, Big Jake, or Lick?

24. Do you think the inclusion of recipes adds to the novel? Are there any that you have tried or plan to try? Do you have any standout dishes like those of the Women's Preservation Club that you would include in a book?

25. What resonates with you and stays with you the most about *Limestone Gumption*? Would you like to see a sequel, following Brad, Gigi, and her sisterfriends? Specifically, which characters would you like to see highlighted in a sequel and why?

ABOUT THE AUTHOR

Bryan E. Robinson is author, psychotherapist, and Professor Emeritus at the University of North Carolina at Charlotte. He has authored thirty-five nonfiction books, including his latest, *The Smart Guide to Managing Stress.* His books have been translated into thirteen languages, and he has written for over one-hundred professional journals and popular magazines. He has won two awards for writing and has lectured across the United States and throughout the world. His work has been featured on every major television network. He maintains a private clinical practice in Asheville, North Carolina, and resides in the Blue Ridge Mountains with his life partner, four dogs, and occasional bears at night. Visit his website: bryanrobinson novels.com or email: bryanrobinson@bryanrobinsononline.com. *Limestone Gumption* is his debut novel.